TRANSFORMERS PRIME
BEAST HUNTERS

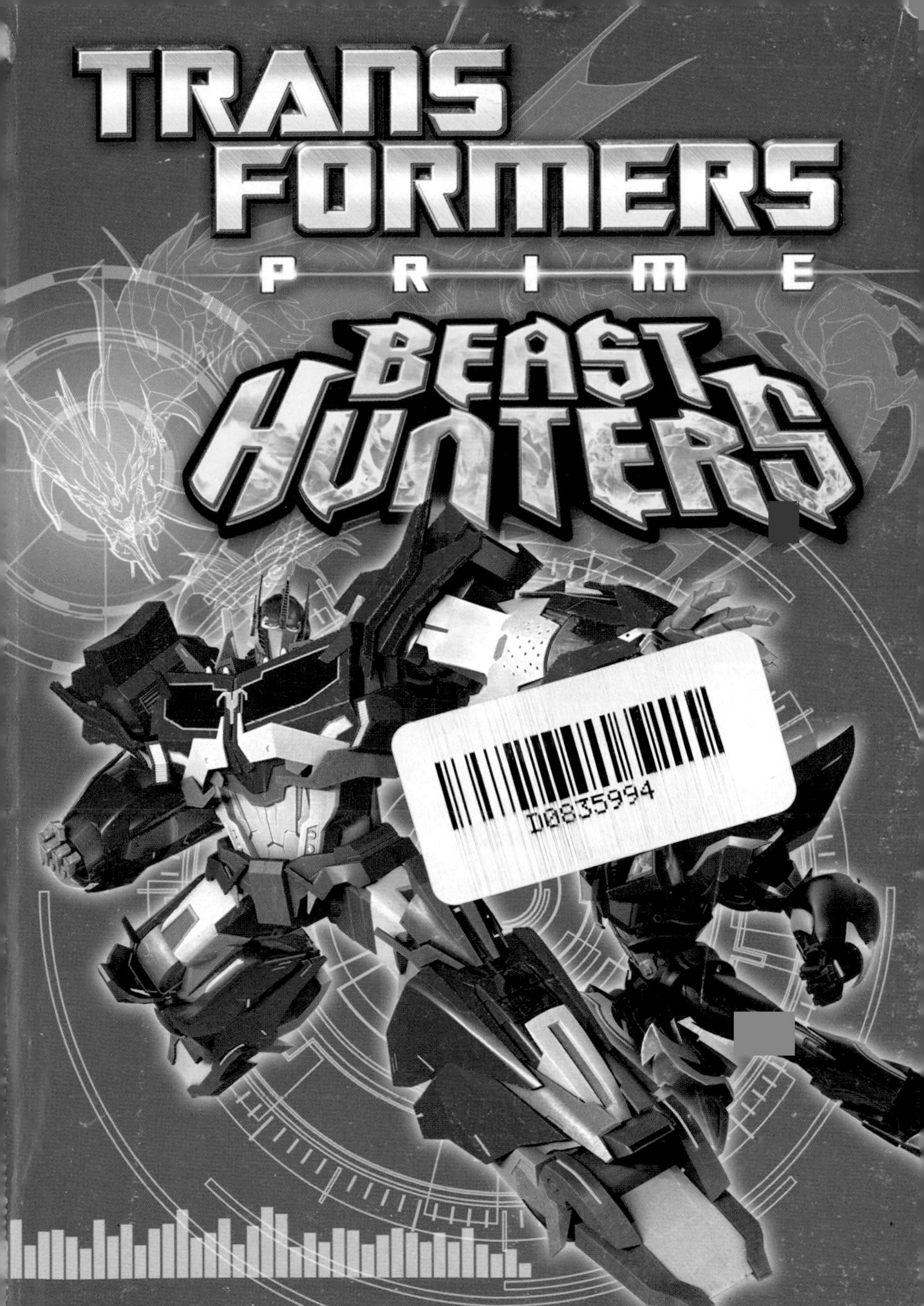

TRANSFORMERS PRIME

BEAST HUNTERS

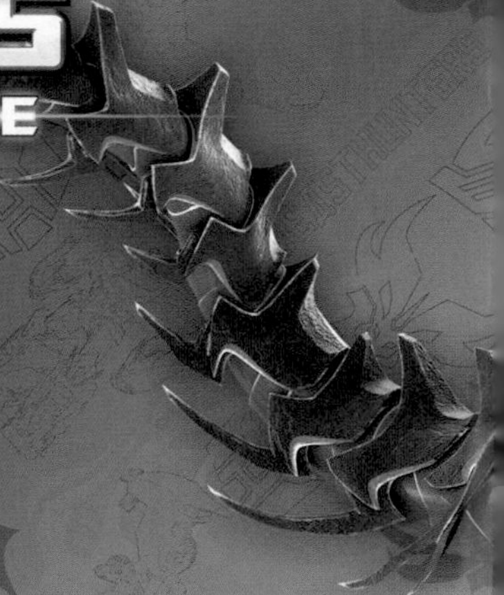

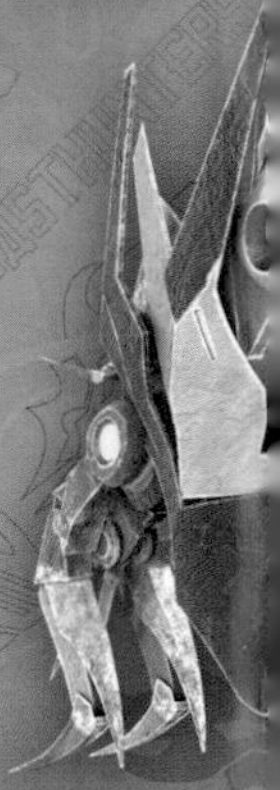

DARKMOUNT, NEVADA PARTS 1–4

WRITTEN BY

MARSHA GRIFFIN

AND

STEVEN MELCHING

ADAPTATION BY:
JUSTIN EISINGER

EDITS BY:
ALONZO SIMON

LETTERS AND DESIGN BY:
TOM B. LONG

Special thanks to Hasbro's Clint Chapman, Jerry Jivoin, Joshua Lamb, Ed Lane, Joe Furfaro, Heather Hopkins, and Michael Kelly for their invaluable assistance.

Licensed By: Hasbro

ISBN: 978-1-61377-715-2
16 15 14 13   1 2 3 4
www.IDWPUBLISHING.com

Ted Adams, CEO & Publisher
Greg Goldstein, President & COO
Robbie Robbins, EVP/Sr. Graphic Artist
Chris Ryall, Chief Creative Officer/Editor-in-Chief
Matthew Ruzicka, CPA, Chief Financial Officer
Alan Payne, VP of Sales
Dirk Wood, VP of Marketing
Lorelei Bunjes, VP of Digital Services

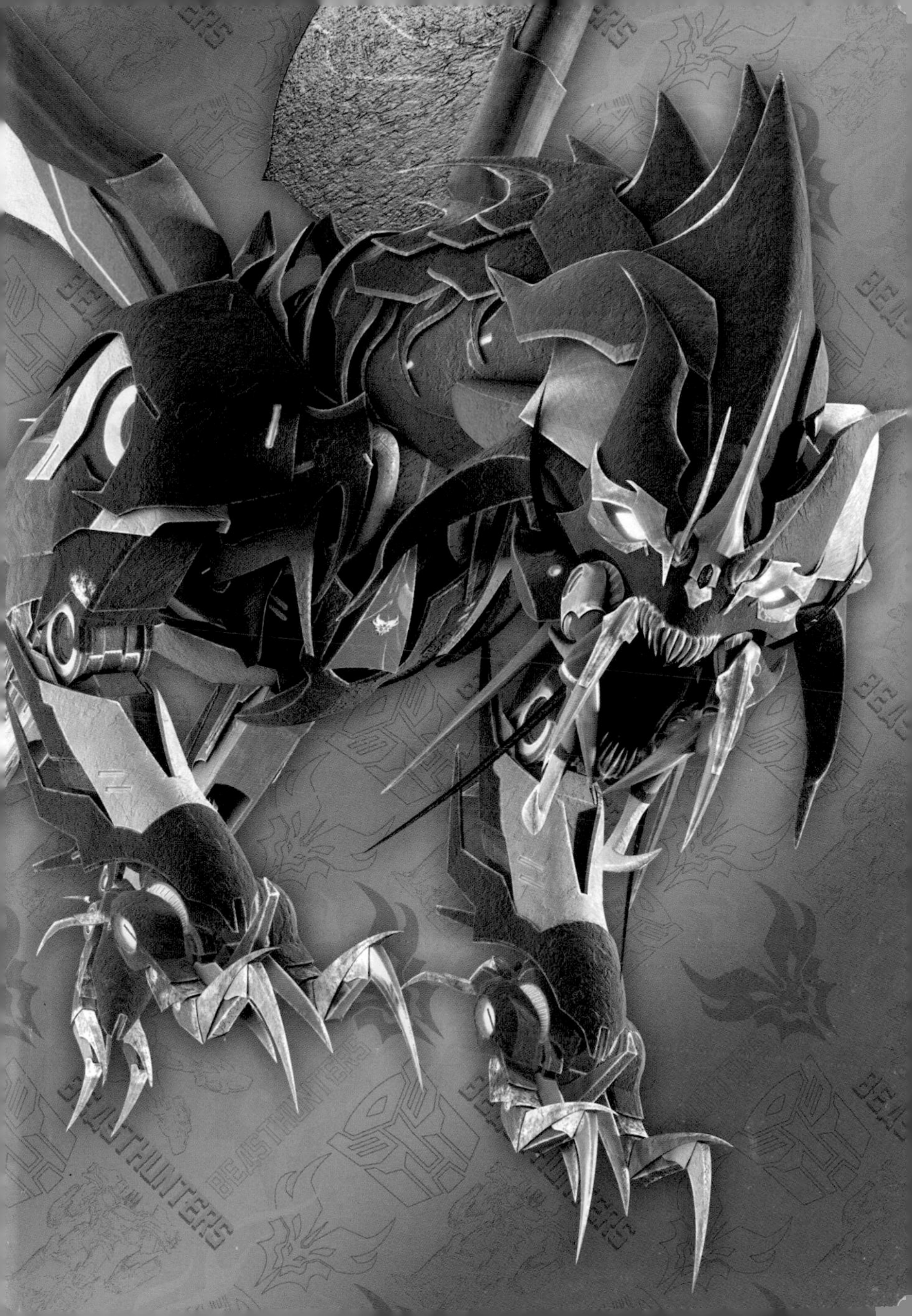
BEASTHUNTERS

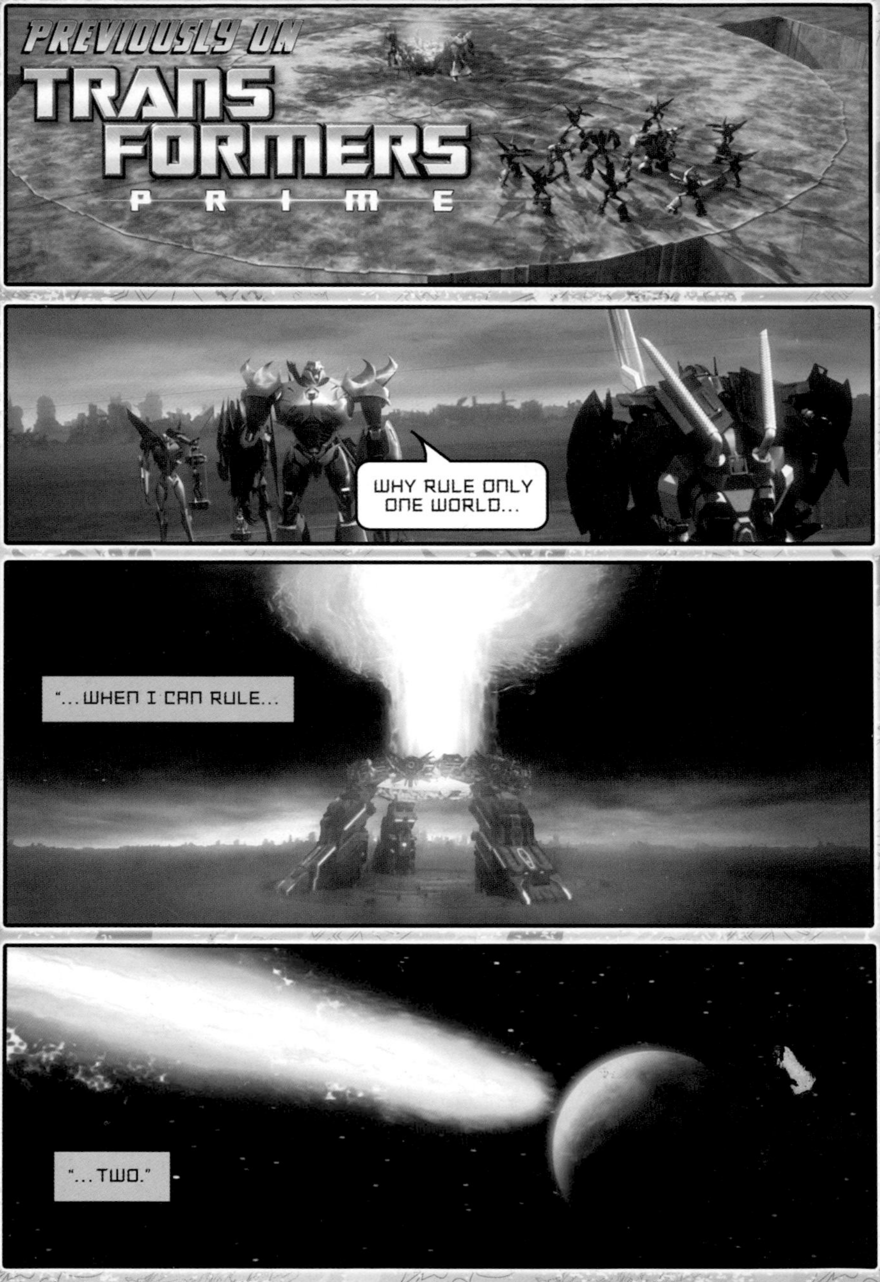
PREVIOUSLY ON
TRANSFORMERS PRIME
WHY RULE ONLY ONE WORLD...
"...WHEN I CAN RULE...
"...TWO."

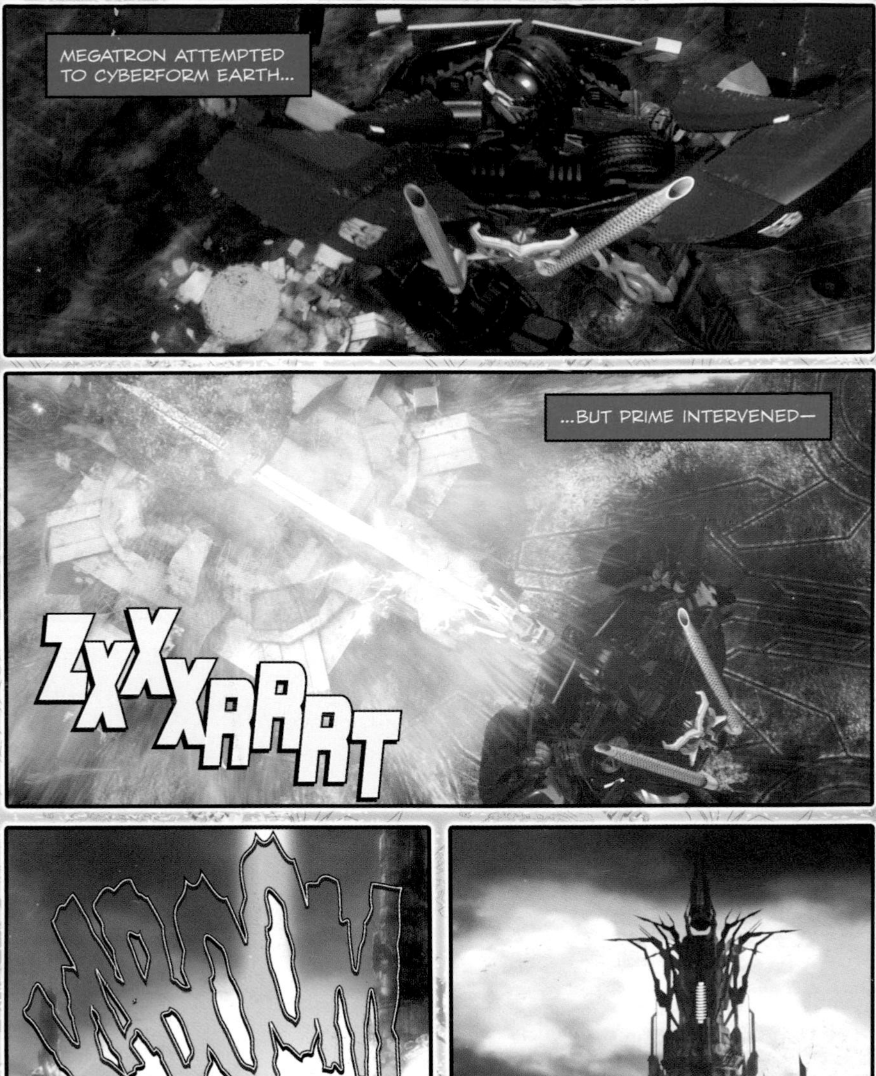
MEGATRON ATTEMPTED TO CYBERFORM EARTH...
...BUT PRIME INTERVENED—
ZXXXXRRRT
—TOO LATE.
"MEGATRON HAS SUCCEEDED IN BUILDING HIS FORTRESS."

IN JASPER, NEVADA?!

BLEEED BLURRP

BUT I DON'T GET IT... WHY HERE?!

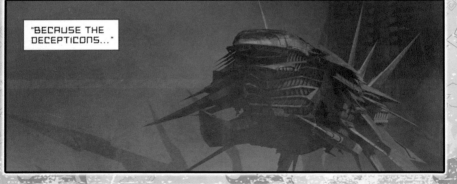

"BECAUSE THE DECEPTICONS..."

...HAVE DISCOVERED THE LOCATION OF OUR BASE.

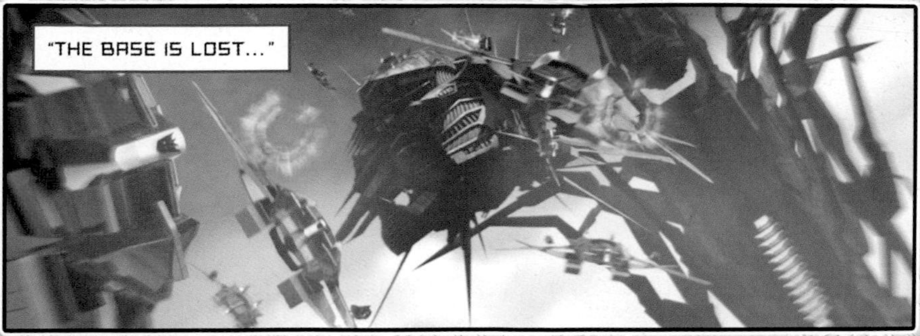
"THE BASE IS LOST..."

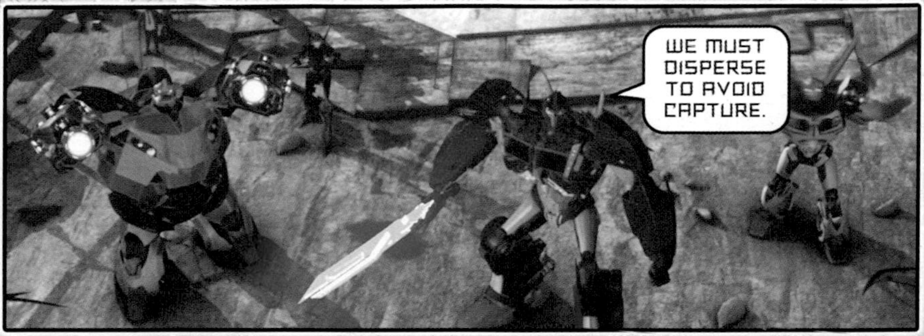
WE MUST DISPERSE TO AVOID CAPTURE.

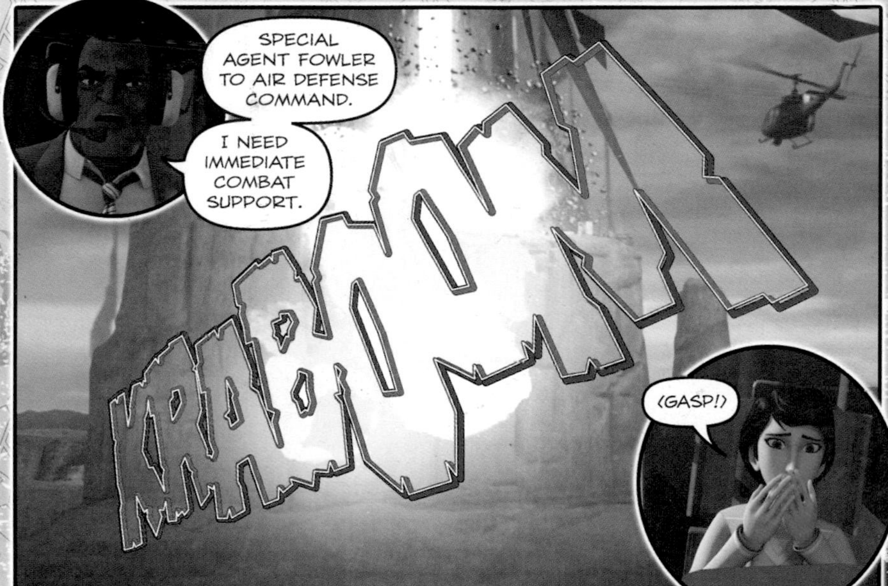
SPECIAL AGENT FOWLER TO AIR DEFENSE COMMAND.
I NEED IMMEDIATE COMBAT SUPPORT.
KRABOOM
(GASP!)

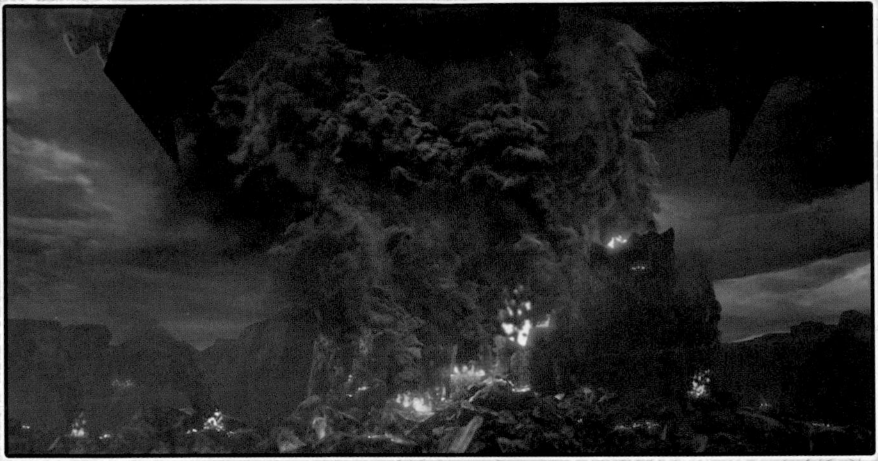

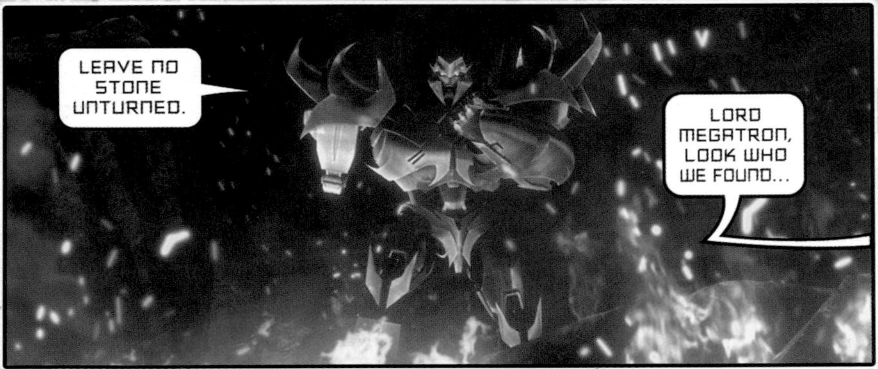
LEAVE NO STONE UNTURNED.
LORD MEGATRON, LOOK WHO WE FOUND...

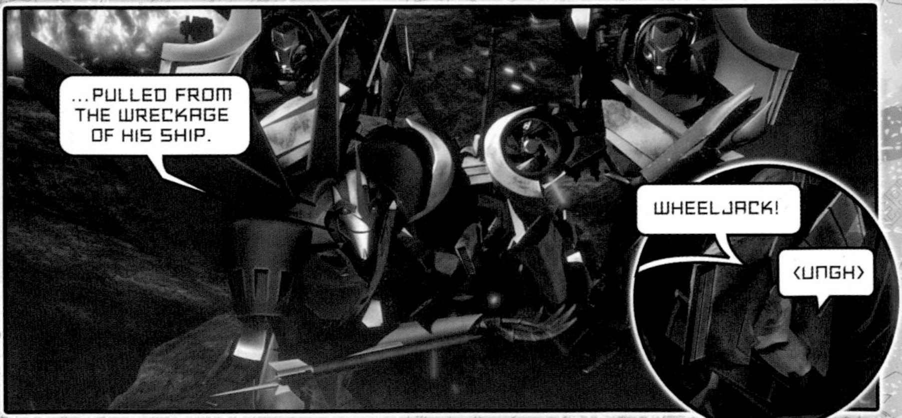
...PULLED FROM THE WRECKAGE OF HIS SHIP.
WHEELJACK!
<UNGH>

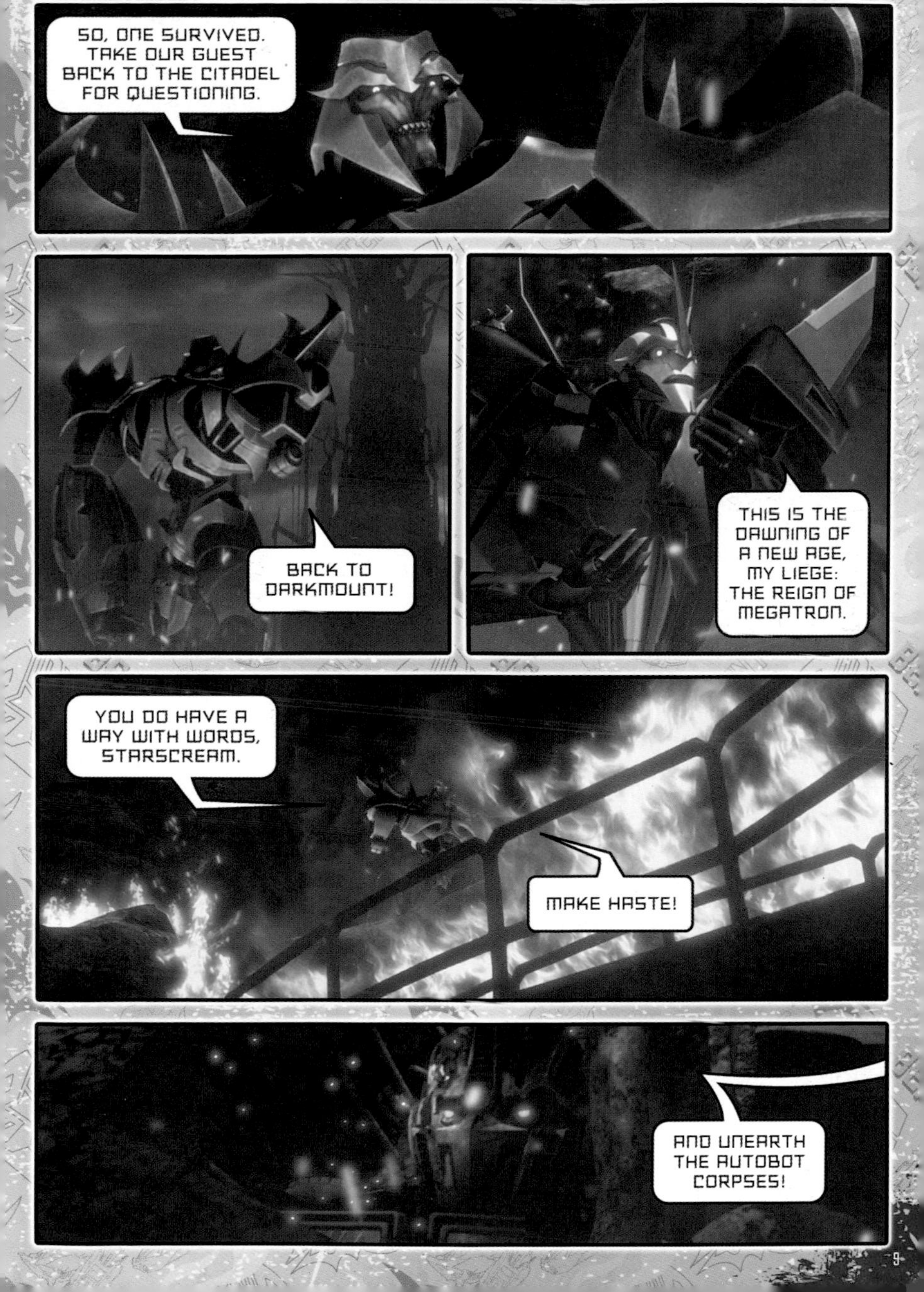
SO, ONE SURVIVED. TAKE OUR GUEST BACK TO THE CITADEL FOR QUESTIONING.
BACK TO DARKMOUNT!
THIS IS THE DAWNING OF A NEW AGE, MY LIEGE: THE REIGN OF MEGATRON.
YOU DO HAVE A WAY WITH WORDS, STARSCREAM.
MAKE HASTE!
AND UNEARTH THE AUTOBOT CORPSES!

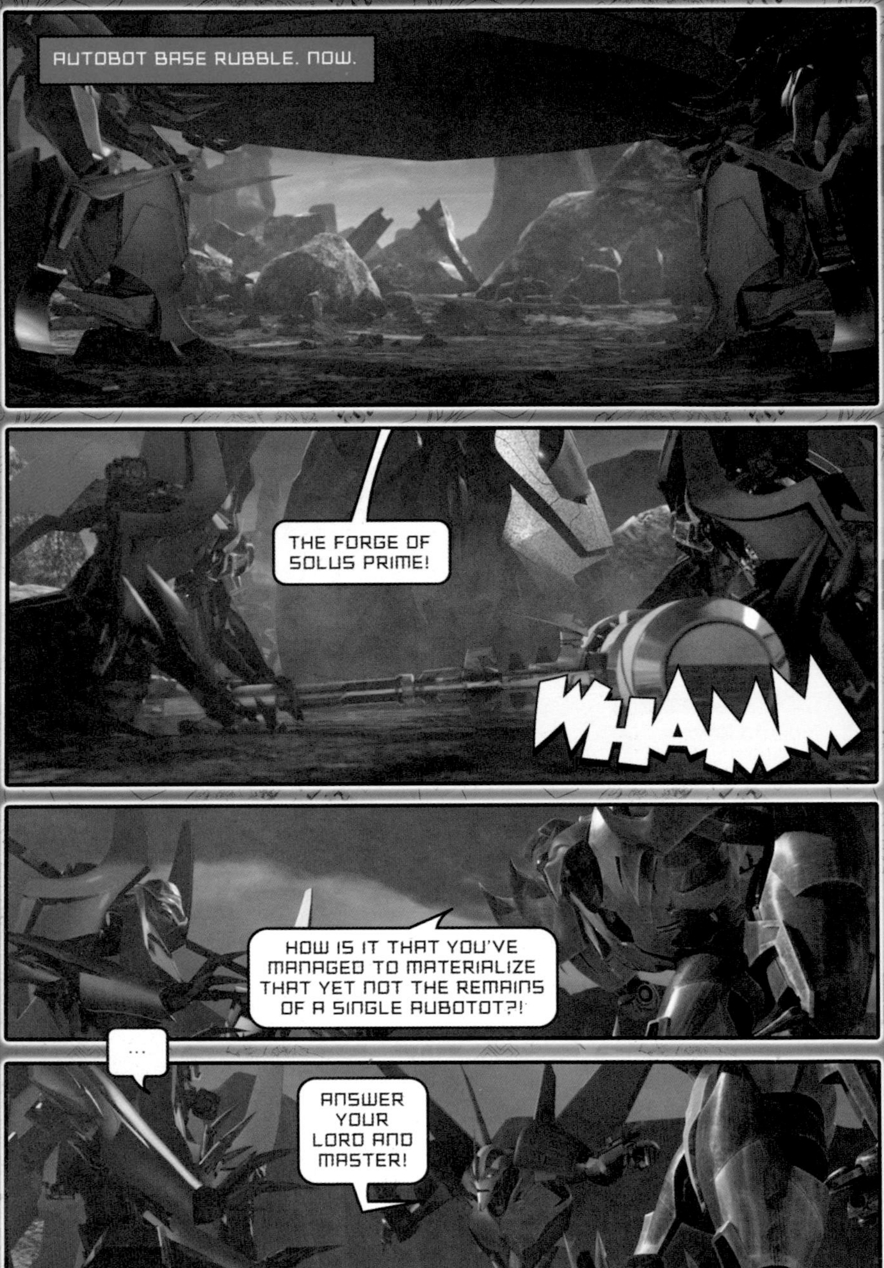
AUTOBOT BASE RUBBLE. NOW.
THE FORGE OF SOLUS PRIME!
WHAMM
HOW IS IT THAT YOU'VE MANAGED TO MATERIALIZE THAT YET NOT THE REMAINS OF A SINGLE AUBOTOT?!
...
ANSWER YOUR LORD AND MASTER!

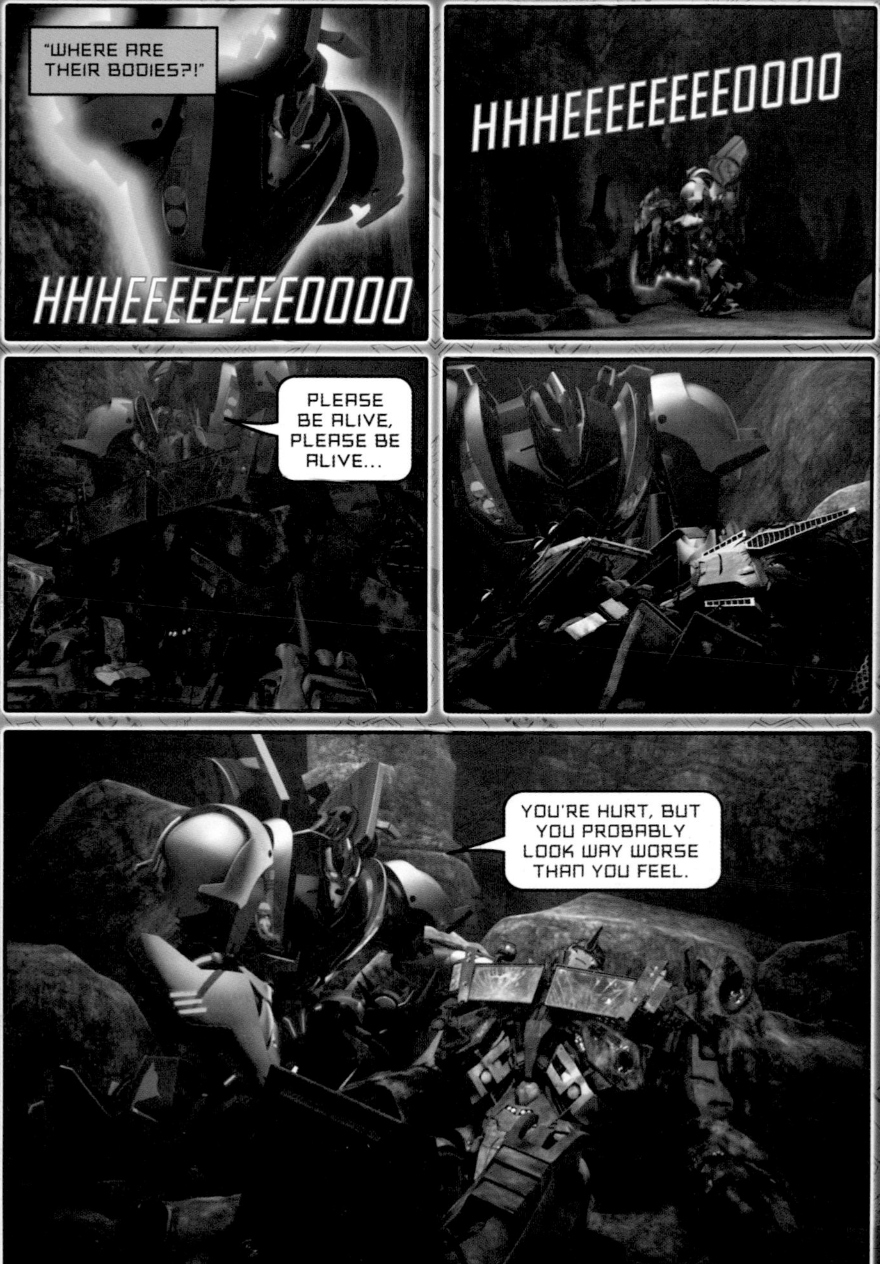

"WHERE ARE THEIR BODIES?!"
HHHEEEEEEEEOOOO
HHHEEEEEEEEOOOO
PLEASE BE ALIVE, PLEASE BE ALIVE...
YOU'RE HURT, BUT YOU PROBABLY LOOK WAY WORSE THAN YOU FEEL.

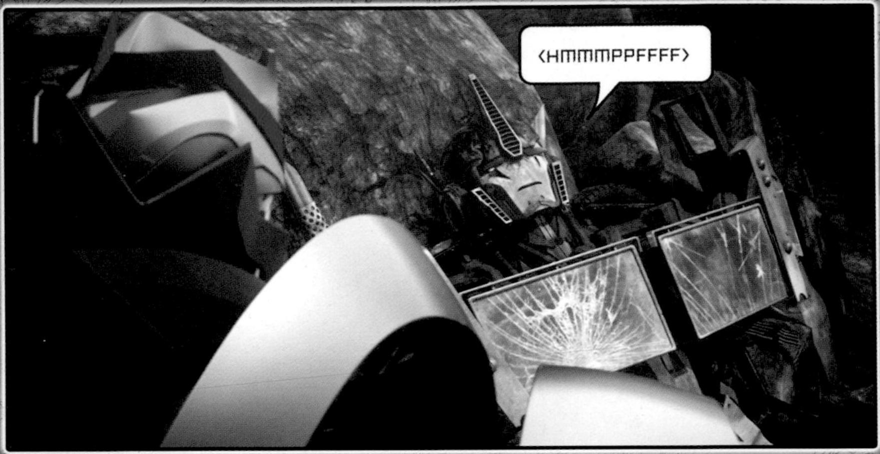
<HMMMPPFFFF>

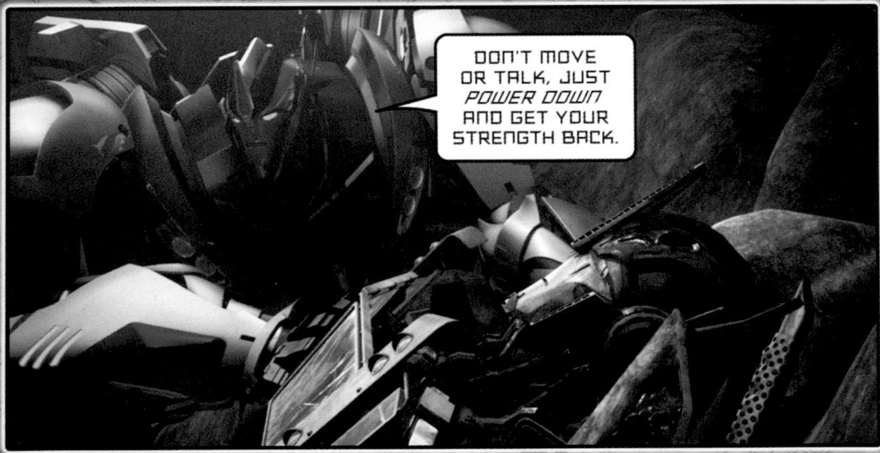
DON'T MOVE OR TALK, JUST *POWER DOWN* AND GET YOUR STRENGTH BACK.

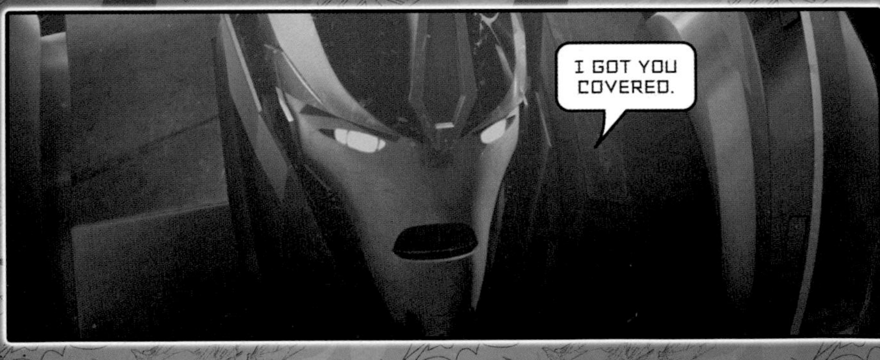
I GOT YOU COVERED.

THE AUTOBOTS CLEARLY GROUNDBRIDGED FROM THEIR BASE BEFORE IT WAS DESTROYED...

...THEY COULD BE ANYWHERE.

WE MUST INITIATE GLOBAL SURVEILLANCE, MY LORD.

SOUNDWAVE, MONITOR ALL EARTH-BASED TRANSMISSIONS FOR ANY AUTOBOT COMMUNICATION—WITH EACH OTHER, OR THEIR HUMAN COUNTERPARTS.

MASTER...

"FOOLISH HUMANS. I SHALL DEPLOY THE ARMADA."

RUMBLE RUMBLE

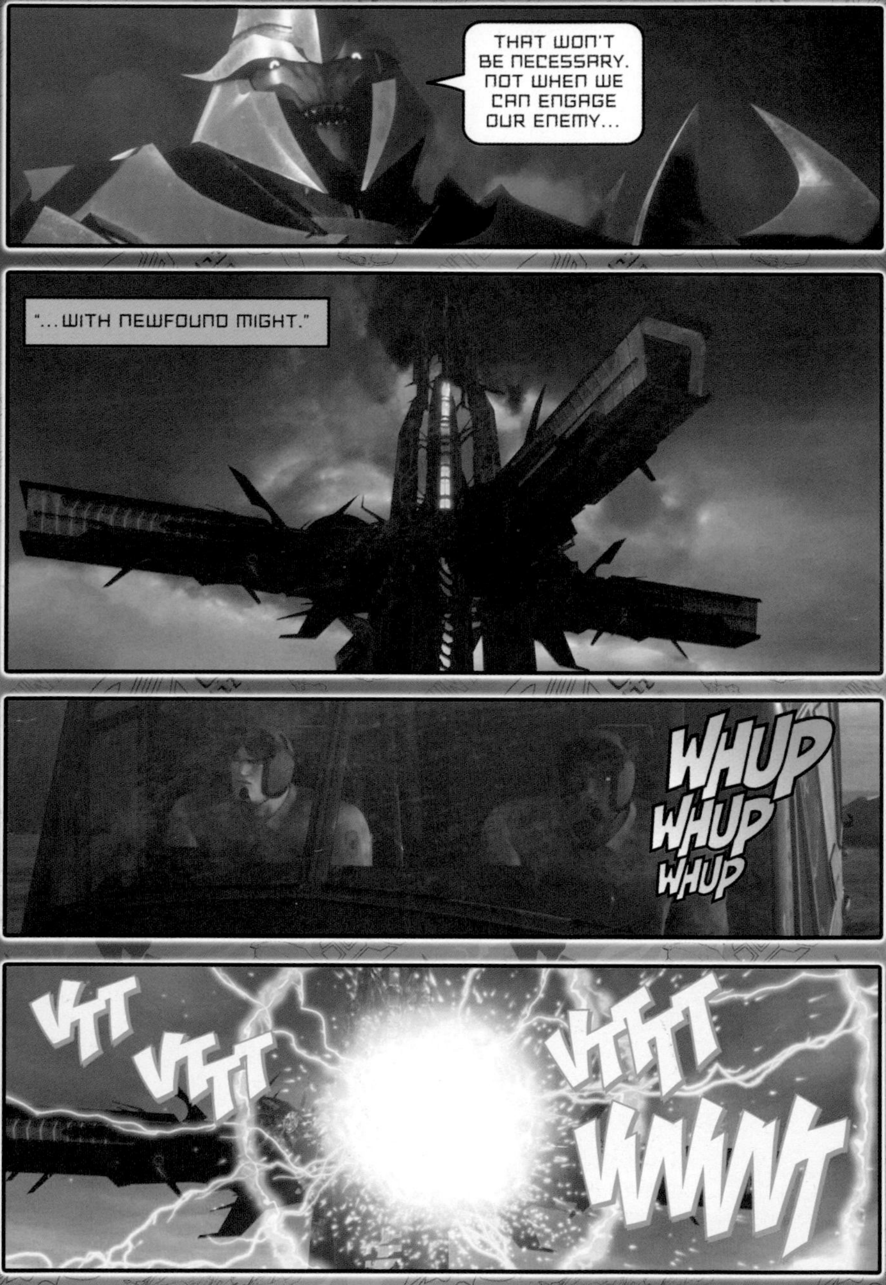
THAT WON'T BE NECESSARY. NOT WHEN WE CAN ENGAGE OUR ENEMY...
"...WITH NEWFOUND MIGHT."
WHUP WHUP WHUP
VTT VTTT VTTTT
VVVVVT

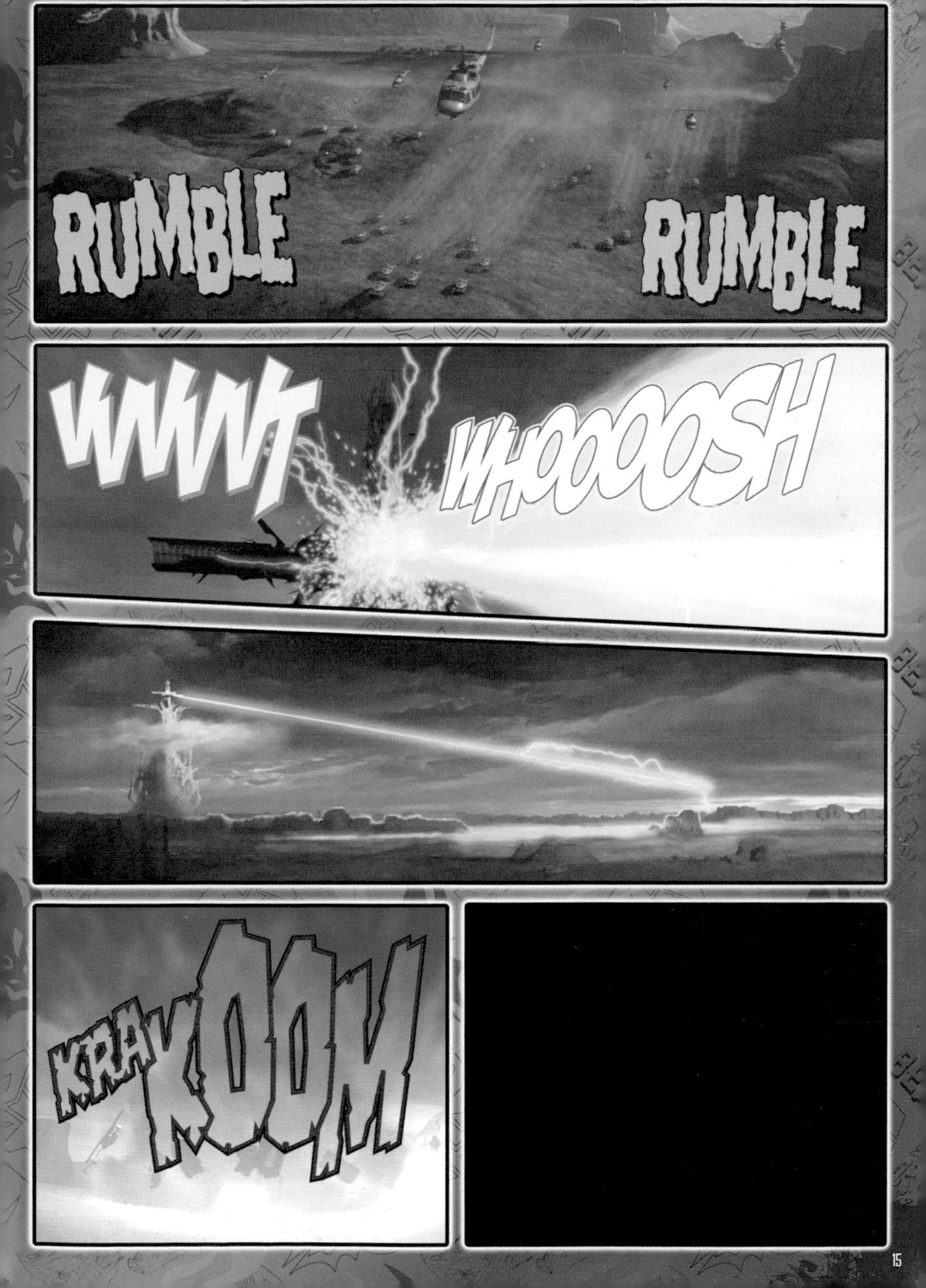
RUMBLE
RUMBLE
WHOOOOSH
KRAKOOM

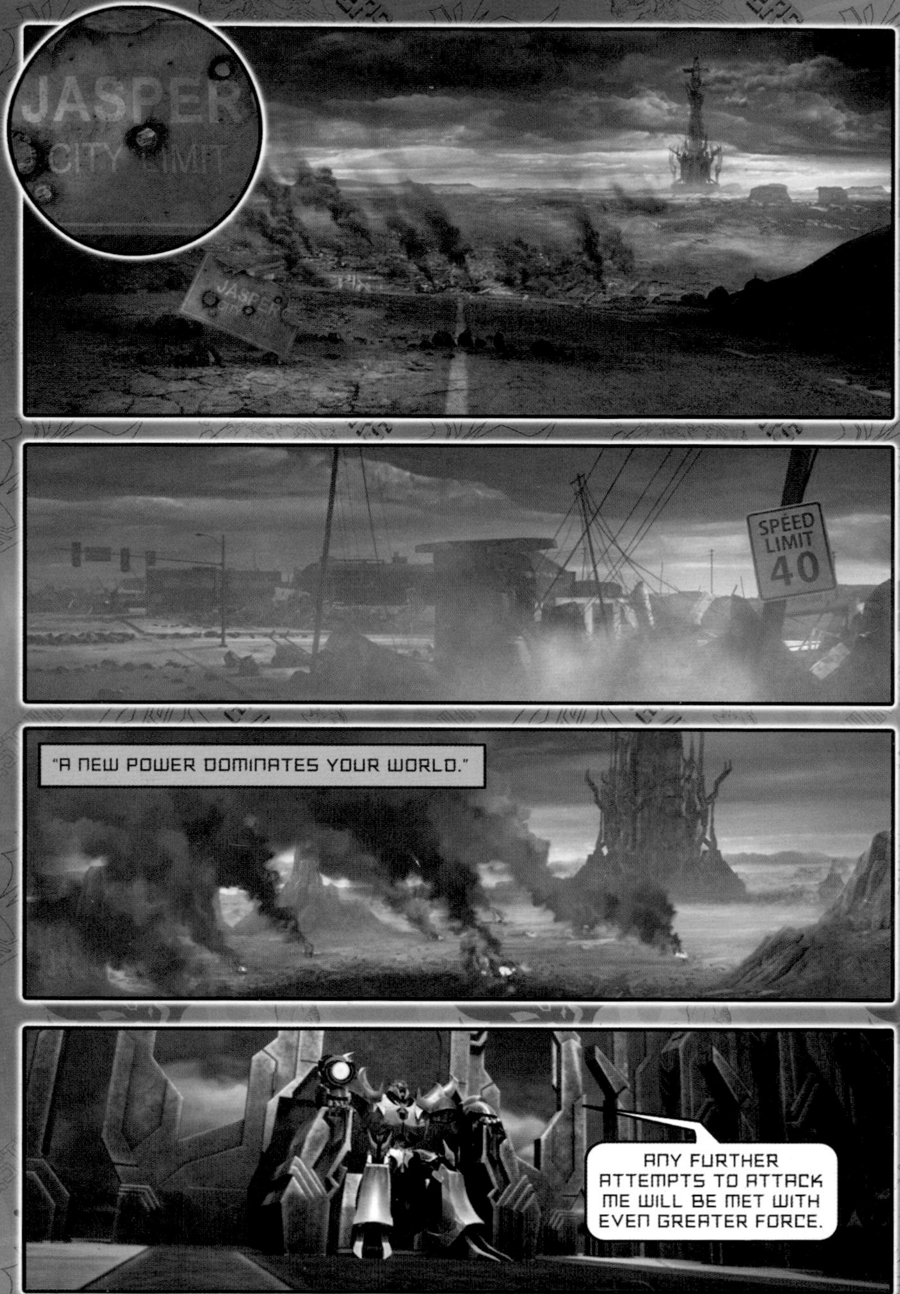
JASPER
CITY LIMIT
SPEED LIMIT
40
"A NEW POWER DOMINATES YOUR WORLD."
ANY FURTHER ATTEMPTS TO ATTACK ME WILL BE MET WITH EVEN GREATER FORCE.

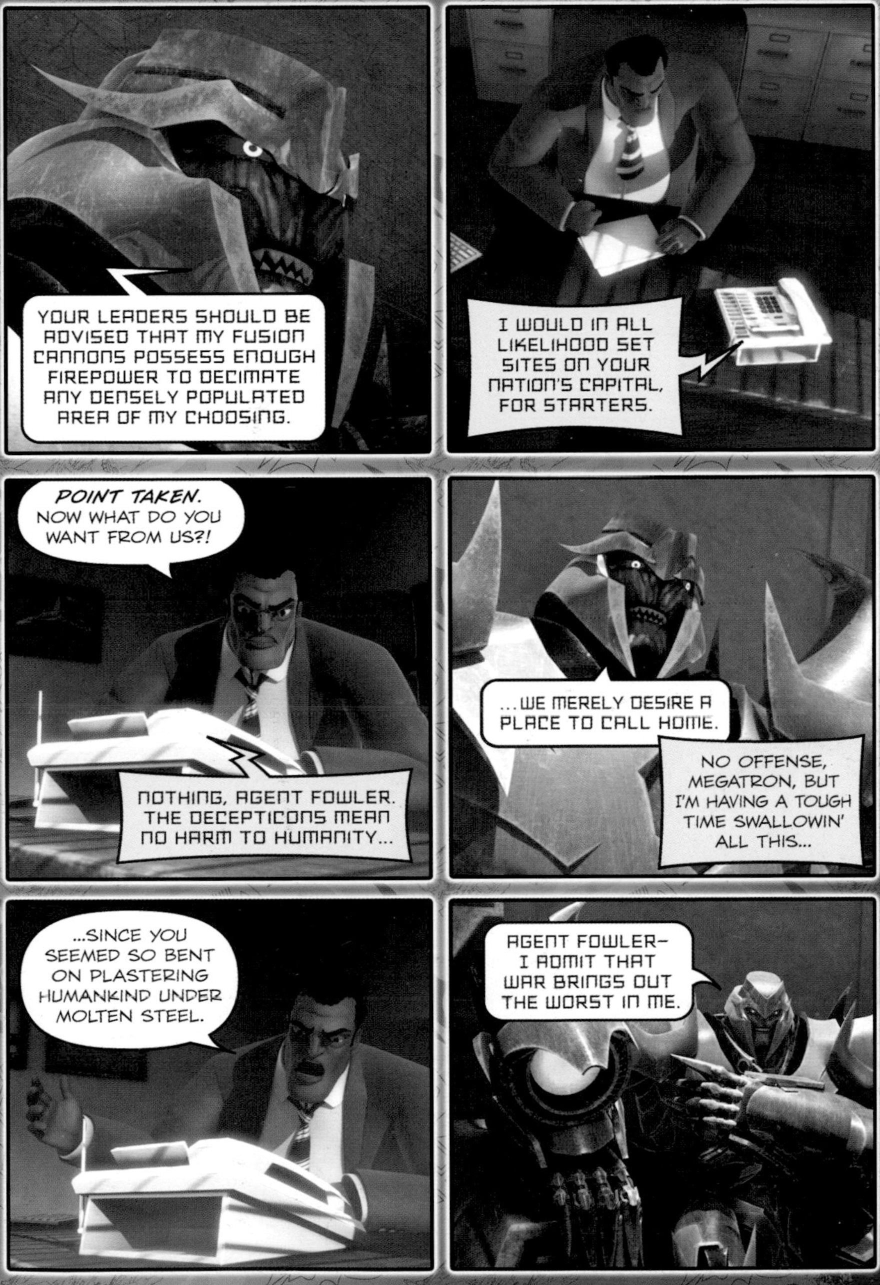
YOUR LEADERS SHOULD BE ADVISED THAT MY FUSION CANNONS POSSESS ENOUGH FIREPOWER TO DECIMATE ANY DENSELY POPULATED AREA OF MY CHOOSING.
I WOULD IN ALL LIKELIHOOD SET SITES ON YOUR NATION'S CAPITAL, FOR STARTERS.
POINT TAKEN. NOW WHAT DO YOU WANT FROM US?!
NOTHING, AGENT FOWLER. THE DECEPTICONS MEAN NO HARM TO HUMANITY...
...WE MERELY DESIRE A PLACE TO CALL HOME.
NO OFFENSE, MEGATRON, BUT I'M HAVING A TOUGH TIME SWALLOWIN' ALL THIS...
...SINCE YOU SEEMED SO BENT ON PLASTERING HUMANKIND UNDER MOLTEN STEEL.
AGENT FOWLER– I ADMIT THAT WAR BRINGS OUT THE WORST IN ME.

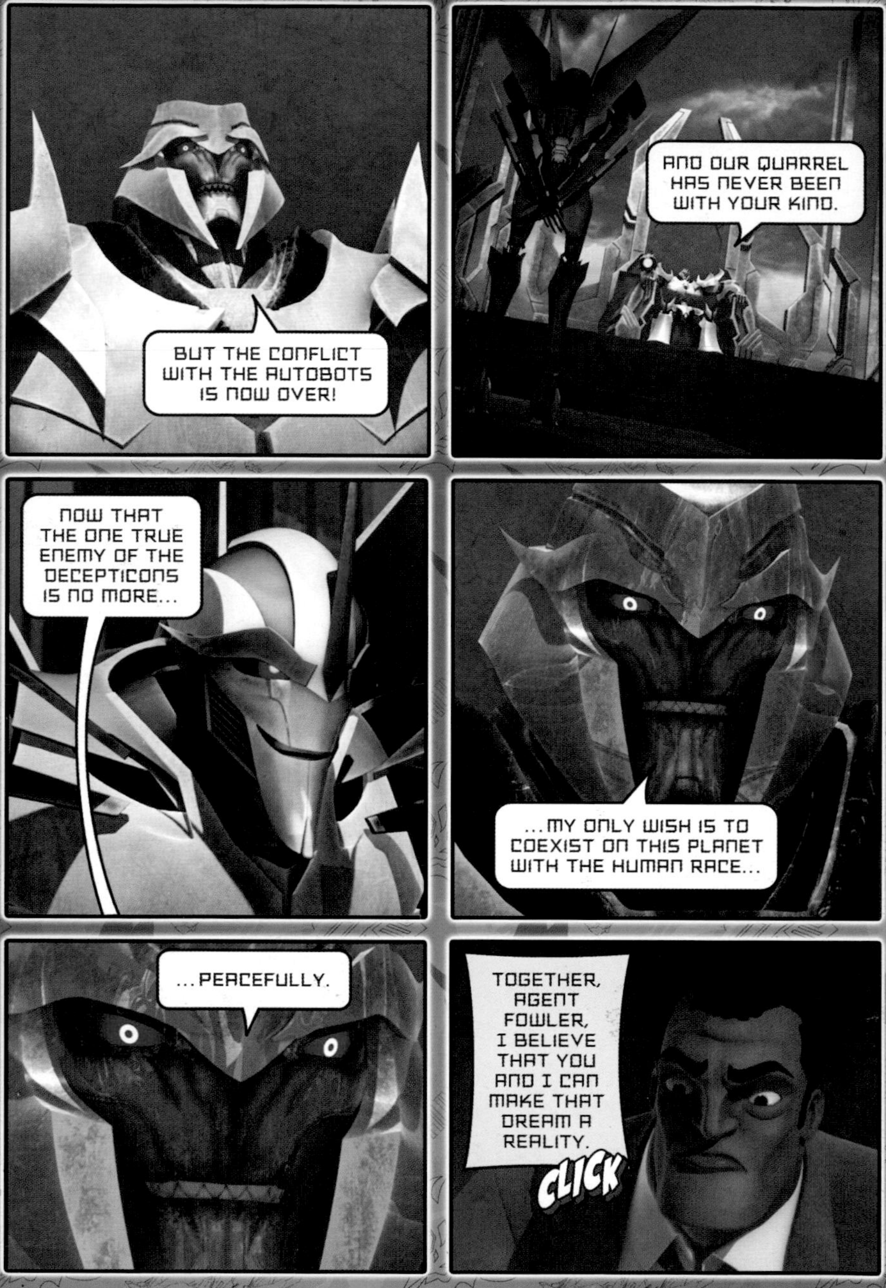
BUT THE CONFLICT WITH THE AUTOBOTS IS NOW OVER!
AND OUR QUARREL HAS NEVER BEEN WITH YOUR KIND.
NOW THAT THE ONE TRUE ENEMY OF THE DECEPTICONS IS NO MORE...
...MY ONLY WISH IS TO COEXIST ON THIS PLANET WITH THE HUMAN RACE...
...PEACEFULLY.
TOGETHER, AGENT FOWLER, I BELIEVE THAT YOU AND I CAN MAKE THAT DREAM A REALITY.
CLICK

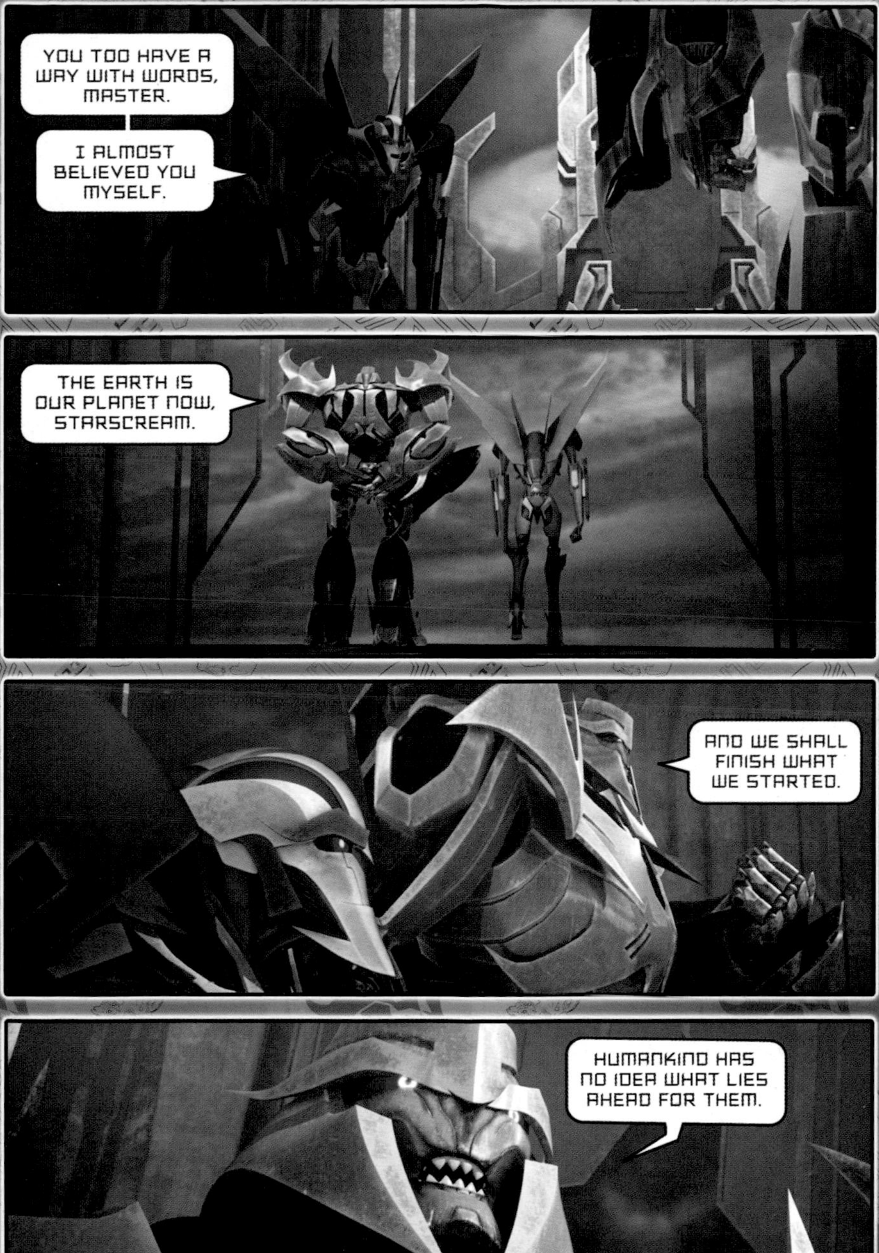
YOU TOO HAVE A WAY WITH WORDS, MASTER.
I ALMOST BELIEVED YOU MYSELF.
THE EARTH IS OUR PLANET NOW, STARSCREAM.
AND WE SHALL FINISH WHAT WE STARTED.
HUMANKIND HAS NO IDEA WHAT LIES AHEAD FOR THEM.

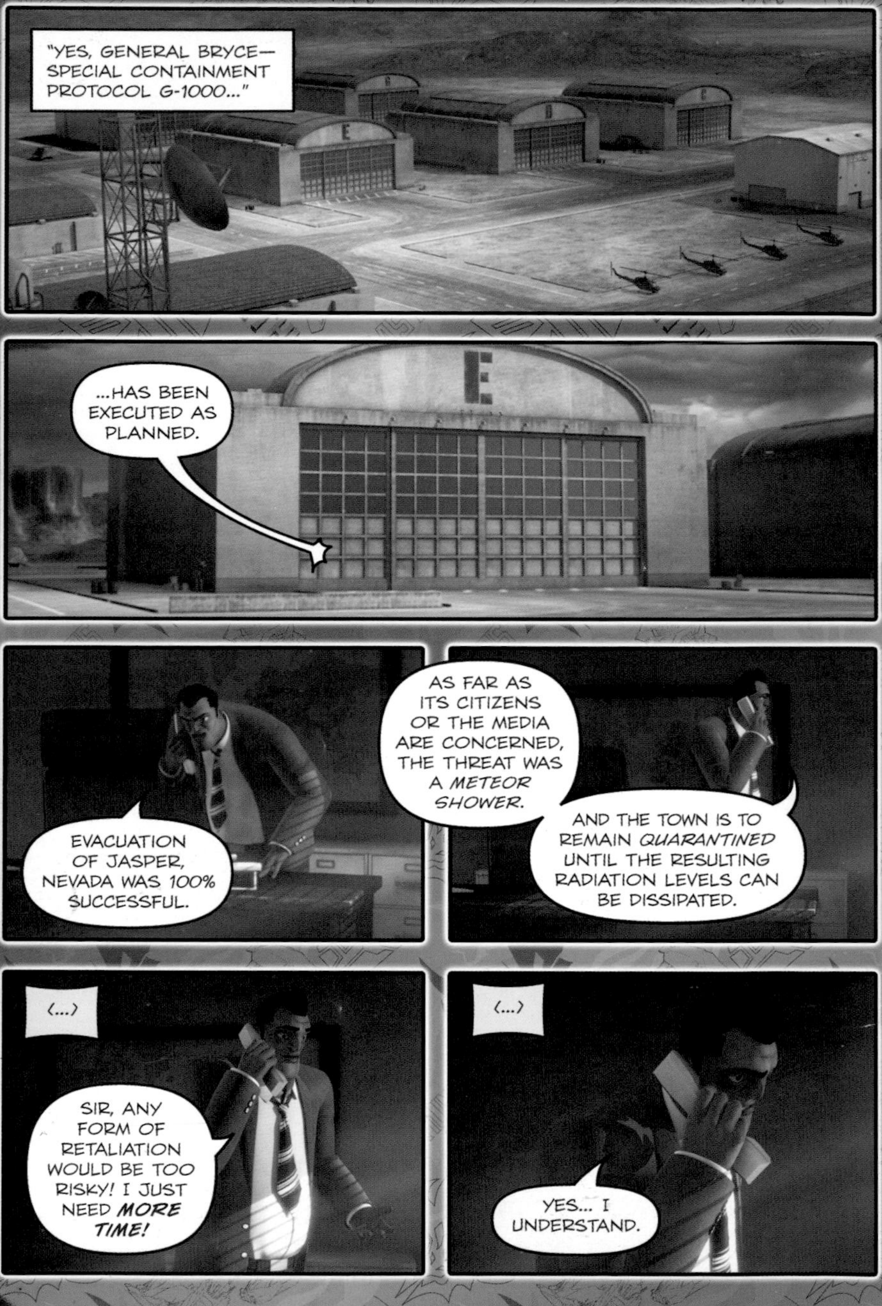
"YES, GENERAL BRYCE— SPECIAL CONTAINMENT PROTOCOL G-1000..."
...HAS BEEN EXECUTED AS PLANNED.
EVACUATION OF JASPER, NEVADA WAS 100% SUCCESSFUL.
AS FAR AS ITS CITIZENS OR THE MEDIA ARE CONCERNED, THE THREAT WAS A *METEOR SHOWER*.
AND THE TOWN IS TO REMAIN *QUARANTINED* UNTIL THE RESULTING RADIATION LEVELS CAN BE DISSIPATED.
<...>
SIR, ANY FORM OF RETALIATION WOULD BE TOO RISKY! I JUST NEED ***MORE TIME!***
<...>
YES... I UNDERSTAND.

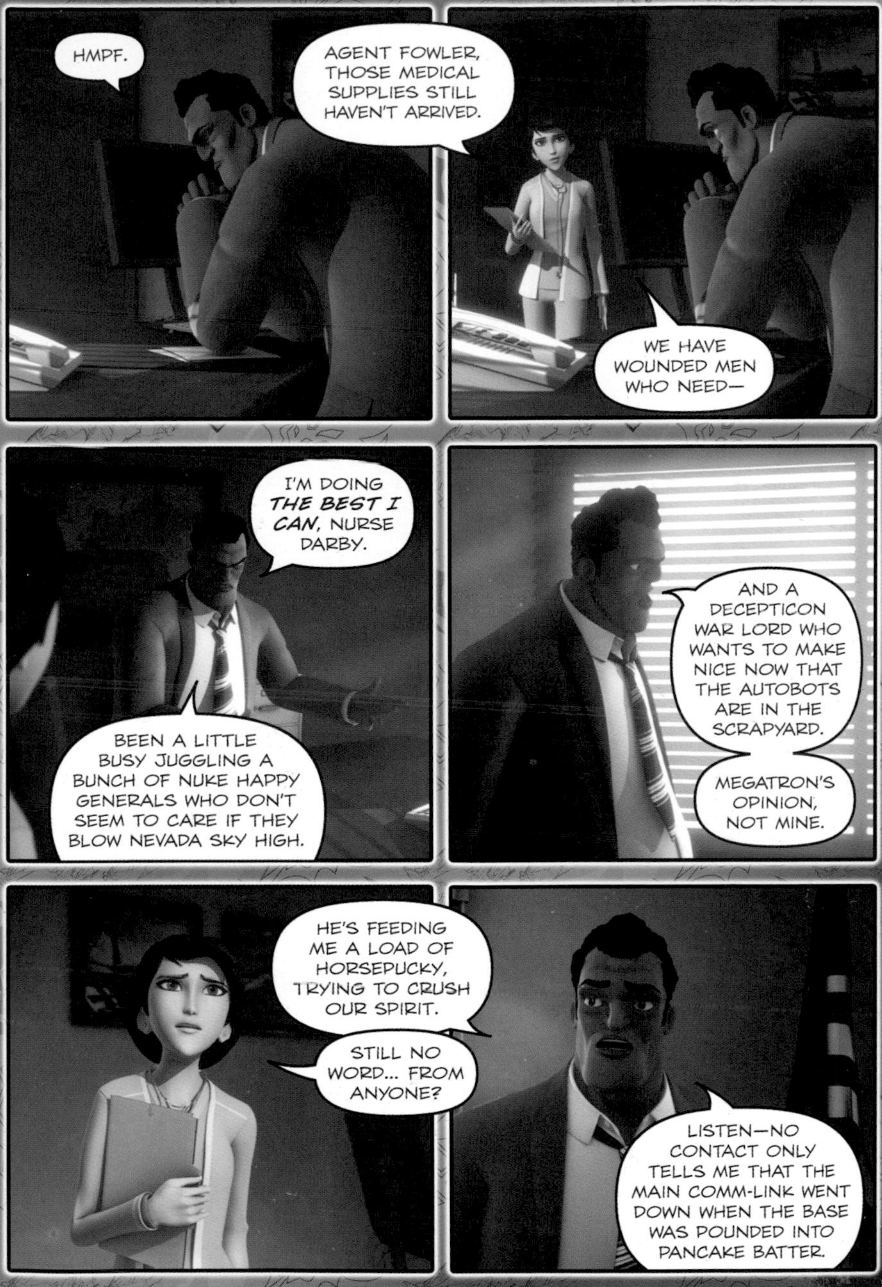
HMPF.
AGENT FOWLER, THOSE MEDICAL SUPPLIES STILL HAVEN'T ARRIVED.
WE HAVE WOUNDED MEN WHO NEED—
I'M DOING ***THE BEST I CAN***, NURSE DARBY.
BEEN A LITTLE BUSY JUGGLING A BUNCH OF NUKE HAPPY GENERALS WHO DON'T SEEM TO CARE IF THEY BLOW NEVADA SKY HIGH.
AND A DECEPTICON WAR LORD WHO WANTS TO MAKE NICE NOW THAT THE AUTOBOTS ARE IN THE SCRAPYARD.
MEGATRON'S OPINION, NOT MINE.
HE'S FEEDING ME A LOAD OF HORSEPUCKY, TRYING TO CRUSH OUR SPIRIT.
STILL NO WORD... FROM ANYONE?
LISTEN—NO CONTACT ONLY TELLS ME THAT THE MAIN COMM-LINK WENT DOWN WHEN THE BASE WAS POUNDED INTO PANCAKE BATTER.

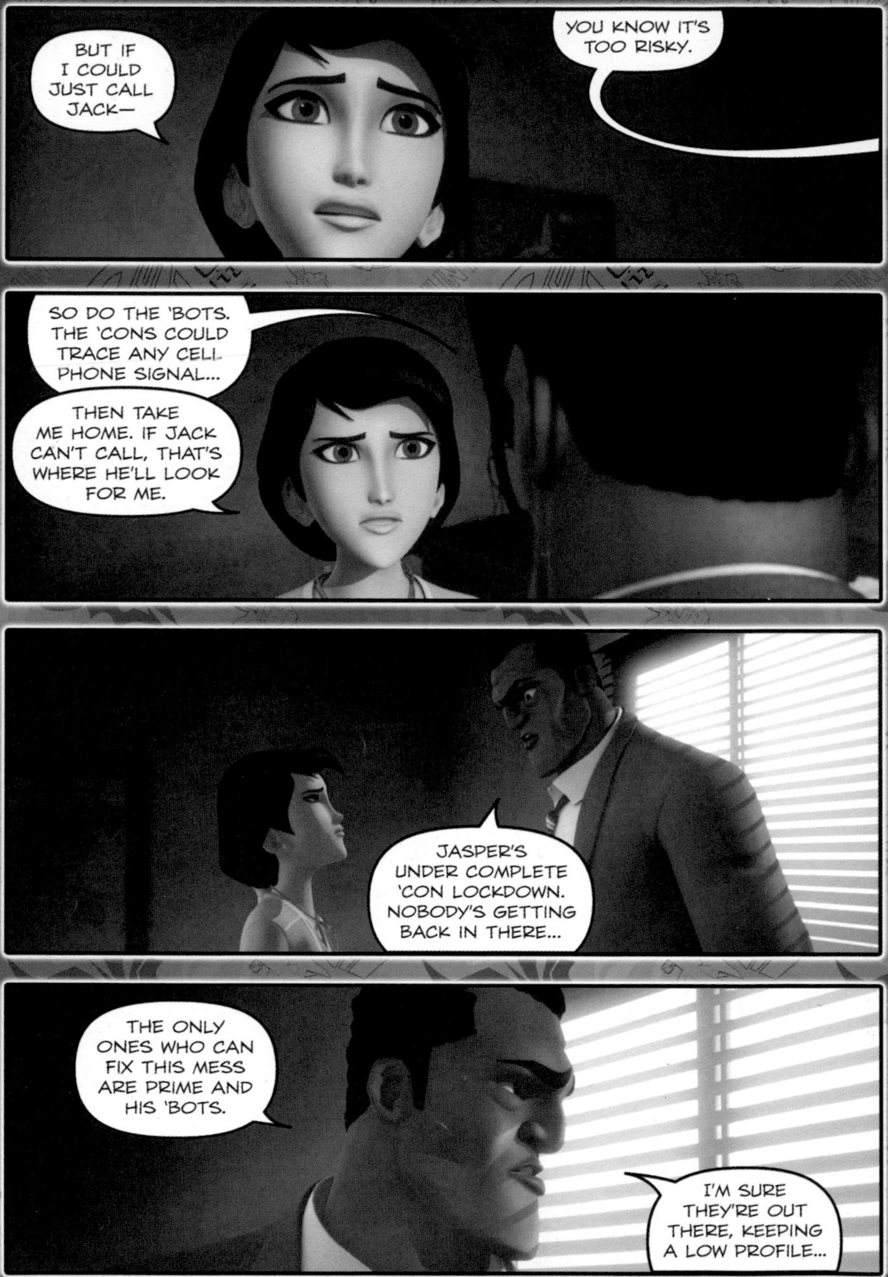
BUT IF I COULD JUST CALL JACK—
YOU KNOW IT'S TOO RISKY.
SO DO THE 'BOTS. THE 'CONS COULD TRACE ANY CELL PHONE SIGNAL...
THEN TAKE ME HOME. IF JACK CAN'T CALL, THAT'S WHERE HE'LL LOOK FOR ME.
JASPER'S UNDER COMPLETE 'CON LOCKDOWN. NOBODY'S GETTING BACK IN THERE...
THE ONLY ONES WHO CAN FIX THIS MESS ARE PRIME AND HIS 'BOTS.
I'M SURE THEY'RE OUT THERE, KEEPING A LOW PROFILE...

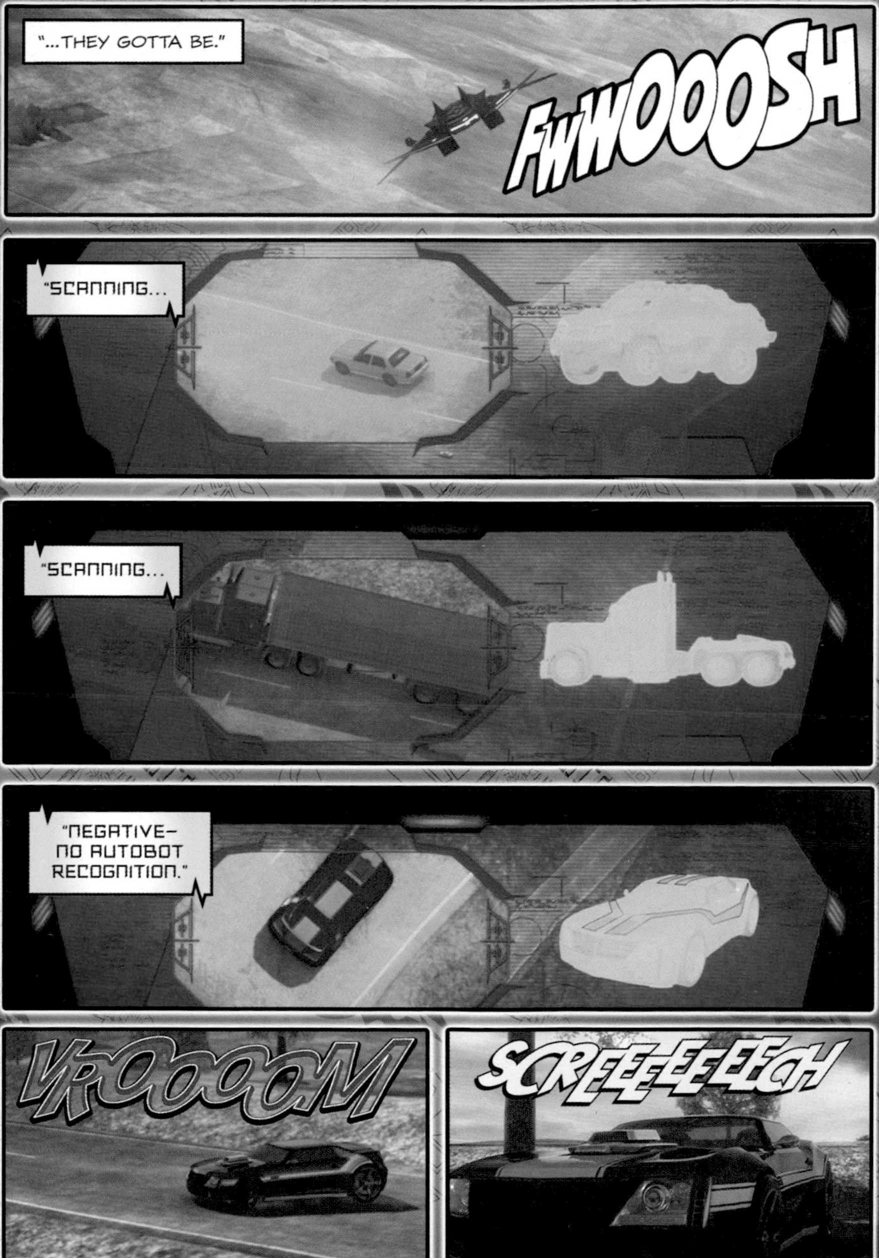

"...THEY GOTTA BE."
FWWOOOSH
"SCANNING...
"SCANNING...
"NEGATIVE— NO AUTOBOT RECOGNITION."
VROOOOM
SCREEEEEEECH

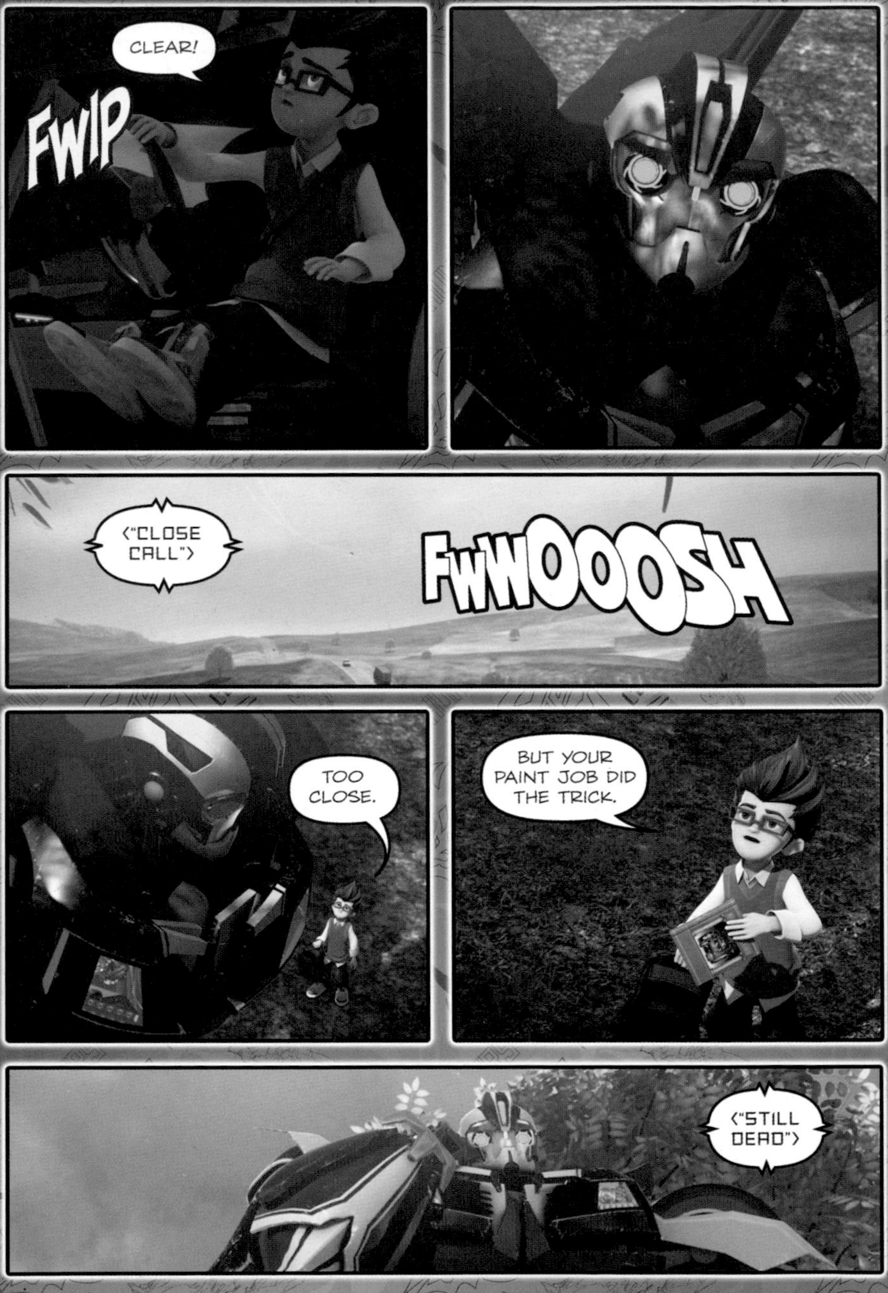
CLEAR!
FWIP
<"CLOSE CALL">
FWWOOOOSH
TOO CLOSE.
BUT YOUR PAINT JOB DID THE TRICK.
<"STILL DEAD">

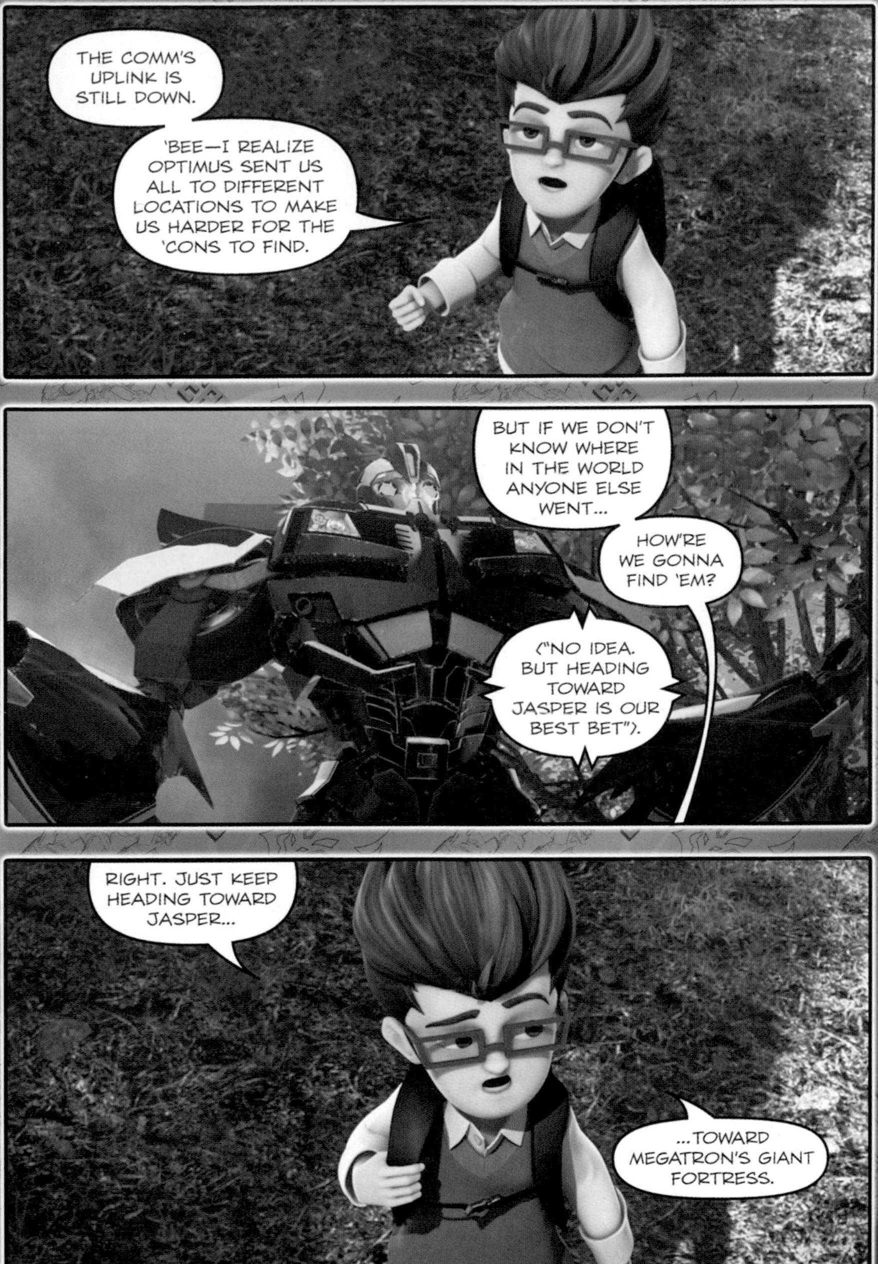
THE COMM'S UPLINK IS STILL DOWN.
'BEE—I REALIZE OPTIMUS SENT US ALL TO DIFFERENT LOCATIONS TO MAKE US HARDER FOR THE 'CONS TO FIND.
BUT IF WE DON'T KNOW WHERE IN THE WORLD ANYONE ELSE WENT...
HOW'RE WE GONNA FIND 'EM?
("NO IDEA. BUT HEADING TOWARD JASPER IS OUR BEST BET").
RIGHT. JUST KEEP HEADING TOWARD JASPER...
...TOWARD MEGATRON'S GIANT FORTRESS.

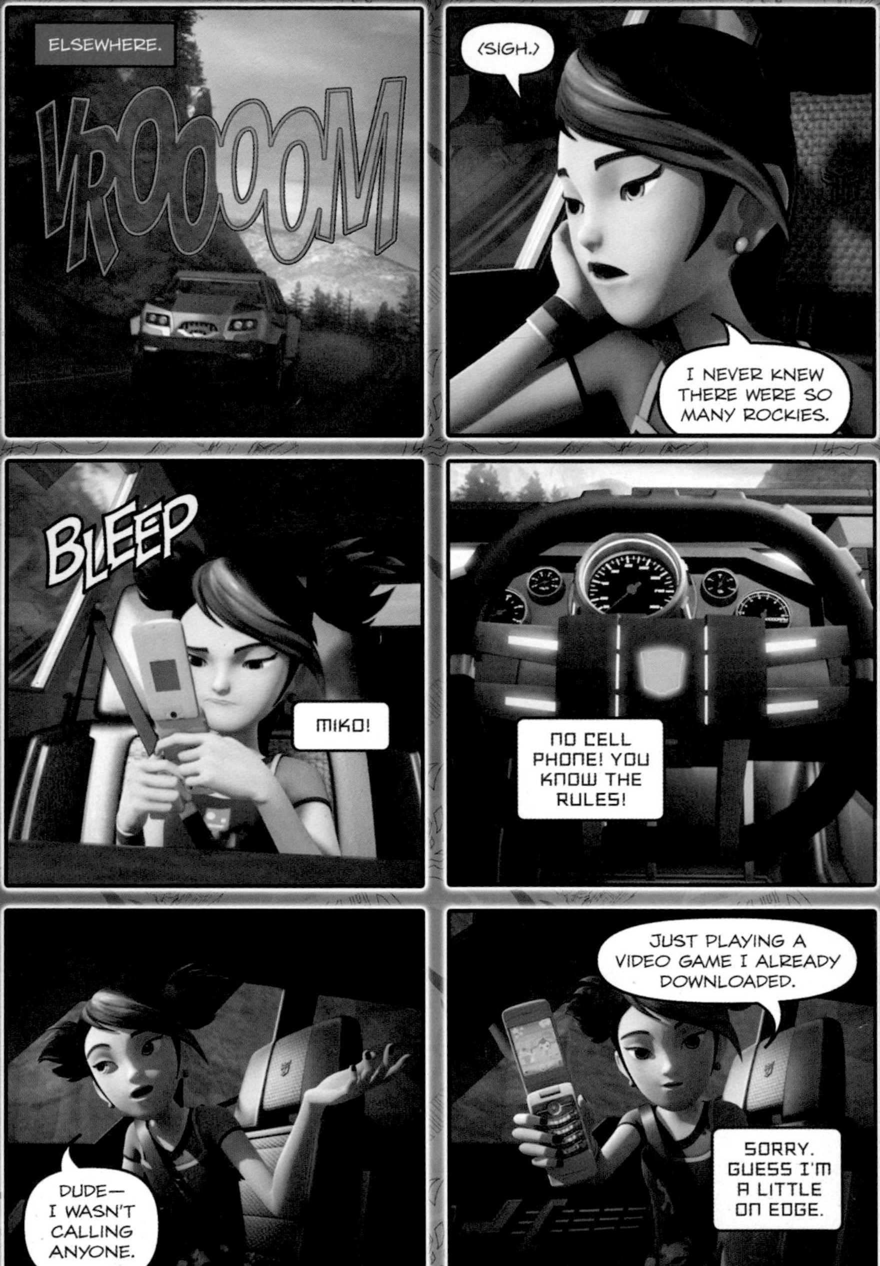
ELSEWHERE.
VROOOOM
(SIGH.)
I NEVER KNEW THERE WERE SO MANY ROCKIES.
BLEEP
MIKO!
NO CELL PHONE! YOU KNOW THE RULES!
DUDE— I WASN'T CALLING ANYONE.
JUST PLAYING A VIDEO GAME I ALREADY DOWNLOADED.
SORRY. GUESS I'M A LITTLE ON EDGE.

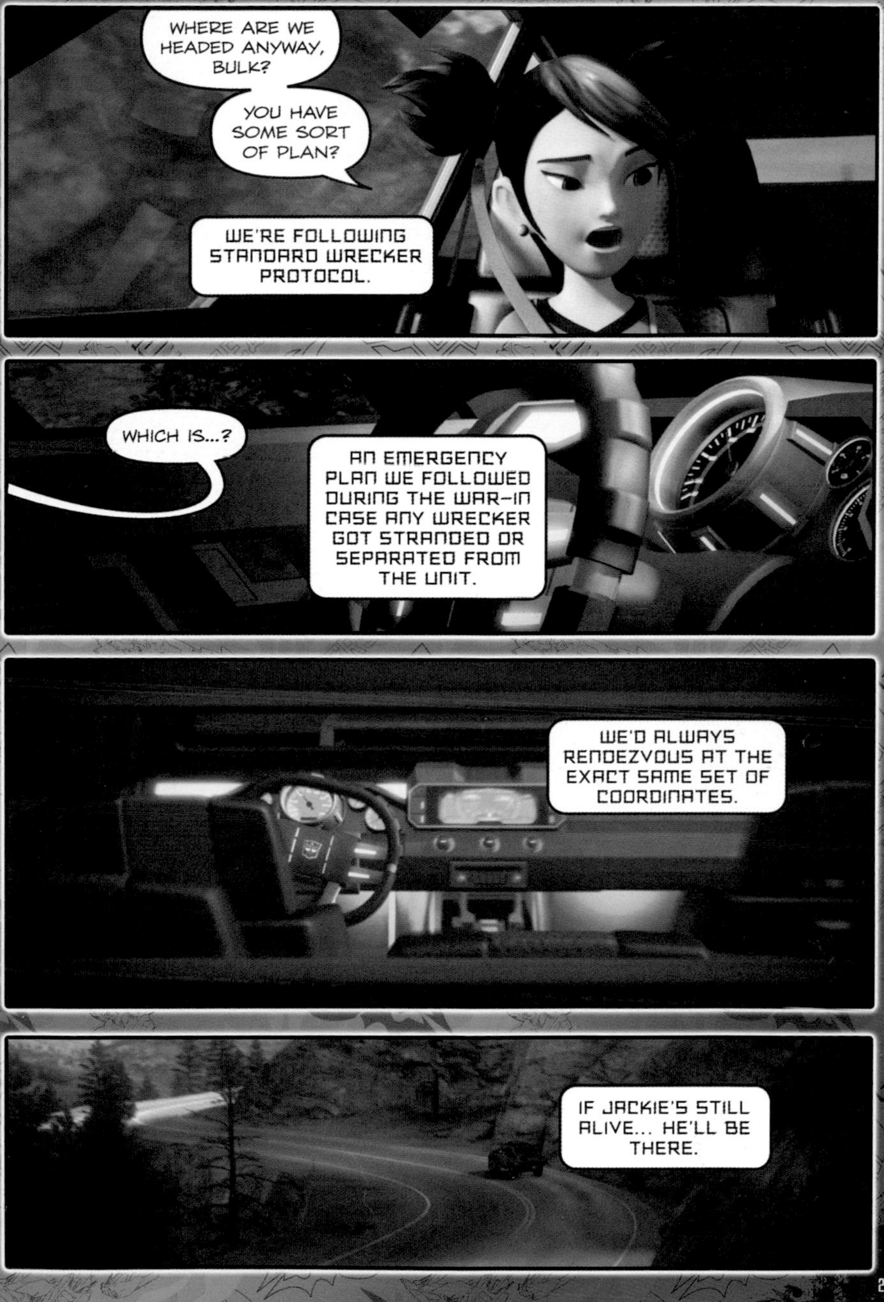
WHERE ARE WE HEADED ANYWAY, BULK?
YOU HAVE SOME SORT OF PLAN?
WE'RE FOLLOWING STANDARD WRECKER PROTOCOL.
WHICH IS...?
AN EMERGENCY PLAN WE FOLLOWED DURING THE WAR–IN CASE ANY WRECKER GOT STRANDED OR SEPARATED FROM THE UNIT.
WE'D ALWAYS RENDEZVOUS AT THE EXACT SAME SET OF COORDINATES.
IF JACKIE'S STILL ALIVE... HE'LL BE THERE.

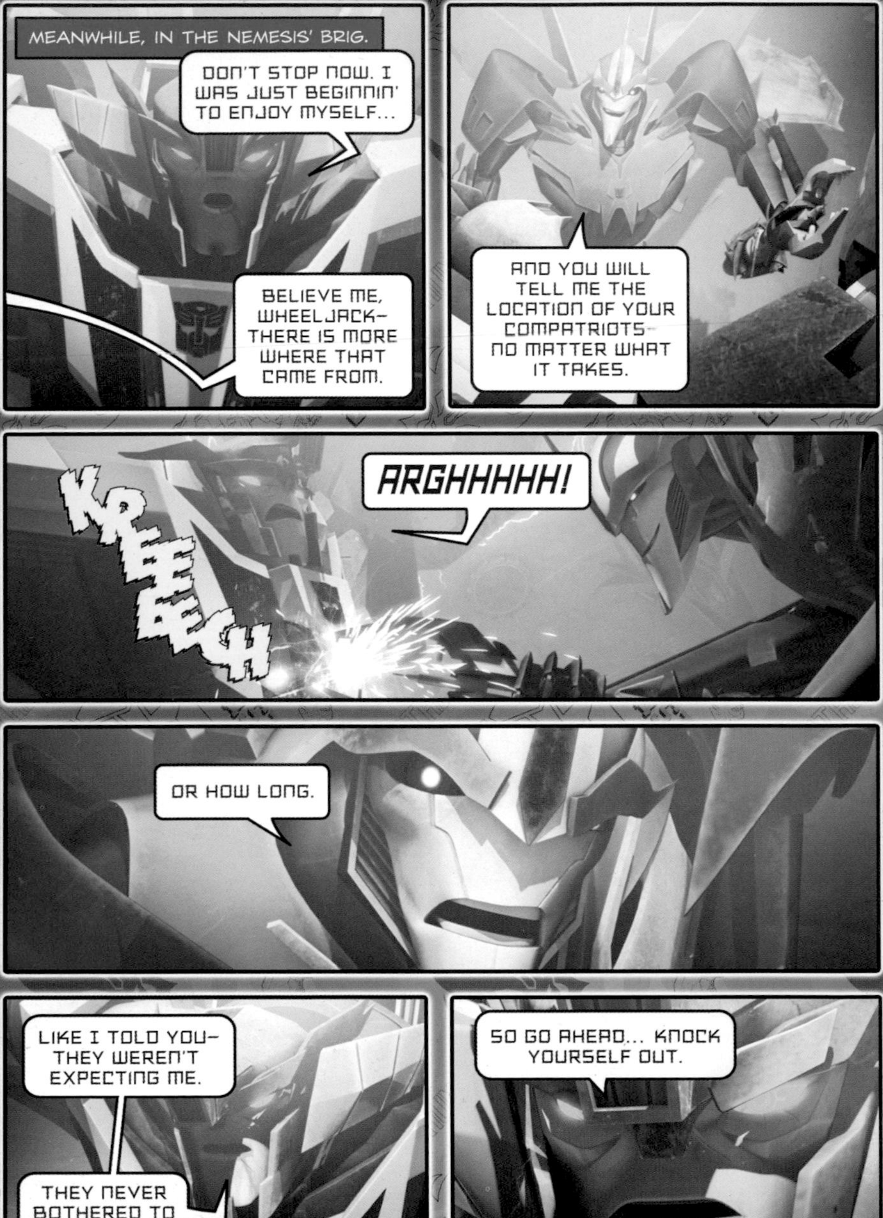

MEANWHILE, IN THE NEMESIS' BRIG.
DON'T STOP NOW. I WAS JUST BEGINNIN' TO ENJOY MYSELF...
BELIEVE ME, WHEELJACK– THERE IS MORE WHERE THAT CAME FROM.
AND YOU WILL TELL ME THE LOCATION OF YOUR COMPATRIOTS– NO MATTER WHAT IT TAKES.
KREEEECH
ARGHHHHH!
OR HOW LONG.
LIKE I TOLD YOU– THEY WEREN'T EXPECTING ME.
THEY NEVER BOTHERED TO FILL ME IN.
SO GO AHEAD... KNOCK YOURSELF OUT.

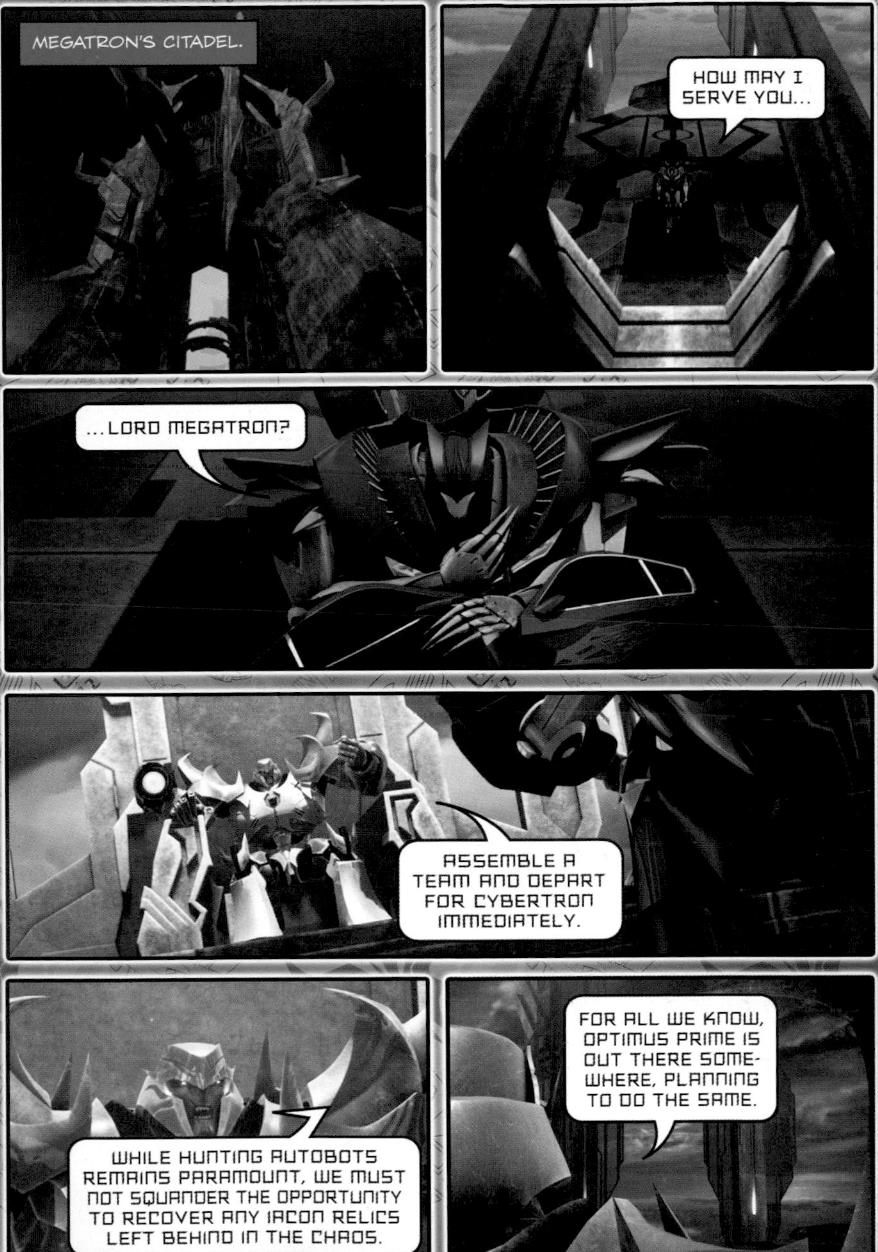
MEGATRON'S CITADEL.
HOW MAY I SERVE YOU...
...LORD MEGATRON?
ASSEMBLE A TEAM AND DEPART FOR CYBERTRON IMMEDIATELY.
WHILE HUNTING AUTOBOTS REMAINS PARAMOUNT, WE MUST NOT SQUANDER THE OPPORTUNITY TO RECOVER ANY IACON RELICS LEFT BEHIND IN THE CHAOS.
FOR ALL WE KNOW, OPTIMUS PRIME IS OUT THERE SOME-WHERE, PLANNING TO DO THE SAME.

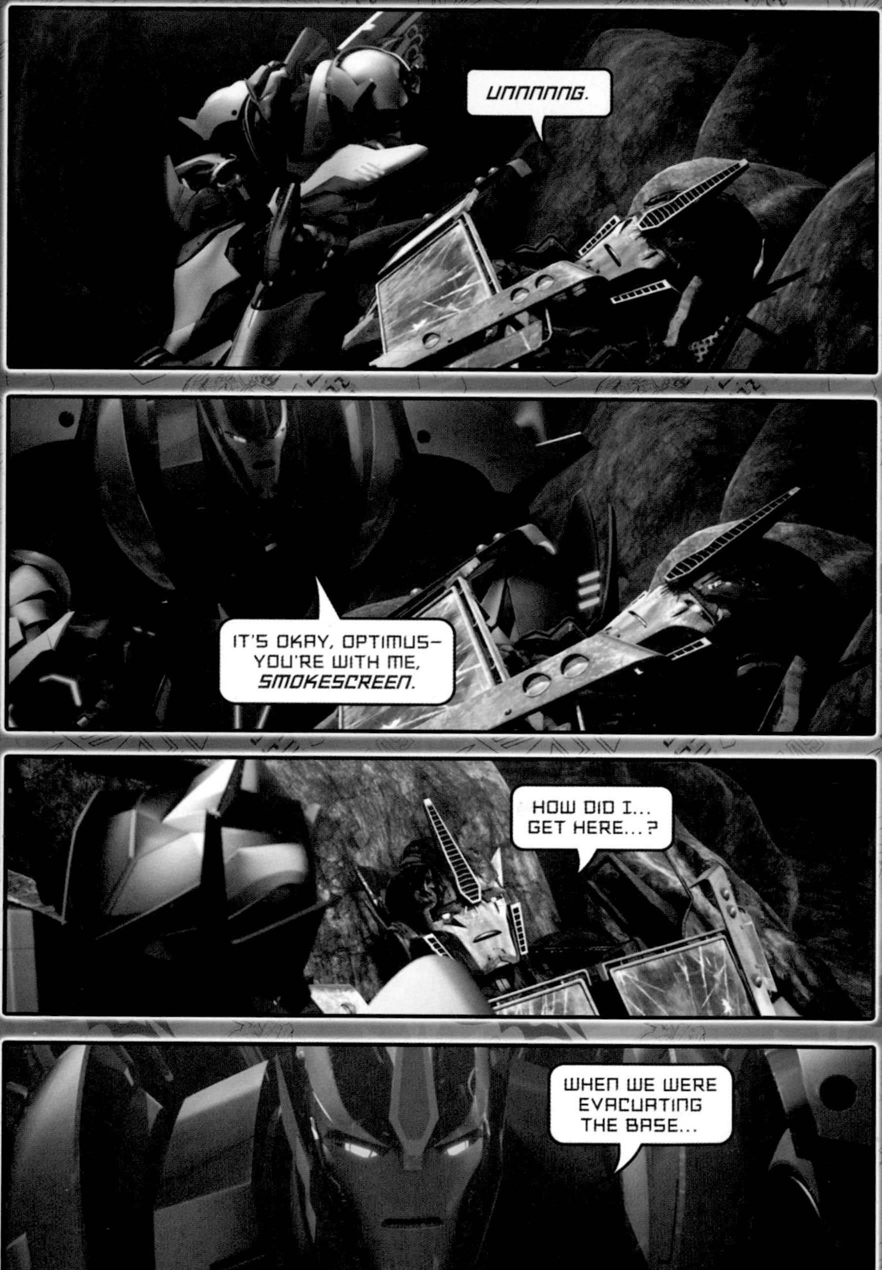
UNNNNNG.
IT'S OKAY, OPTIMUS— YOU'RE WITH ME, SMOKESCREEN.
HOW DID I... GET HERE...?
WHEN WE WERE EVACUATING THE BASE...

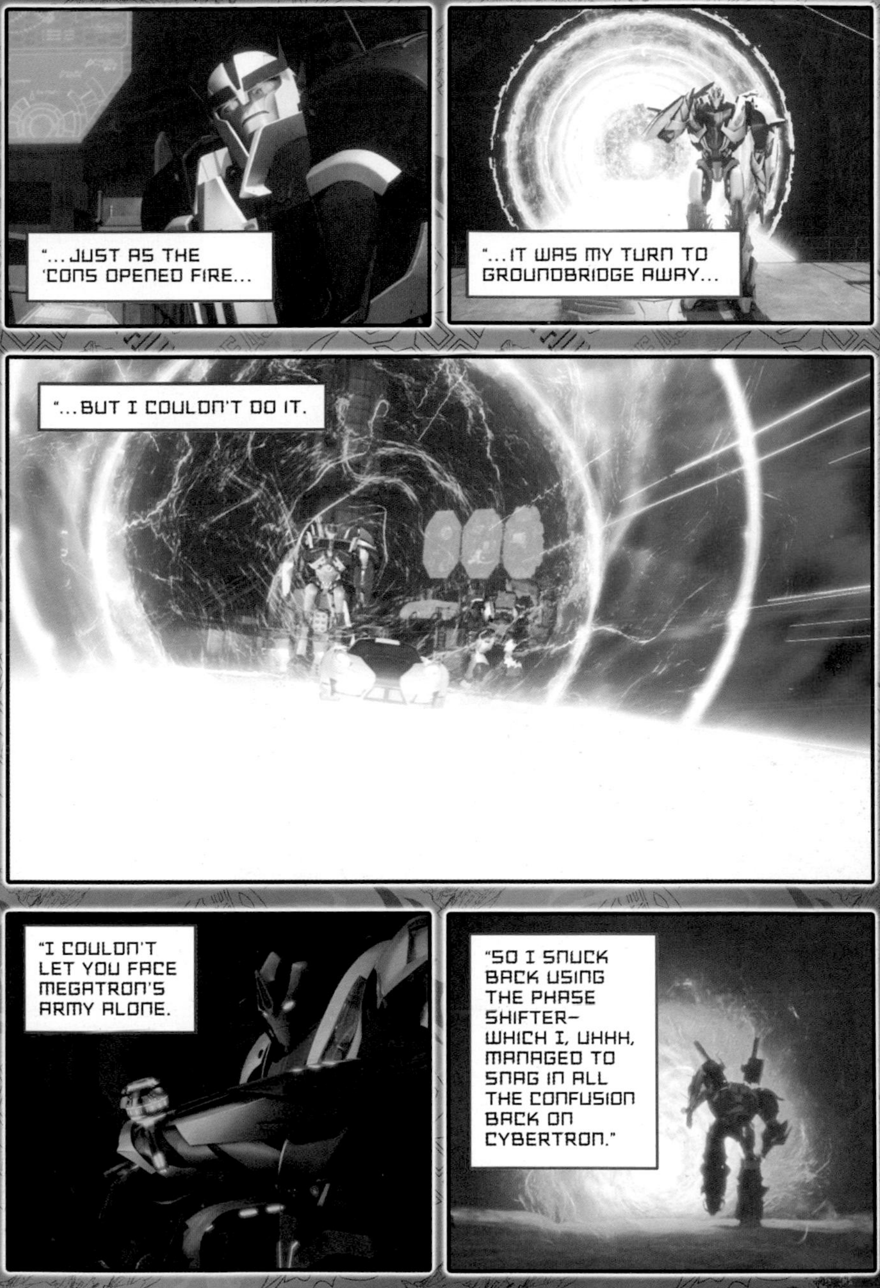
"...JUST AS THE 'CONS OPENED FIRE...
"...IT WAS MY TURN TO GROUNDBRIDGE AWAY...
"...BUT I COULDN'T DO IT.
"I COULDN'T LET YOU FACE MEGATRON'S ARMY ALONE.
"SO I SNUCK BACK USING THE PHASE SHIFTER—WHICH I, UHHH, MANAGED TO SNAG IN ALL THE CONFUSION BACK ON CYBERTRON."

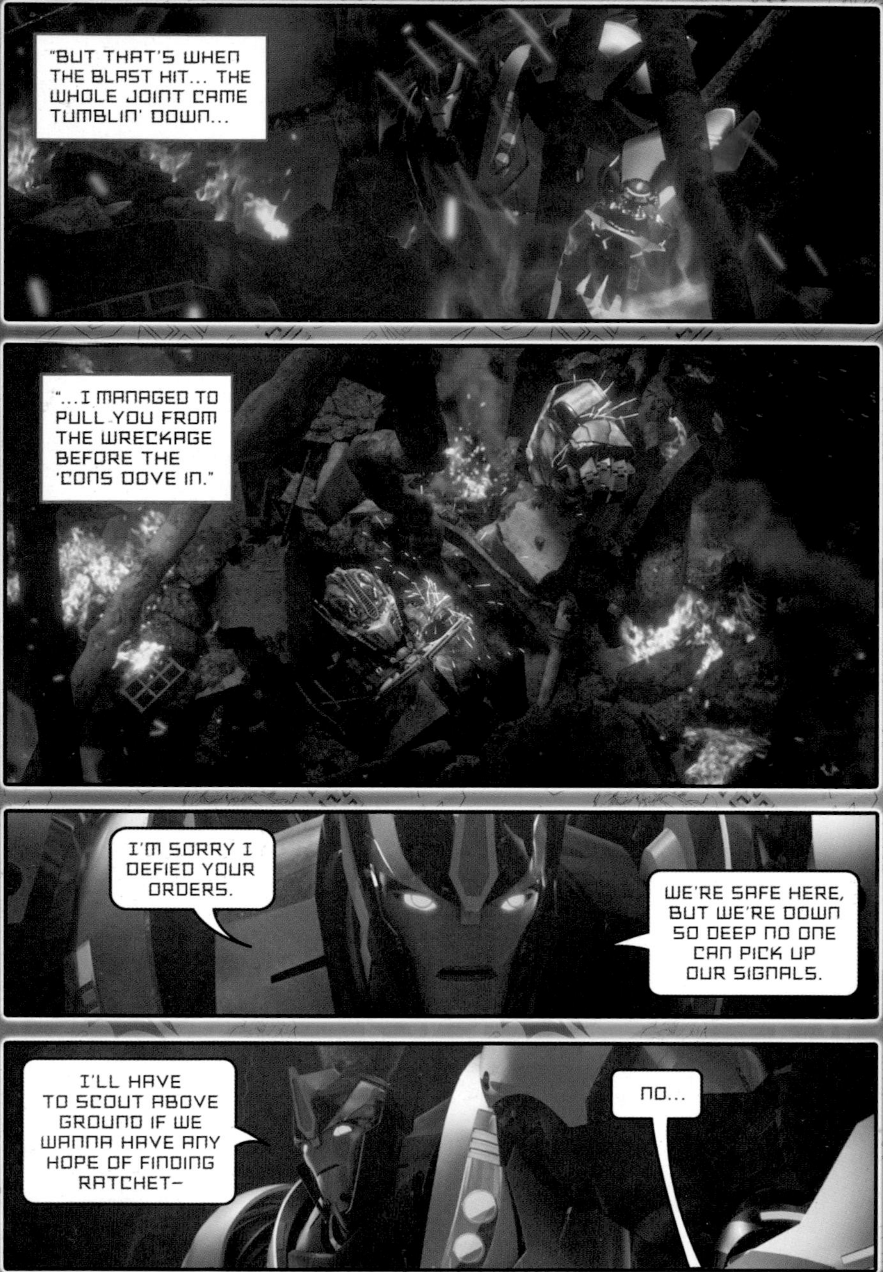
"BUT THAT'S WHEN THE BLAST HIT... THE WHOLE JOINT CAME TUMBLIN' DOWN...
"...I MANAGED TO PULL YOU FROM THE WRECKAGE BEFORE THE 'CONS DOVE IN."
I'M SORRY I DEFIED YOUR ORDERS.
WE'RE SAFE HERE, BUT WE'RE DOWN SO DEEP NO ONE CAN PICK UP OUR SIGNALS.
I'LL HAVE TO SCOUT ABOVE GROUND IF WE WANNA HAVE ANY HOPE OF FINDING RATCHET–
NO...

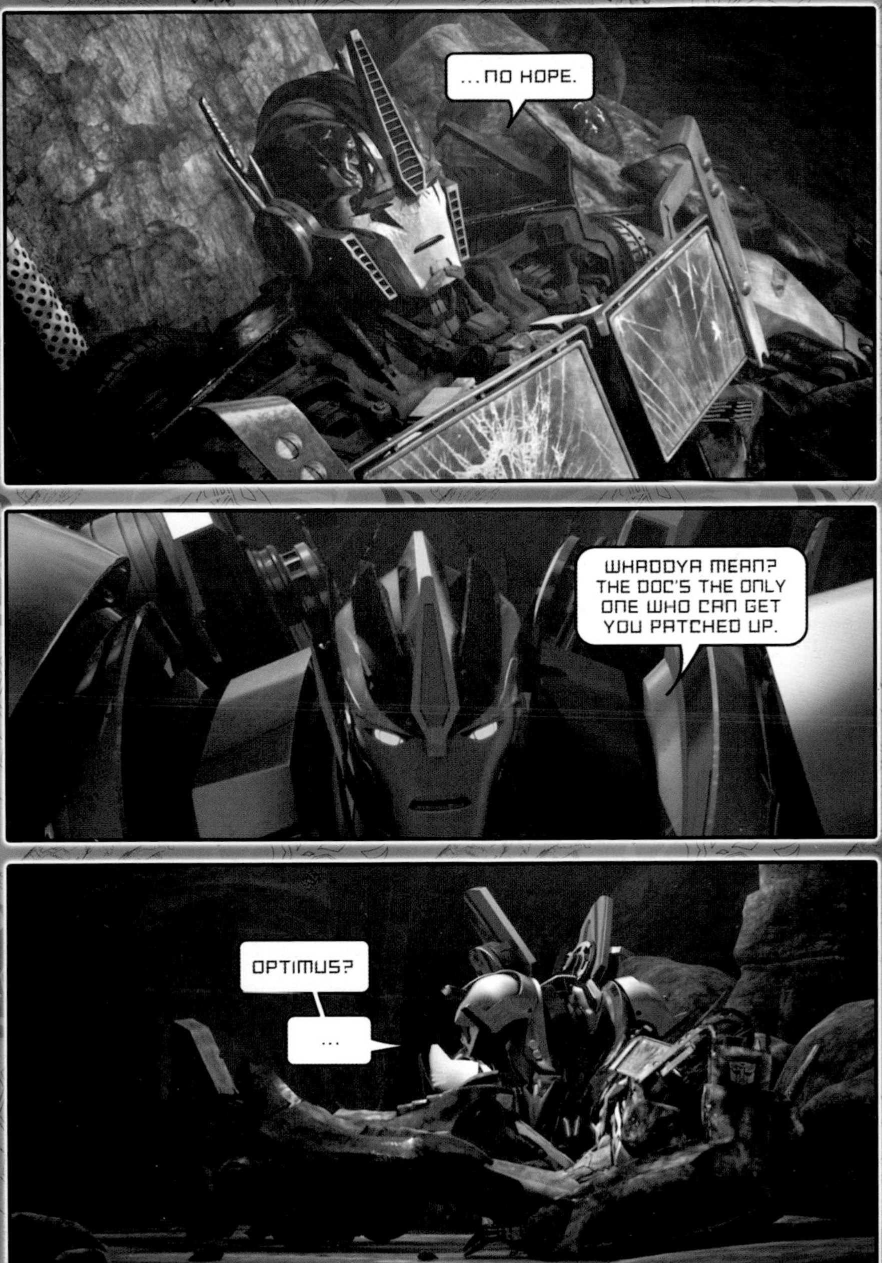
...NO HOPE.
WHADDYA MEAN? THE DOC'S THE ONLY ONE WHO CAN GET YOU PATCHED UP.
OPTIMUS?
...

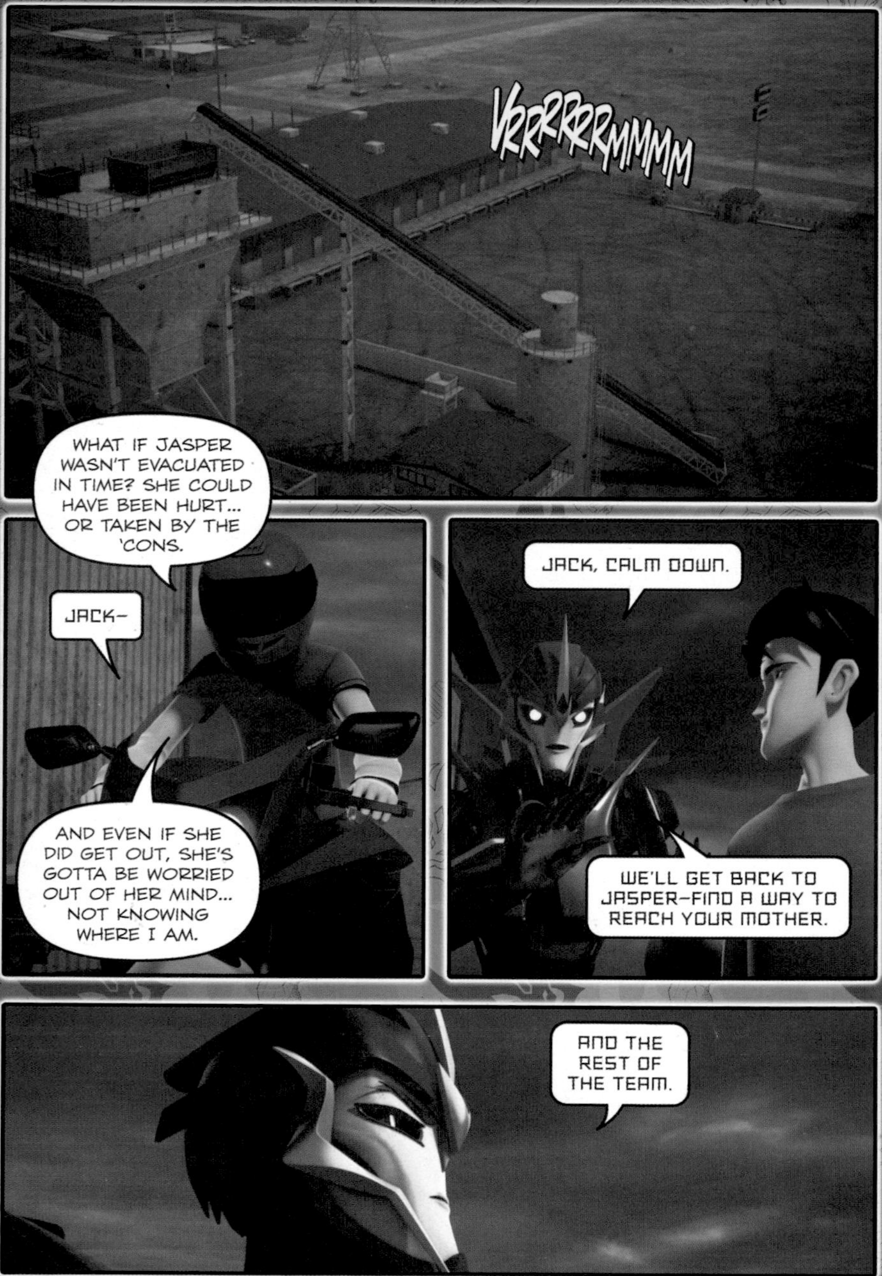
VRRRRRRMMMM
WHAT IF JASPER WASN'T EVACUATED IN TIME? SHE COULD HAVE BEEN HURT... OR TAKEN BY THE 'CONS.
JACK–
AND EVEN IF SHE DID GET OUT, SHE'S GOTTA BE WORRIED OUT OF HER MIND... NOT KNOWING WHERE I AM.
JACK, CALM DOWN.
WE'LL GET BACK TO JASPER–FIND A WAY TO REACH YOUR MOTHER.
AND THE REST OF THE TEAM.

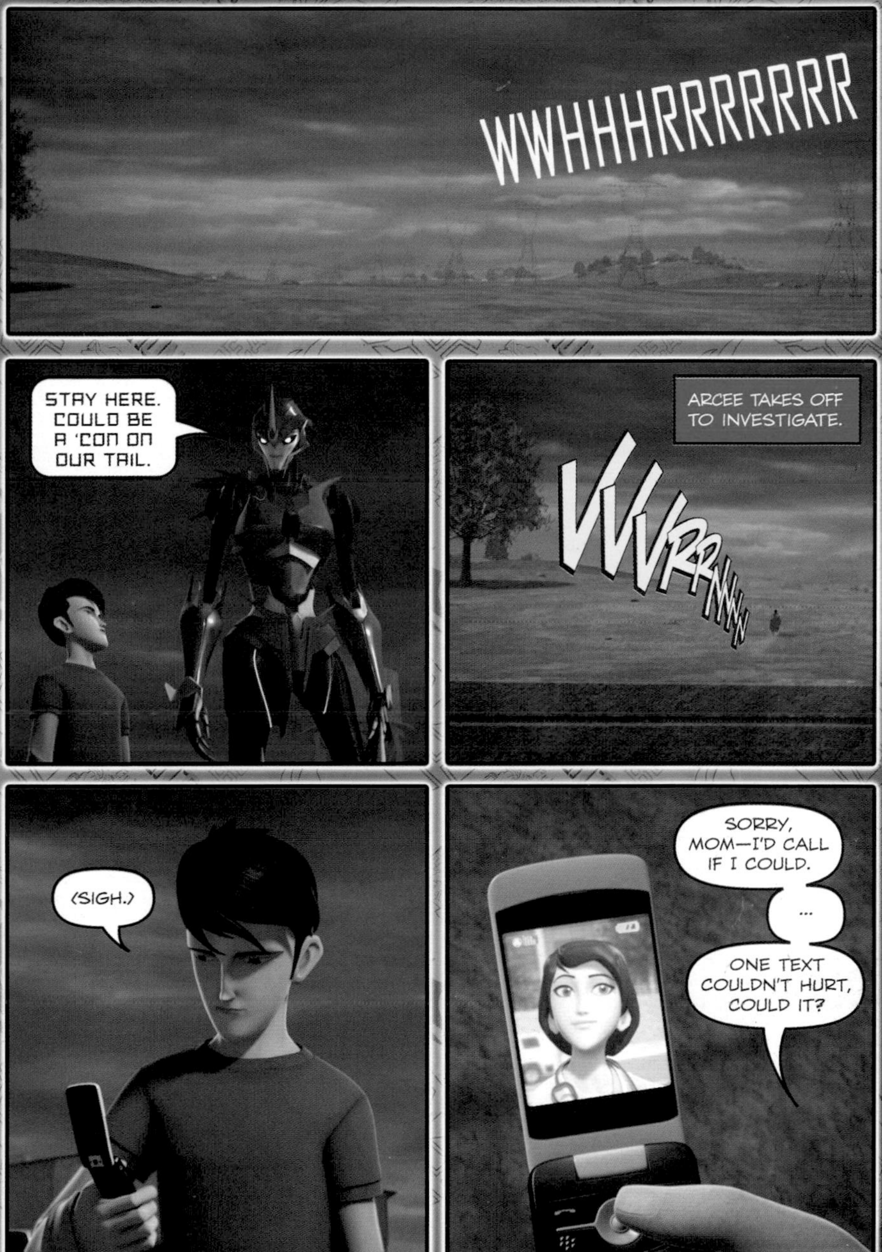
WWHHHRRRRRRR
STAY HERE. COULD BE A 'CON ON OUR TAIL.
ARCEE TAKES OFF TO INVESTIGATE.
VVVRRNNN
(SIGH.)
SORRY, MOM—I'D CALL IF I COULD.
...
ONE TEXT COULDN'T HURT, COULD IT?

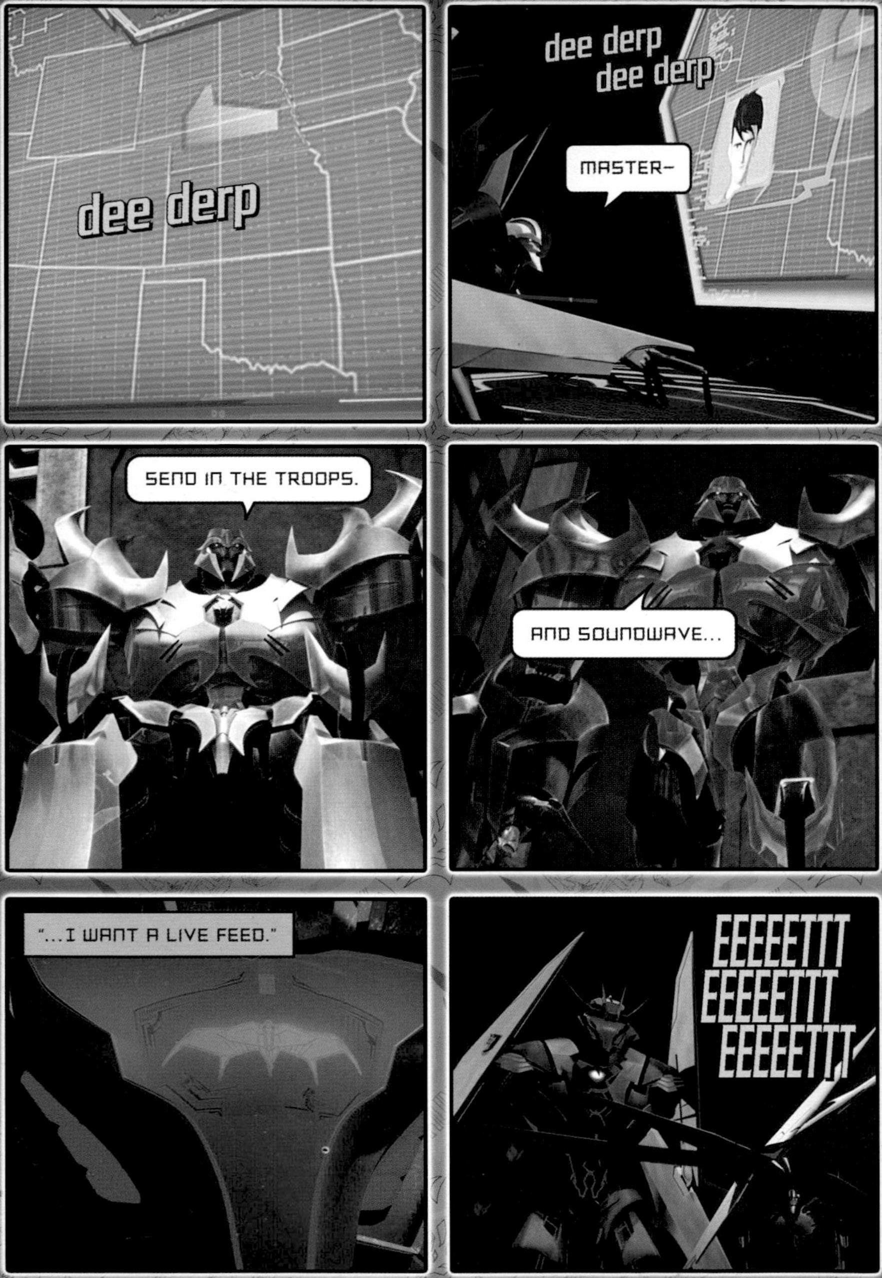

dee derp
dee derp
dee derp
MASTER–
SEND IN THE TROOPS.
AND SOUNDWAVE...
"...I WANT A LIVE FEED."
EEEEETTT
EEEEETTT
EEEEETTT

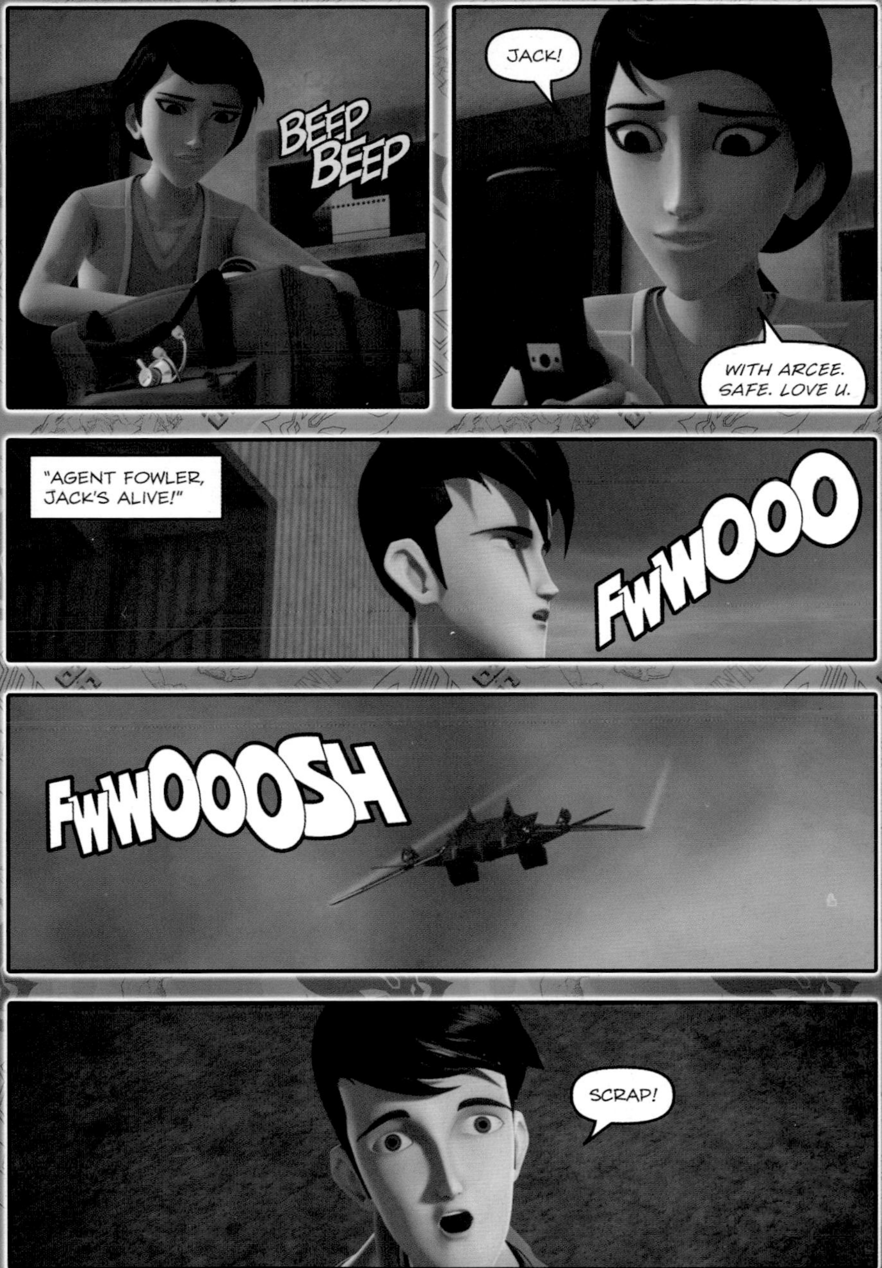

BEEP BEEP
JACK!
WITH ARCEE. SAFE. LOVE U.
"AGENT FOWLER, JACK'S ALIVE!"
FWWOOO
FWWOOOSH
SCRAP!

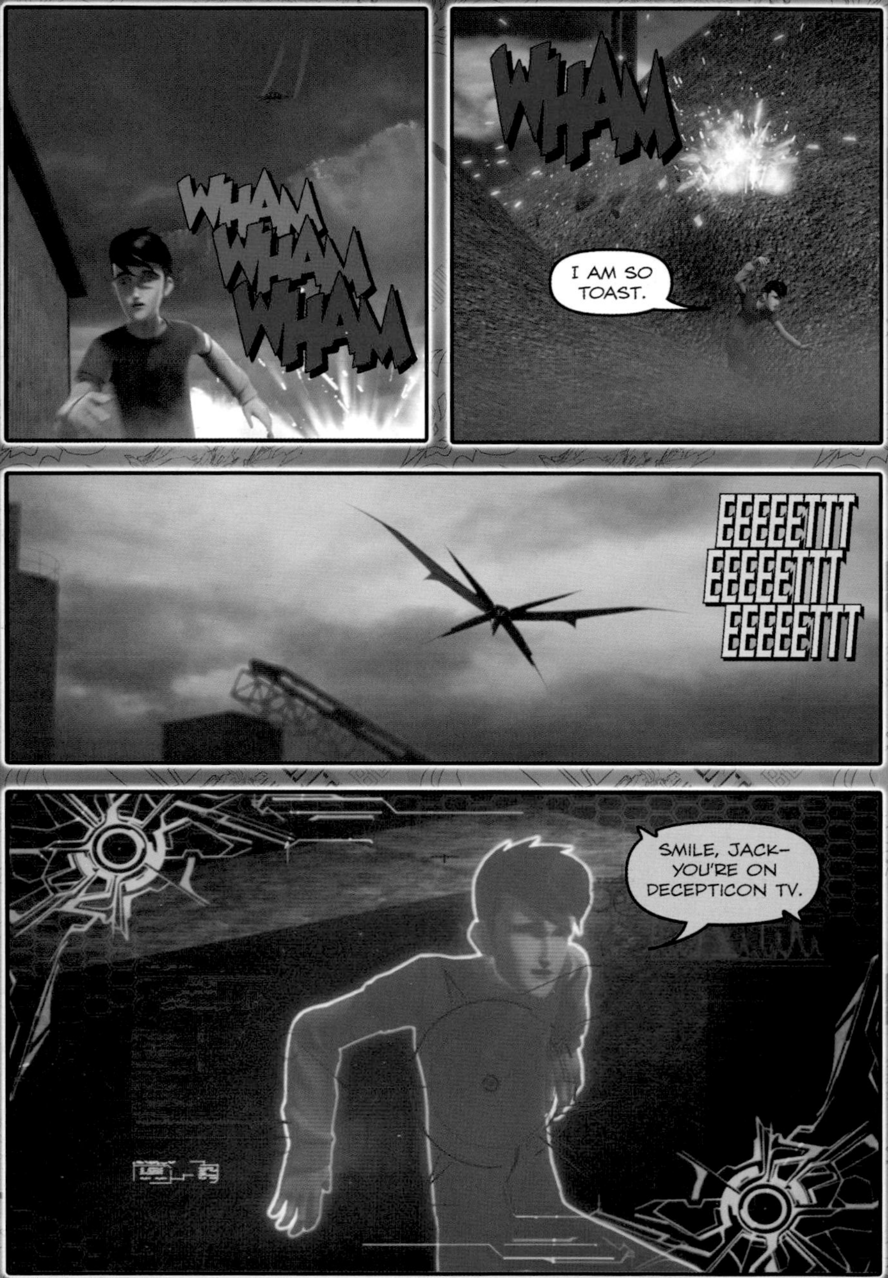
WHAM
WHAM
WHAM
WHAM
I AM SO TOAST.
EEEEETTT
EEEEETTT
EEEEETTT
SMILE, JACK— YOU'RE ON DECEPTICON TV.

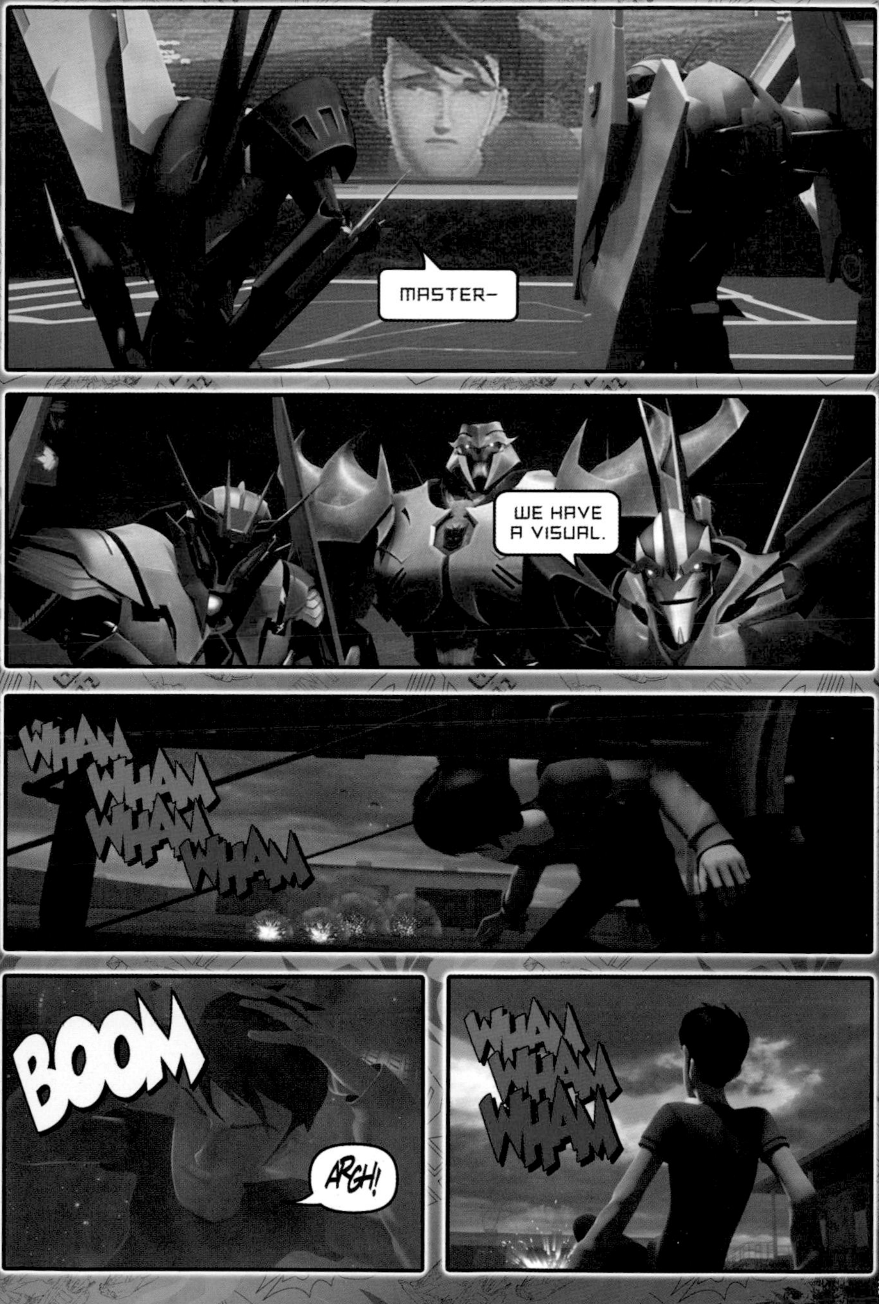
MASTER–
WE HAVE A VISUAL.
WHAM WHAM WHAM WHAM
BOOM
ARGH!
WHAM WHAM WHAM

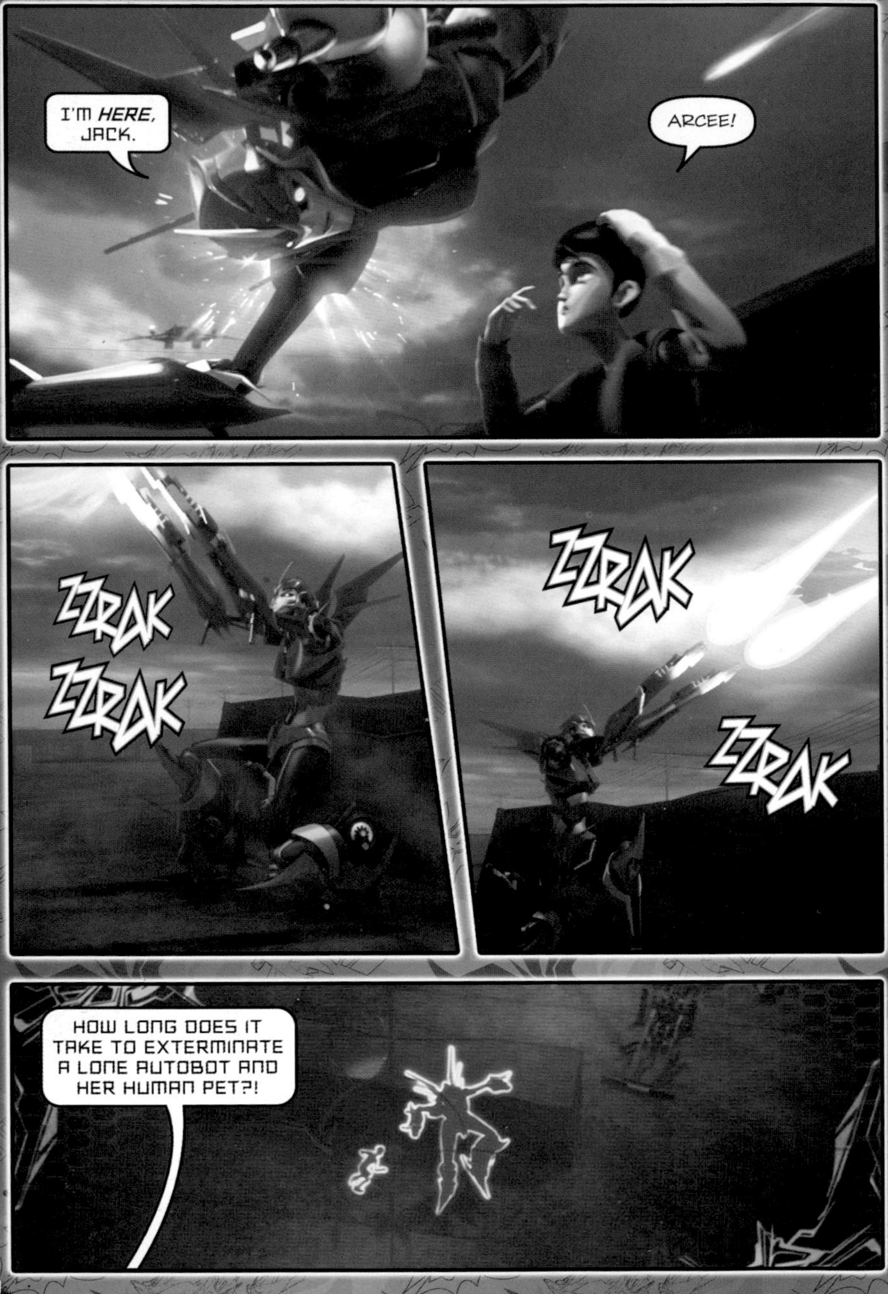

I'M *HERE*, JACK.
ARCEE!
ZZRAK
ZZRAK
ZZRAK
ZZRAK
HOW LONG DOES IT TAKE TO EXTERMINATE A LONE AUTOBOT AND HER HUMAN PET?!

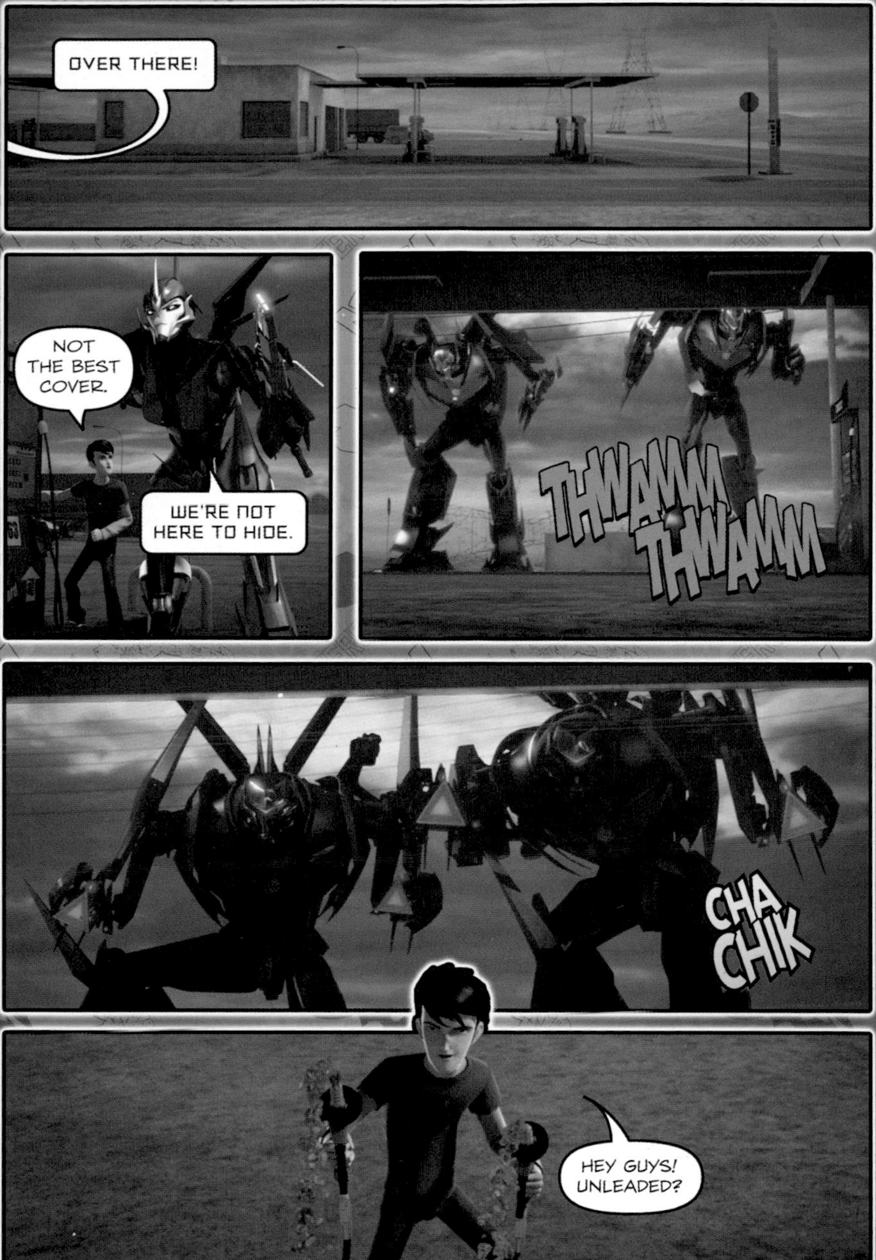
OVER THERE!
NOT THE BEST COVER.
WE'RE NOT HERE TO HIDE.
THWAMM THWAMM
CHA CHIK
HEY GUYS! UNLEADED?

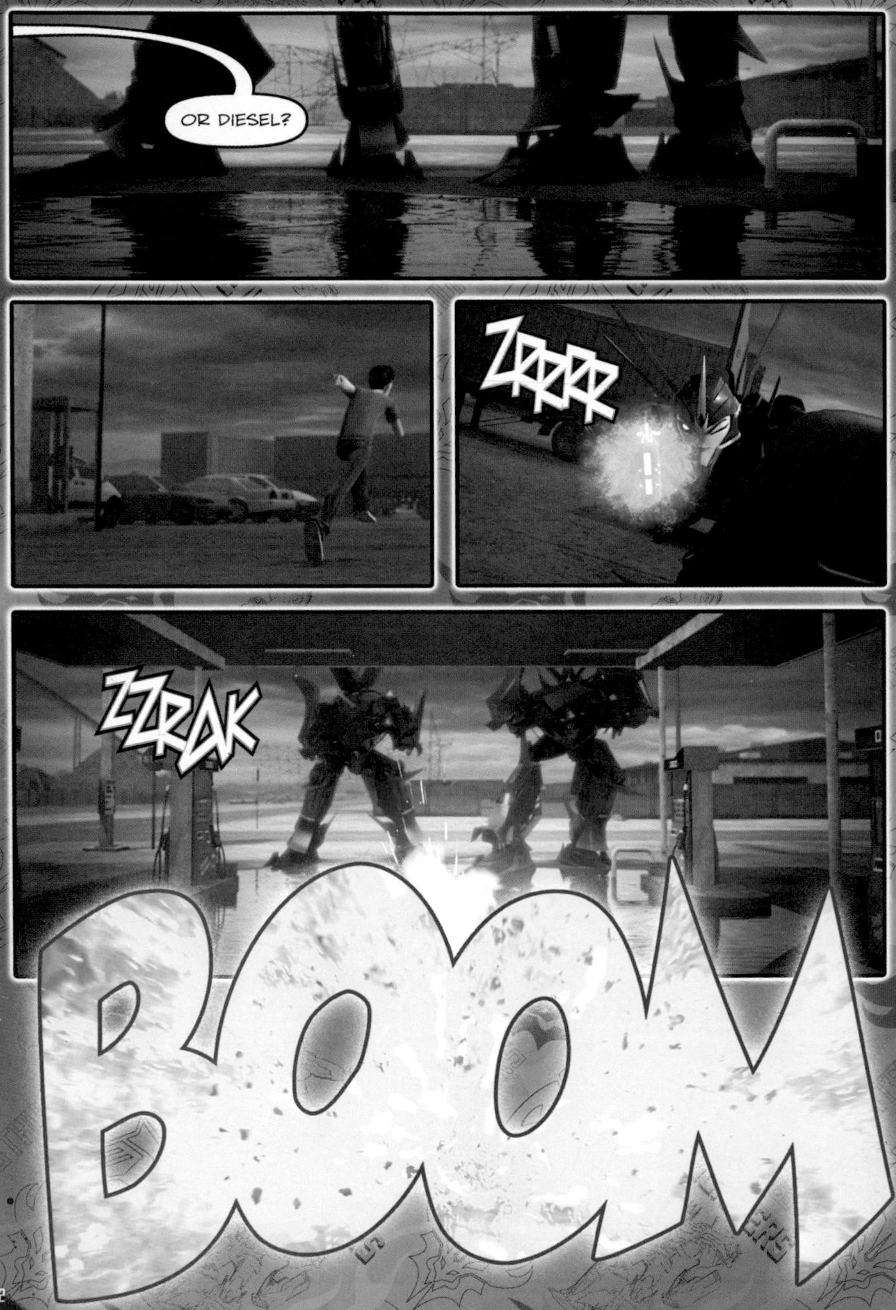
OR DIESEL?
ZRRRR
ZZRAK
BOOM

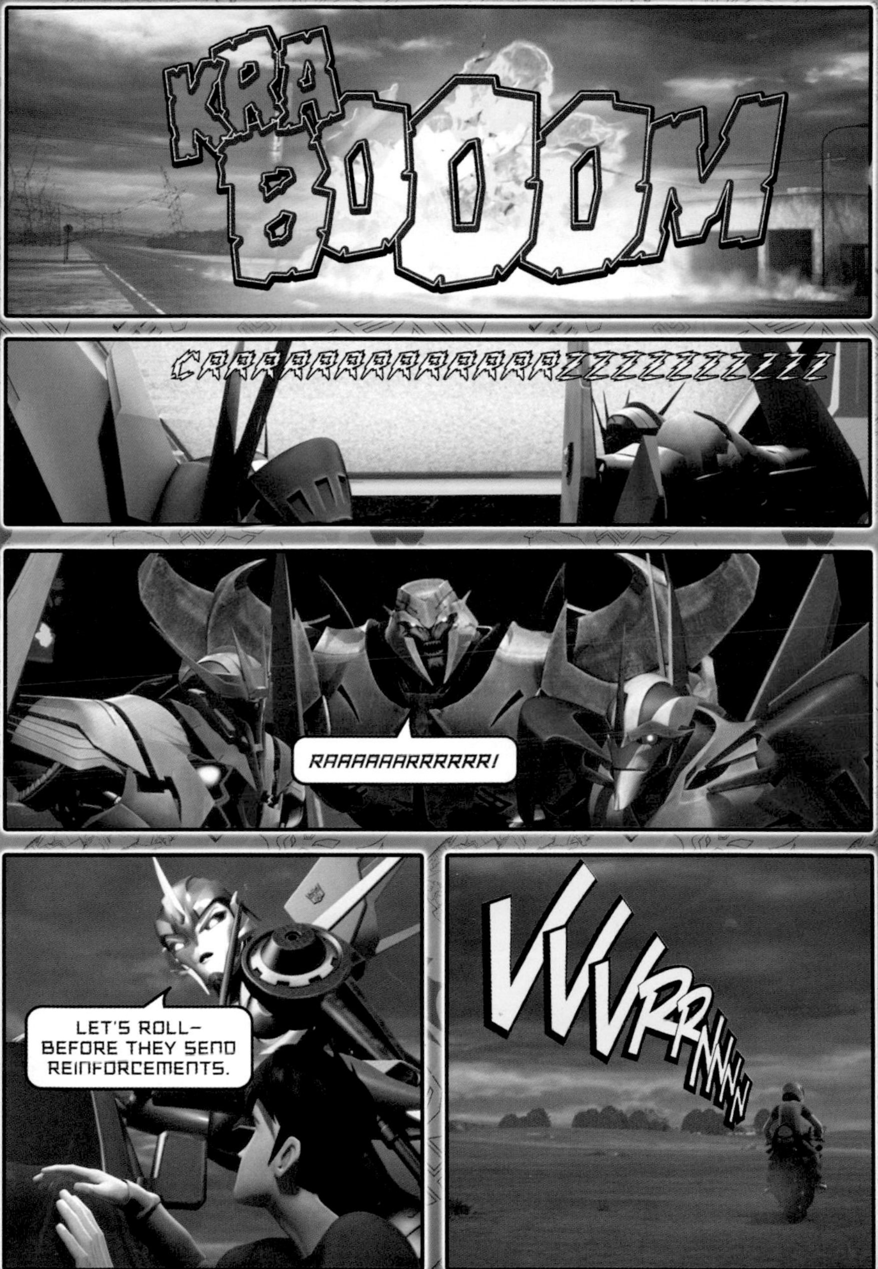
KRA BOOOM
CRRRRRRRRRRRRRRRZZZZZZZZZZZZ
RAAAAAARRRRRR!
LET'S ROLL—
BEFORE THEY SEND
REINFORCEMENTS.
VVVRRNNNN

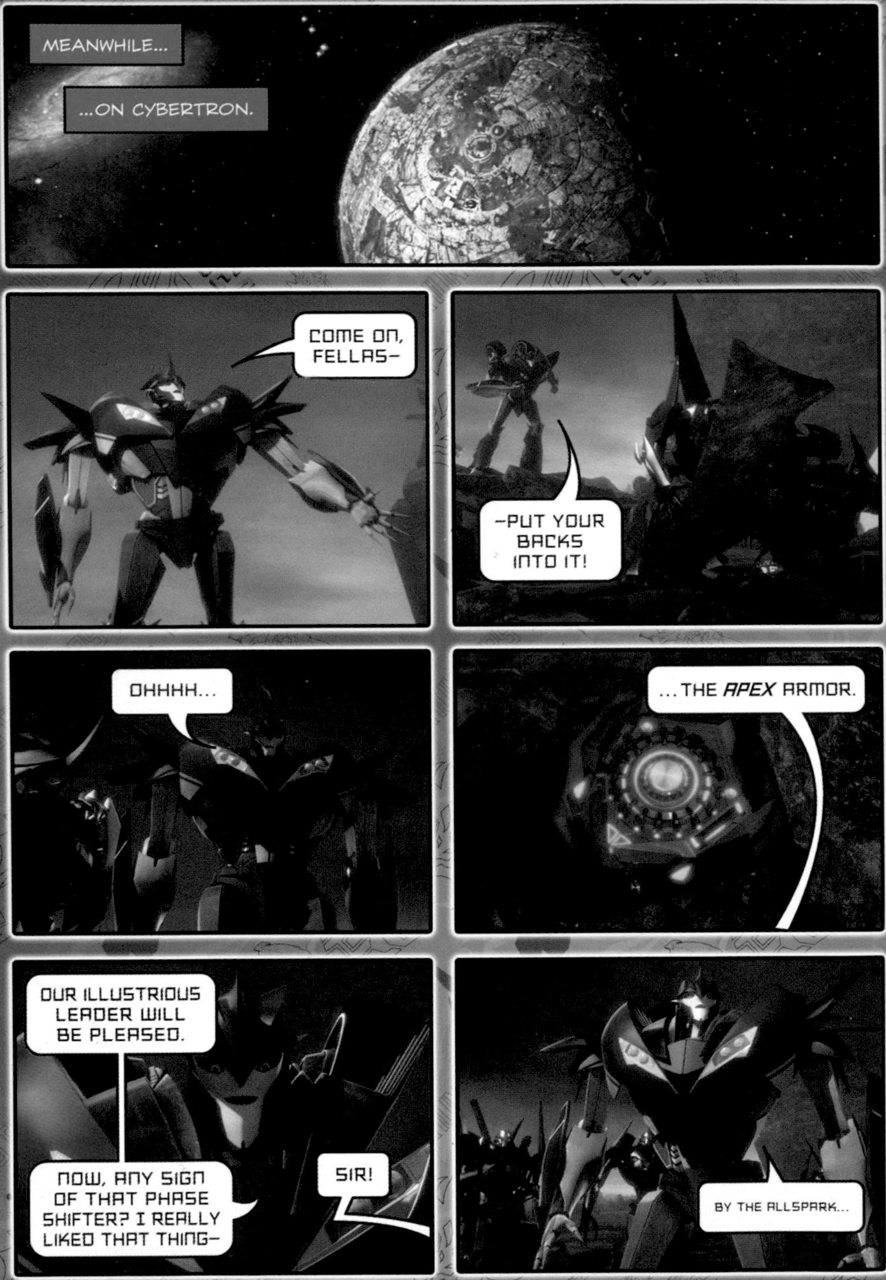
MEANWHILE...
...ON CYBERTRON.
COME ON, FELLAS–
–PUT YOUR BACKS INTO IT!
OHHHH...
...THE *APEX* ARMOR.
OUR ILLUSTRIOUS LEADER WILL BE PLEASED.
NOW, ANY SIGN OF THAT PHASE SHIFTER? I REALLY LIKED THAT THING–
SIR!
BY THE ALLSPARK...

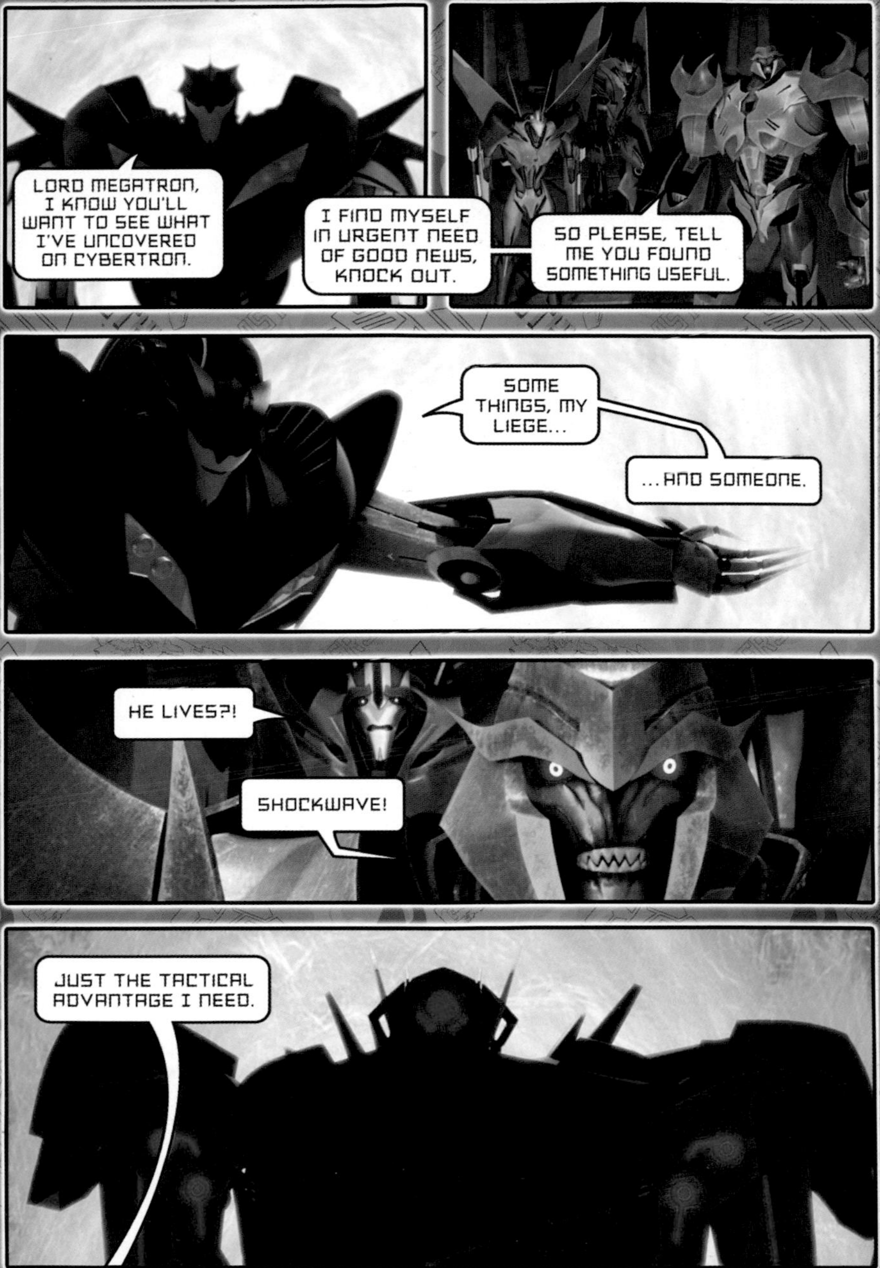
LORD MEGATRON, I KNOW YOU'LL WANT TO SEE WHAT I'VE UNCOVERED ON CYBERTRON.
I FIND MYSELF IN URGENT NEED OF GOOD NEWS, KNOCK OUT.
SO PLEASE, TELL ME YOU FOUND SOMETHING USEFUL.
SOME THINGS, MY LIEGE...
...AND SOMEONE.
HE LIVES?!
SHOCKWAVE!
JUST THE TACTICAL ADVANTAGE I NEED.

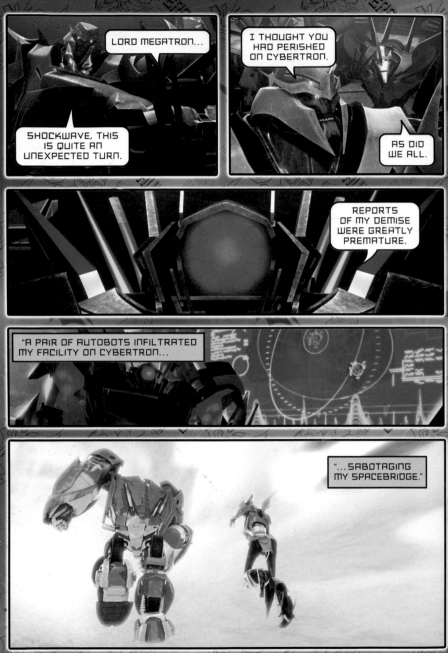

LORD MEGATRON...

I THOUGHT YOU HAD PERISHED ON CYBERTRON.

SHOCKWAVE, THIS IS QUITE AN UNEXPECTED TURN.

AS DID WE ALL.

REPORTS OF MY DEMISE WERE GREATLY PREMATURE.

"A PAIR OF AUTOBOTS INFILTRATED MY FACILITY ON CYBERTRON...

"...SABOTAGING MY SPACEBRIDGE."

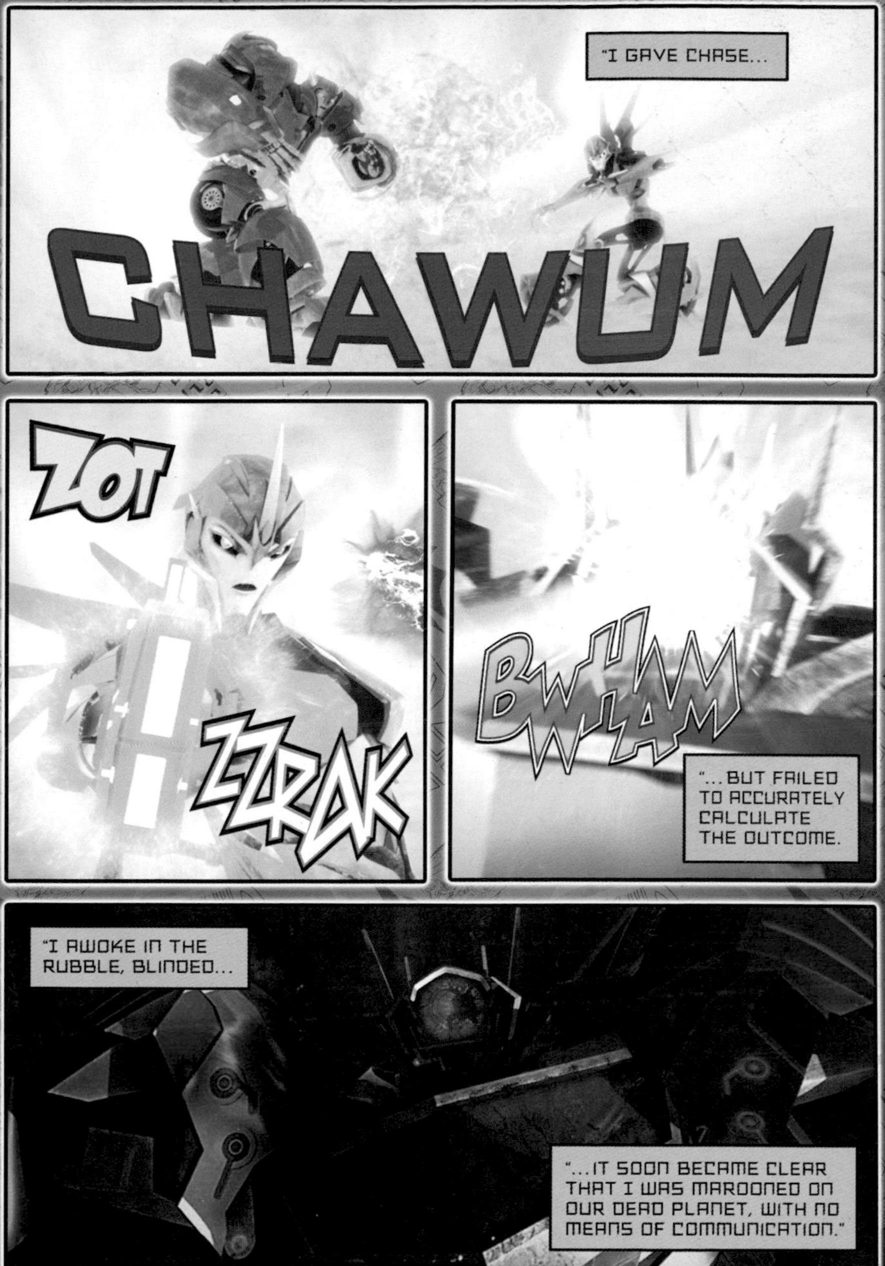
"I GAVE CHASE...
CHAWUM
ZOT
ZZZRAK
BWHAM
"...BUT FAILED TO ACCURATELY CALCULATE THE OUTCOME.
"I AWOKE IN THE RUBBLE, BLINDED...
"...IT SOON BECAME CLEAR THAT I WAS MAROONED ON OUR DEAD PLANET, WITH NO MEANS OF COMMUNICATION."

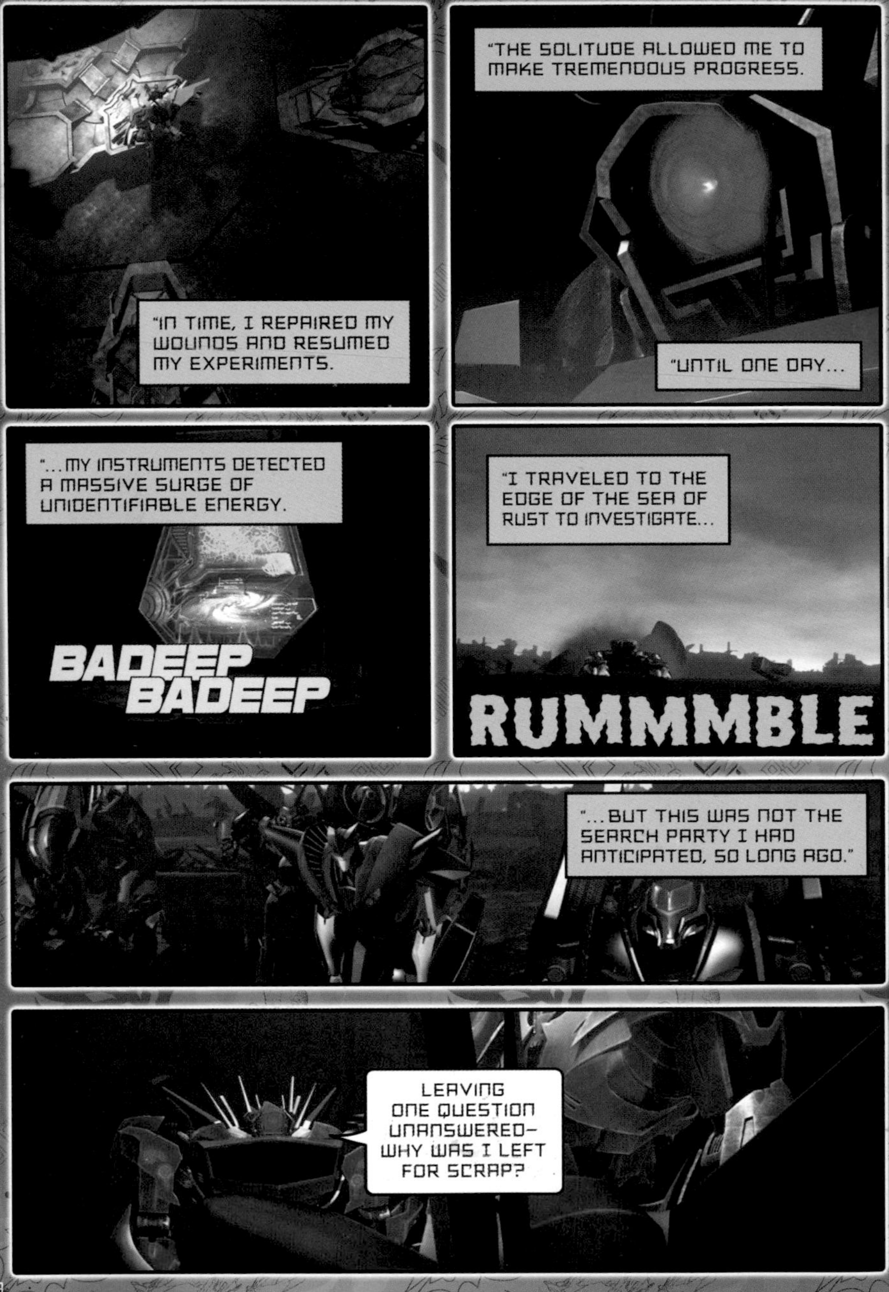

"IN TIME, I REPAIRED MY WOUNDS AND RESUMED MY EXPERIMENTS.
"THE SOLITUDE ALLOWED ME TO MAKE TREMENDOUS PROGRESS.
"UNTIL ONE DAY...
"...MY INSTRUMENTS DETECTED A MASSIVE SURGE OF UNIDENTIFIABLE ENERGY.
BADEEP BADEEP
"I TRAVELED TO THE EDGE OF THE SEA OF RUST TO INVESTIGATE...
RUMMMBLE
"...BUT THIS WAS NOT THE SEARCH PARTY I HAD ANTICIPATED, SO LONG AGO."
LEAVING ONE QUESTION UNANSWERED— WHY WAS I LEFT FOR SCRAP?

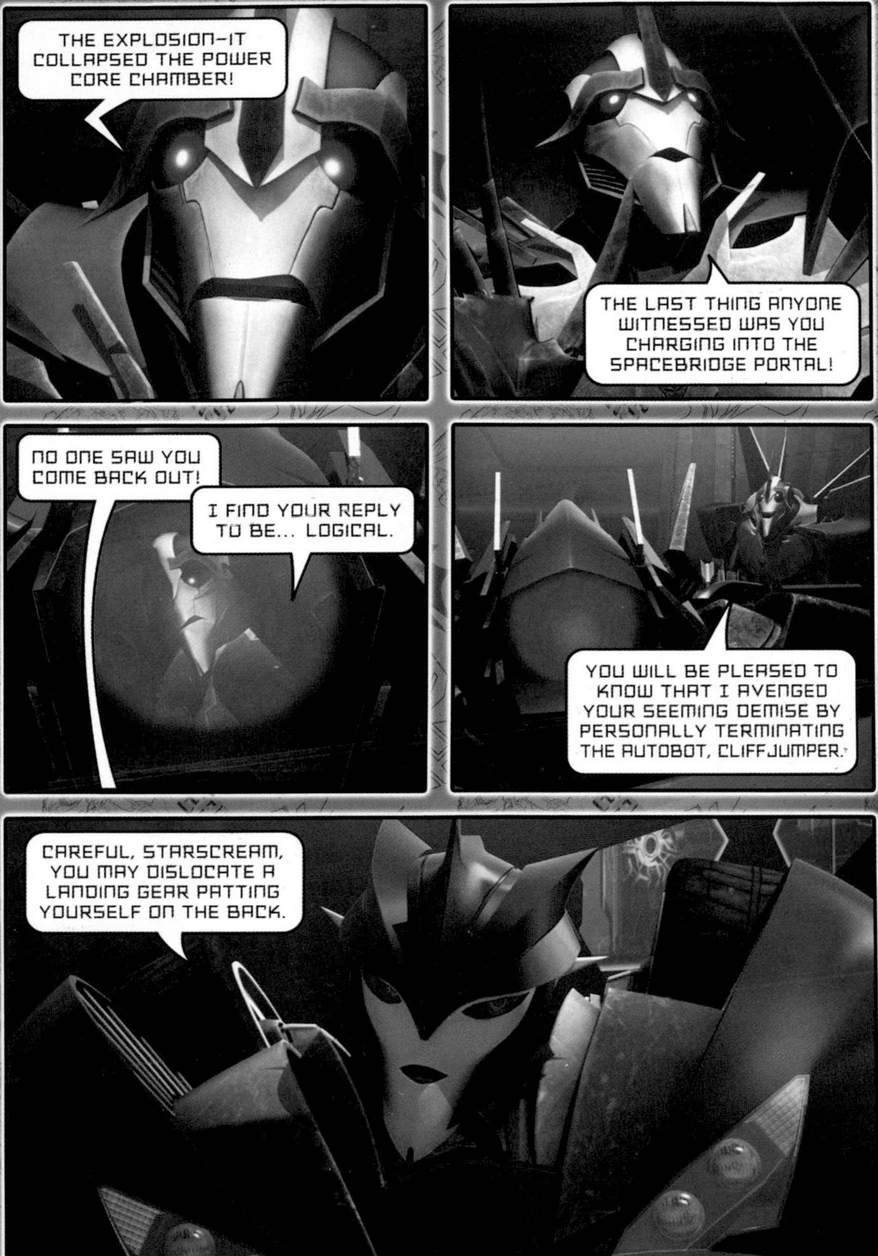
THE EXPLOSION—IT COLLAPSED THE POWER CORE CHAMBER!
THE LAST THING ANYONE WITNESSED WAS YOU CHARGING INTO THE SPACEBRIDGE PORTAL!
NO ONE SAW YOU COME BACK OUT!
I FIND YOUR REPLY TO BE... LOGICAL.
YOU WILL BE PLEASED TO KNOW THAT I AVENGED YOUR SEEMING DEMISE BY PERSONALLY TERMINATING THE AUTOBOT, CLIFFJUMPER.
CAREFUL, STARSCREAM, YOU MAY DISLOCATE A LANDING GEAR PATTING YOURSELF ON THE BACK.

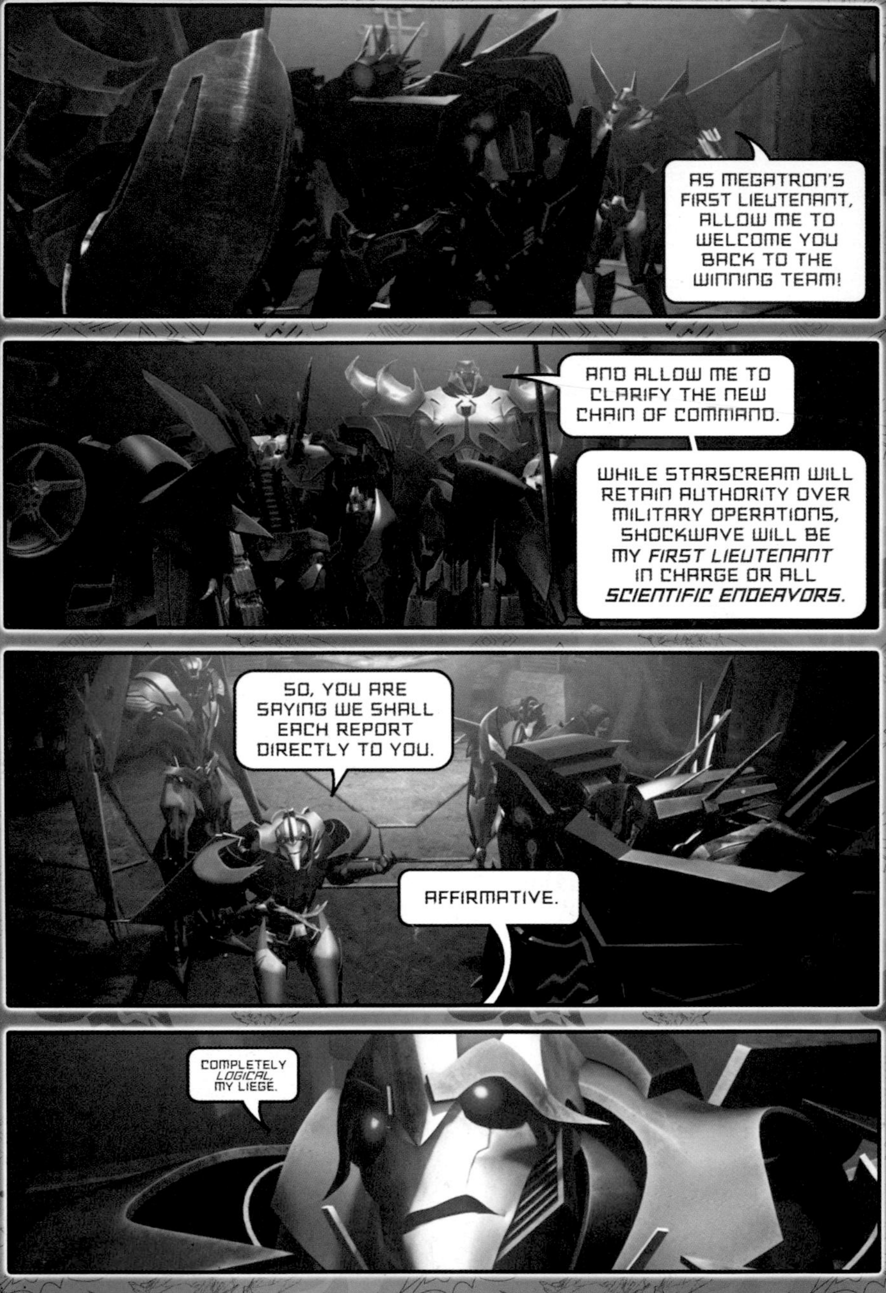
AS MEGATRON'S FIRST LIEUTENANT, ALLOW ME TO WELCOME YOU BACK TO THE WINNING TEAM!
AND ALLOW ME TO CLARIFY THE NEW CHAIN OF COMMAND.
WHILE STARSCREAM WILL RETAIN AUTHORITY OVER MILITARY OPERATIONS, SHOCKWAVE WILL BE MY *FIRST LIEUTENANT* IN CHARGE OR ALL *SCIENTIFIC ENDEAVORS*.
SO, YOU ARE SAYING WE SHALL EACH REPORT DIRECTLY TO YOU.
AFFIRMATIVE.
COMPLETELY *LOGICAL*, MY LIEGE.

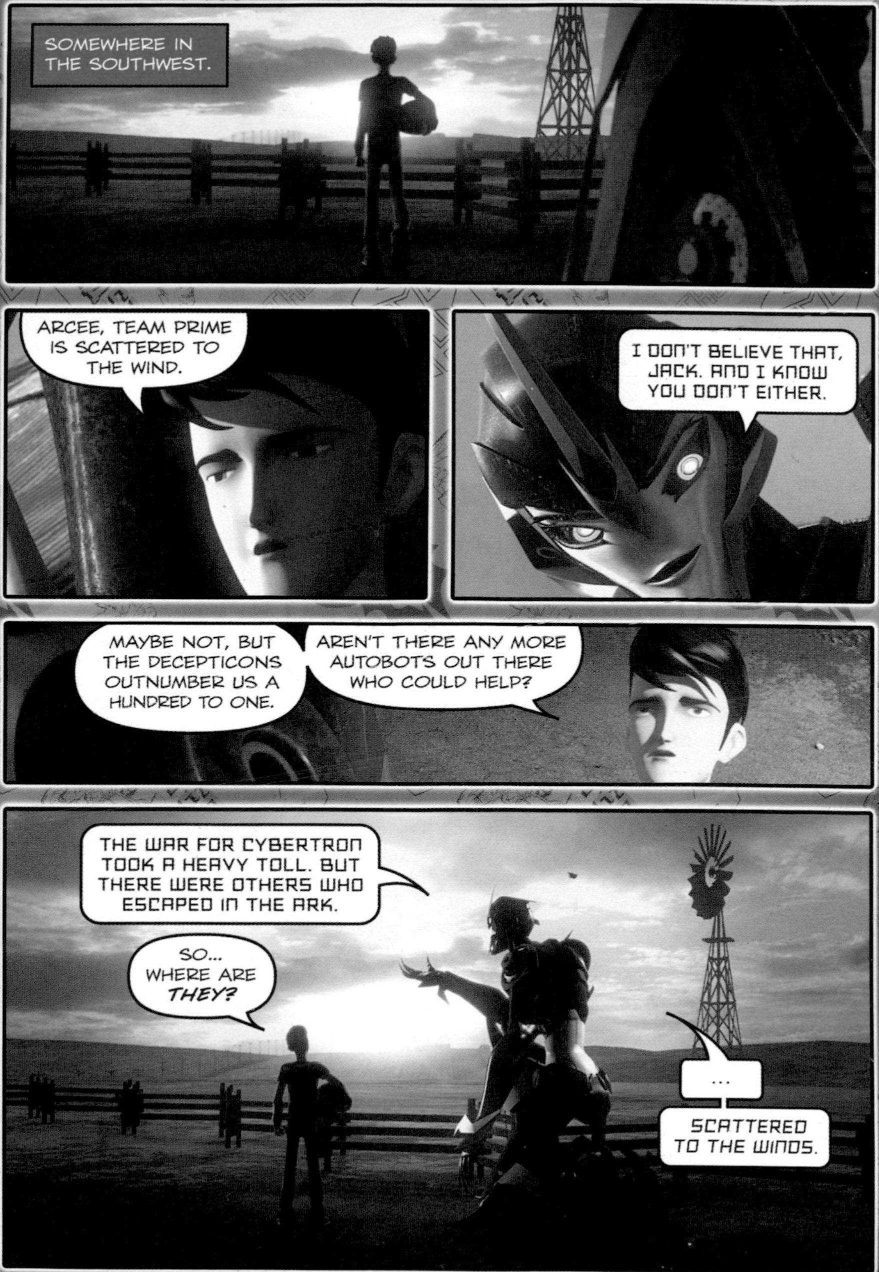
SOMEWHERE IN THE SOUTHWEST.
ARCEE, TEAM PRIME IS SCATTERED TO THE WIND.
I DON'T BELIEVE THAT, JACK. AND I KNOW YOU DON'T EITHER.
MAYBE NOT, BUT THE DECEPTICONS OUTNUMBER US A HUNDRED TO ONE.
AREN'T THERE ANY MORE AUTOBOTS OUT THERE WHO COULD HELP?
THE WAR FOR CYBERTRON TOOK A HEAVY TOLL. BUT THERE WERE OTHERS WHO ESCAPED IN THE ARK.
SO... WHERE ARE *THEY?*
...
SCATTERED TO THE WINDS.

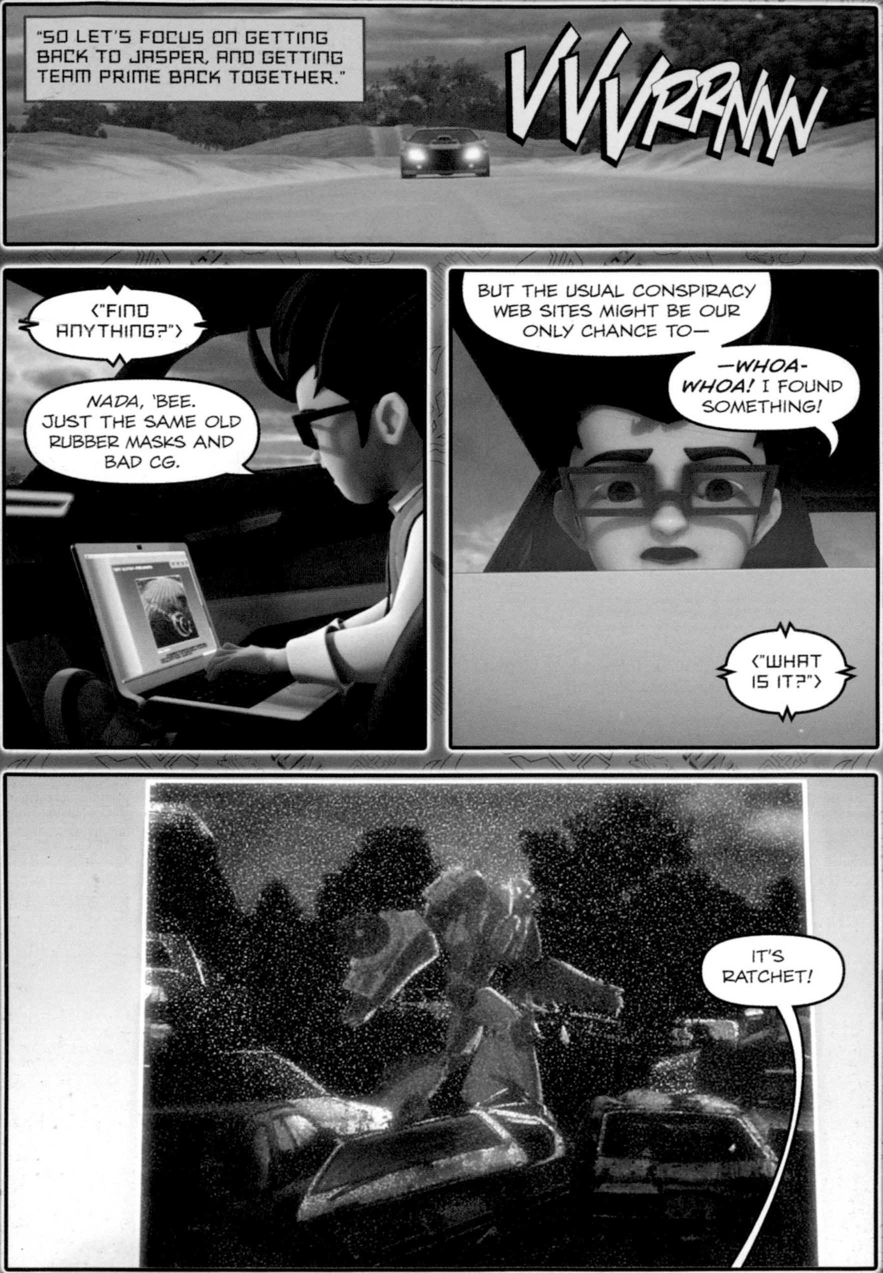
"SO LET'S FOCUS ON GETTING BACK TO JASPER, AND GETTING TEAM PRIME BACK TOGETHER."
VVVRRNNN
<"FIND ANYTHING?">
NADA, 'BEE. JUST THE SAME OLD RUBBER MASKS AND BAD CG.
BUT THE USUAL CONSPIRACY WEB SITES MIGHT BE OUR ONLY CHANCE TO—
—WHOA-WHOA! I FOUND SOMETHING!
<"WHAT IS IT?">
IT'S RATCHET!

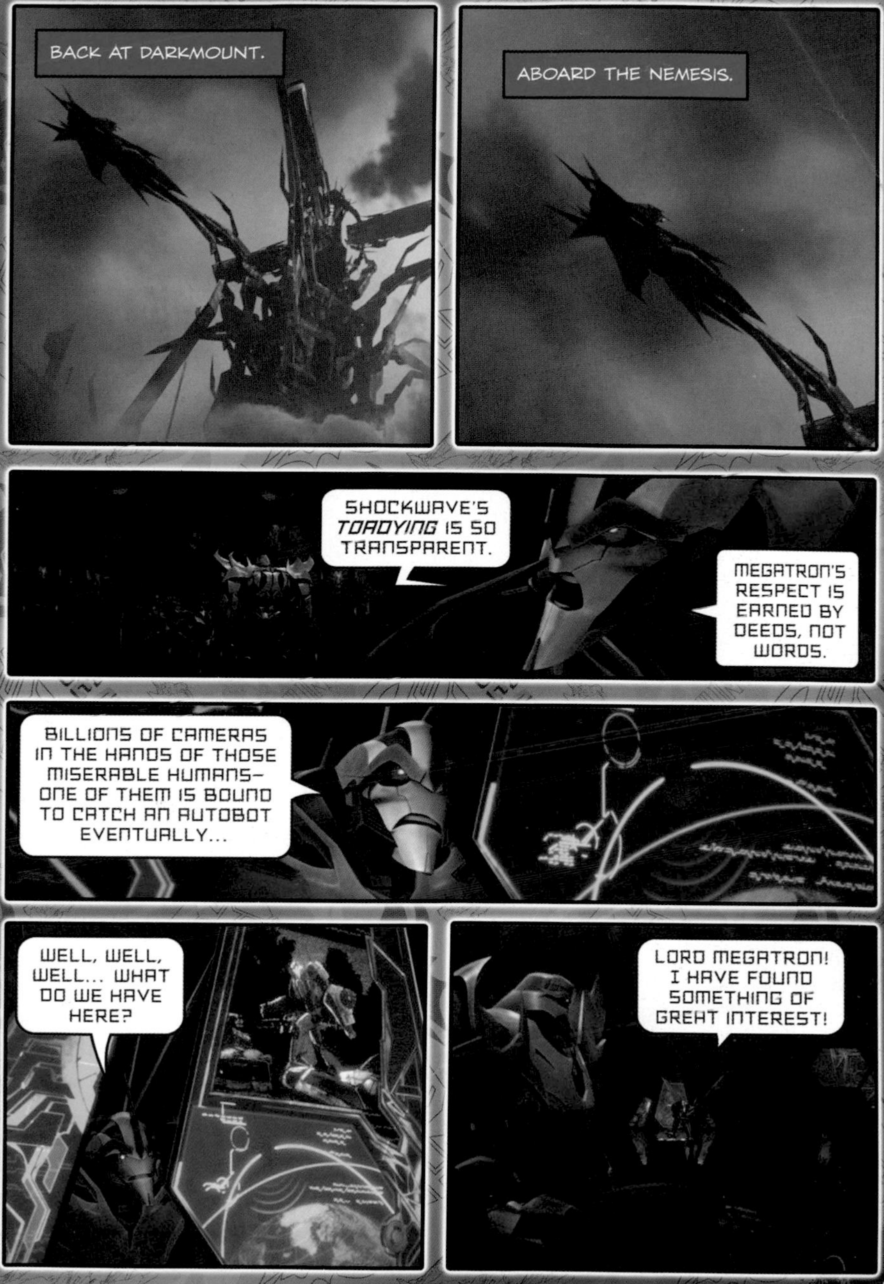
BACK AT DARKMOUNT.
ABOARD THE NEMESIS.
SHOCKWAVE'S *TOADYING* IS SO TRANSPARENT.
MEGATRON'S RESPECT IS EARNED BY DEEDS, NOT WORDS.
BILLIONS OF CAMERAS IN THE HANDS OF THOSE MISERABLE HUMANS— ONE OF THEM IS BOUND TO CATCH AN AUTOBOT EVENTUALLY...
WELL, WELL, WELL... WHAT DO WE HAVE HERE?
LORD MEGATRON! I HAVE FOUND SOMETHING OF GREAT INTEREST!

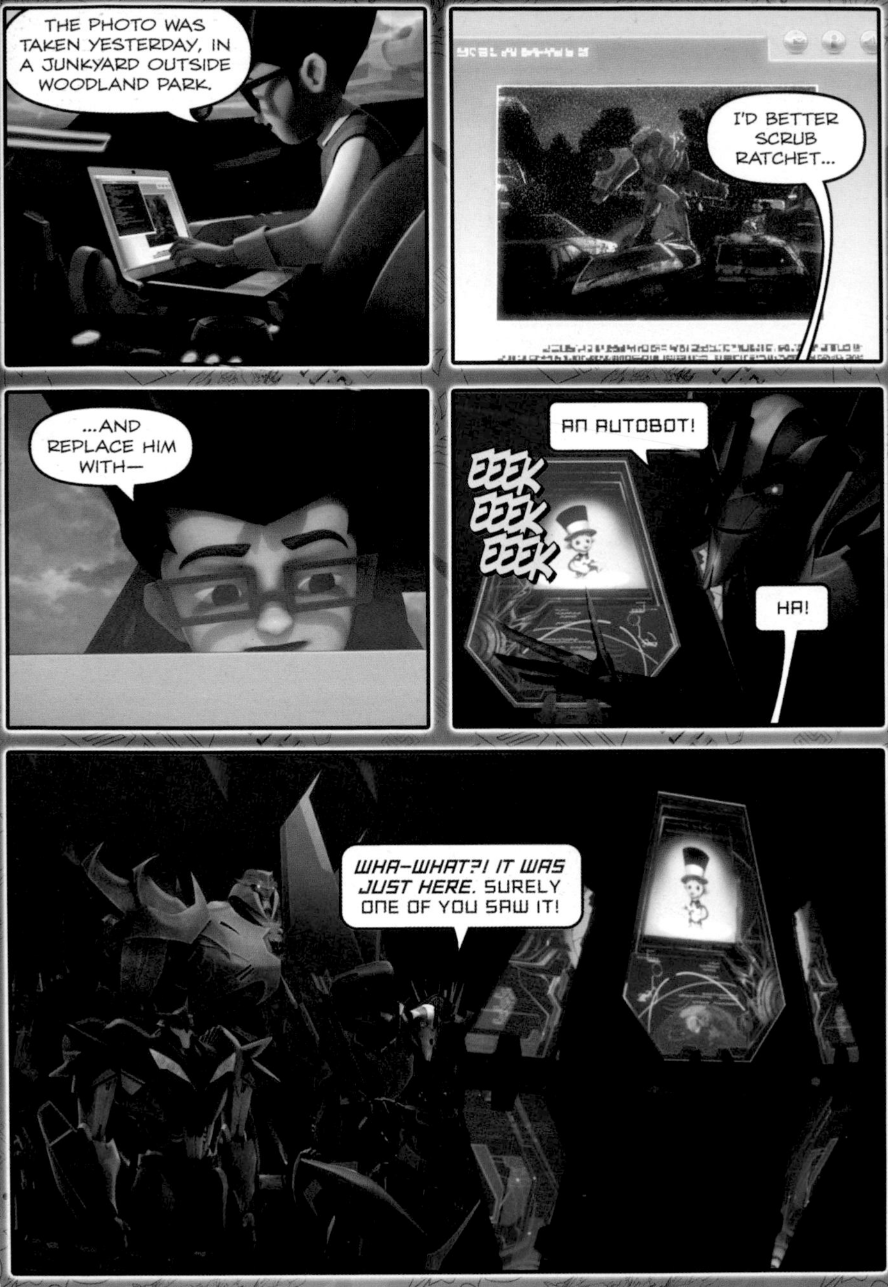
THE PHOTO WAS TAKEN YESTERDAY, IN A JUNKYARD OUTSIDE WOODLAND PARK.
I'D BETTER SCRUB RATCHET...
...AND REPLACE HIM WITH—
AN AUTOBOT!
EEEK EEEK EEEK
HA!
WHA-WHAT?! IT WAS JUST HERE. SURELY ONE OF YOU SAW IT!

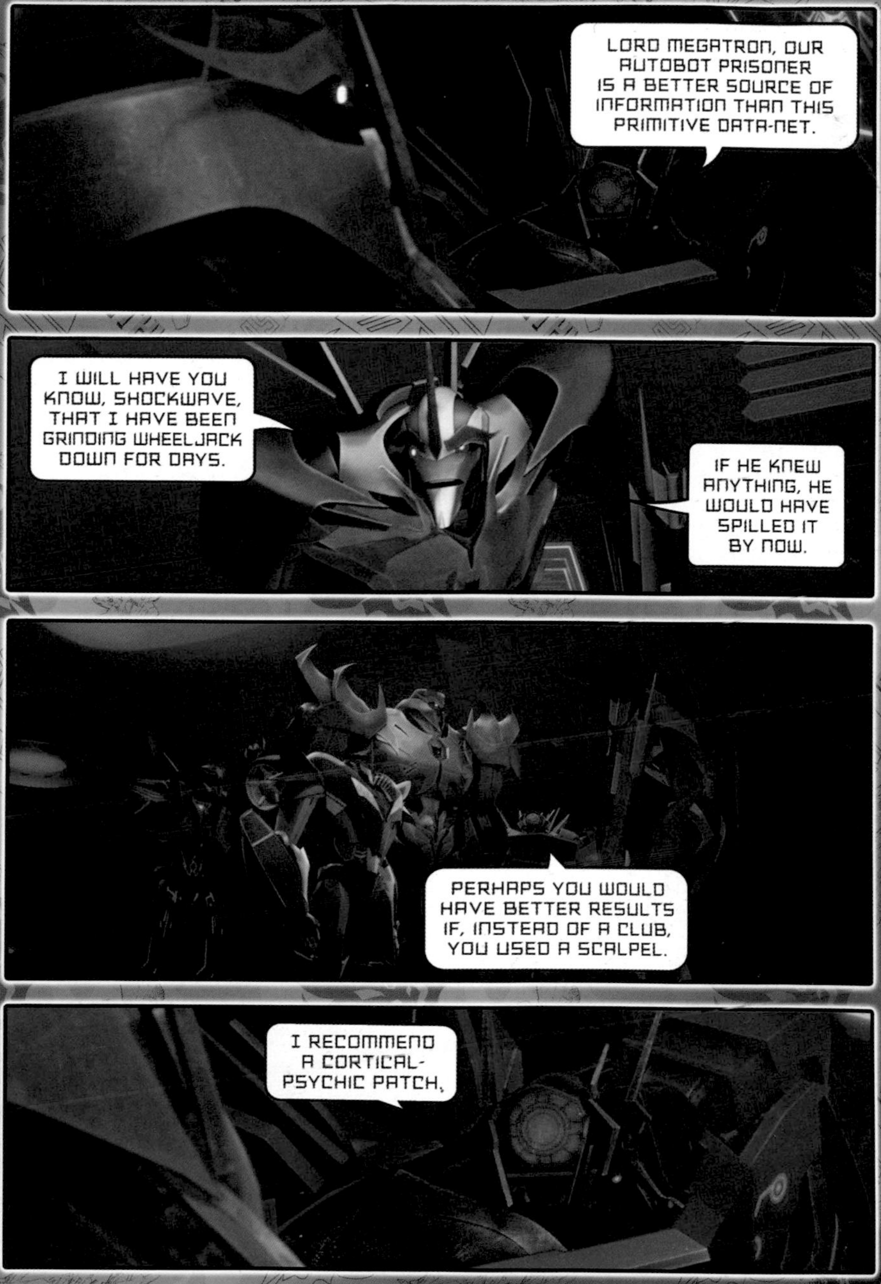
LORD MEGATRON, OUR AUTOBOT PRISONER IS A BETTER SOURCE OF INFORMATION THAN THIS PRIMITIVE DATA-NET.
I WILL HAVE YOU KNOW, SHOCKWAVE, THAT I HAVE BEEN GRINDING WHEELJACK DOWN FOR DAYS.
IF HE KNEW ANYTHING, HE WOULD HAVE SPILLED IT BY NOW.
PERHAPS YOU WOULD HAVE BETTER RESULTS IF, INSTEAD OF A CLUB, YOU USED A SCALPEL.
I RECOMMEND A CORTICAL-PSYCHIC PATCH.

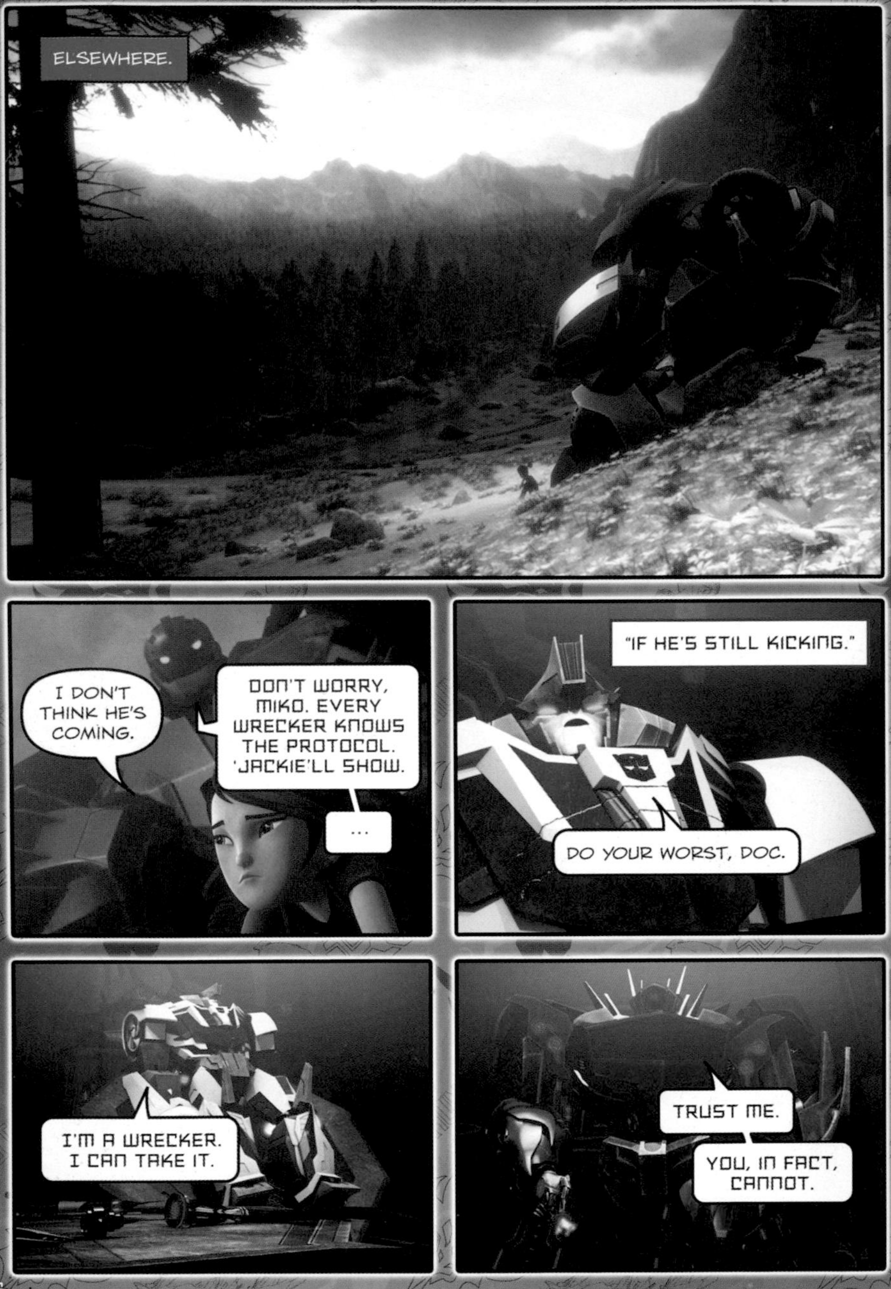
ELSEWHERE.
I DON'T THINK HE'S COMING.
DON'T WORRY, MIKO. EVERY WRECKER KNOWS THE PROTOCOL. 'JACKIE'LL SHOW.
...
"IF HE'S STILL KICKING."
DO YOUR WORST, DOC.
I'M A WRECKER. I CAN TAKE IT.
TRUST ME.
YOU, IN FACT, CANNOT.

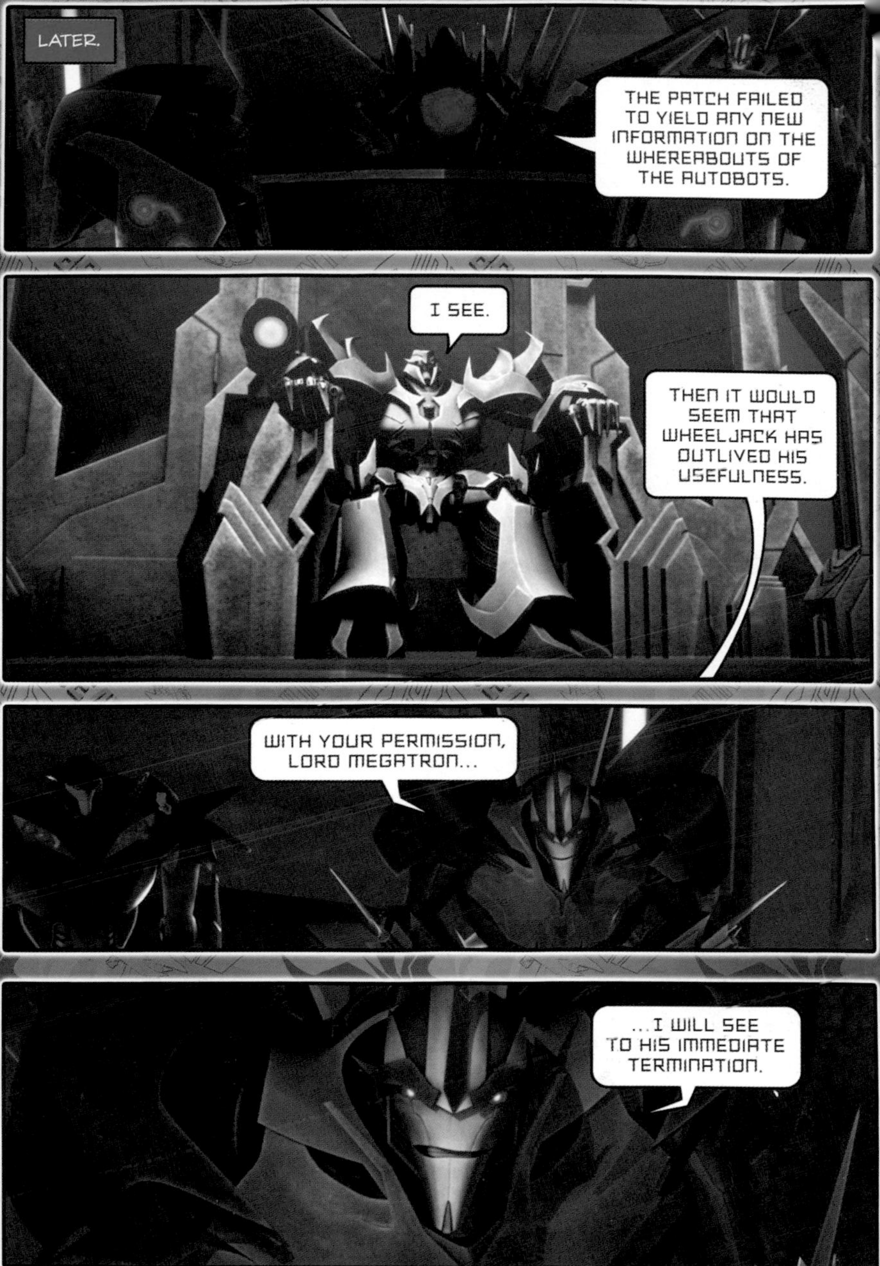
LATER.
THE PATCH FAILED TO YIELD ANY NEW INFORMATION ON THE WHEREABOUTS OF THE AUTOBOTS.
I SEE.
THEN IT WOULD SEEM THAT WHEELJACK HAS OUTLIVED HIS USEFULNESS.
WITH YOUR PERMISSION, LORD MEGATRON...
...I WILL SEE TO HIS IMMEDIATE TERMINATION.

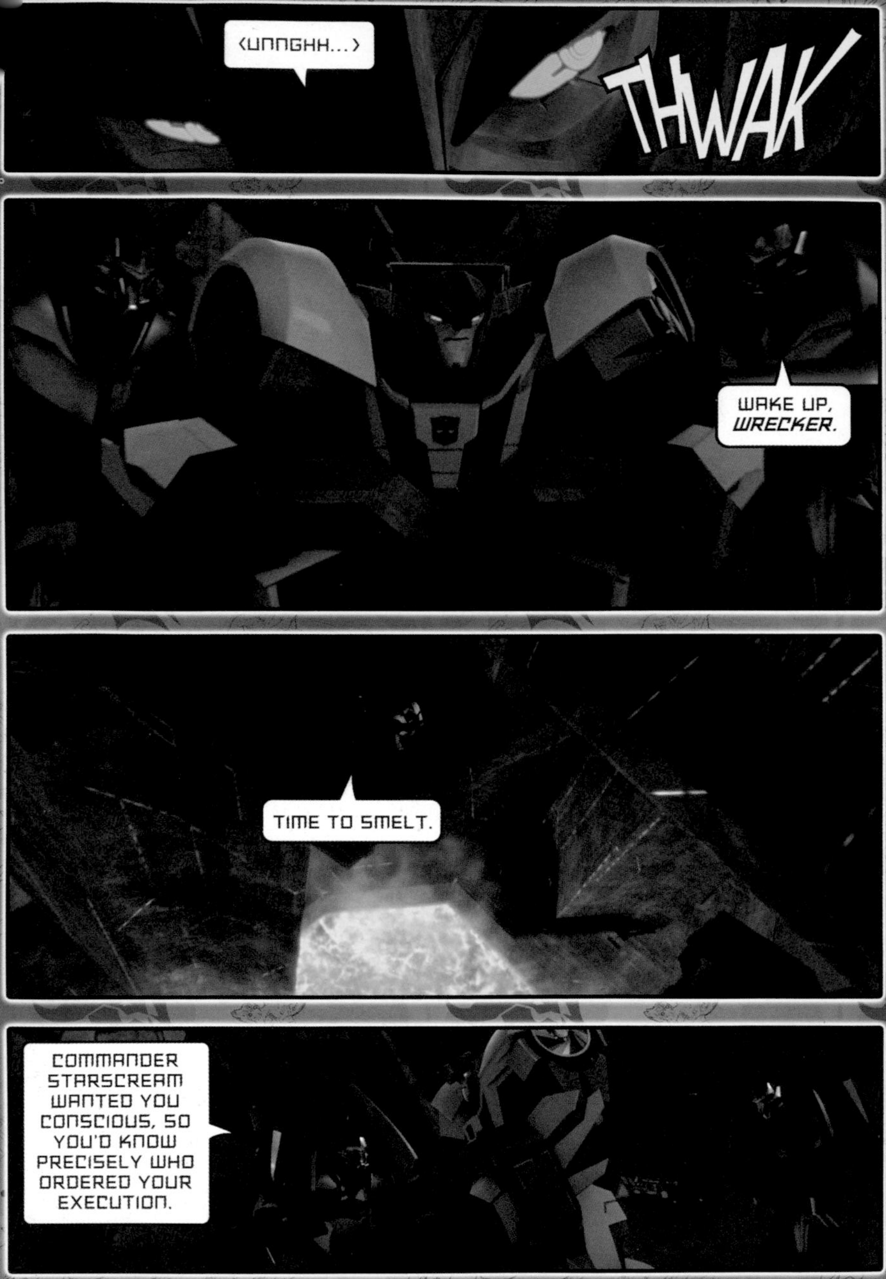
‹UNNGHH...›
THWAK
WAKE UP, *WRECKER*.
TIME TO SMELT.
COMMANDER STARSCREAM WANTED YOU CONSCIOUS, SO YOU'D KNOW PRECISELY WHO ORDERED YOUR EXECUTION.

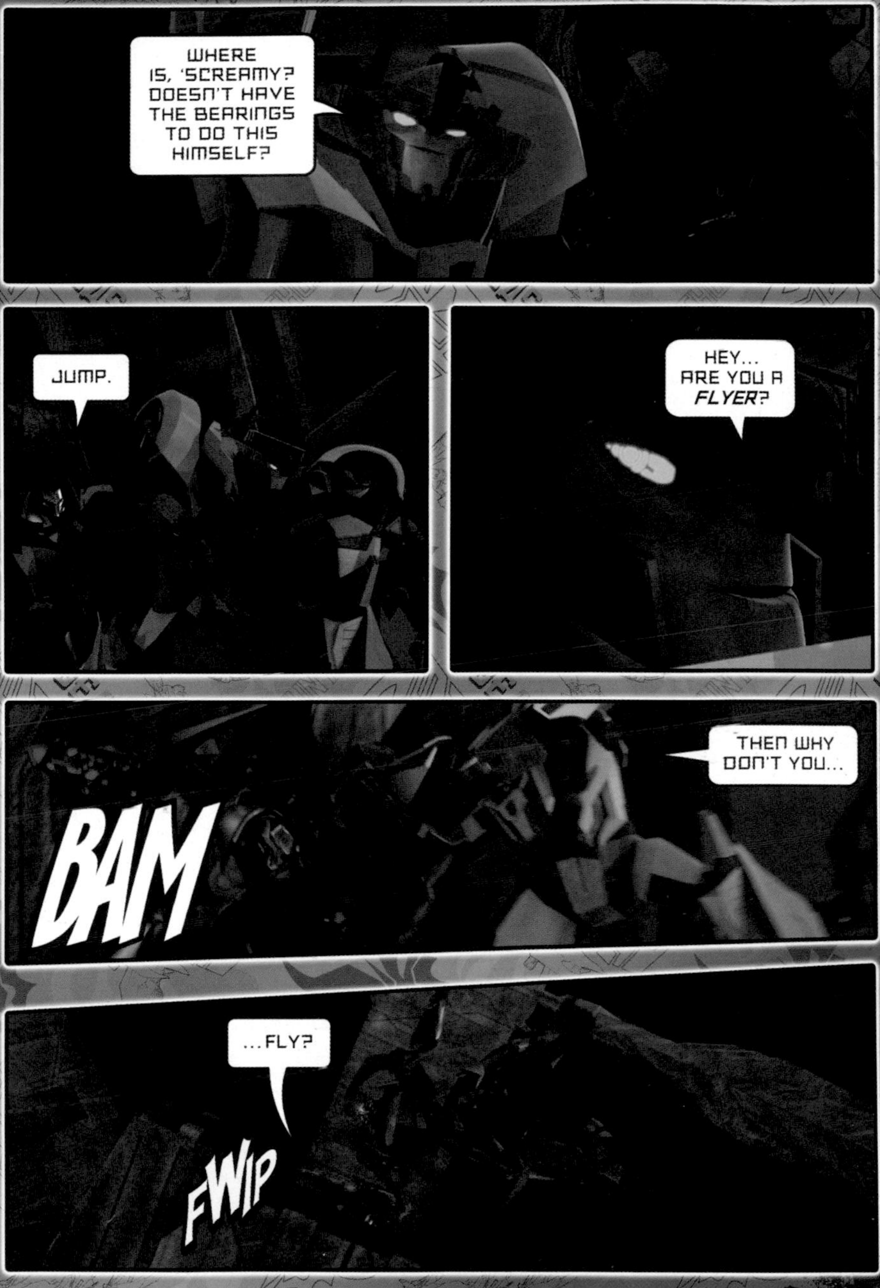
WHERE IS, 'SCREAMY? DOESN'T HAVE THE BEARINGS TO DO THIS HIMSELF?
JUMP.
HEY... ARE YOU A *FLYER*?
THEN WHY DON'T YOU...
BAM
...FLY?
FWIP

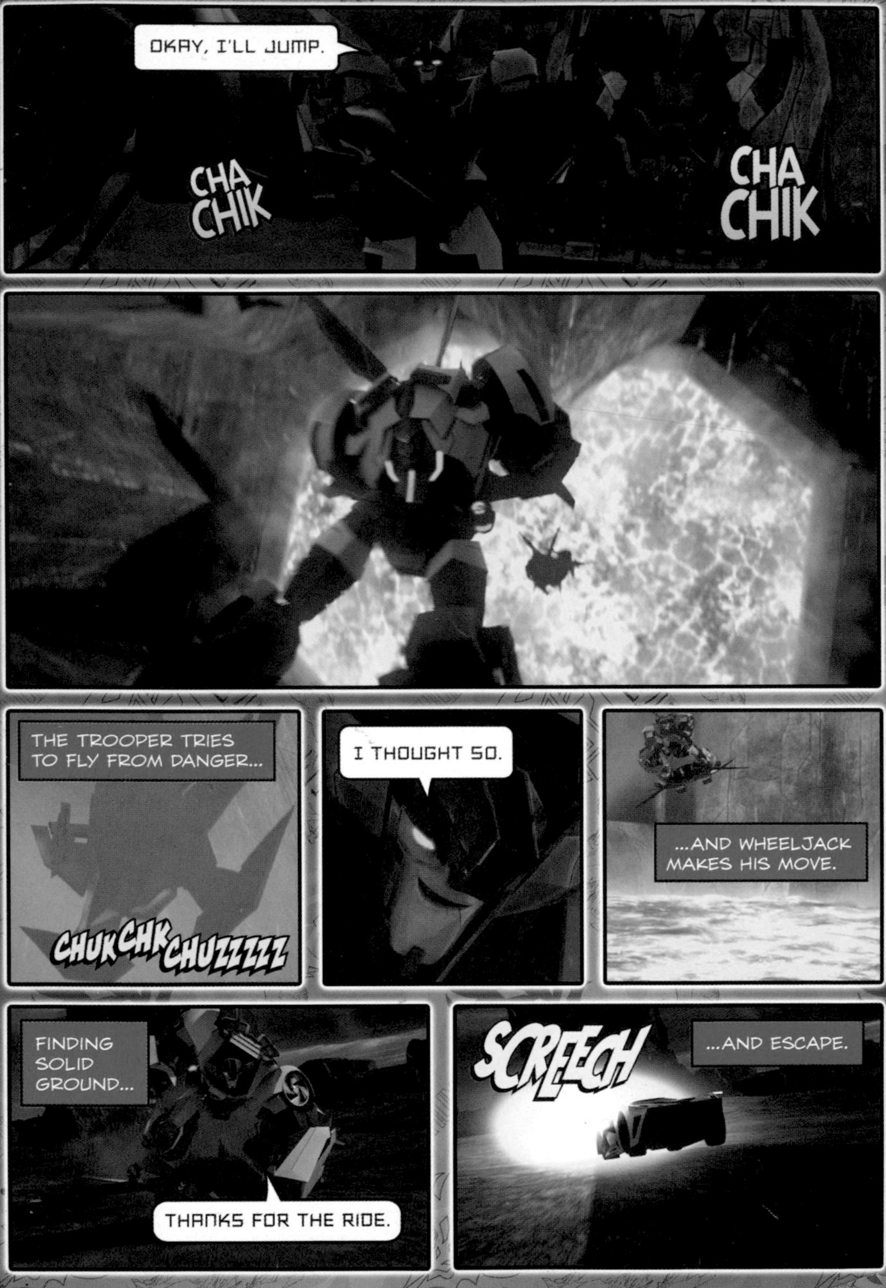
OKAY, I'LL JUMP.
CHA CHIK
CHA CHIK
THE TROOPER TRIES TO FLY FROM DANGER...
CHUKCHKCHUZZZZZ
I THOUGHT SO.
...AND WHEELJACK MAKES HIS MOVE.
FINDING SOLID GROUND...
THANKS FOR THE RIDE.
SCREECH
...AND ESCAPE.

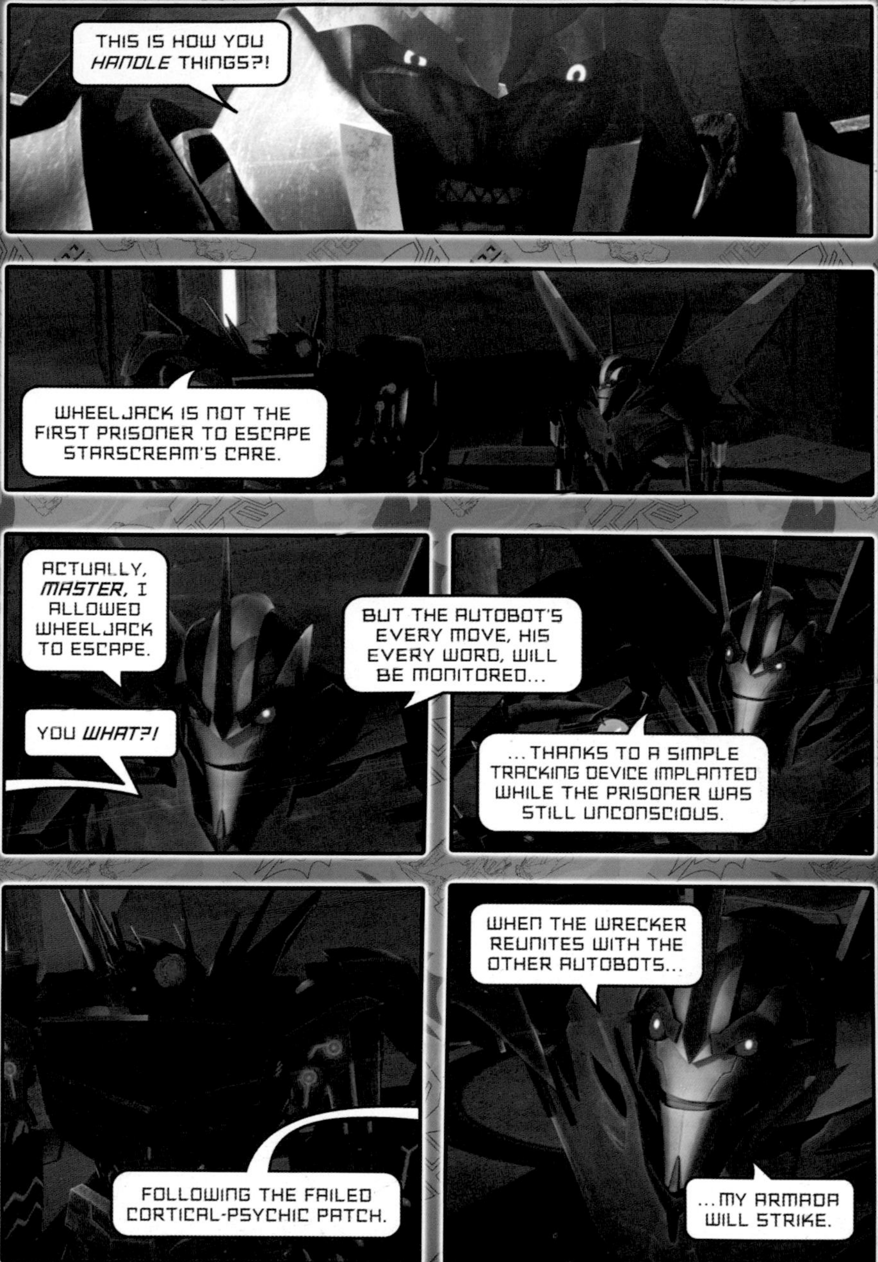
THIS IS HOW YOU *HANDLE* THINGS?!
WHEELJACK IS NOT THE FIRST PRISONER TO ESCAPE STARSCREAM'S CARE.
ACTUALLY, *MASTER,* I ALLOWED WHEELJACK TO ESCAPE.
YOU *WHAT?!*
BUT THE AUTOBOT'S EVERY MOVE, HIS EVERY WORD, WILL BE MONITORED...
...THANKS TO A SIMPLE TRACKING DEVICE IMPLANTED WHILE THE PRISONER WAS STILL UNCONSCIOUS.
FOLLOWING THE FAILED CORTICAL-PSYCHIC PATCH.
WHEN THE WRECKER REUNITES WITH THE OTHER AUTOBOTS...
...MY ARMADA WILL STRIKE.

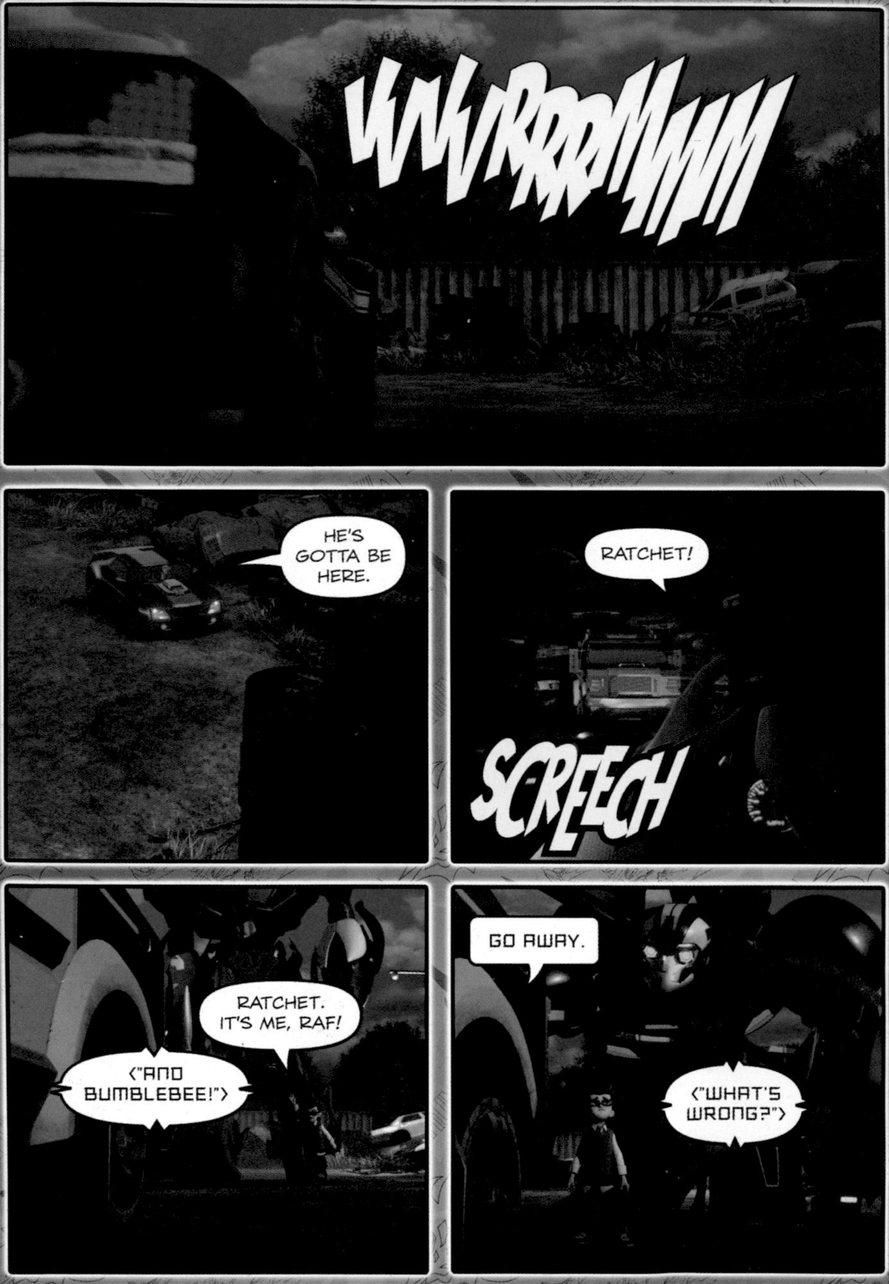
VVVVVRRRRMMMM
HE'S GOTTA BE HERE.
RATCHET!
SCREECH
RATCHET. IT'S ME, RAF!
<"AND BUMBLEBEE!">
GO AWAY.
<"WHAT'S WRONG?">

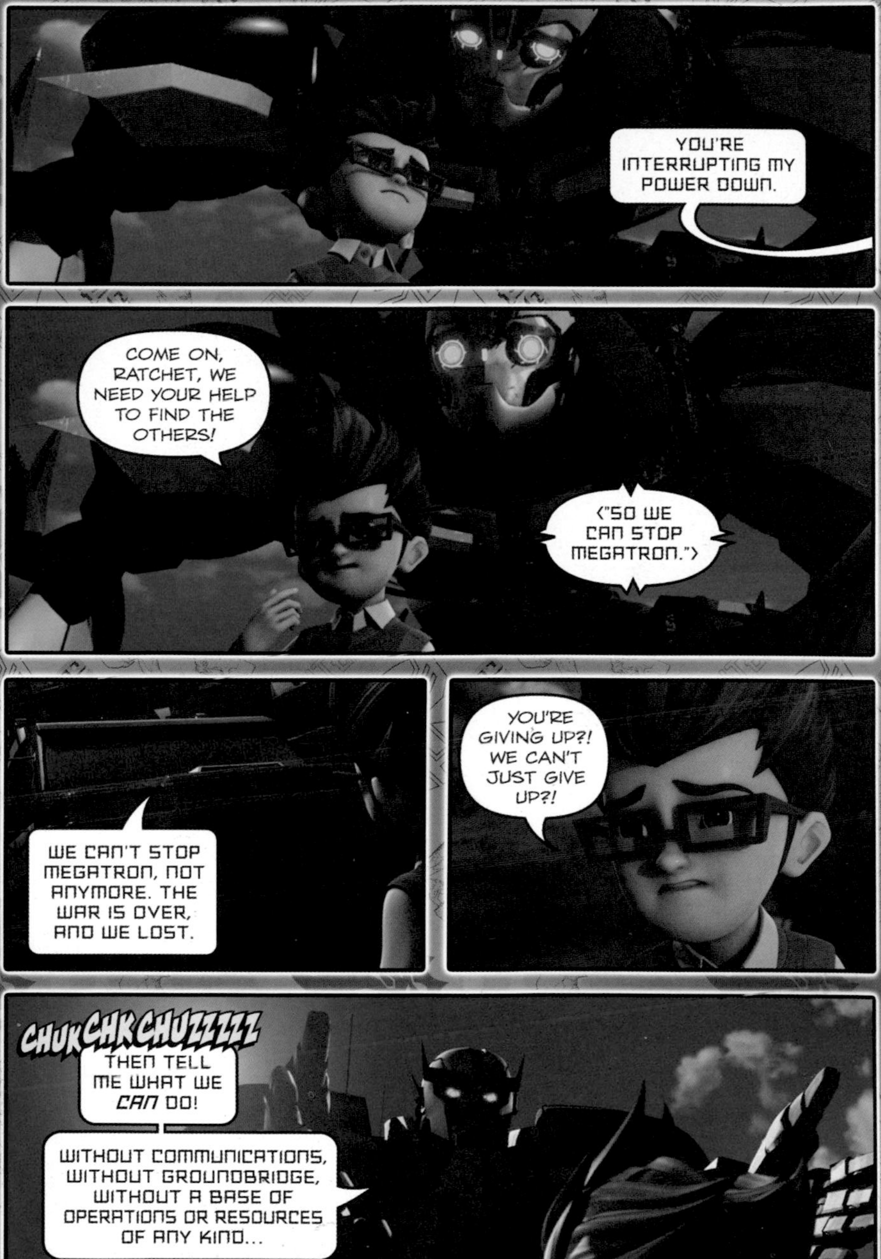
YOU'RE INTERRUPTING MY POWER DOWN.
COME ON, RATCHET, WE NEED YOUR HELP TO FIND THE OTHERS!
<"SO WE CAN STOP MEGATRON.">
WE CAN'T STOP MEGATRON, NOT ANYMORE. THE WAR IS OVER, AND WE LOST.
YOU'RE GIVING UP?! WE CAN'T JUST GIVE UP?!
CHUKCHKCHUZZZZZZ
THEN TELL ME WHAT WE *CAN* DO!
WITHOUT COMMUNICATIONS, WITHOUT GROUNDBRIDGE, WITHOUT A BASE OF OPERATIONS OR RESOURCES OF ANY KIND...

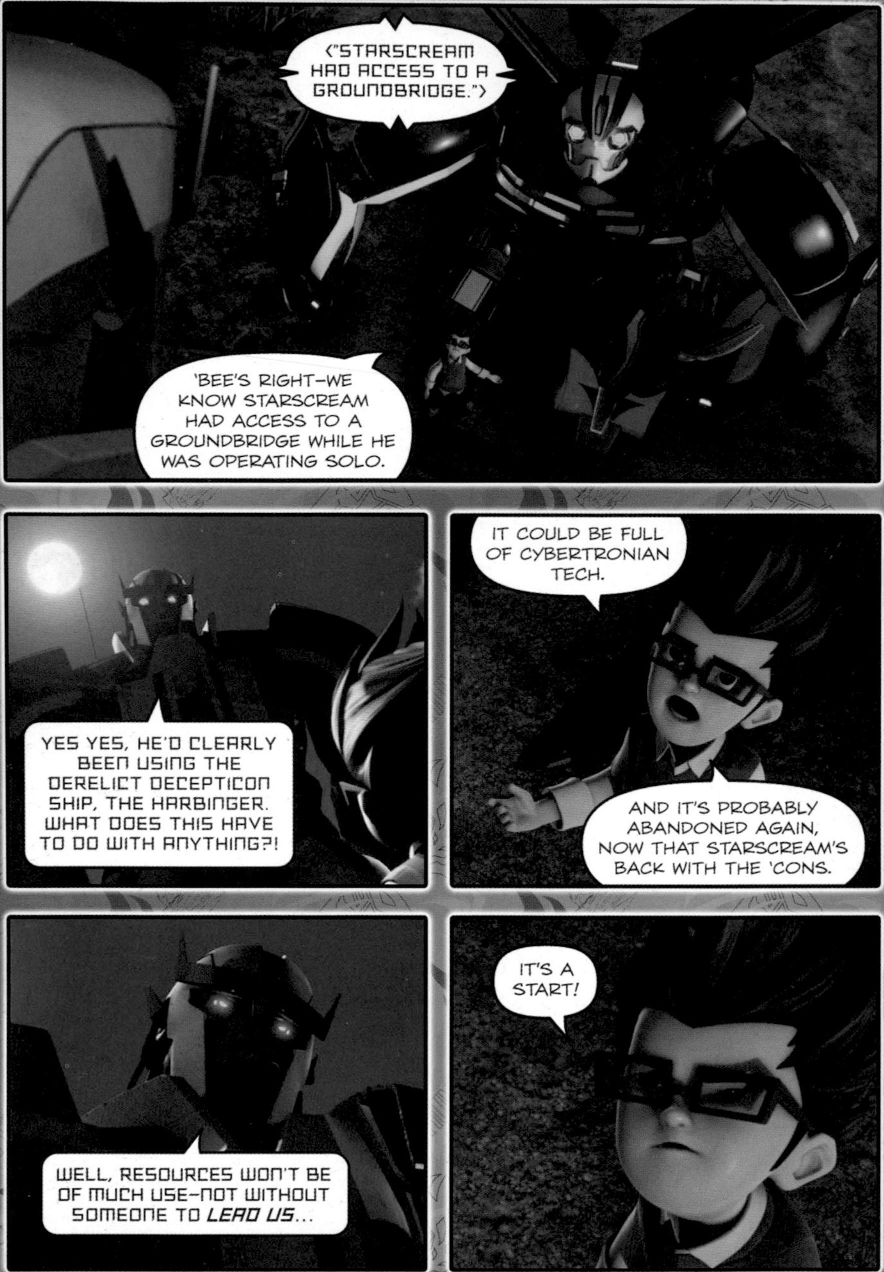

<("STARSCREAM HAD ACCESS TO A GROUNDBRIDGE.")>
'BEE'S RIGHT—WE KNOW STARSCREAM HAD ACCESS TO A GROUNDBRIDGE WHILE HE WAS OPERATING SOLO.
YES YES, HE'D CLEARLY BEEN USING THE DERELICT DECEPTICON SHIP, THE HARBINGER. WHAT DOES THIS HAVE TO DO WITH ANYTHING?!
IT COULD BE FULL OF CYBERTRONIAN TECH.
AND IT'S PROBABLY ABANDONED AGAIN, NOW THAT STARSCREAM'S BACK WITH THE 'CONS.
WELL, RESOURCES WON'T BE OF MUCH USE—NOT WITHOUT SOMEONE TO *LEAD US*...
IT'S A START!

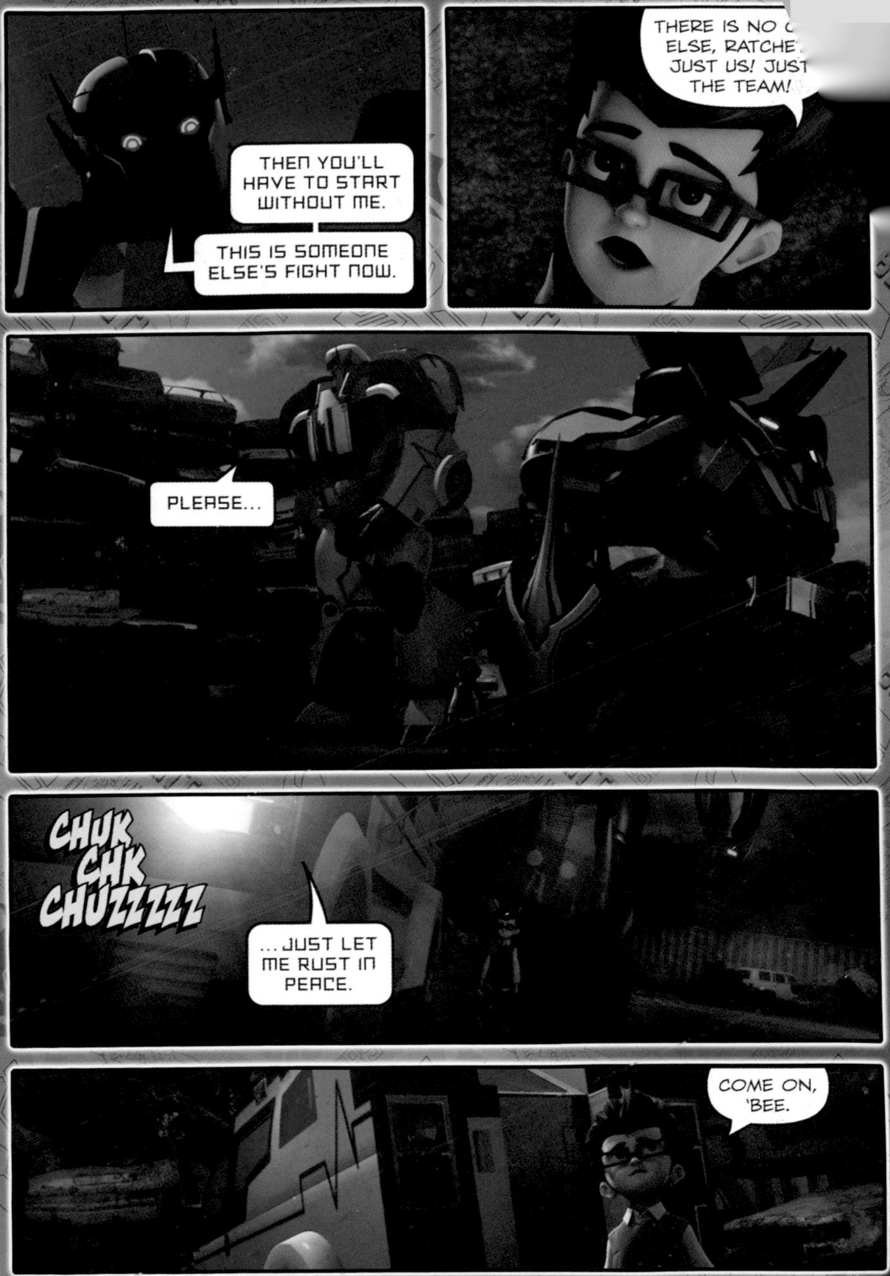
THEN YOU'LL HAVE TO START WITHOUT ME.
THIS IS SOMEONE ELSE'S FIGHT NOW.
THERE IS NO
ELSE,
JUST US!
THE TEAM!
PLEASE...
CHUK CHK CHUZZZZZ
...JUST LET ME RUST IN PEACE.
COME ON, 'BEE.

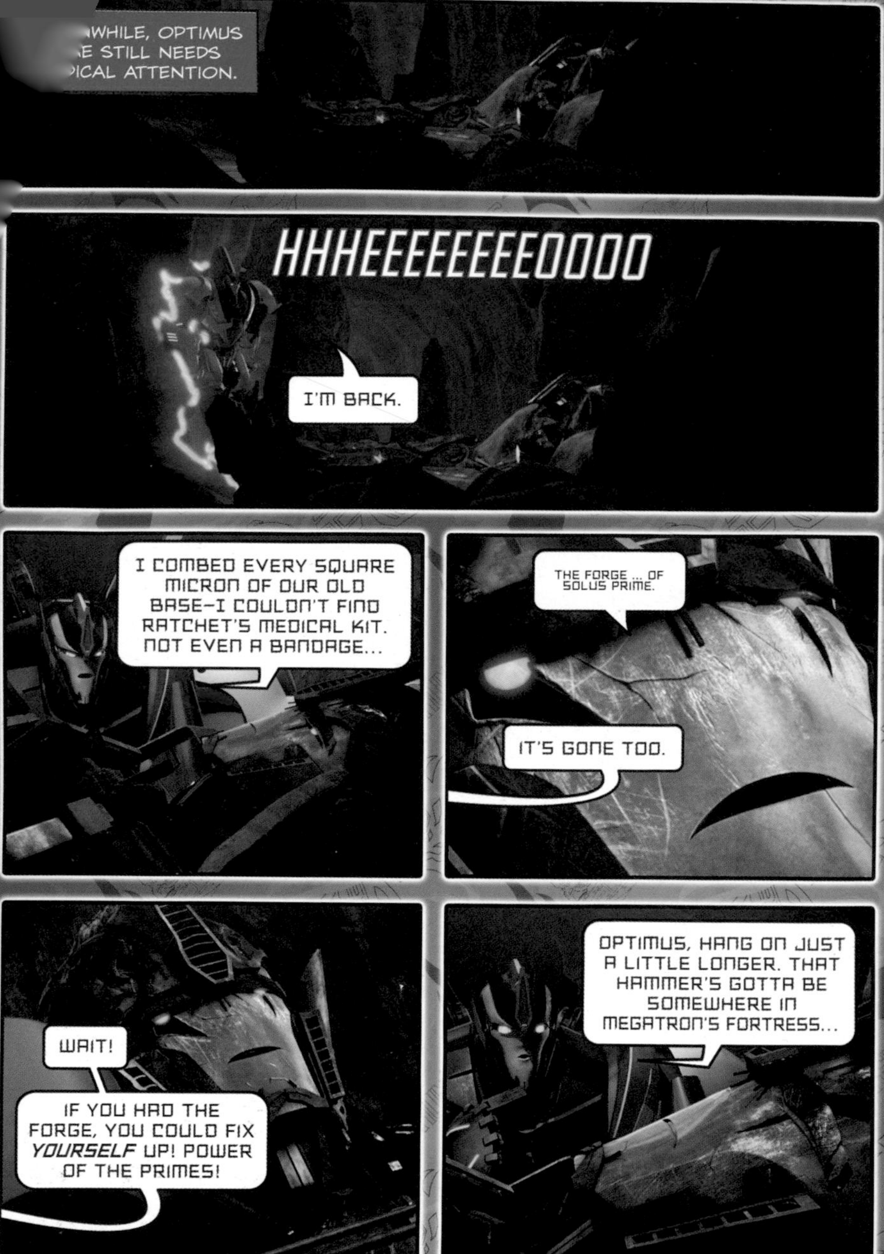

NWHILE, OPTIMUS E STILL NEEDS DICAL ATTENTION.
HHHEEEEEEEEOOOO
I'M BACK.
I COMBED EVERY SQUARE MICRON OF OUR OLD BASE—I COULDN'T FIND RATCHET'S MEDICAL KIT. NOT EVEN A BANDAGE...
THE FORGE ... OF SOLUS PRIME.
IT'S GONE TOO.
WAIT!
IF YOU HAD THE FORGE, YOU COULD FIX *YOURSELF* UP! POWER OF THE PRIMES!
OPTIMUS, HANG ON JUST A LITTLE LONGER. THAT HAMMER'S GOTTA BE SOMEWHERE IN MEGATRON'S FORTRESS...

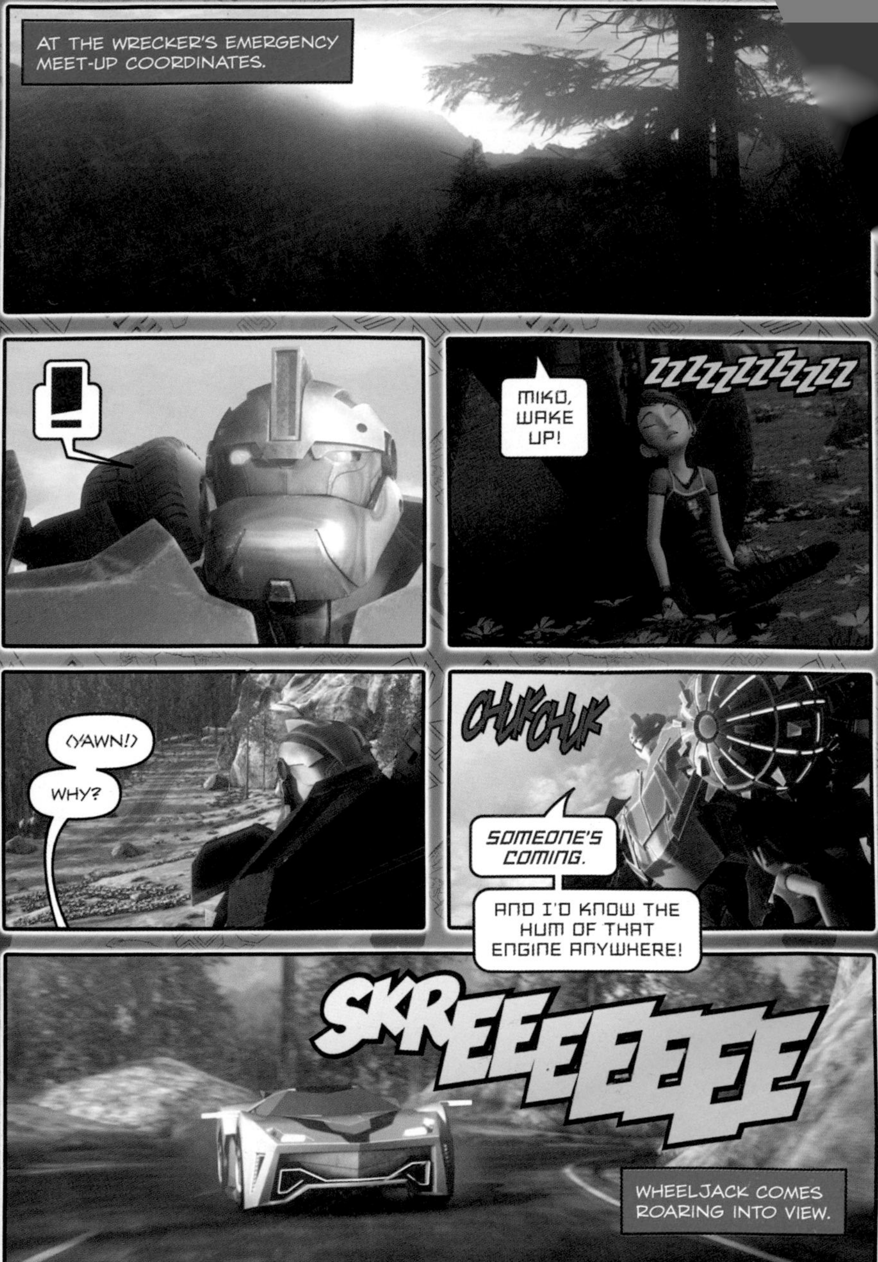

AT THE WRECKER'S EMERGENCY MEET-UP COORDINATES.
MIKO, WAKE UP!
ZZZZZZZZZZZZZ
(YAWN!)
WHY?
CHUKCHUK
SOMEONE'S COMING.
AND I'D KNOW THE HUM OF THAT ENGINE ANYWHERE!
SKREEEEEEEE
WHEELJACK COMES ROARING INTO VIEW.

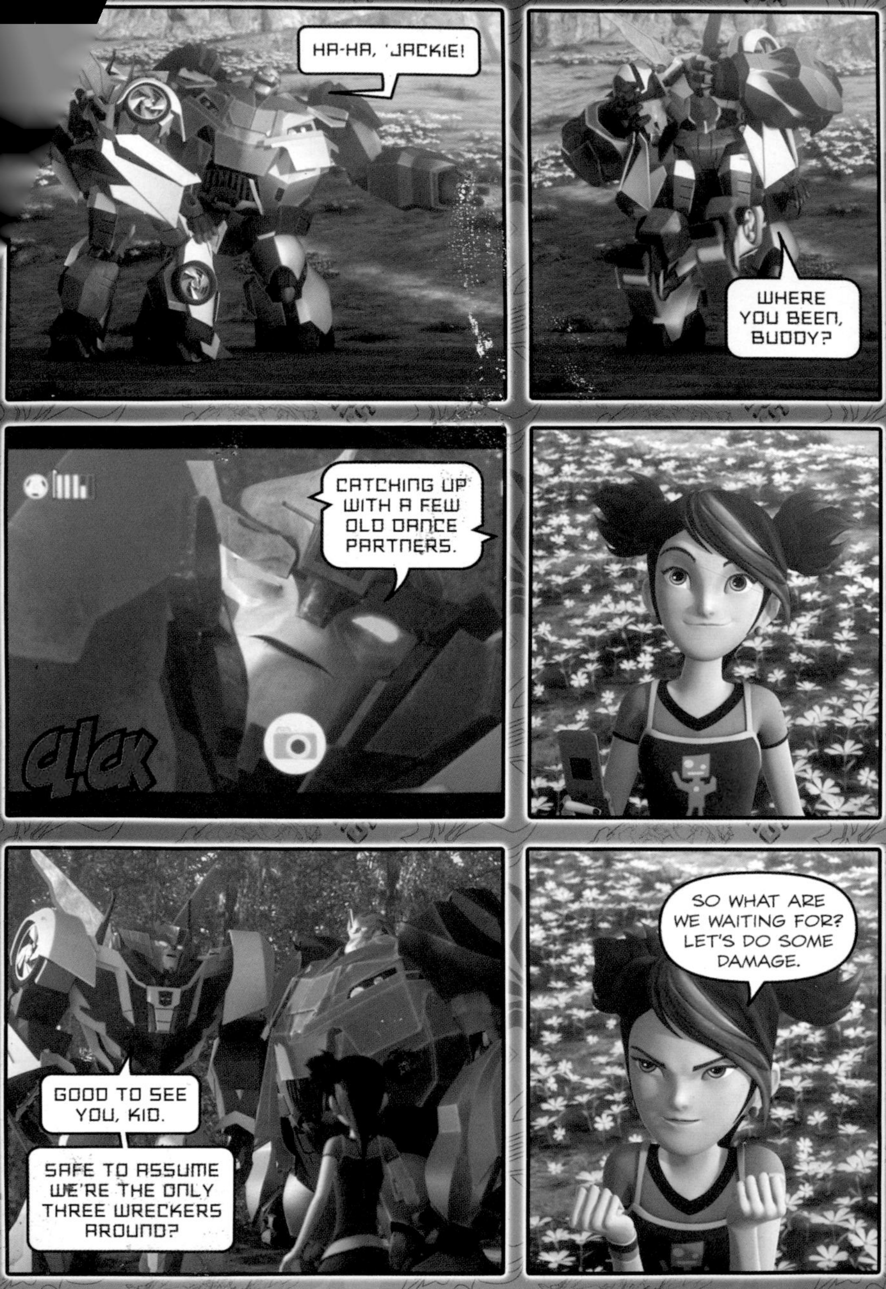
HA-HA, 'JACKIE!
WHERE YOU BEEN, BUDDY?
CATCHING UP WITH A FEW OLD DANCE PARTNERS.
CLICK
GOOD TO SEE YOU, KID.
SAFE TO ASSUME WE'RE THE ONLY THREE WRECKERS AROUND?
SO WHAT ARE WE WAITING FOR? LET'S DO SOME DAMAGE.

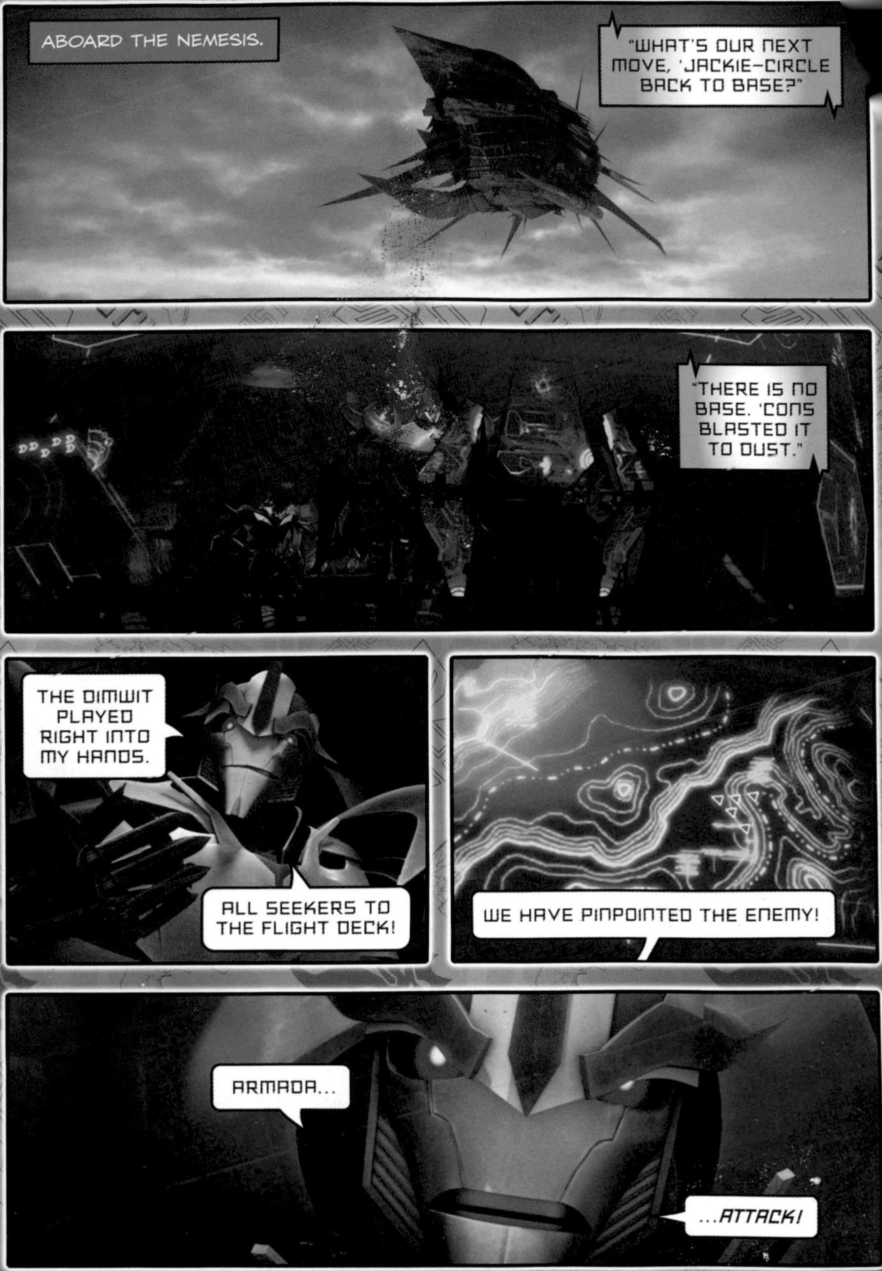
ABOARD THE NEMESIS.
"WHAT'S OUR NEXT MOVE, 'JACKIE–CIRCLE BACK TO BASE?"
"THERE IS NO BASE. 'CONS BLASTED IT TO DUST."
THE DIMWIT PLAYED RIGHT INTO MY HANDS.
ALL SEEKERS TO THE FLIGHT DECK!
WE HAVE PINPOINTED THE ENEMY!
ARMADA...
...ATTACK!

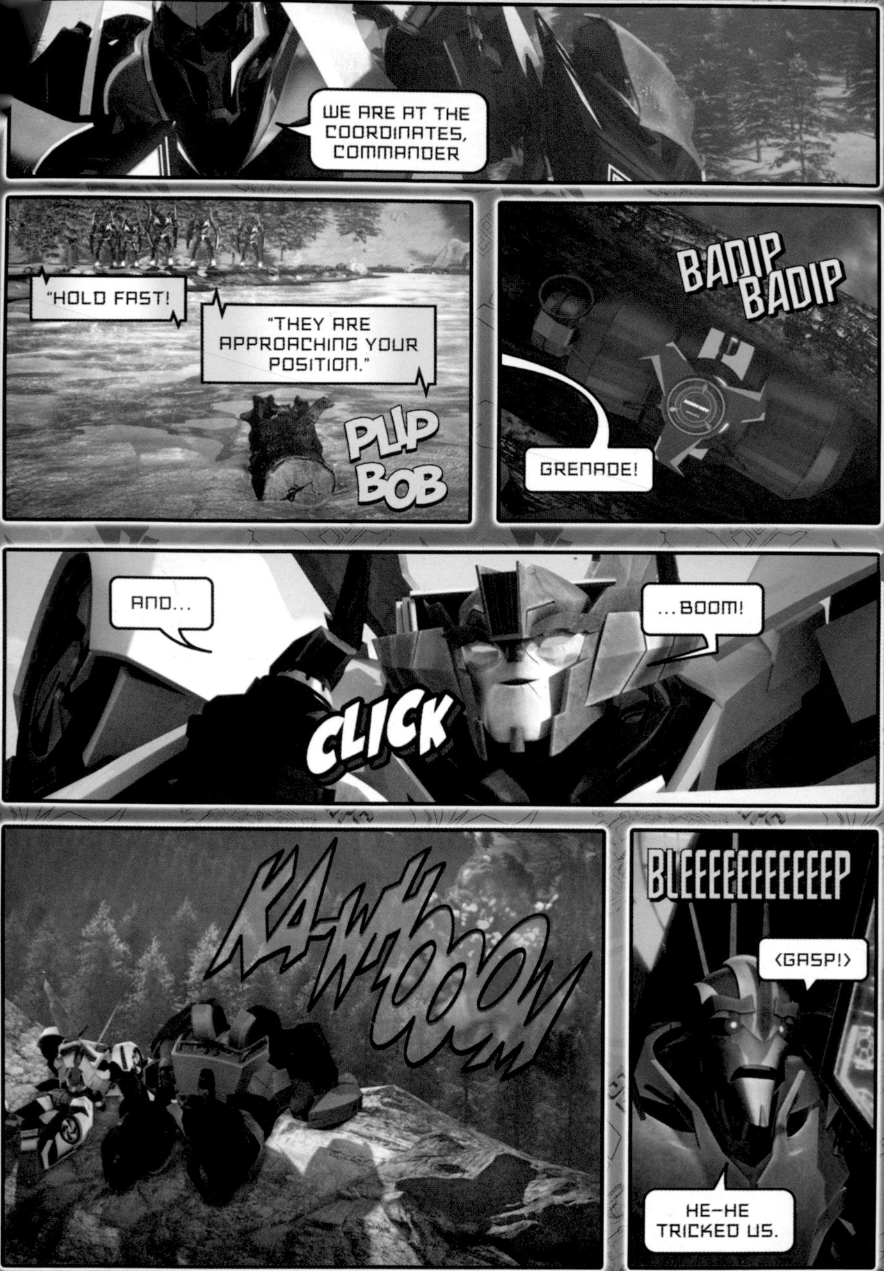
WE ARE AT THE COORDINATES, COMMANDER
"HOLD FAST!
"THEY ARE APPROACHING YOUR POSITION."
PLIP BOB
BADIP BADIP
GRENADE!
AND...
...BOOM!
CLICK
KA-WHOOOOM
BLEEEEEEEEEEEP
<GASP!>
HE-HE TRICKED US.

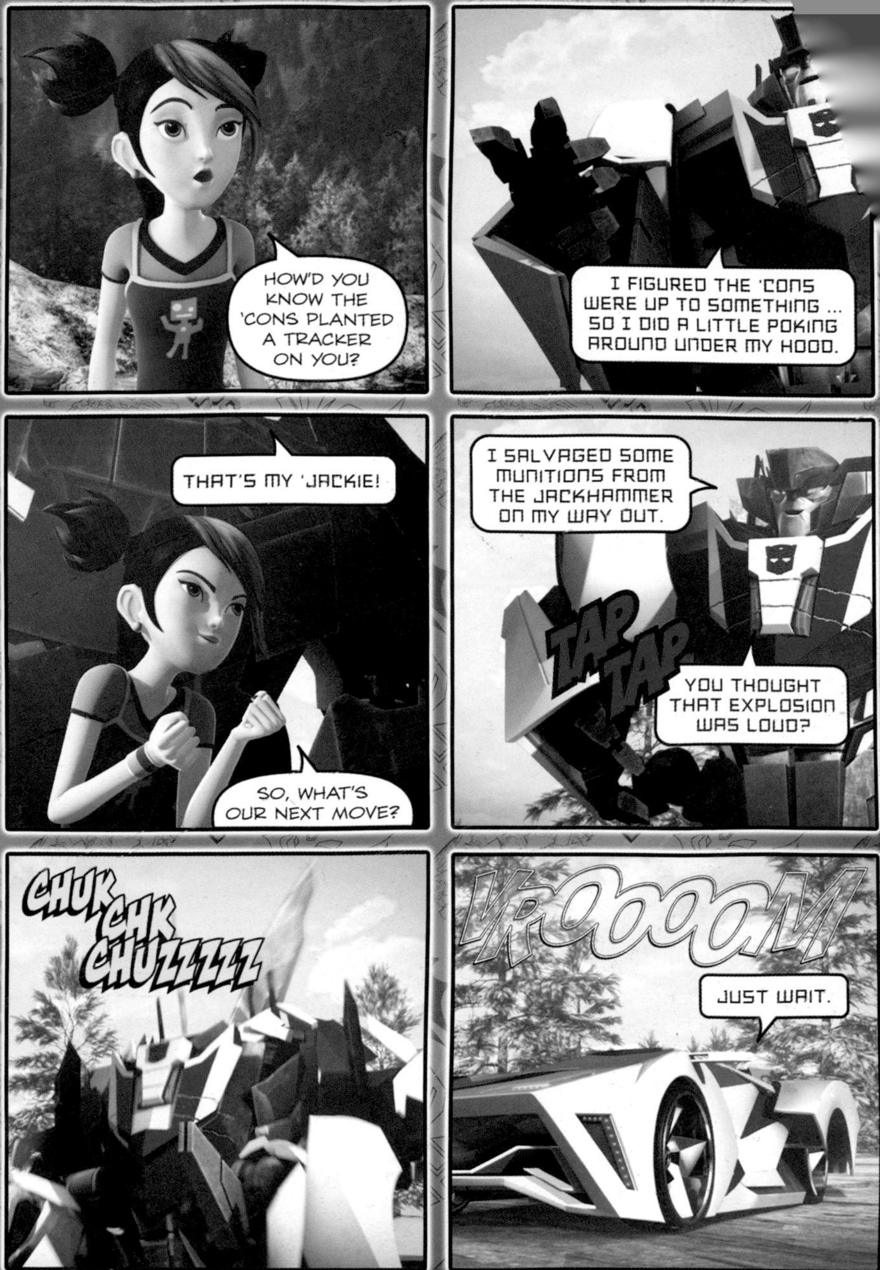
HOW'D YOU KNOW THE 'CONS PLANTED A TRACKER ON YOU?
I FIGURED THE 'CONS WERE UP TO SOMETHING ... SO I DID A LITTLE POKING AROUND UNDER MY HOOD.
THAT'S MY 'JACKIE!
SO, WHAT'S OUR NEXT MOVE?
I SALVAGED SOME MUNITIONS FROM THE JACKHAMMER ON MY WAY OUT.
TAP TAP
YOU THOUGHT THAT EXPLOSION WAS LOUD?
CHUK CHK CHUZZZZZ
VROOOOOM
JUST WAIT.

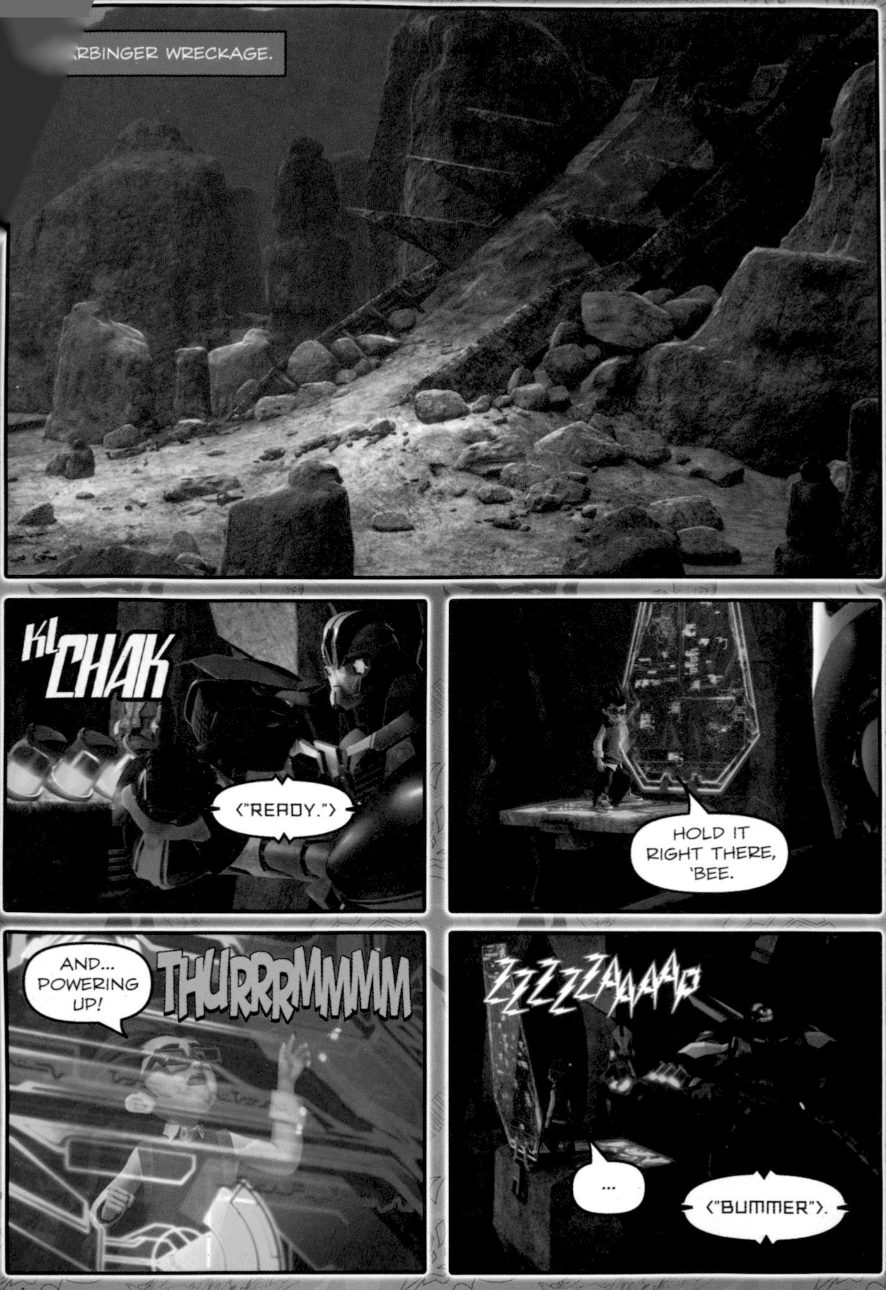
RBINGER WRECKAGE.
KL CHAK
("READY.")
HOLD IT RIGHT THERE, 'BEE.
AND... POWERING UP!
THURRRMMMMM
ZZZZZAAAAP
...
("BUMMER").

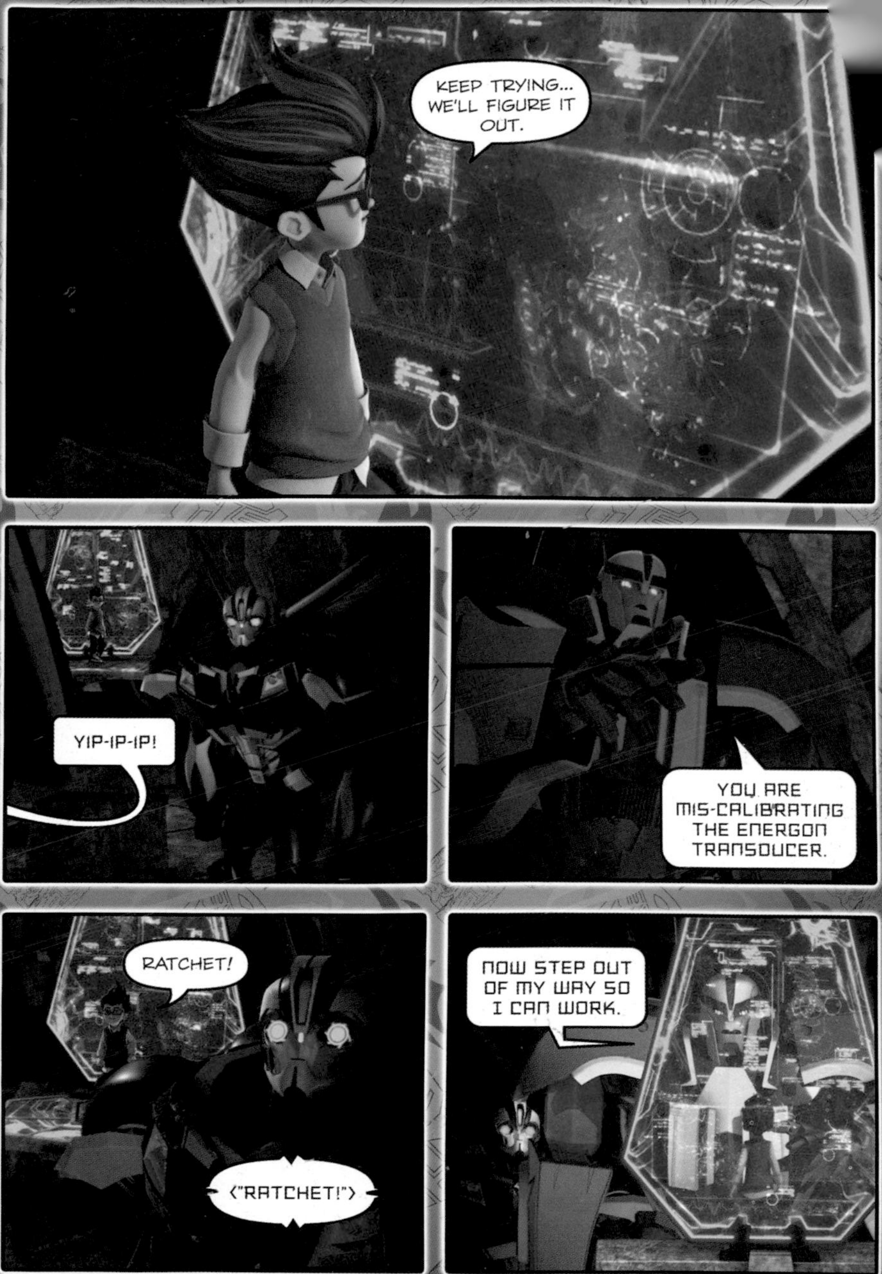
KEEP TRYING... WE'LL FIGURE IT OUT.
YIP-IP-IP!
YOU ARE MIS-CALIBRATING THE ENERGON TRANSDUCER.
RATCHET!
("RATCHET!")
NOW STEP OUT OF MY WAY SO I CAN WORK.

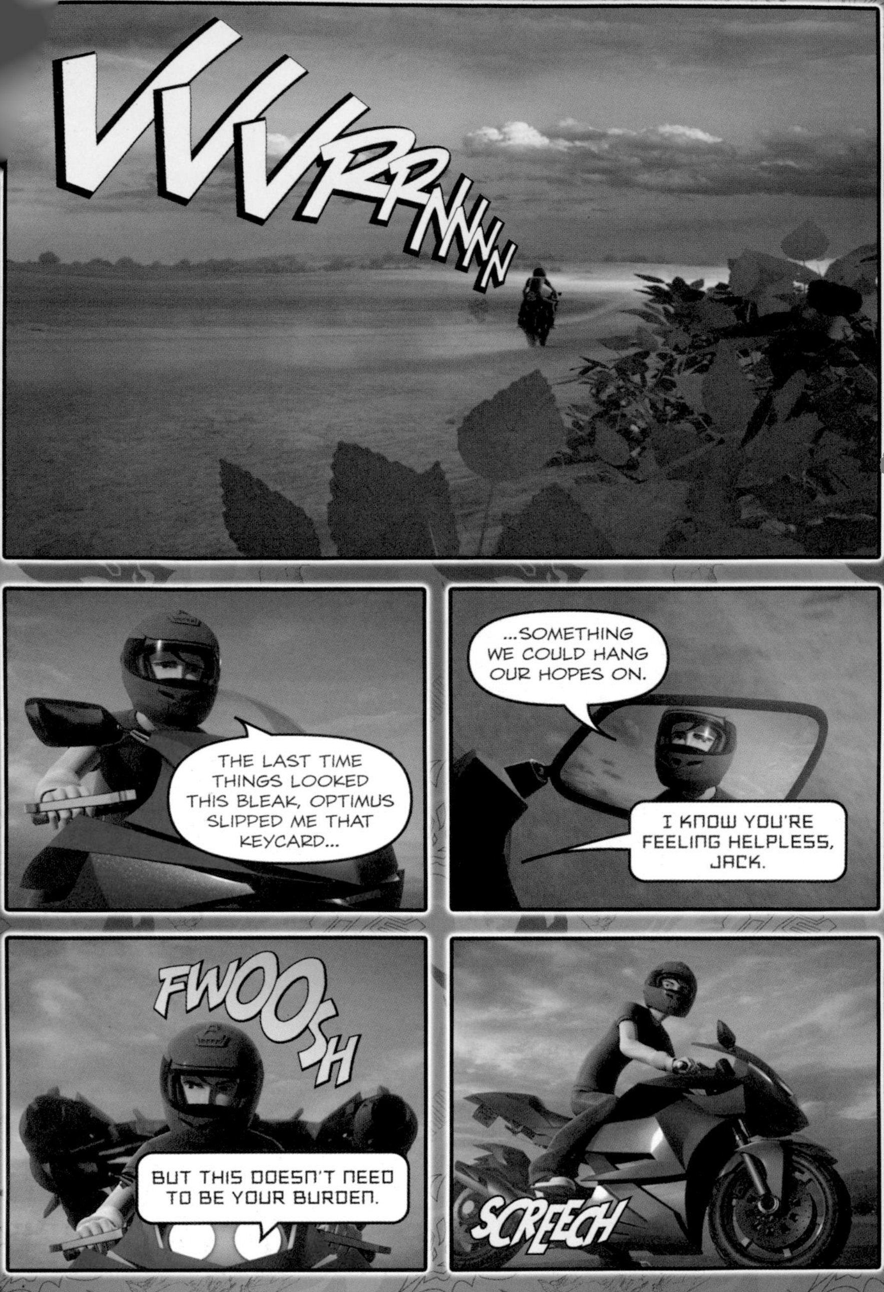
VVVRRNNNN
THE LAST TIME THINGS LOOKED THIS BLEAK, OPTIMUS SLIPPED ME THAT KEYCARD...
...SOMETHING WE COULD HANG OUR HOPES ON.
I KNOW YOU'RE FEELING HELPLESS, JACK.
FWOOSH
BUT THIS DOESN'T NEED TO BE YOUR BURDEN.
SCREECH

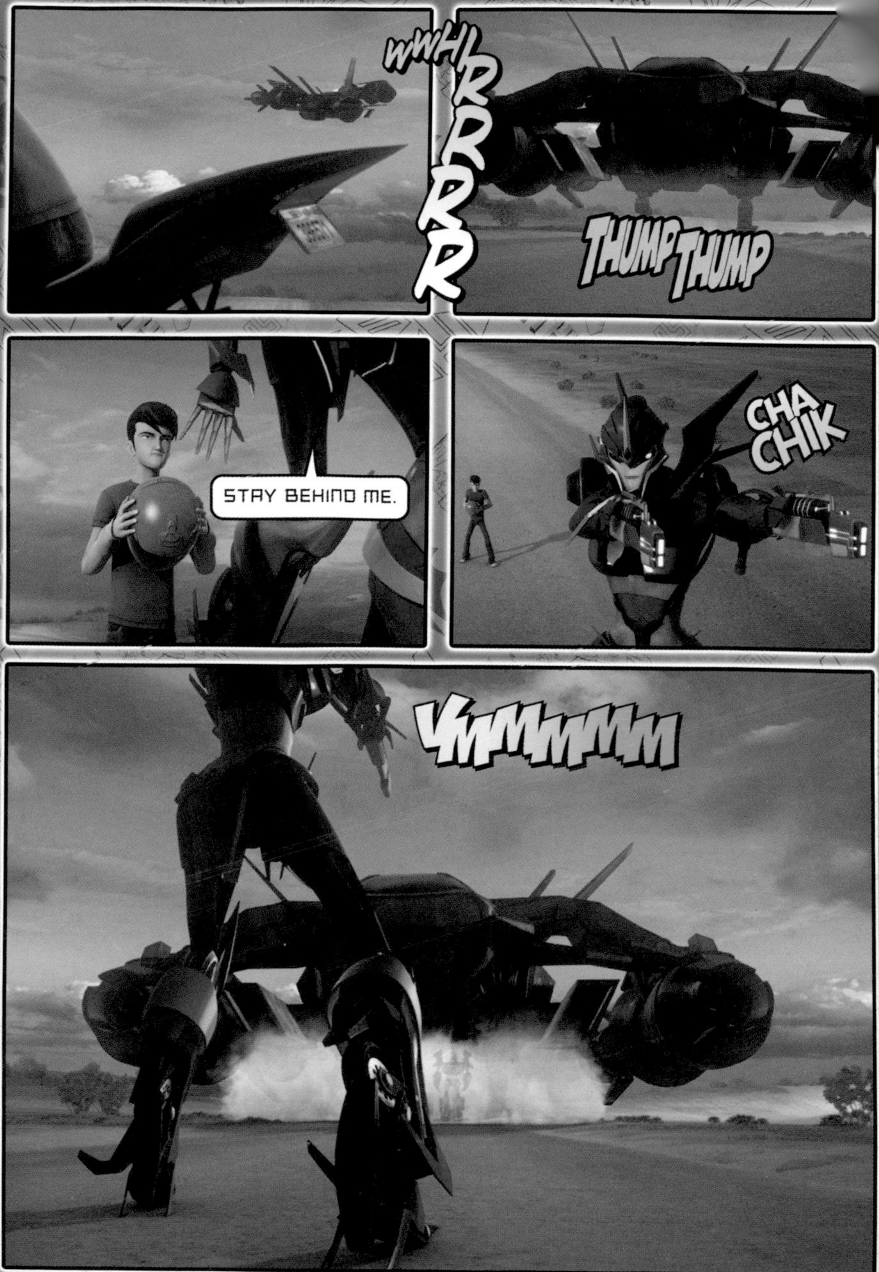
WWHIRRRRR
THUMP THUMP
STAY BEHIND ME.
CHA CHIK
VMMMMM

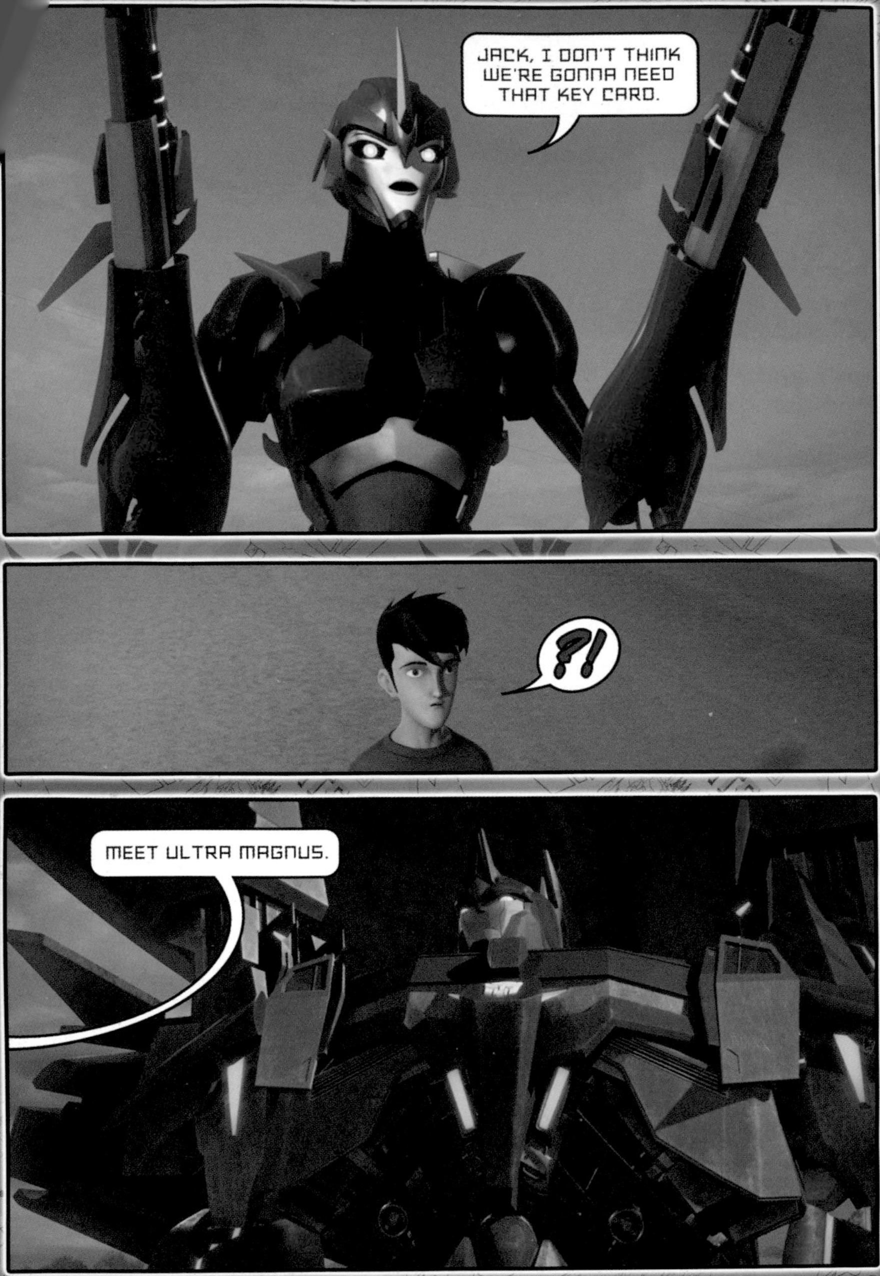
JACK, I DON'T THINK WE'RE GONNA NEED THAT KEY CARD.
?!
MEET ULTRA MAGNUS.

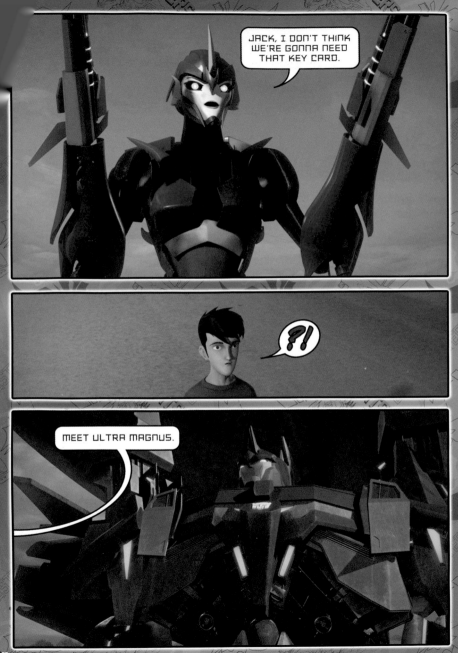

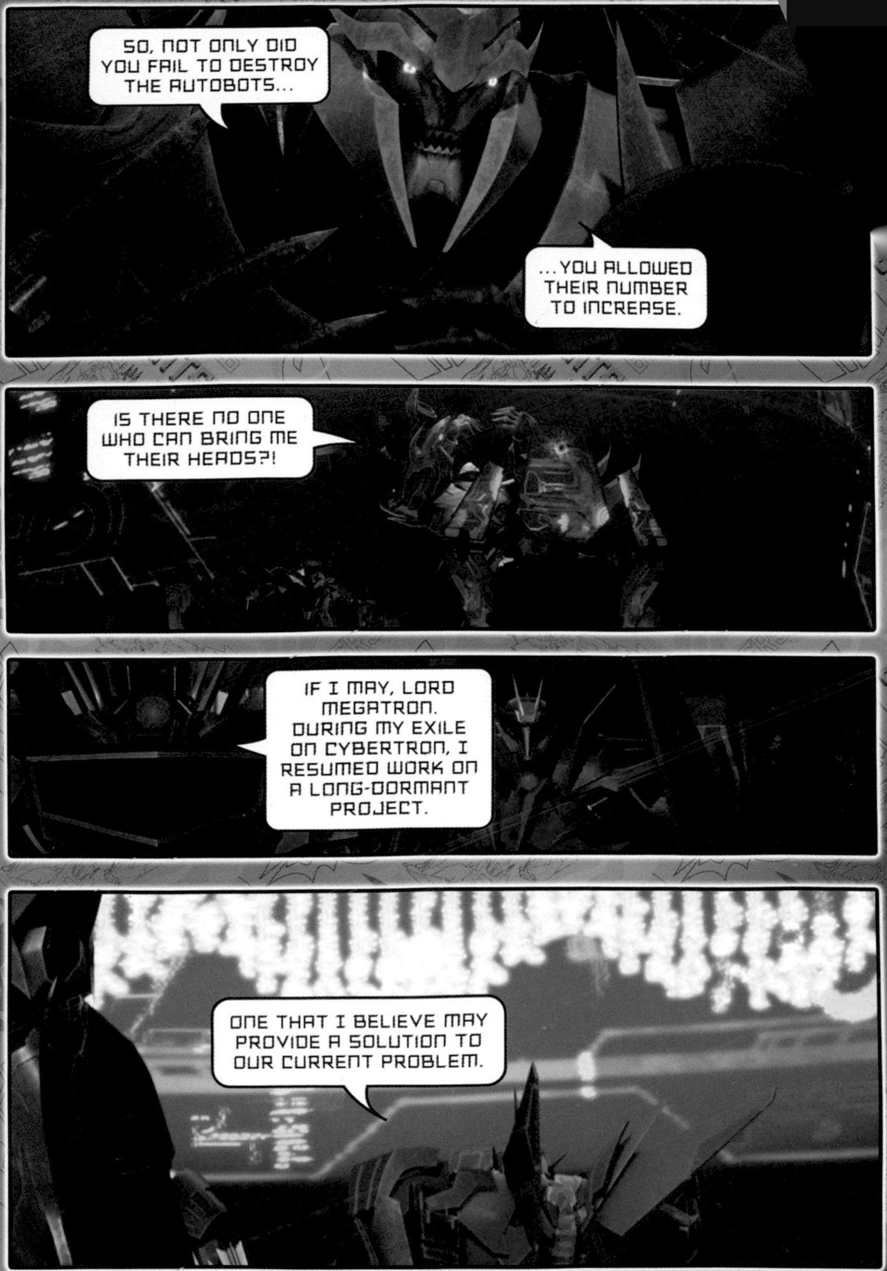
SO, NOT ONLY DID YOU FAIL TO DESTROY THE AUTOBOTS...
...YOU ALLOWED THEIR NUMBER TO INCREASE.
IS THERE NO ONE WHO CAN BRING ME THEIR HEADS?!
IF I MAY, LORD MEGATRON. DURING MY EXILE ON CYBERTRON, I RESUMED WORK ON A LONG-DORMANT PROJECT.
ONE THAT I BELIEVE MAY PROVIDE A SOLUTION TO OUR CURRENT PROBLEM.

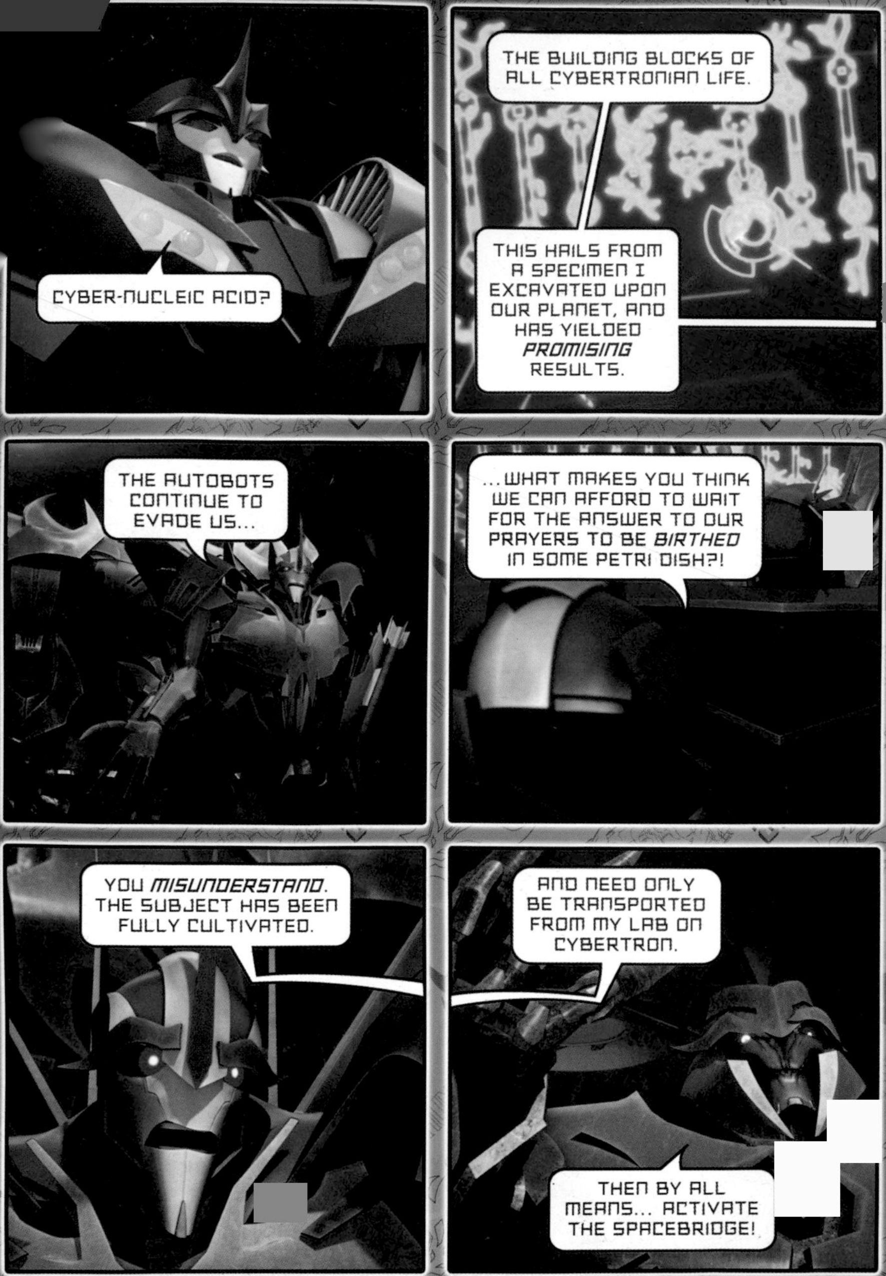
CYBER-NUCLEIC ACID?
THE BUILDING BLOCKS OF ALL CYBERTRONIAN LIFE.
THIS HAILS FROM A SPECIMEN I EXCAVATED UPON OUR PLANET, AND HAS YIELDED *PROMISING* RESULTS.
THE AUTOBOTS CONTINUE TO EVADE US...
...WHAT MAKES YOU THINK WE CAN AFFORD TO WAIT FOR THE ANSWER TO OUR PRAYERS TO BE *BIRTHED* IN SOME PETRI DISH?!
YOU *MISUNDERSTAND*. THE SUBJECT HAS BEEN FULLY CULTIVATED.
AND NEED ONLY BE TRANSPORTED FROM MY LAB ON CYBERTRON.
THEN BY ALL MEANS... ACTIVATE THE SPACEBRIDGE!

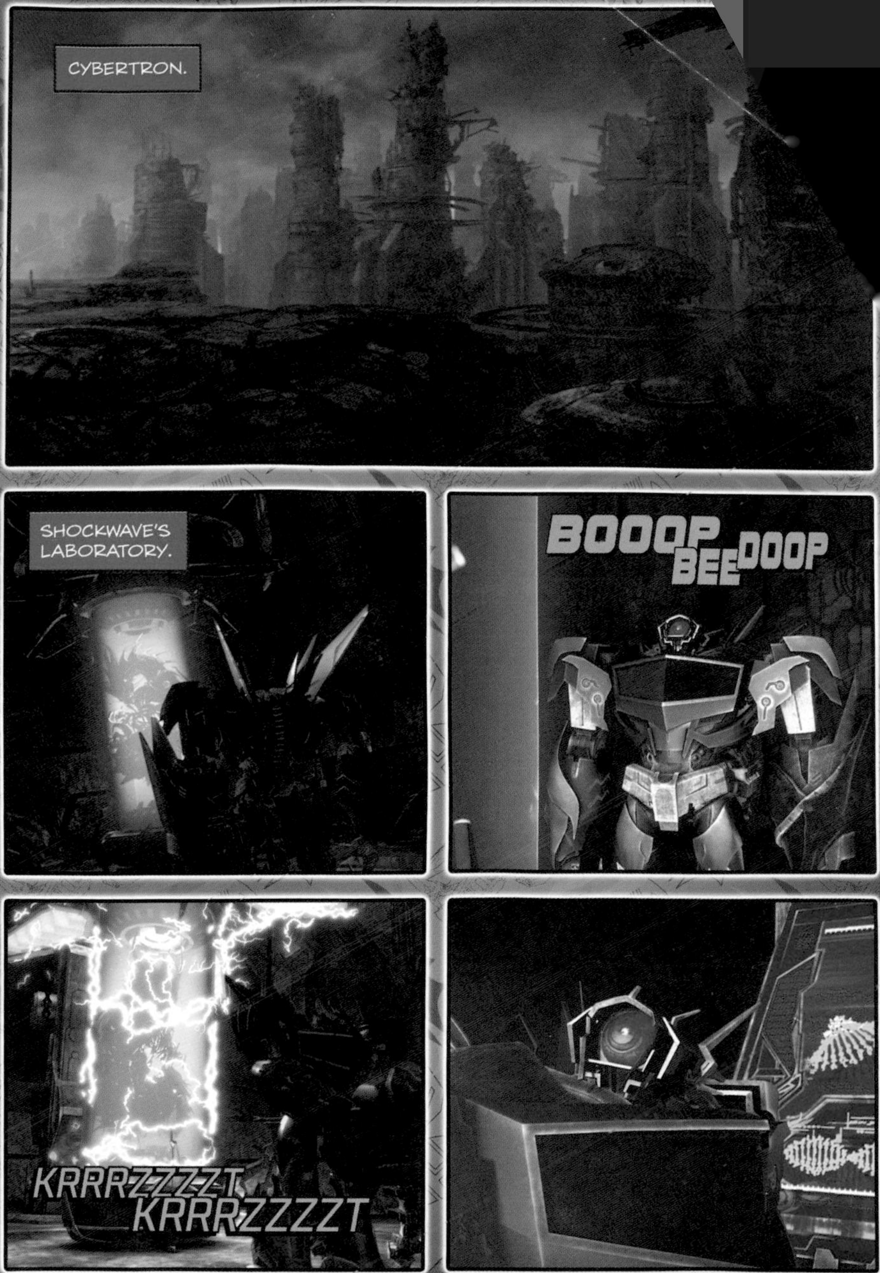
CYBERTRON.
SHOCKWAVE'S LABORATORY.
BOOOP BEEDOOP
KRRRZZZZT
KRRRZZZZT

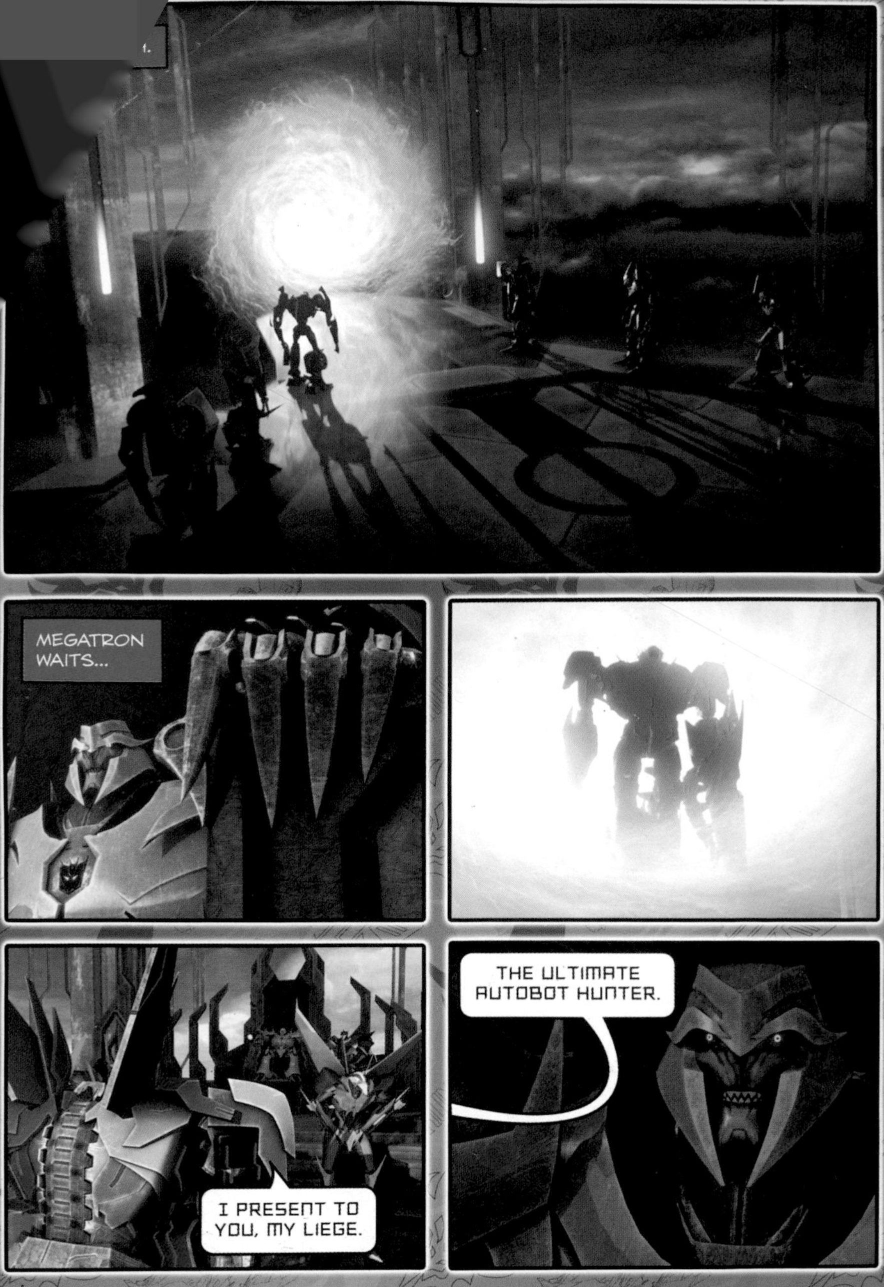
1.
MEGATRON WAITS...
I PRESENT TO YOU, MY LIEGE.
THE ULTIMATE AUTOBOT HUNTER.

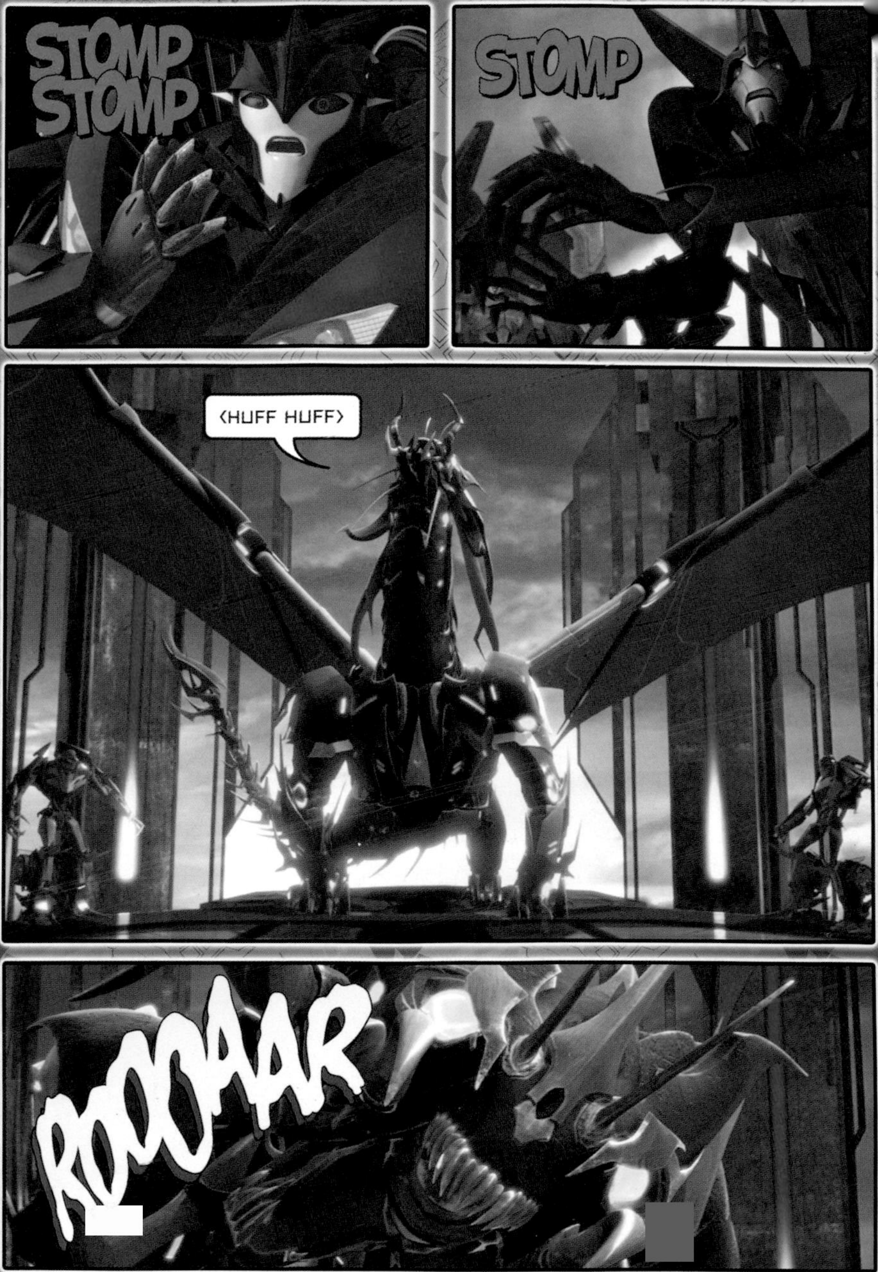
STOMP STOMP
STOMP
<HUFF HUFF>
ROOOAAR

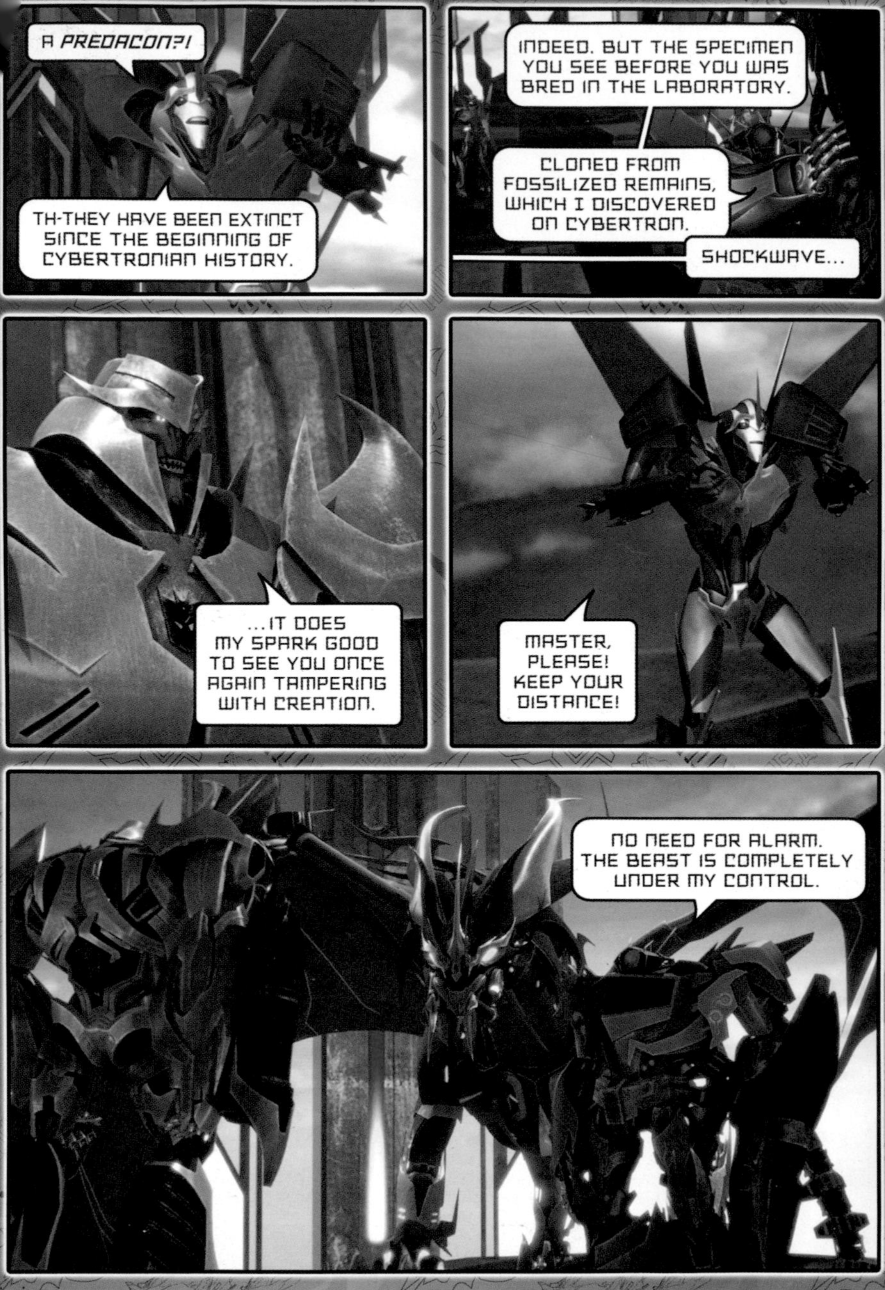
A PREDACON?!
TH-THEY HAVE BEEN EXTINCT SINCE THE BEGINNING OF CYBERTRONIAN HISTORY.
INDEED. BUT THE SPECIMEN YOU SEE BEFORE YOU WAS BRED IN THE LABORATORY.
CLONED FROM FOSSILIZED REMAINS, WHICH I DISCOVERED ON CYBERTRON.
SHOCKWAVE...
...IT DOES MY SPARK GOOD TO SEE YOU ONCE AGAIN TAMPERING WITH CREATION.
MASTER, PLEASE! KEEP YOUR DISTANCE!
NO NEED FOR ALARM. THE BEAST IS COMPLETELY UNDER MY CONTROL.

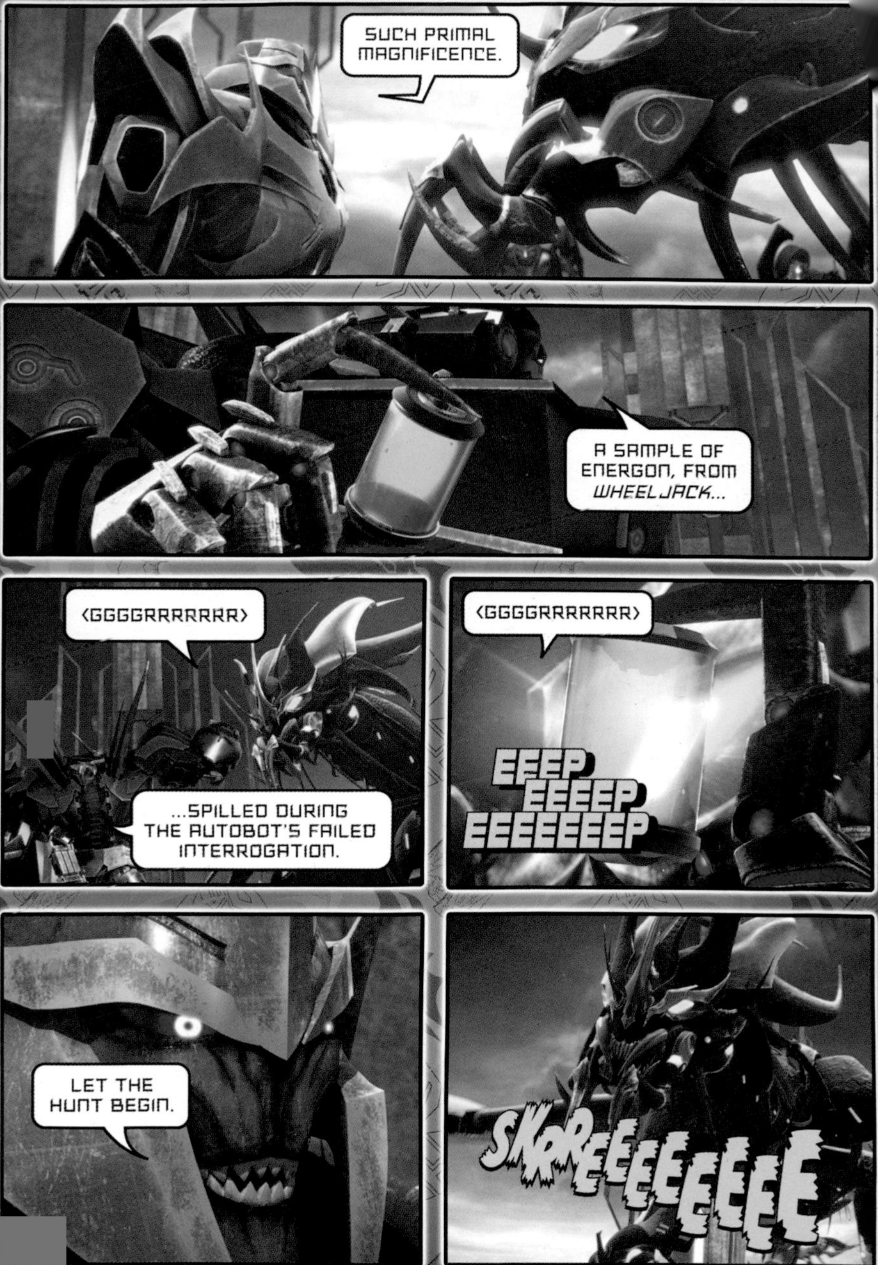
SUCH PRIMAL MAGNIFICENCE.
A SAMPLE OF ENERGON, FROM WHEELJACK...
⟨GGGGRRRRRRR⟩
...SPILLED DURING THE AUTOBOT'S FAILED INTERROGATION.
⟨GGGGRRRRRRR⟩
EEEP EEEEP EEEEEEEP
LET THE HUNT BEGIN.
SKREEEEEEEEEE

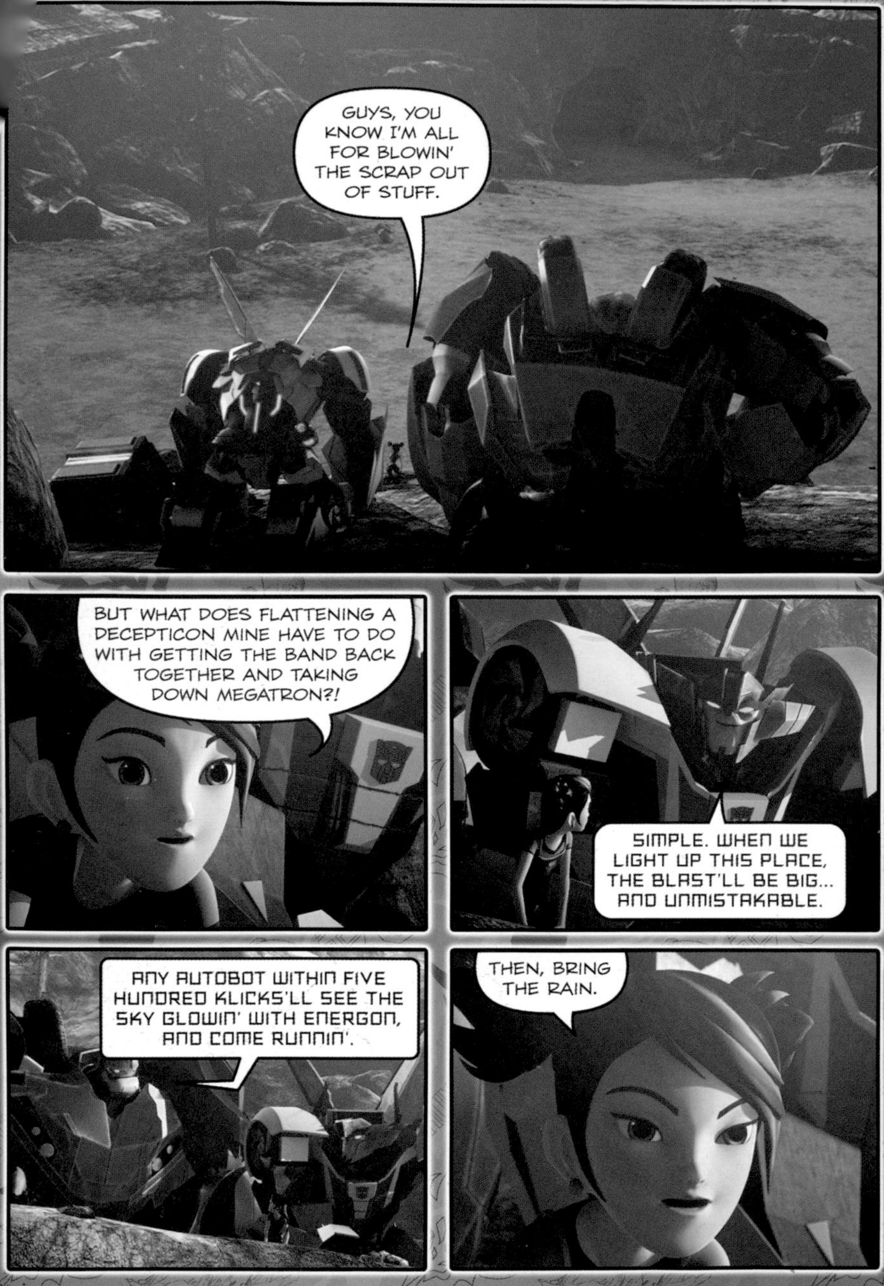
GUYS, YOU KNOW I'M ALL FOR BLOWIN' THE SCRAP OUT OF STUFF.
BUT WHAT DOES FLATTENING A DECEPTICON MINE HAVE TO DO WITH GETTING THE BAND BACK TOGETHER AND TAKING DOWN MEGATRON?!
SIMPLE. WHEN WE LIGHT UP THIS PLACE, THE BLAST'LL BE BIG... AND UNMISTAKABLE.
ANY AUTOBOT WITHIN FIVE HUNDRED KLICKS'LL SEE THE SKY GLOWIN' WITH ENERGON, AND COME RUNNIN'.
THEN, BRING THE RAIN.

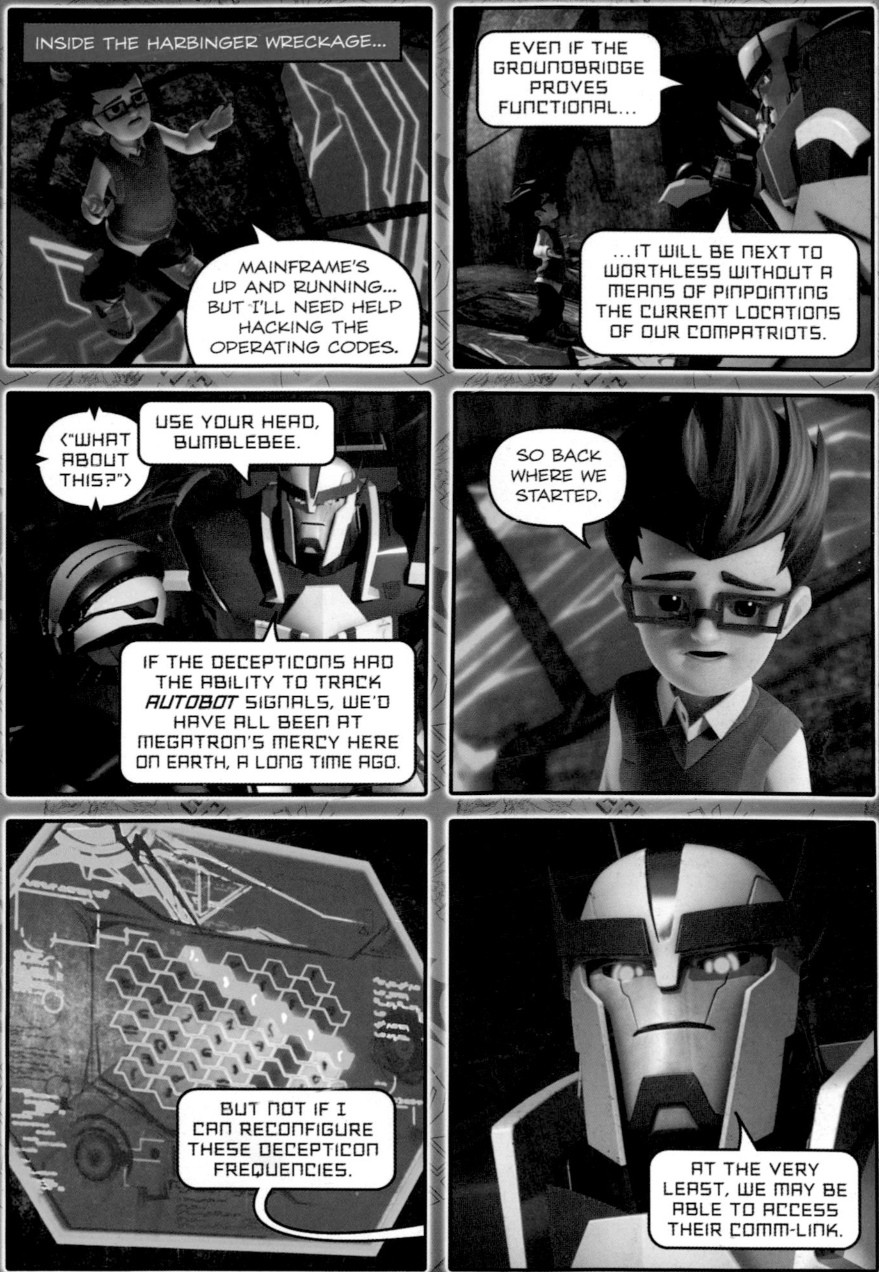
INSIDE THE HARBINGER WRECKAGE...
MAINFRAME'S UP AND RUNNING... BUT I'LL NEED HELP HACKING THE OPERATING CODES.
EVEN IF THE GROUNDBRIDGE PROVES FUNCTIONAL...
...IT WILL BE NEXT TO WORTHLESS WITHOUT A MEANS OF PINPOINTING THE CURRENT LOCATIONS OF OUR COMPATRIOTS.
USE YOUR HEAD, BUMBLEBEE.
<"WHAT ABOUT THIS?">
IF THE DECEPTICONS HAD THE ABILITY TO TRACK *AUTOBOT* SIGNALS, WE'D HAVE ALL BEEN AT MEGATRON'S MERCY HERE ON EARTH, A LONG TIME AGO.
SO BACK WHERE WE STARTED.
BUT NOT IF I CAN RECONFIGURE THESE DECEPTICON FREQUENCIES.
AT THE VERY LEAST, WE MAY BE ABLE TO ACCESS THEIR COMM-LINK.

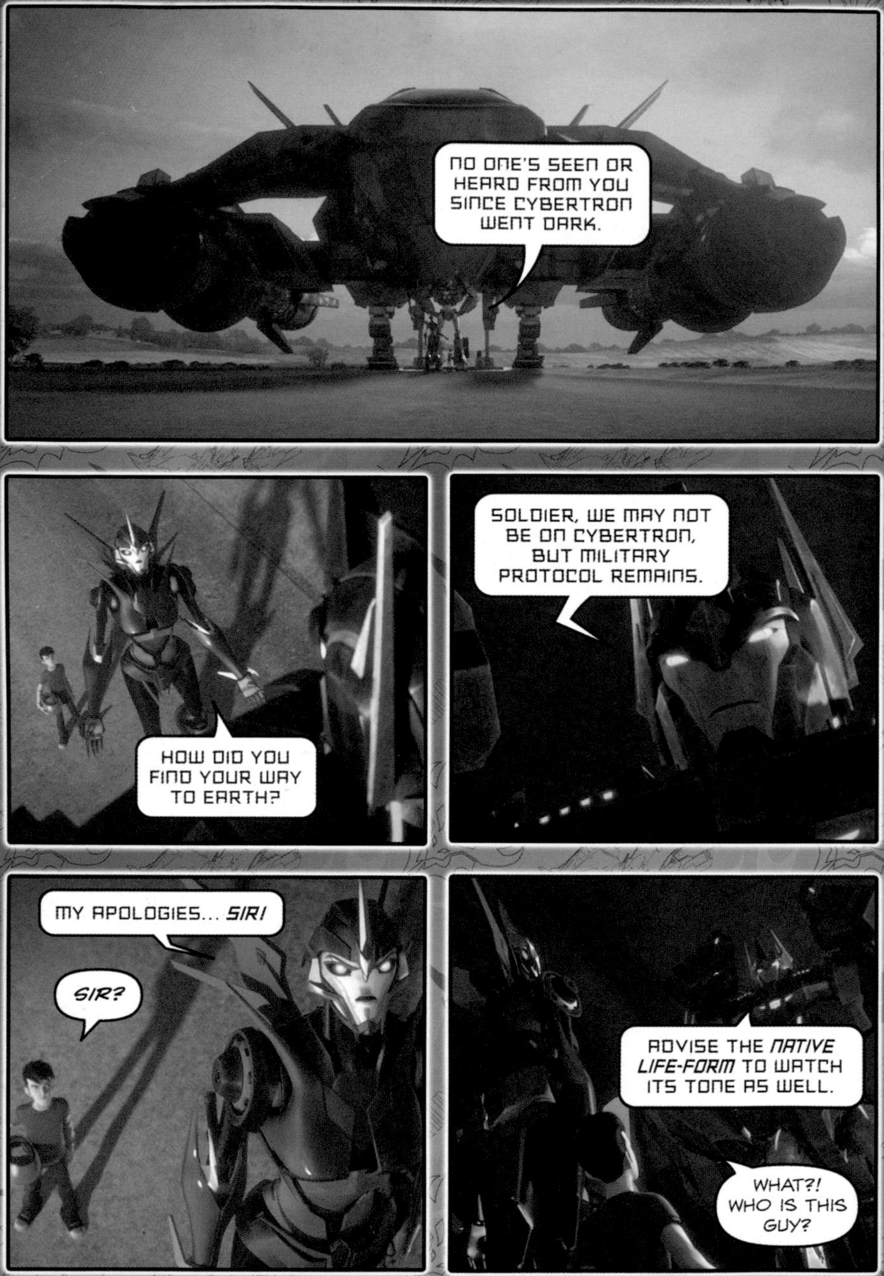
NO ONE'S SEEN OR HEARD FROM YOU SINCE CYBERTRON WENT DARK.
HOW DID YOU FIND YOUR WAY TO EARTH?
SOLDIER, WE MAY NOT BE ON CYBERTRON, BUT MILITARY PROTOCOL REMAINS.
MY APOLOGIES... *SIR!*
SIR?
ADVISE THE *NATIVE LIFE-FORM* TO WATCH ITS TONE AS WELL.
WHAT?! WHO IS THIS GUY?

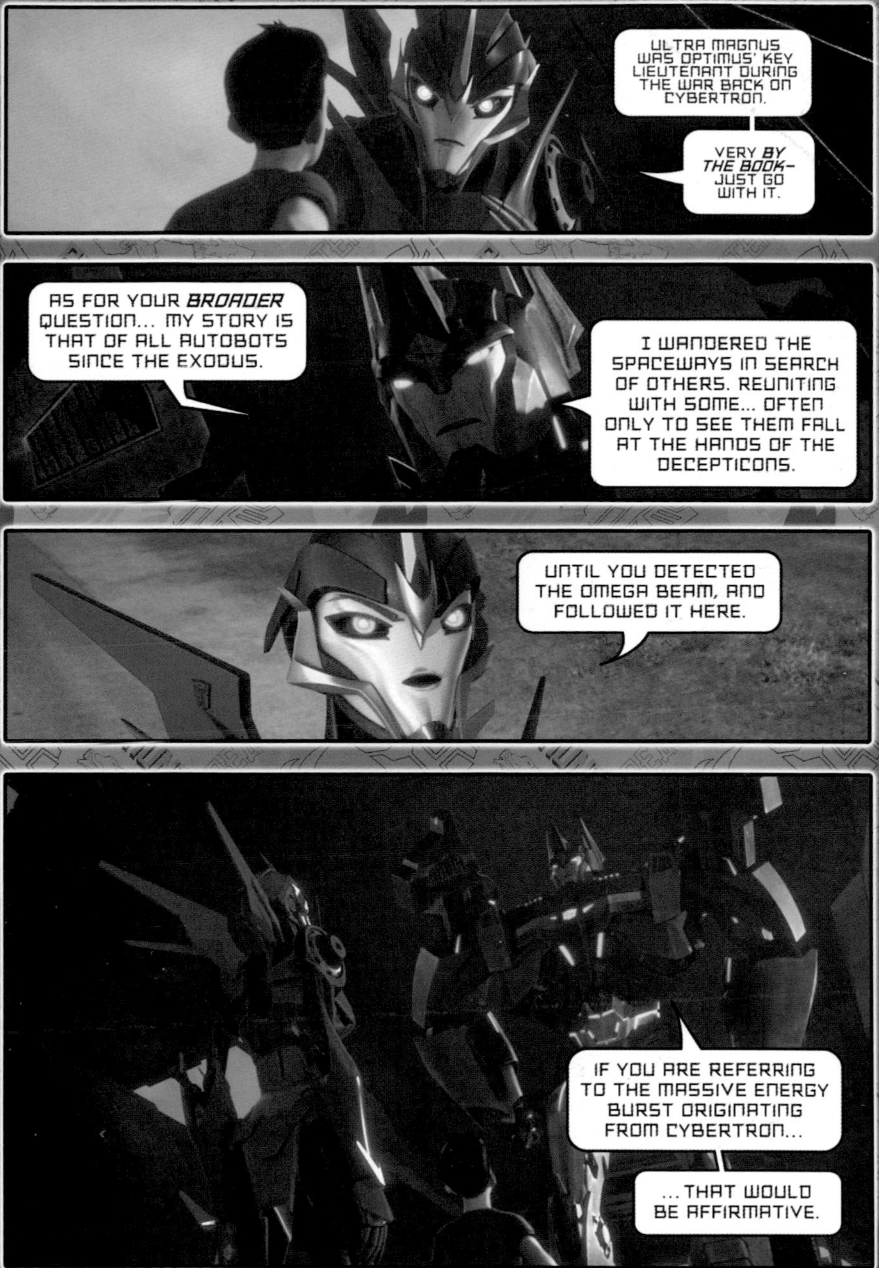
ULTRA MAGNUS WAS OPTIMUS' KEY LIEUTENANT DURING THE WAR BACK ON CYBERTRON.
VERY *BY THE BOOK*– JUST GO WITH IT.
AS FOR YOUR *BROADER* QUESTION... MY STORY IS THAT OF ALL AUTOBOTS SINCE THE EXODUS.
I WANDERED THE SPACEWAYS IN SEARCH OF OTHERS. REUNITING WITH SOME... OFTEN ONLY TO SEE THEM FALL AT THE HANDS OF THE DECEPTICONS.
UNTIL YOU DETECTED THE OMEGA BEAM, AND FOLLOWED IT HERE.
IF YOU ARE REFERRING TO THE MASSIVE ENERGY BURST ORIGINATING FROM CYBERTRON...
...THAT WOULD BE AFFIRMATIVE.

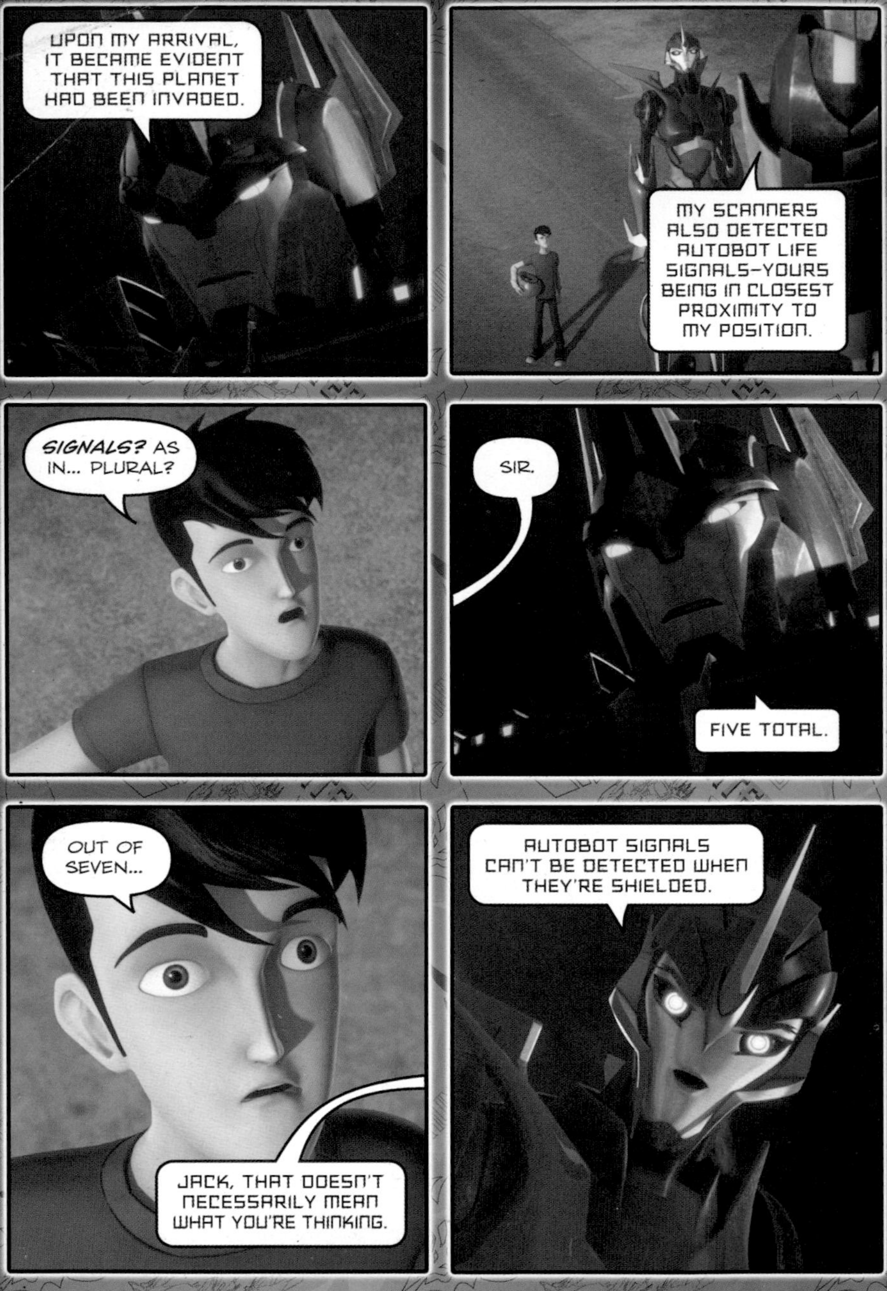
UPON MY ARRIVAL, IT BECAME EVIDENT THAT THIS PLANET HAD BEEN INVADED.
MY SCANNERS ALSO DETECTED AUTOBOT LIFE SIGNALS–YOURS BEING IN CLOSEST PROXIMITY TO MY POSITION.
SIGNALS? AS IN... PLURAL?
SIR.
FIVE TOTAL.
OUT OF SEVEN...
JACK, THAT DOESN'T NECESSARILY MEAN WHAT YOU'RE THINKING.
AUTOBOT SIGNALS CAN'T BE DETECTED WHEN THEY'RE SHIELDED.

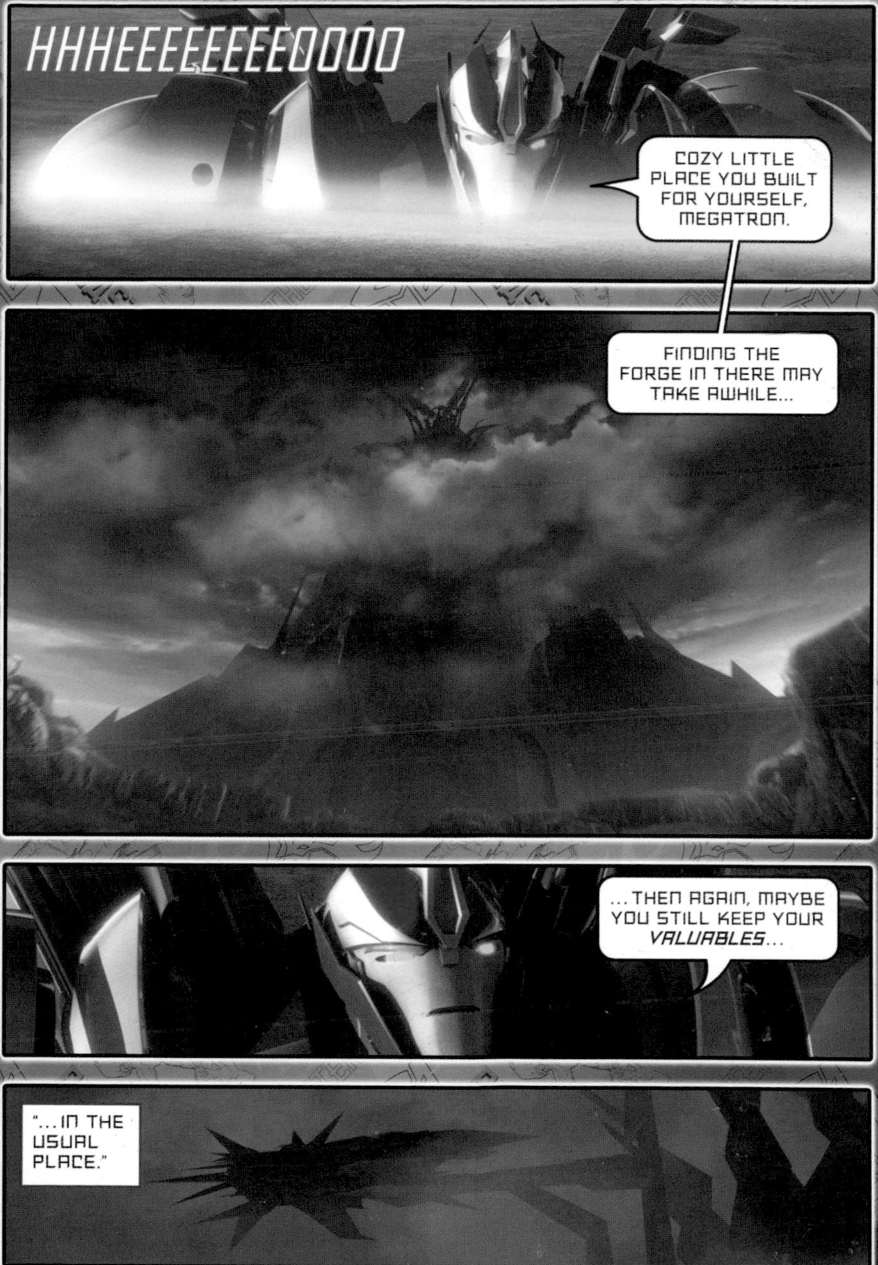
HHHEEEEEEEEEOOOO
COZY LITTLE PLACE YOU BUILT FOR YOURSELF, MEGATRON.
FINDING THE FORGE IN THERE MAY TAKE AWHILE...
...THEN AGAIN, MAYBE YOU STILL KEEP YOUR *VALUABLES*...
"...IN THE USUAL PLACE."

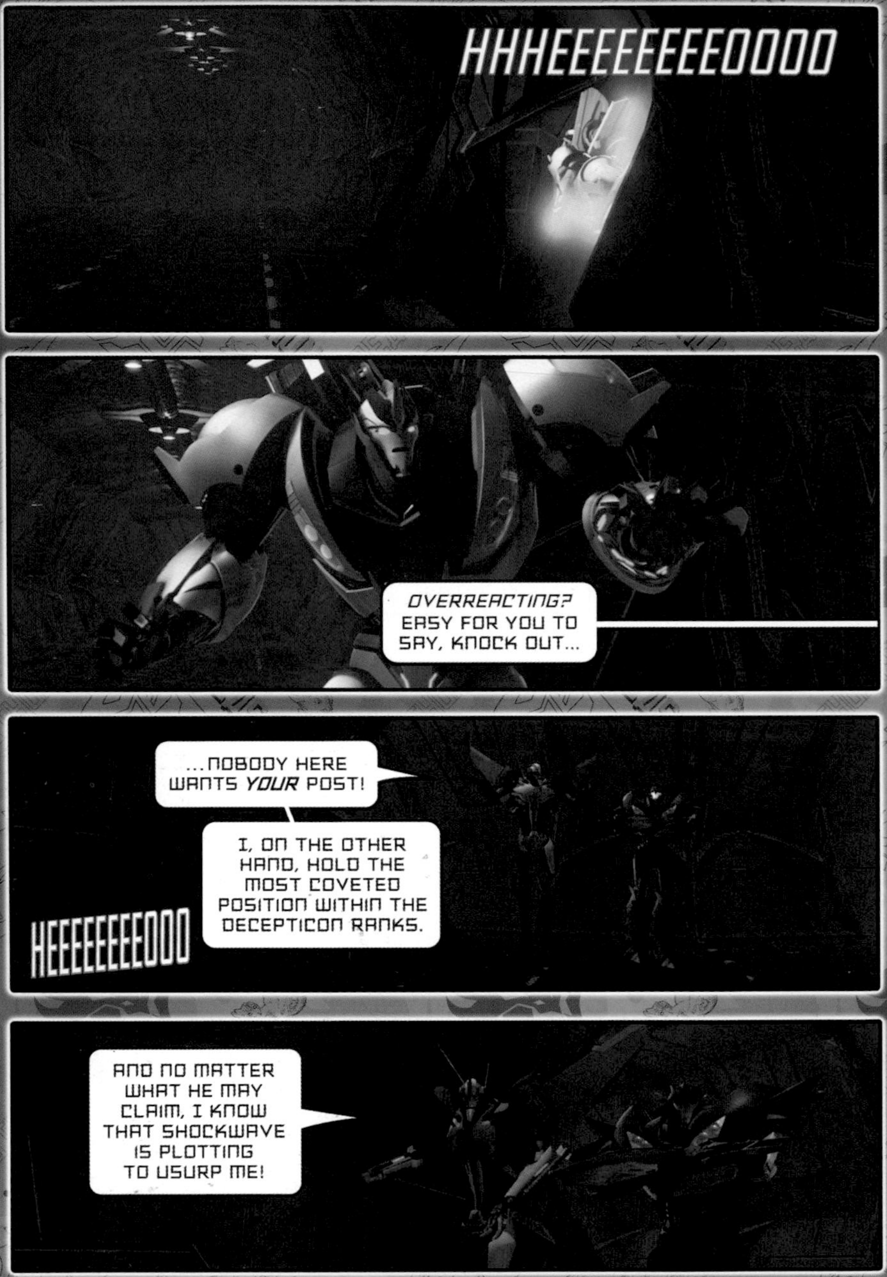
HHHEEEEEEEEEOOOO
OVERREACTING? EASY FOR YOU TO SAY, KNOCK OUT...
...NOBODY HERE WANTS YOUR POST!
I, ON THE OTHER HAND, HOLD THE MOST COVETED POSITION WITHIN THE DECEPTICON RANKS.
HEEEEEEEEOOO
AND NO MATTER WHAT HE MAY CLAIM, I KNOW THAT SHOCKWAVE IS PLOTTING TO USURP ME!

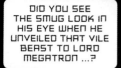
DID YOU SEE THE SMUG LOOK IN HIS EYE WHEN HE UNVEILED THAT VILE BEAST TO LORD MEGATRON ...?

DANGER PASSES, AND SMOKESCREEN CONTINUES HIS SEARCH.

HHHEEEEEEEEOOOO

WELL, WELL...

...HELLO, BEAUTIFUL.

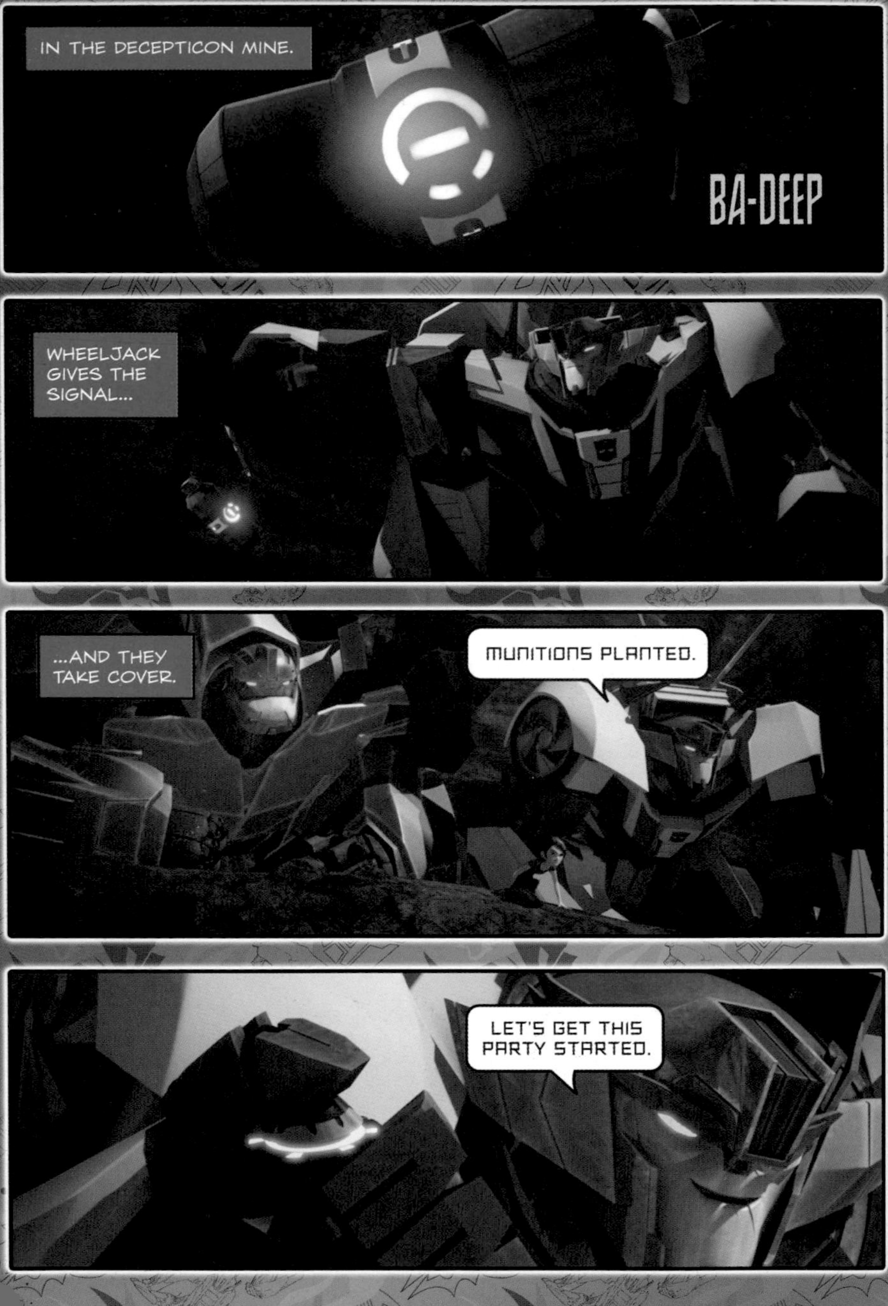
IN THE DECEPTICON MINE.
BA-DEEP
WHEELJACK GIVES THE SIGNAL...
...AND THEY TAKE COVER.
MUNITIONS PLANTED.
LET'S GET THIS PARTY STARTED.

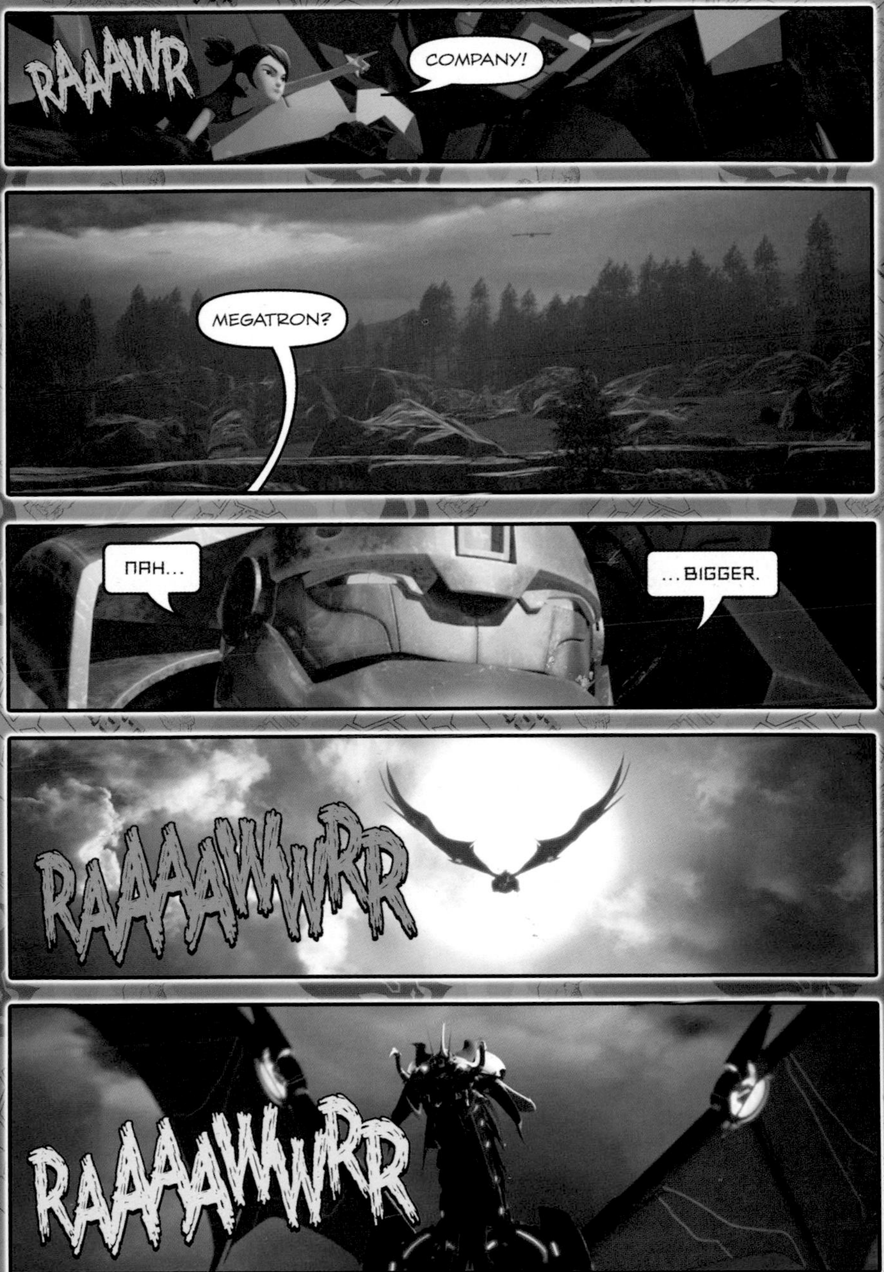
RAAAWR
COMPANY!
MEGATRON?
NAH...
...BIGGER.
RAAAAWWRR
RAAAAWWRR

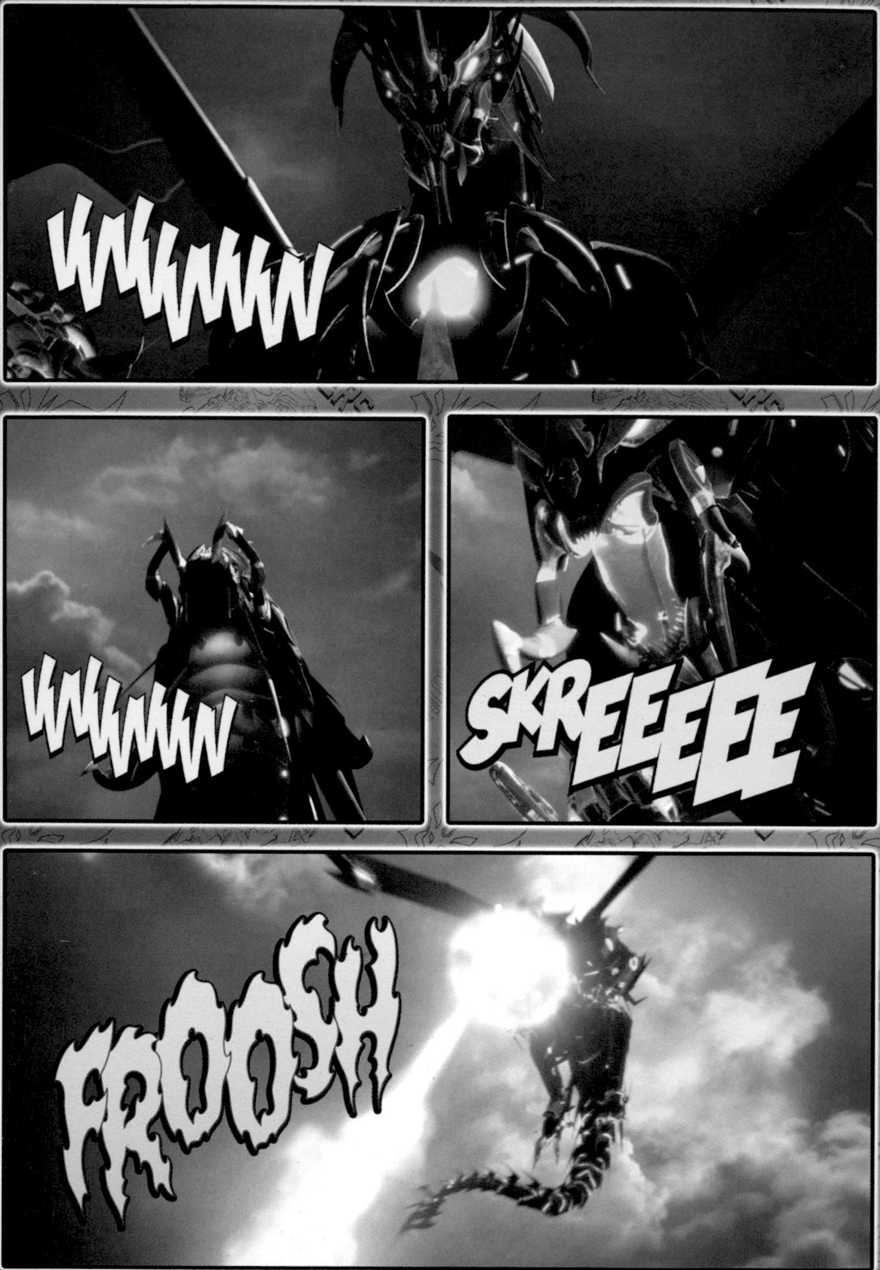
SKREEEEE
FROOSH

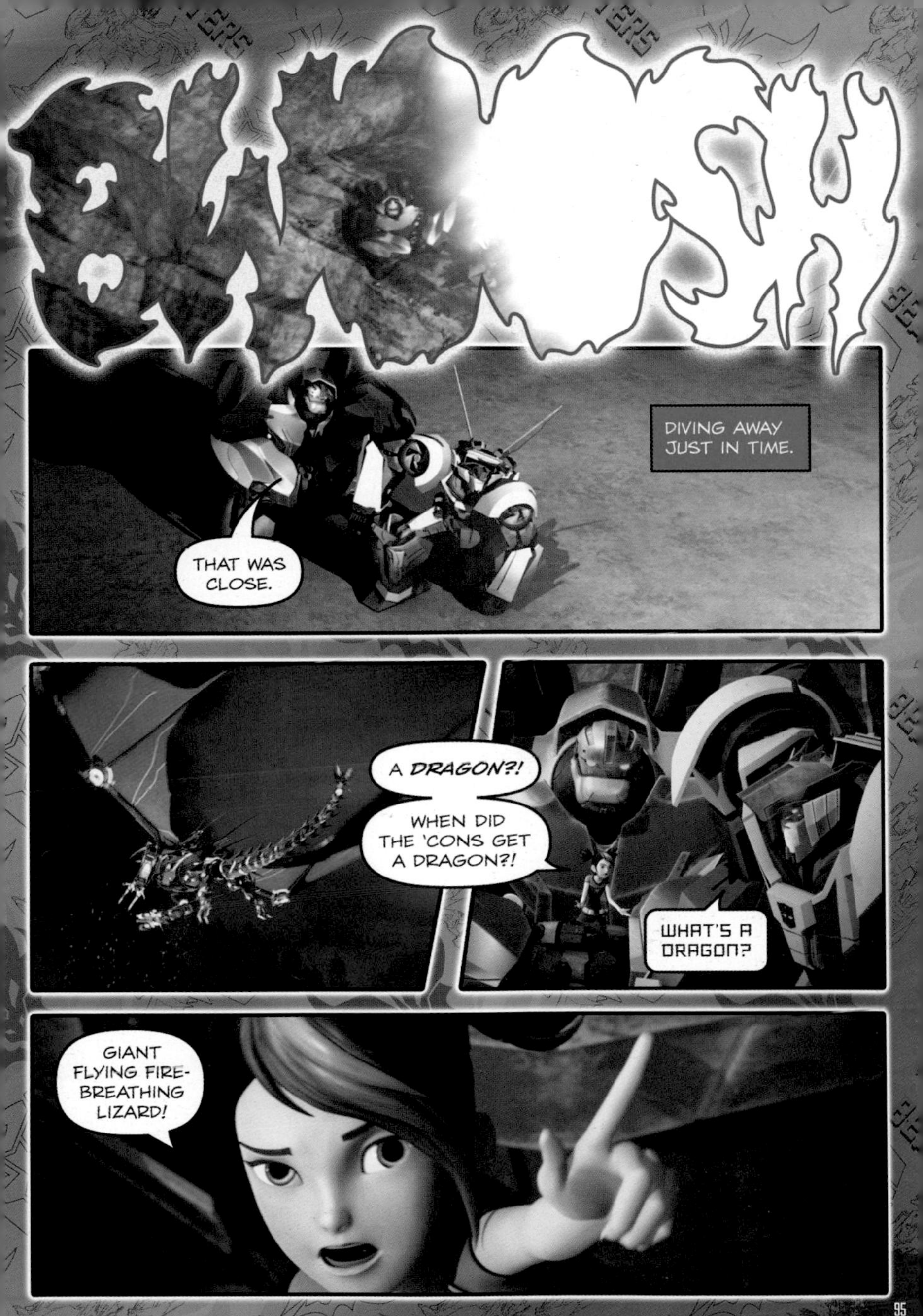
FWOOSH
DIVING AWAY JUST IN TIME.
THAT WAS CLOSE.
A *DRAGON*?!
WHEN DID THE 'CONS GET A DRAGON?!
WHAT'S A DRAGON?
GIANT FLYING FIRE-BREATHING LIZARD!

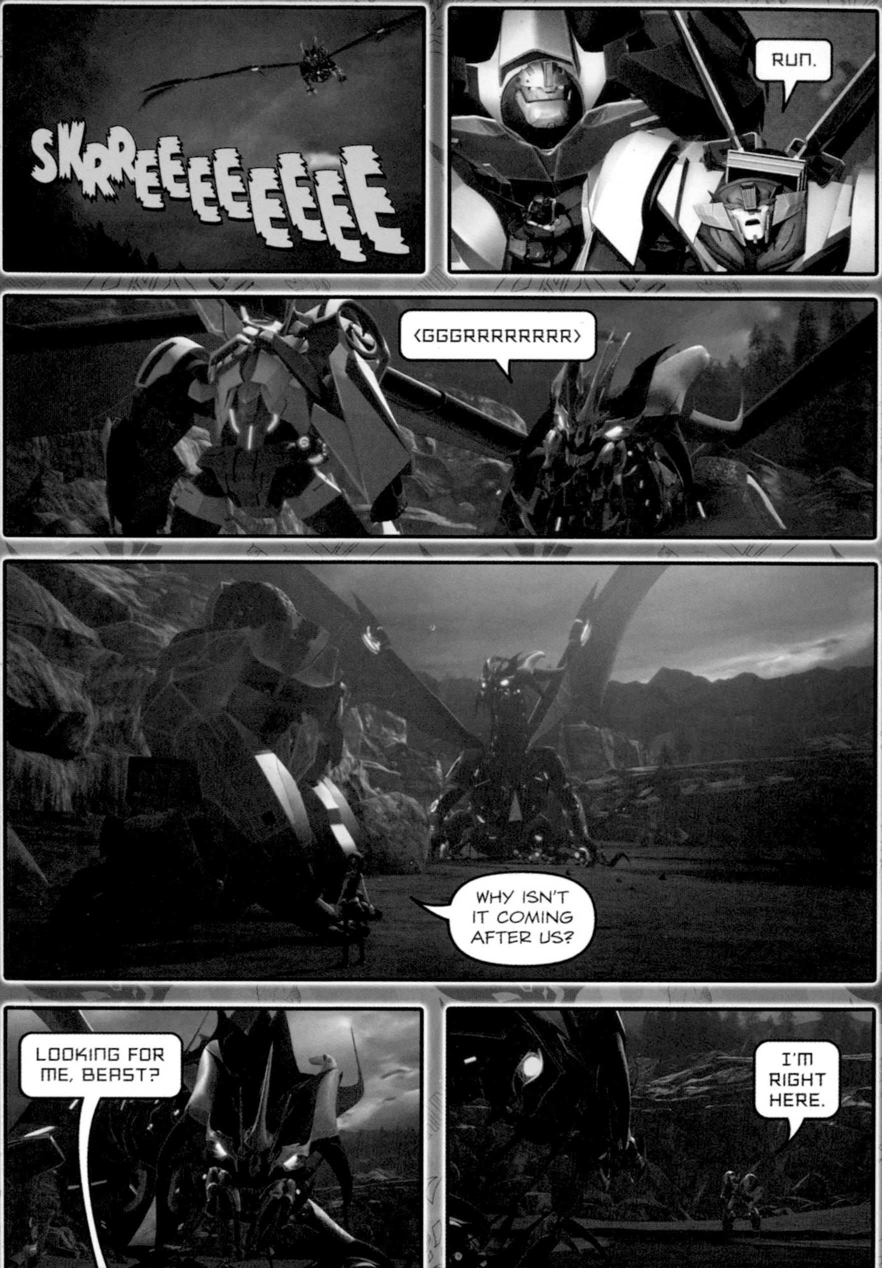
SKRREEEEEEEEEE
RUN.
<GGGRRRRRRRR>
WHY ISN'T IT COMING AFTER US?
LOOKING FOR ME, BEAST?
I'M RIGHT HERE.

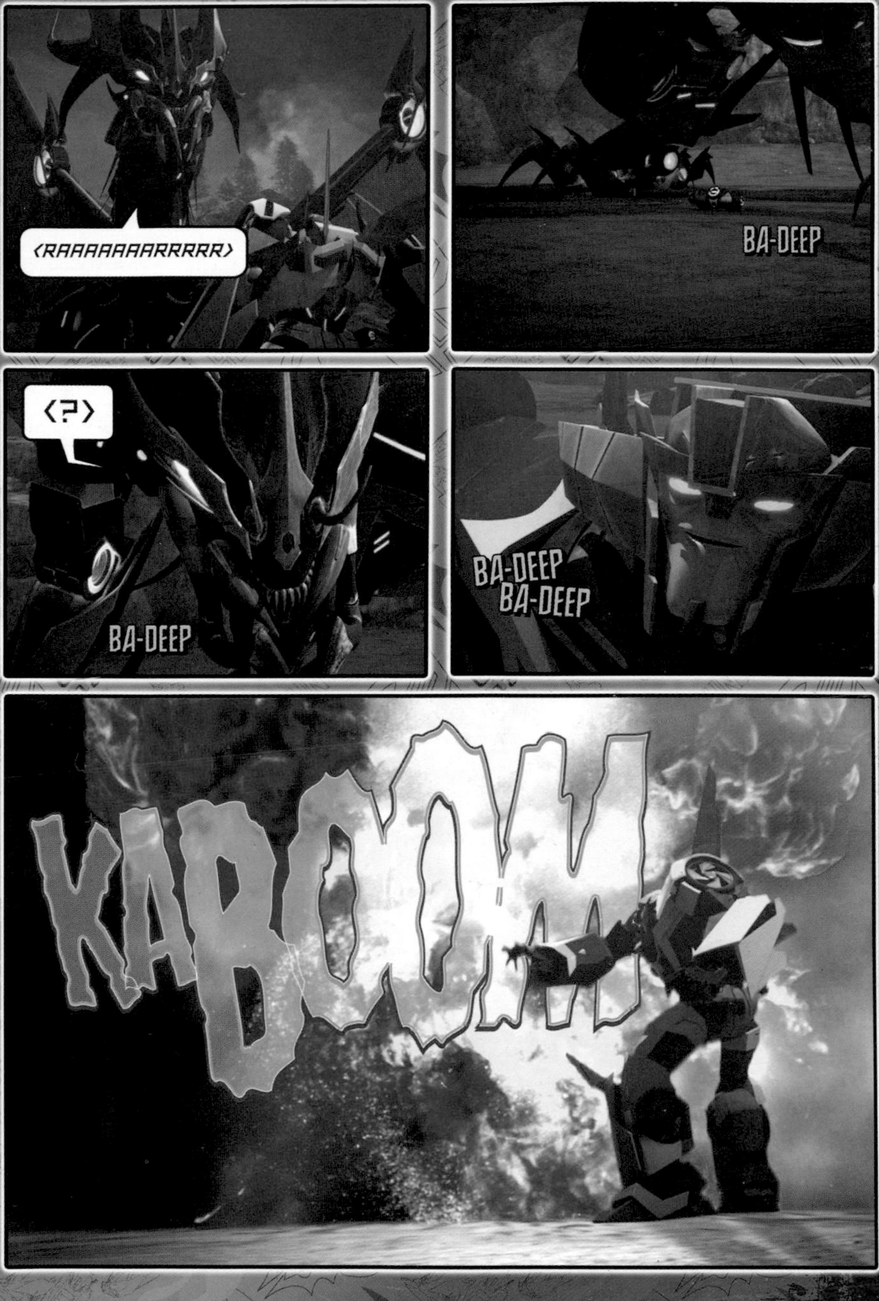
<RAAAAAAAARRRRR>
BA-DEEP
<?>
BA-DEEP
BA-DEEP
BA-DEEP
KABOOM

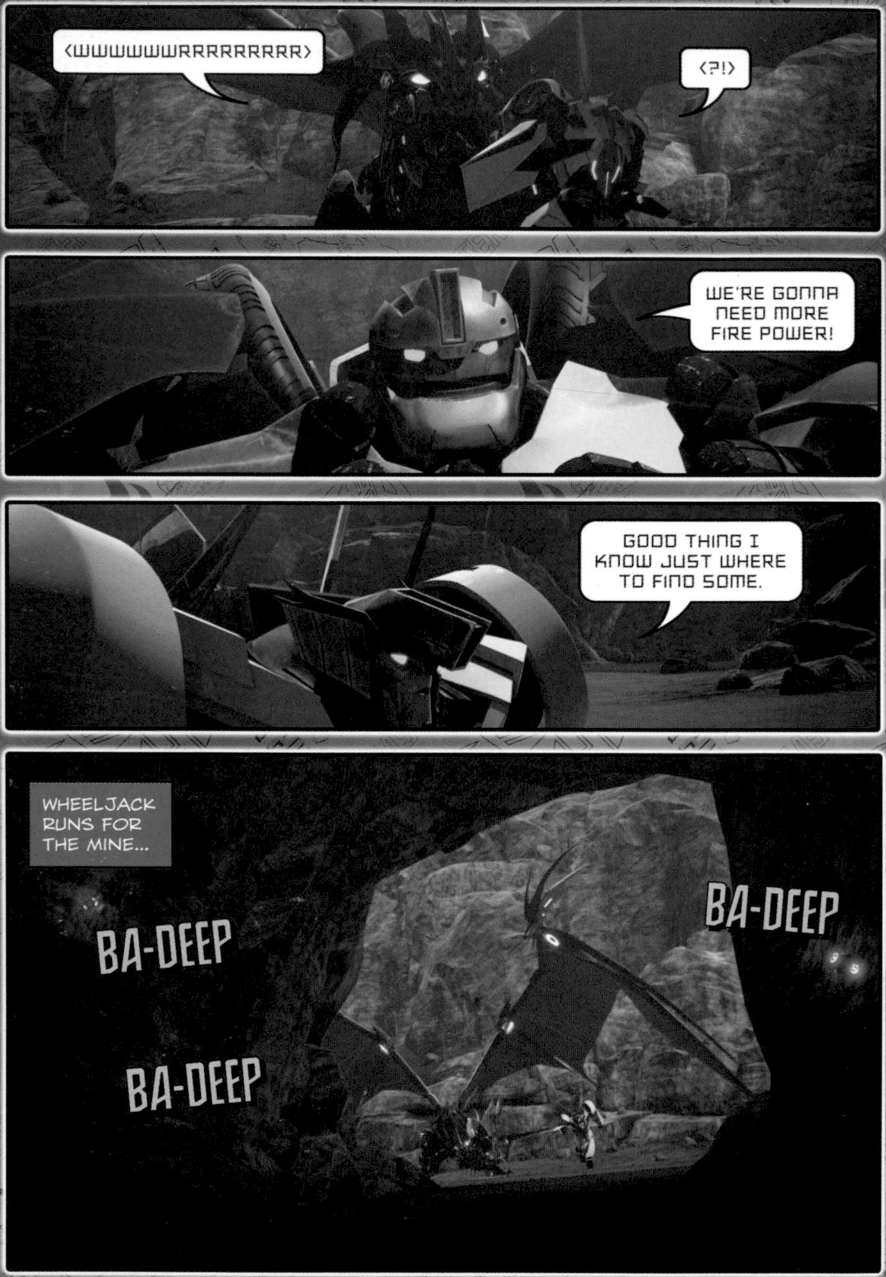
<WWWWWWRRRRRRRRR>
<?!>
WE'RE GONNA NEED MORE FIRE POWER!
GOOD THING I KNOW JUST WHERE TO FIND SOME.
WHEELJACK RUNS FOR THE MINE...
BA-DEEP
BA-DEEP
BA-DEEP

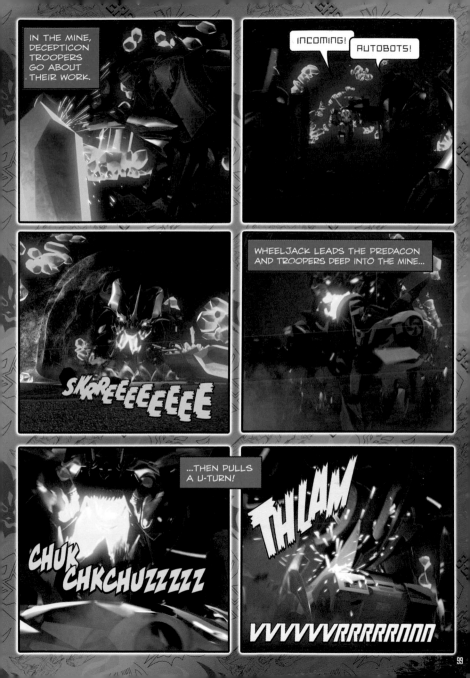

IN THE MINE, DECEPTICON TROOPERS GO ABOUT THEIR WORK.

INCOMING!

AUTOBOTS!

WHEELJACK LEADS THE PREDACON AND TROOPERS DEEP INTO THE MINE...

SKREEEEEEEEE

...THEN PULLS A U-TURN!

CHUK CHKCHUZZZZZ

THLAM

VVVVVVRRRRRNNN

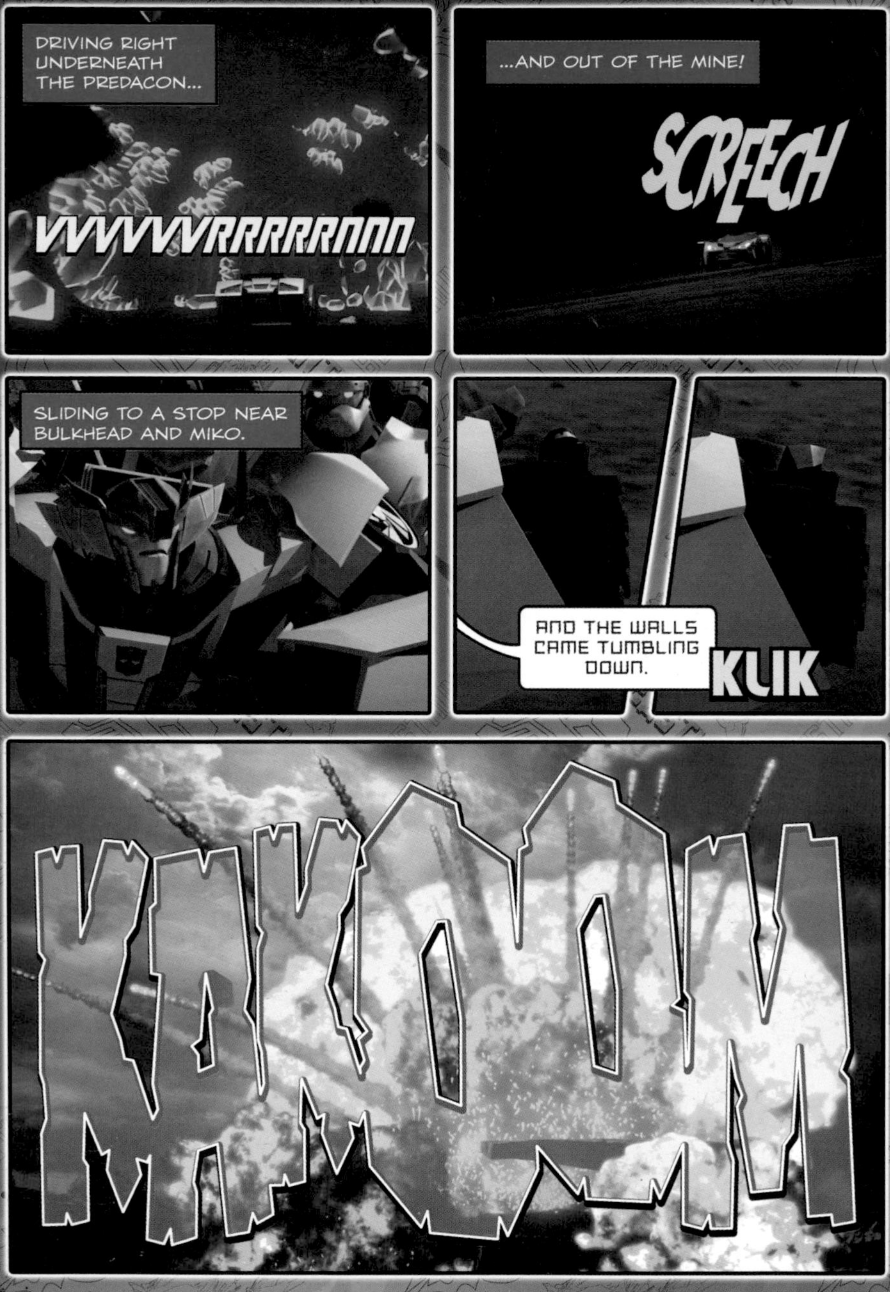
DRIVING RIGHT UNDERNEATH THE PREDACON...
VVVVVVRRRRRNNN
...AND OUT OF THE MINE!
SCREECH
SLIDING TO A STOP NEAR BULKHEAD AND MIKO.
AND THE WALLS CAME TUMBLING DOWN.
KLIK
KAKOOM

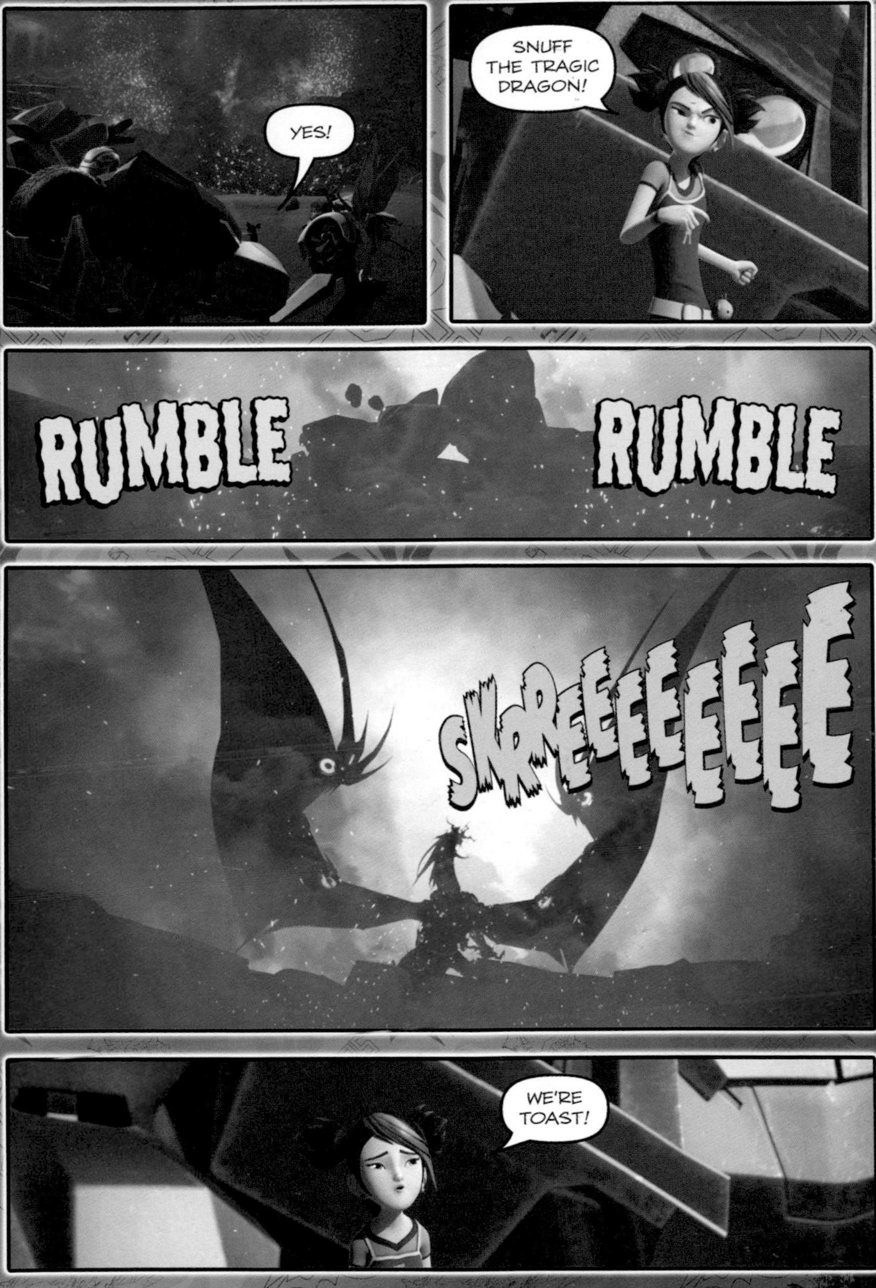
YES!
SNUFF THE TRAGIC DRAGON!
RUMBLE RUMBLE
SKREEEEEEEEEE
WE'RE TOAST!

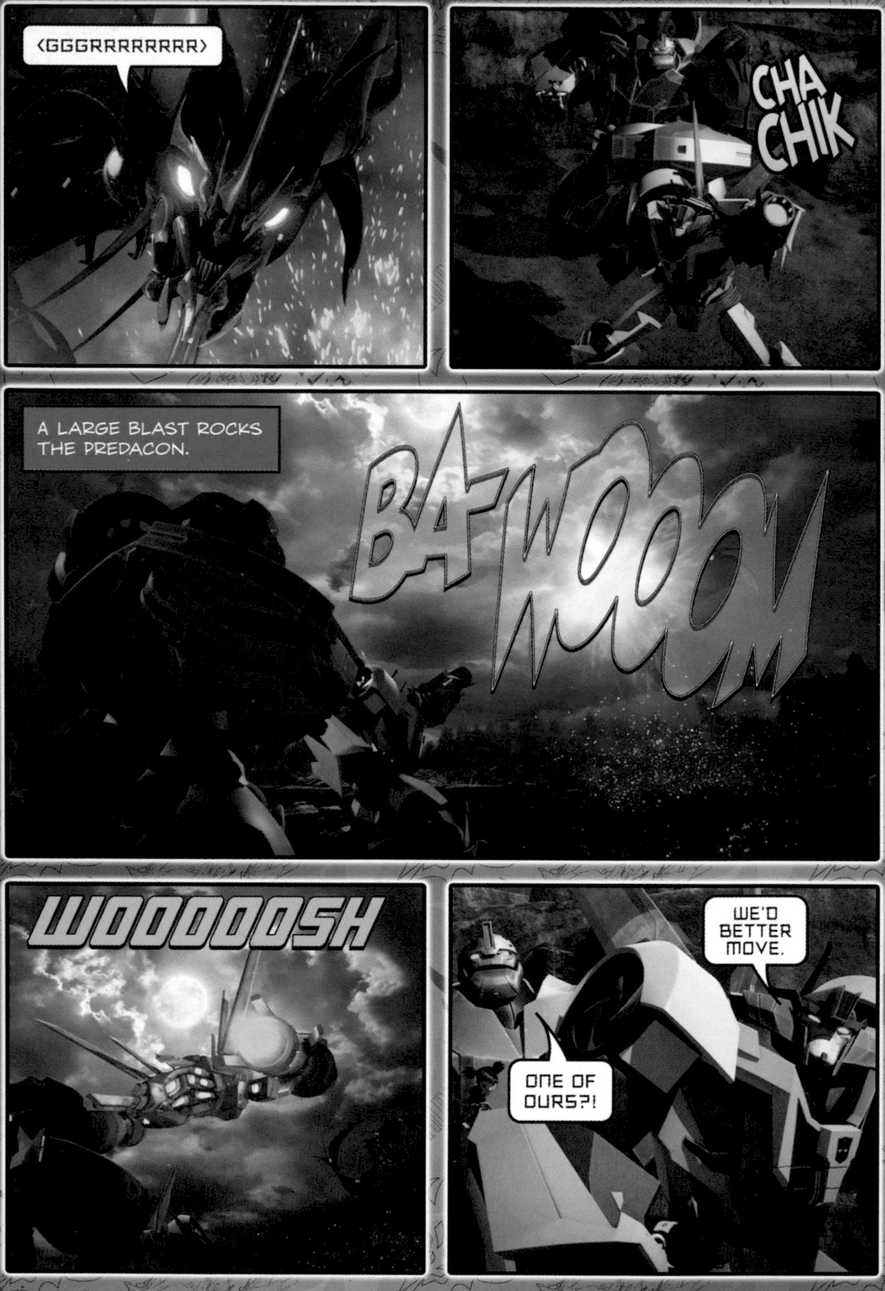
<GGGRRRRRRRR>
CHA CHIK
A LARGE BLAST ROCKS THE PREDACON.
BAWOOOM
WOOOOOSH
WE'D BETTER MOVE.
ONE OF OURS?!

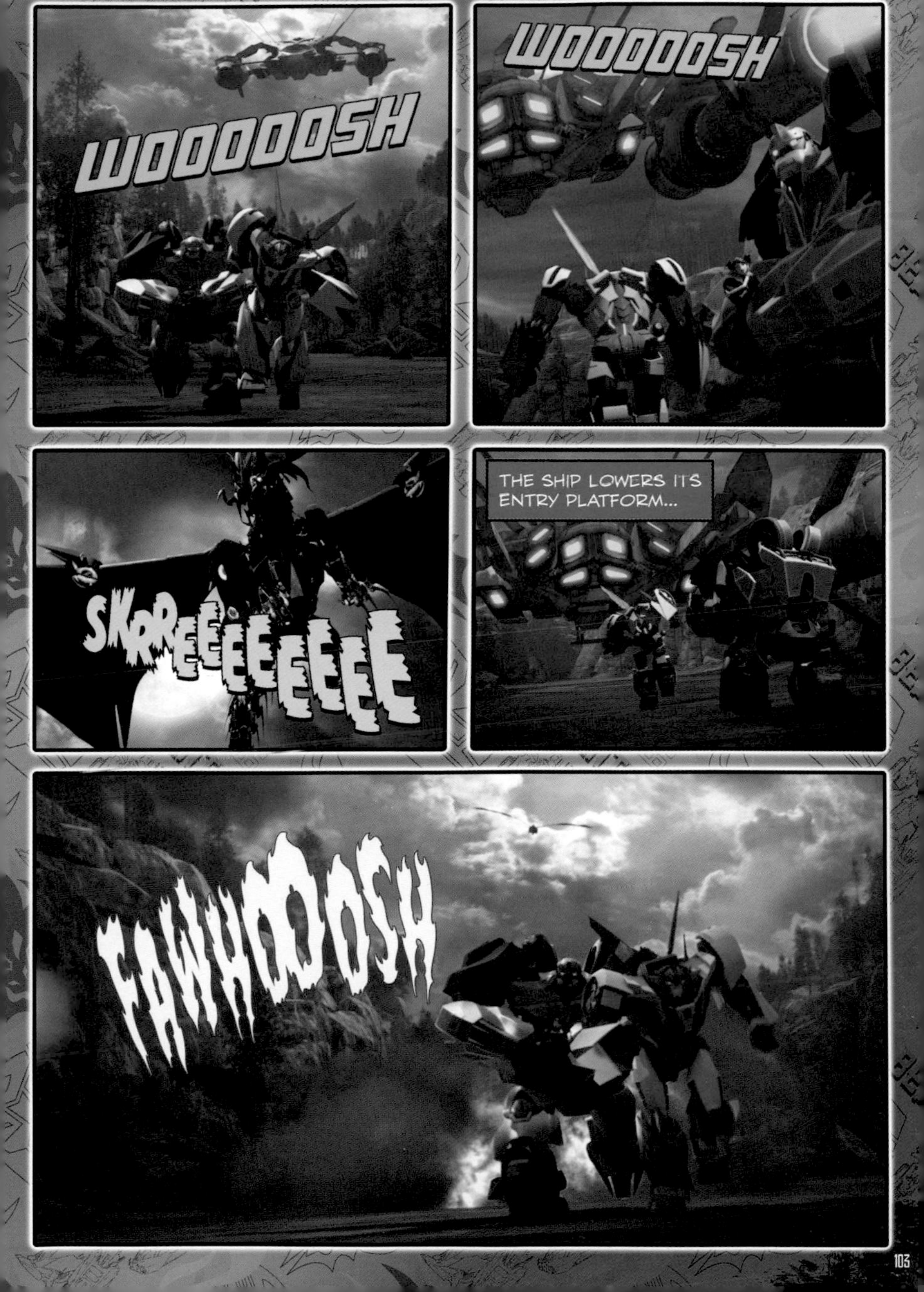
WOOOOOSH
WOOOOOSH
SKREEEEEEEEE
THE SHIP LOWERS ITS ENTRY PLATFORM...
FAWHOOOSH

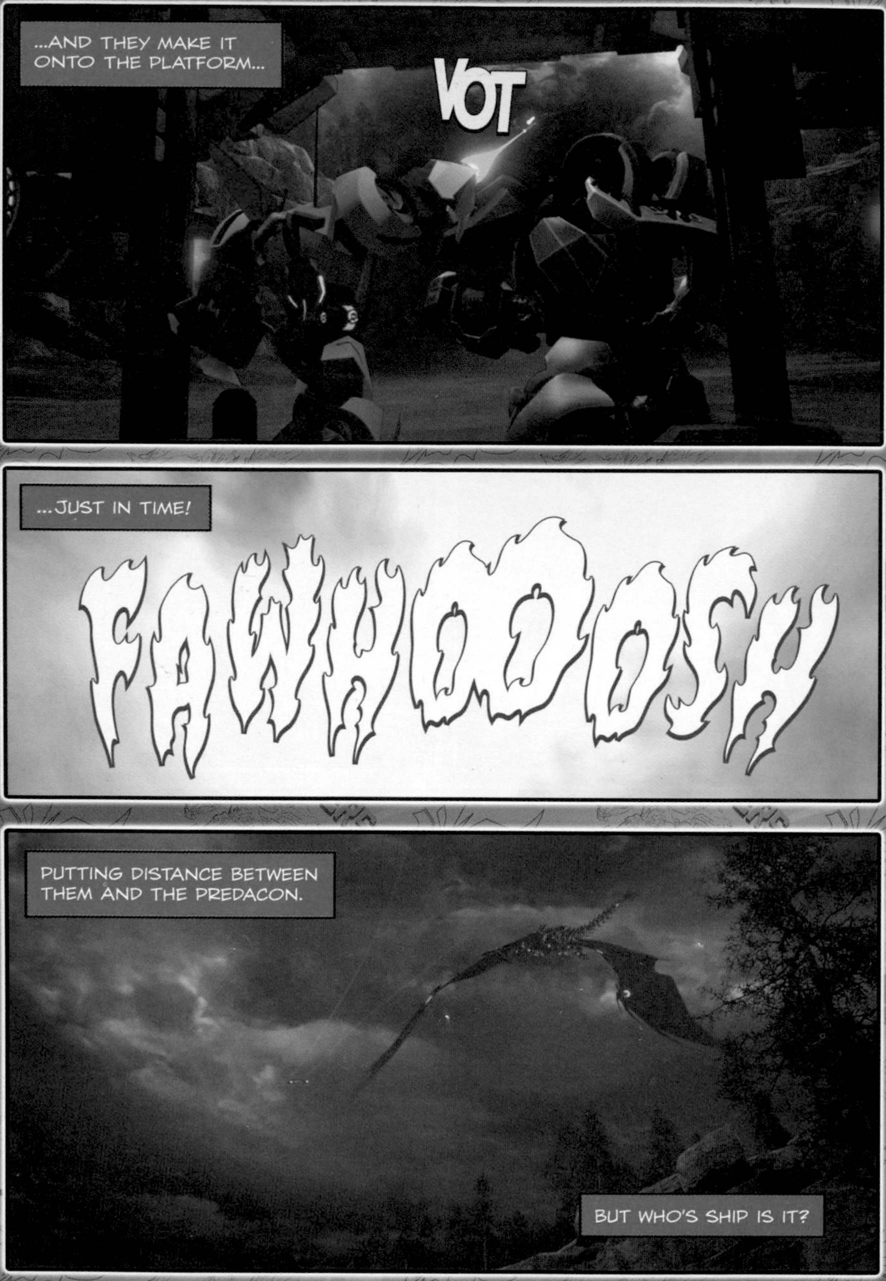
...AND THEY MAKE IT ONTO THE PLATFORM...
VOT
...JUST IN TIME!
FAWHOOOSH
PUTTING DISTANCE BETWEEN THEM AND THE PREDACON.
BUT WHO'S SHIP IS IT?

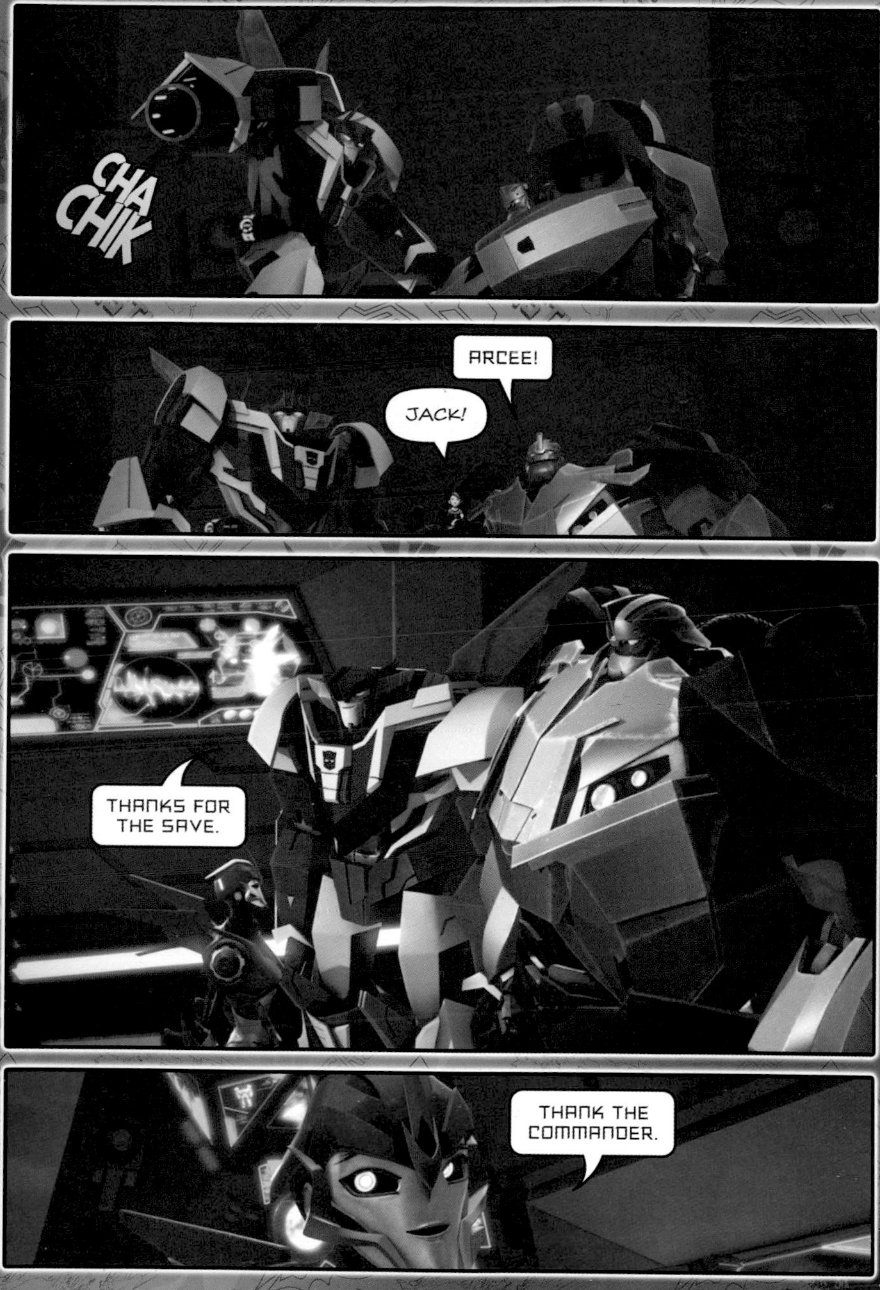

CHA CHIK
ARCEE!
JACK!
THANKS FOR THE SAVE.
THANK THE COMMANDER.

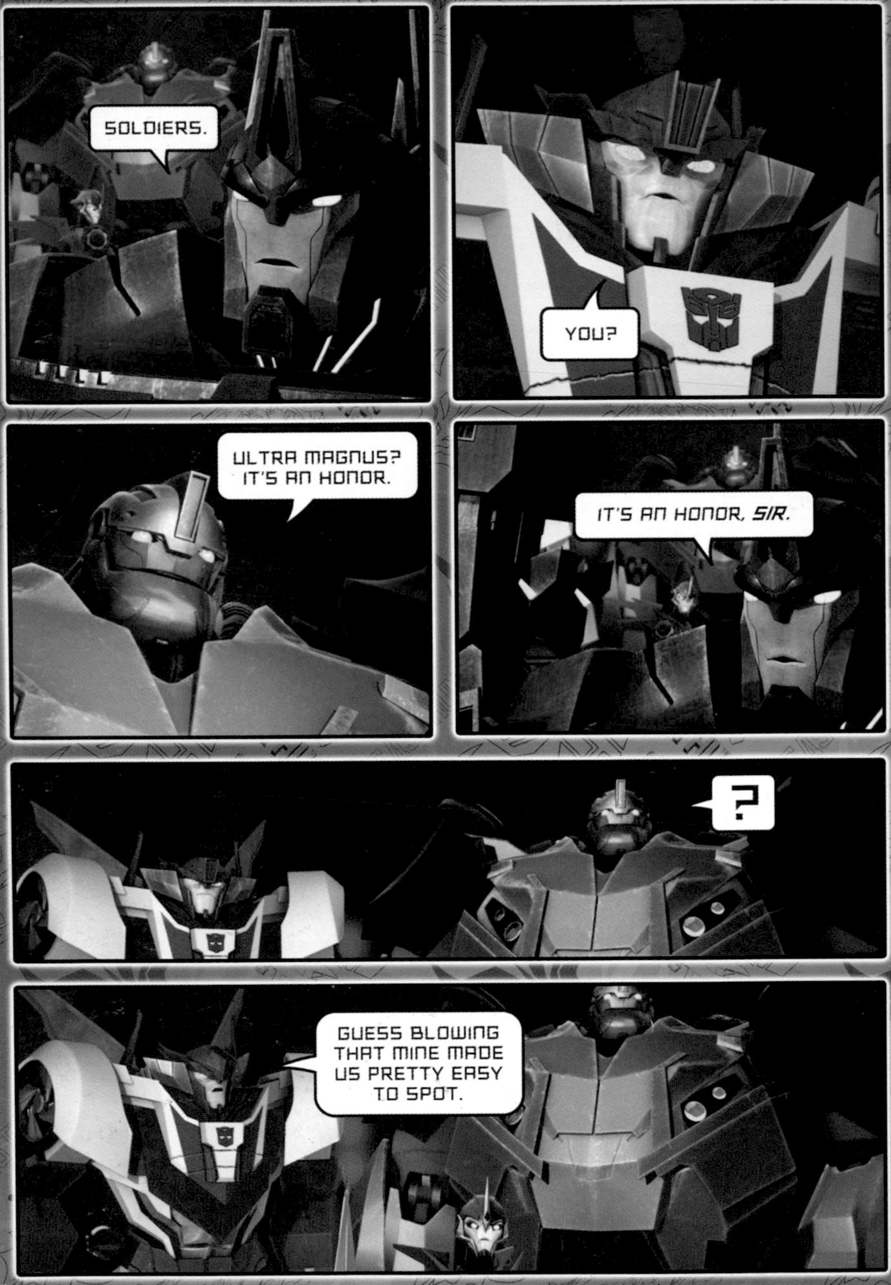
SOLDIERS.
YOU?
ULTRA MAGNUS? IT'S AN HONOR.
IT'S AN HONOR, *SIR*.
?
GUESS BLOWING THAT MINE MADE US PRETTY EASY TO SPOT.

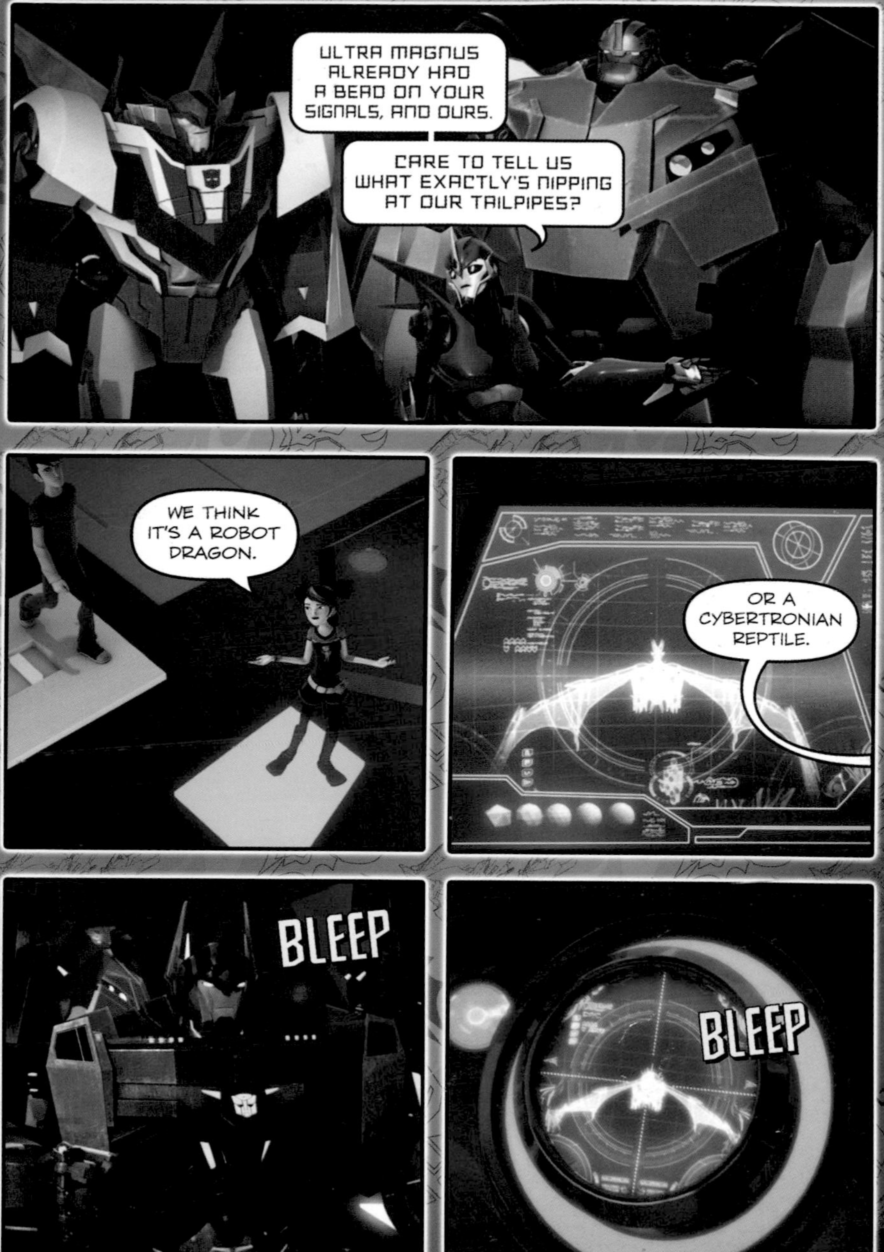
ULTRA MAGNUS ALREADY HAD A BEAD ON YOUR SIGNALS, AND OURS.
CARE TO TELL US WHAT EXACTLY'S NIPPING AT OUR TAILPIPES?
WE THINK IT'S A ROBOT DRAGON.
OR A CYBERTRONIAN REPTILE.
BLEEP
BLEEP

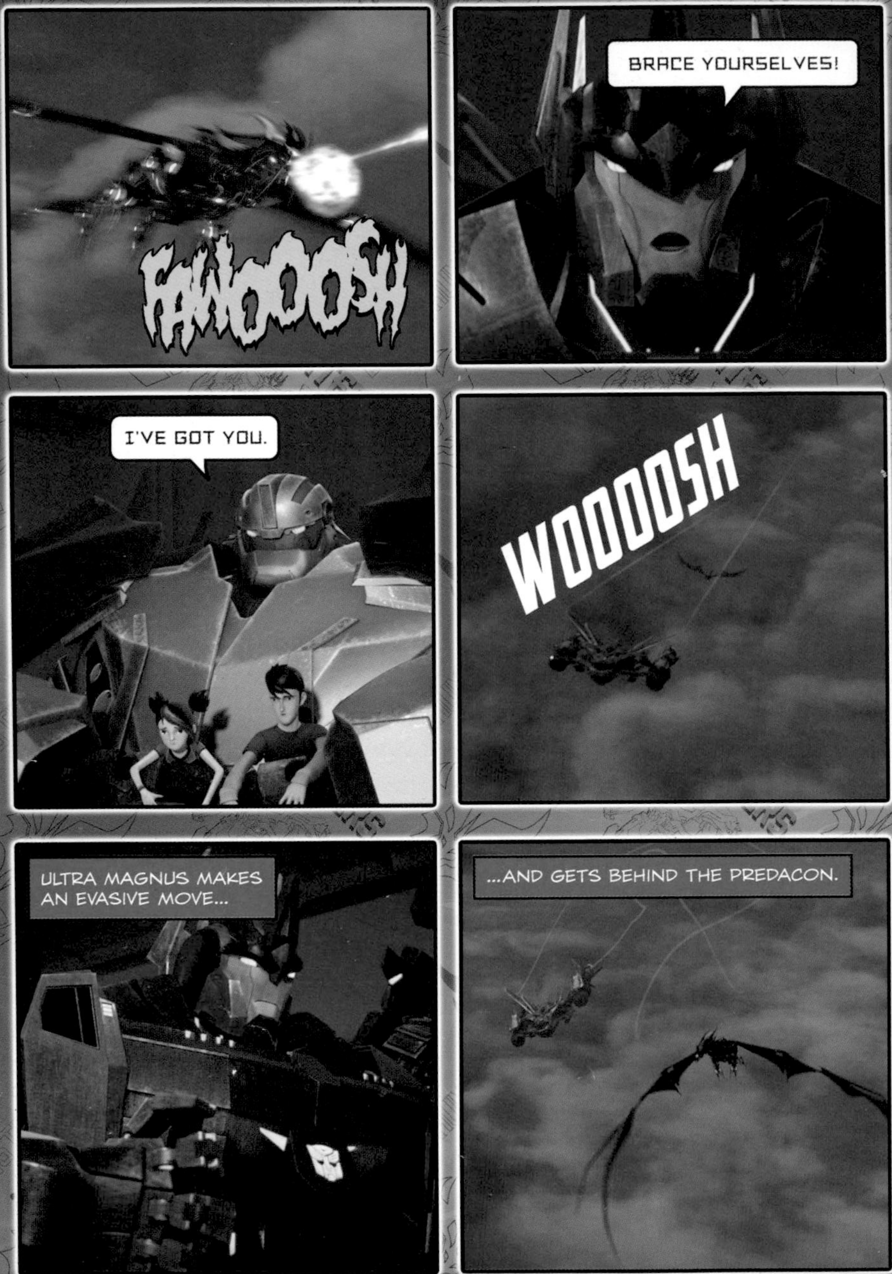
FWOOOSH
BRACE YOURSELVES!
I'VE GOT YOU.
WOOOOSH
ULTRA MAGNUS MAKES AN EVASIVE MOVE...
...AND GETS BEHIND THE PREDACON.

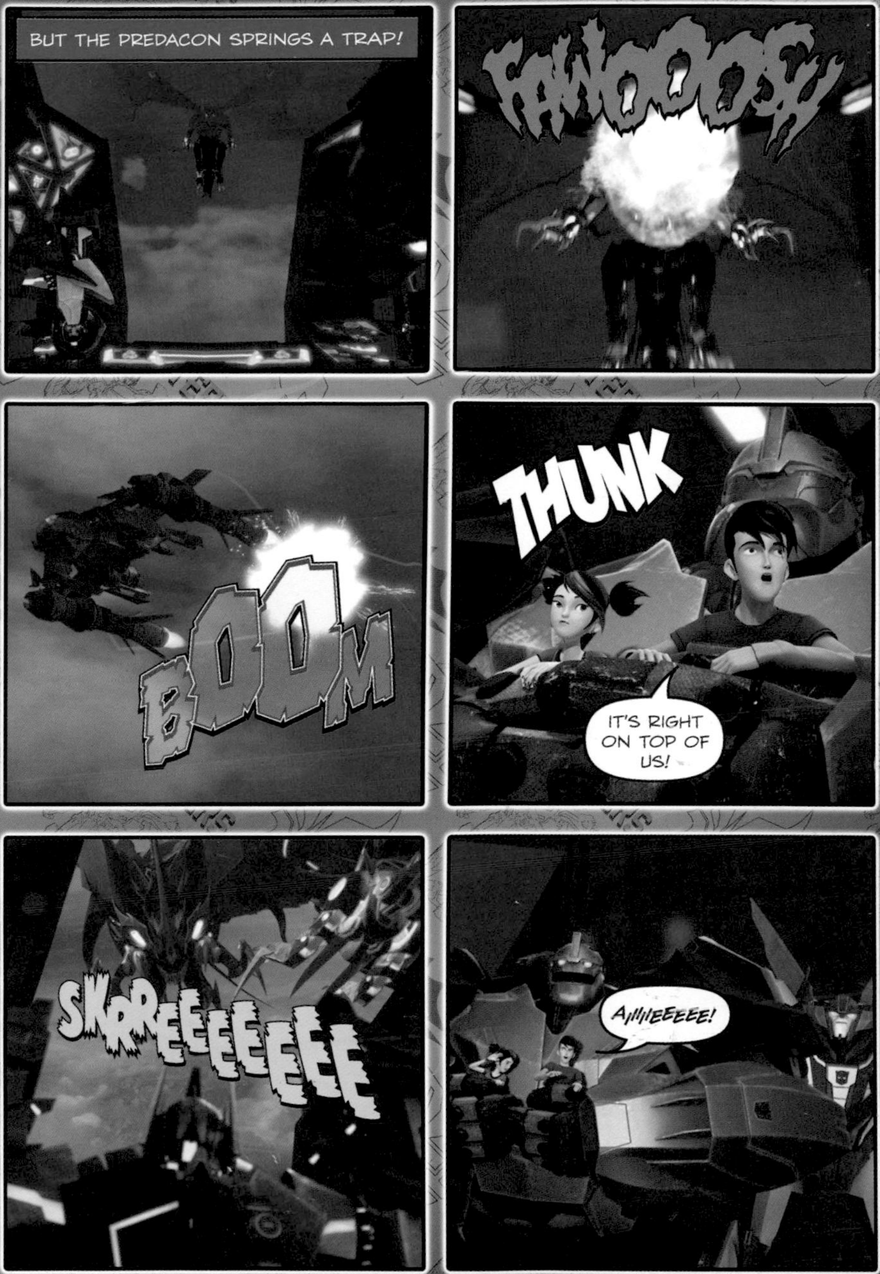
BUT THE PREDACON SPRINGS A TRAP!
FWOOOSH
BOOM
THUNK
IT'S RIGHT ON TOP OF US!
SKREEEEEEEE
AIIIIEEEEE!

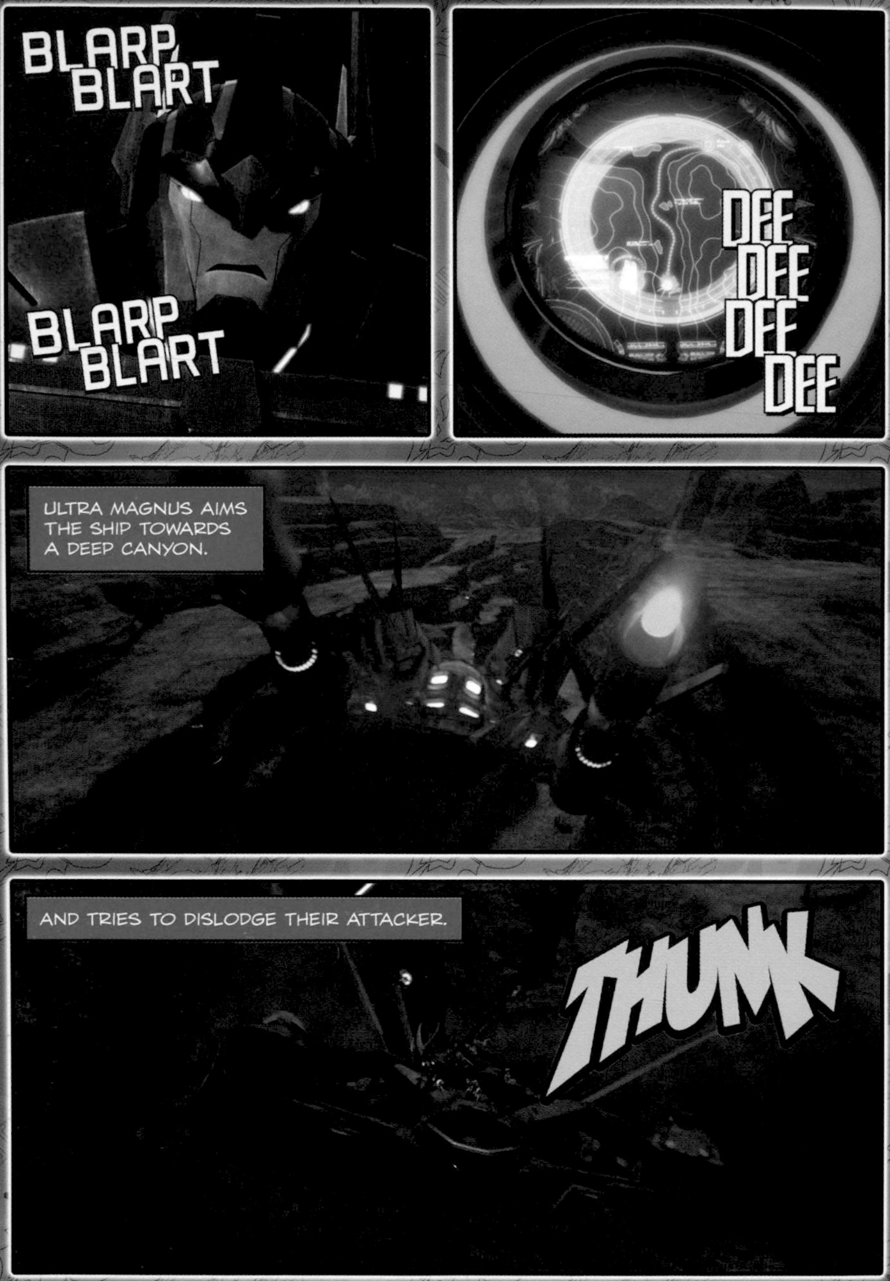
BLARP BLART
BLARP BLART
DEE DEE DEE DEE
ULTRA MAGNUS AIMS THE SHIP TOWARDS A DEEP CANYON.
AND TRIES TO DISLODGE THEIR ATTACKER.
THUNK

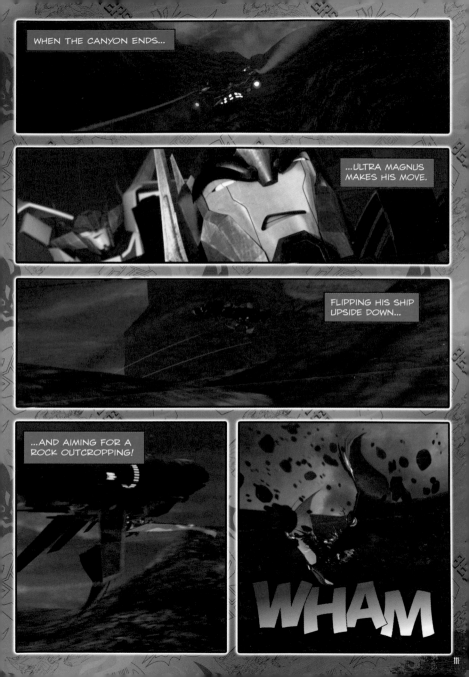

WHEN THE CANYON ENDS...

...ULTRA MAGNUS MAKES HIS MOVE.

FLIPPING HIS SHIP UPSIDE DOWN...

...AND AIMING FOR A ROCK OUTCROPPING!

WHAM

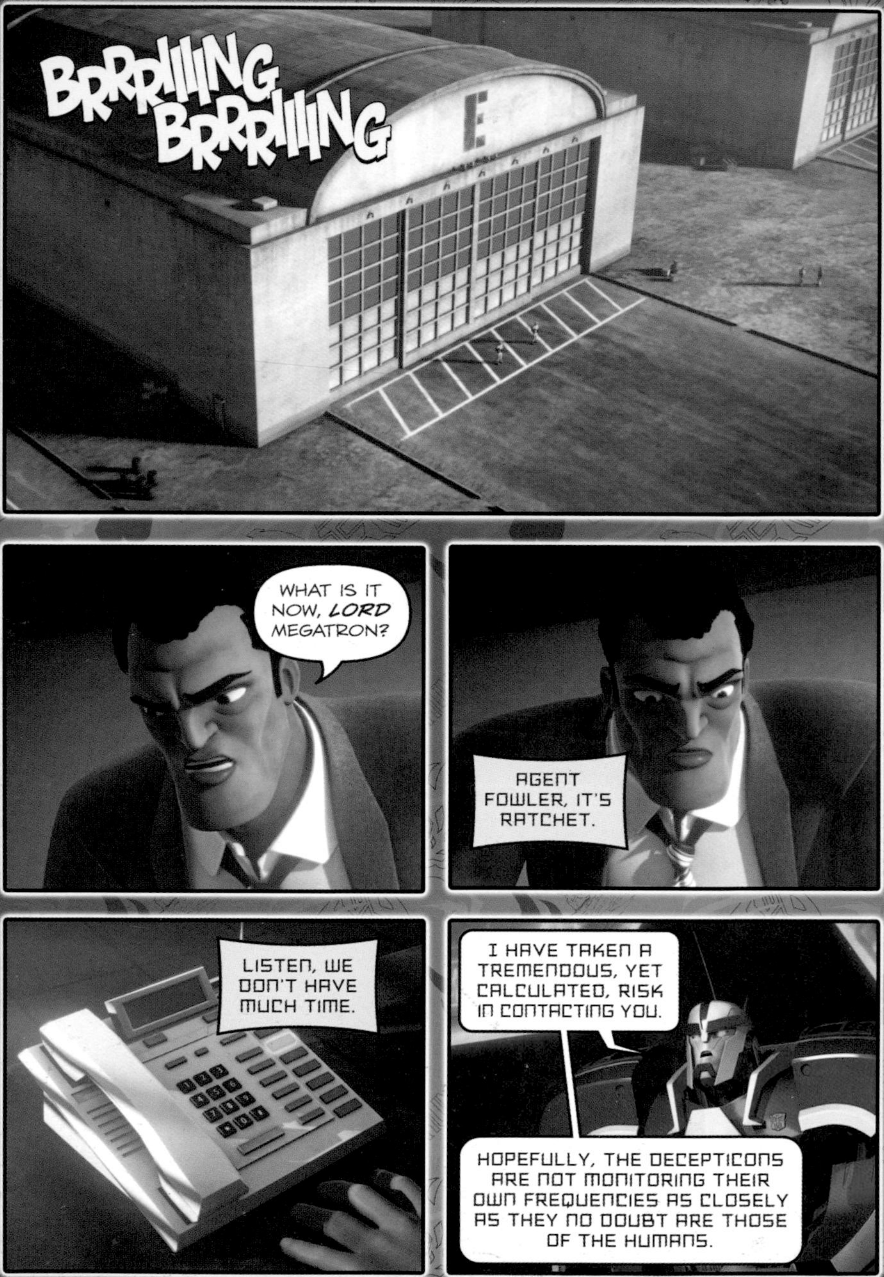
BRRRIIIING BRRRIIIING
WHAT IS IT NOW, LORD MEGATRON?
AGENT FOWLER, IT'S RATCHET.
LISTEN, WE DON'T HAVE MUCH TIME.
I HAVE TAKEN A TREMENDOUS, YET CALCULATED, RISK IN CONTACTING YOU.
HOPEFULLY, THE DECEPTICONS ARE NOT MONITORING THEIR OWN FREQUENCIES AS CLOSELY AS THEY NO DOUBT ARE THOSE OF THE HUMANS.

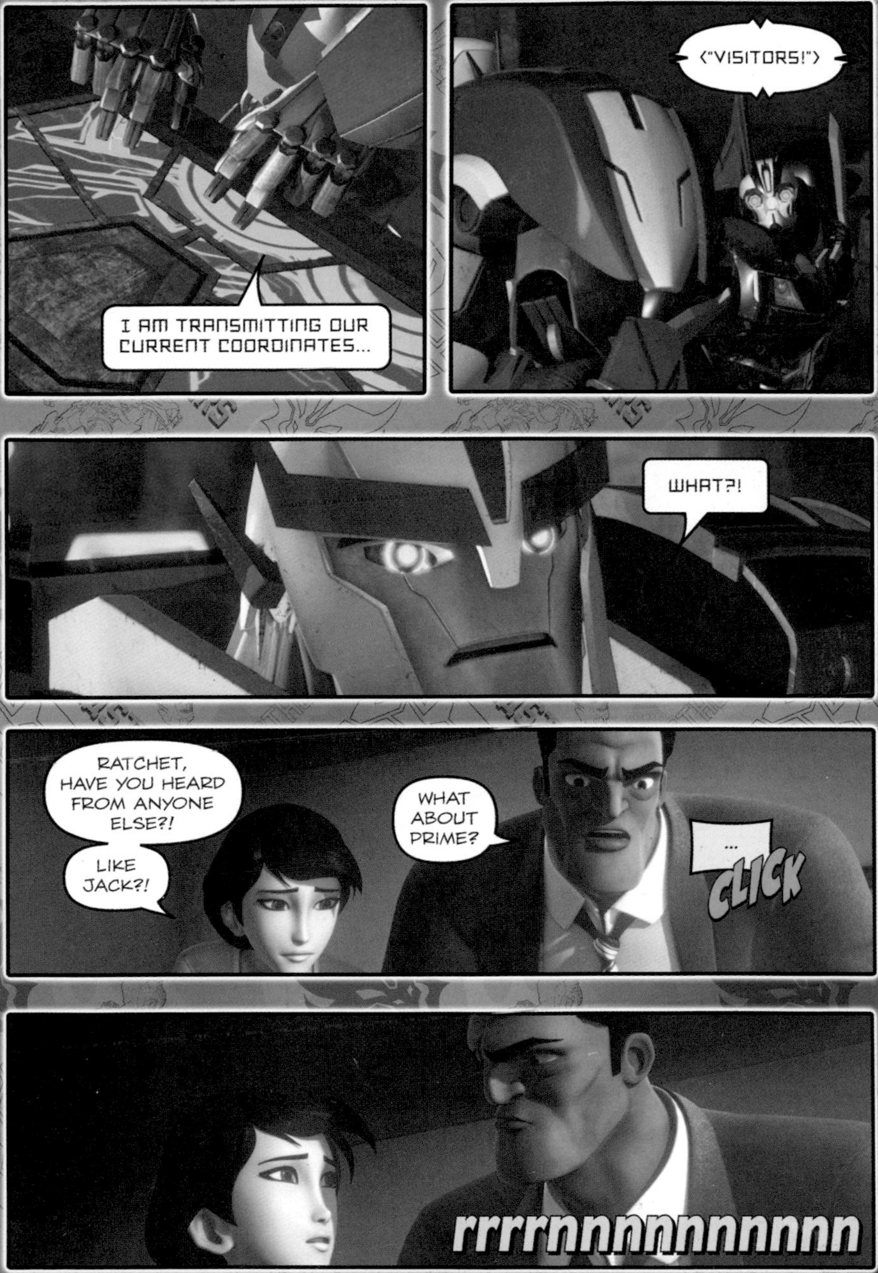
I AM TRANSMITTING OUR CURRENT COORDINATES...
<"VISITORS!">
WHAT?!
RATCHET, HAVE YOU HEARD FROM ANYONE ELSE?!
LIKE JACK?!
WHAT ABOUT PRIME?
...
CLICK
rrrrnnnnnnnnnnn

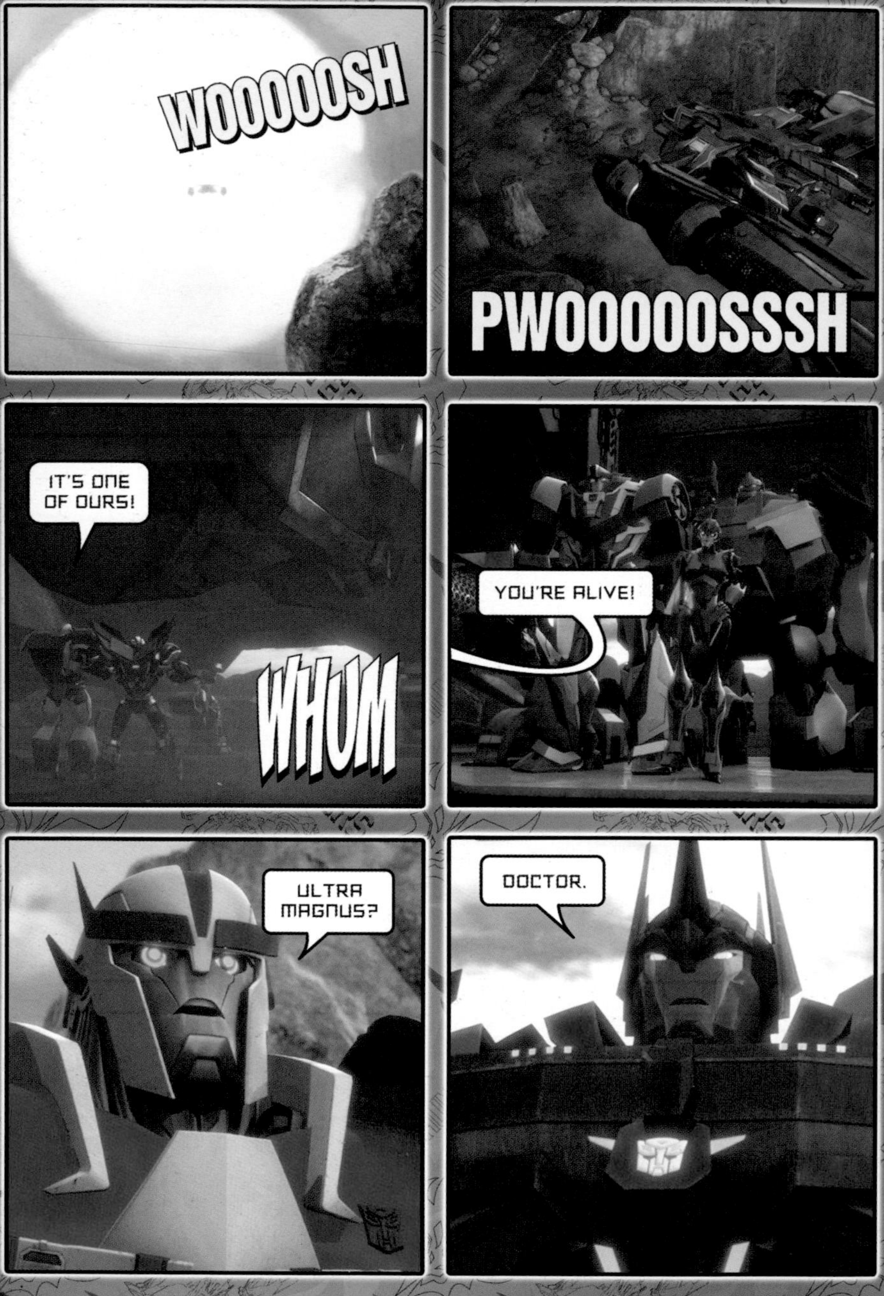
WOOOOOSH
PWOOOOOOSSSH
IT'S ONE OF OURS!
WHUM
YOU'RE ALIVE!
ULTRA MAGNUS?
DOCTOR.

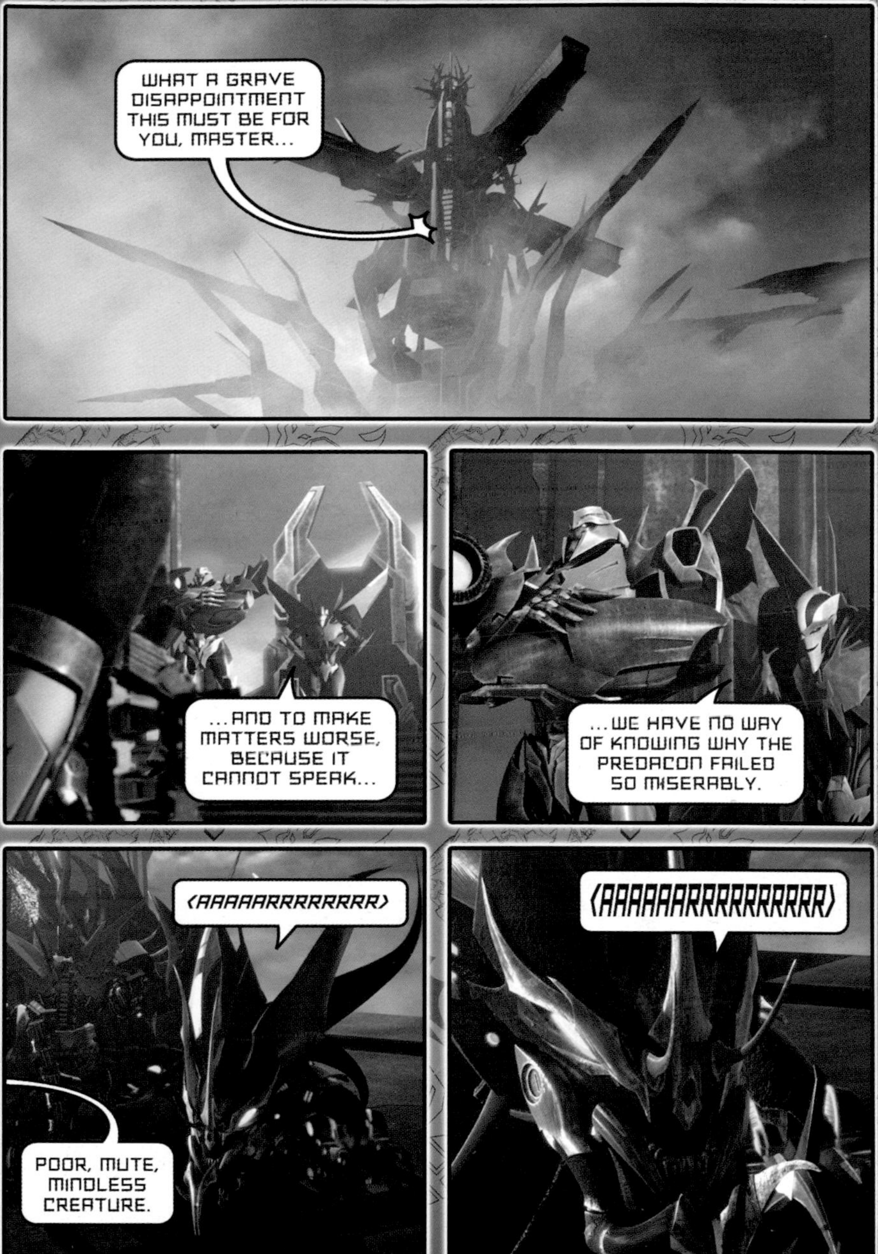
WHAT A GRAVE DISAPPOINTMENT THIS MUST BE FOR YOU, MASTER...
...AND TO MAKE MATTERS WORSE, BECAUSE IT CANNOT SPEAK...
...WE HAVE NO WAY OF KNOWING WHY THE PREDACON FAILED SO MISERABLY.
<AAAAAARRRRRRRR>
POOR, MUTE, MINDLESS CREATURE.
<AAAAAARRRRRRRRRR>

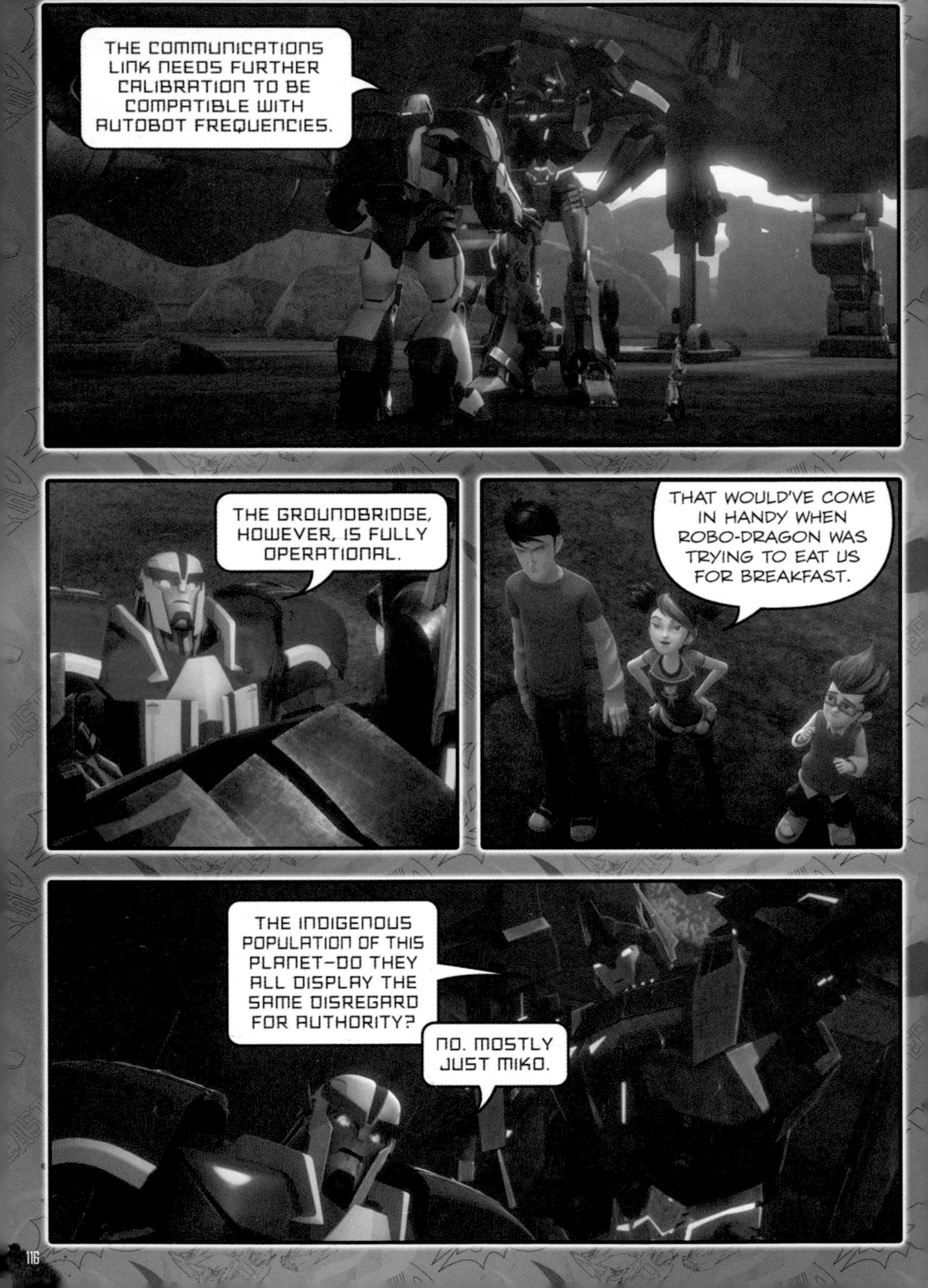
THE COMMUNICATIONS LINK NEEDS FURTHER CALIBRATION TO BE COMPATIBLE WITH AUTOBOT FREQUENCIES.
THE GROUNDBRIDGE, HOWEVER, IS FULLY OPERATIONAL.
THAT WOULD'VE COME IN HANDY WHEN ROBO-DRAGON WAS TRYING TO EAT US FOR BREAKFAST.
THE INDIGENOUS POPULATION OF THIS PLANET—DO THEY ALL DISPLAY THE SAME DISREGARD FOR AUTHORITY?
NO. MOSTLY JUST MIKO.

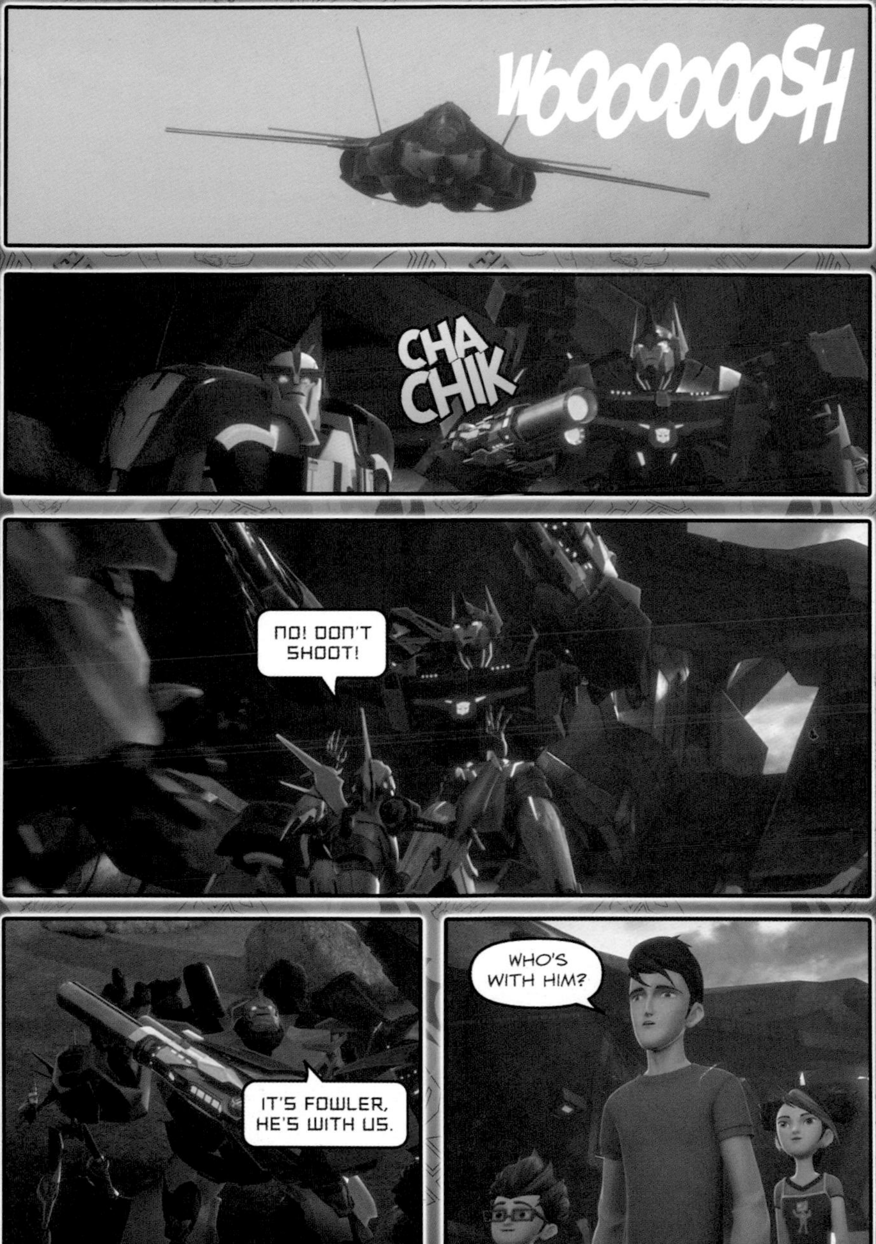
WOOOOOOOSH
CHA CHIK
NO! DON'T SHOOT!
IT'S FOWLER, HE'S WITH US.
WHO'S WITH HIM?

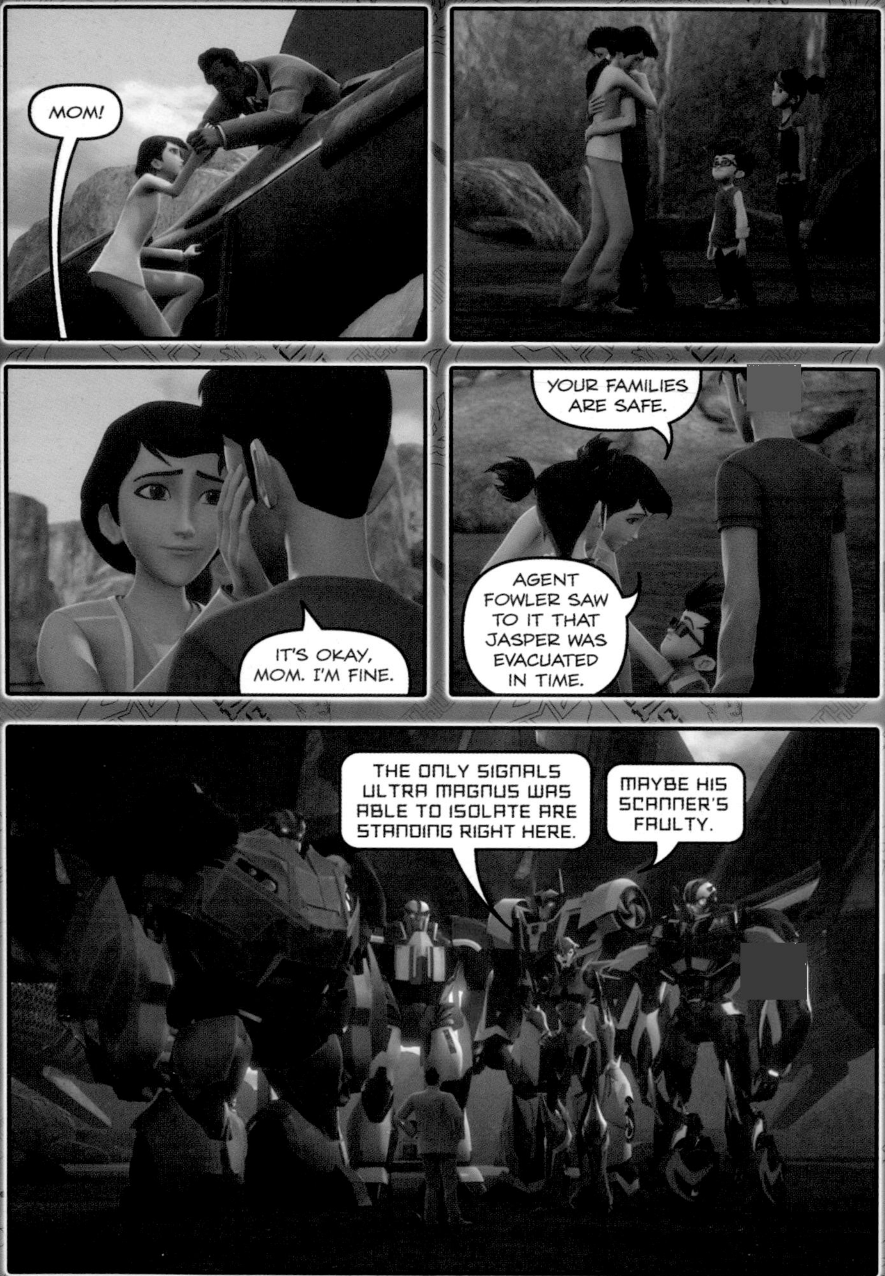
MOM!
IT'S OKAY, MOM. I'M FINE.
YOUR FAMILIES ARE SAFE.
AGENT FOWLER SAW TO IT THAT JASPER WAS EVACUATED IN TIME.
THE ONLY SIGNALS ULTRA MAGNUS WAS ABLE TO ISOLATE ARE STANDING RIGHT HERE.
MAYBE HIS SCANNER'S FAULTY.

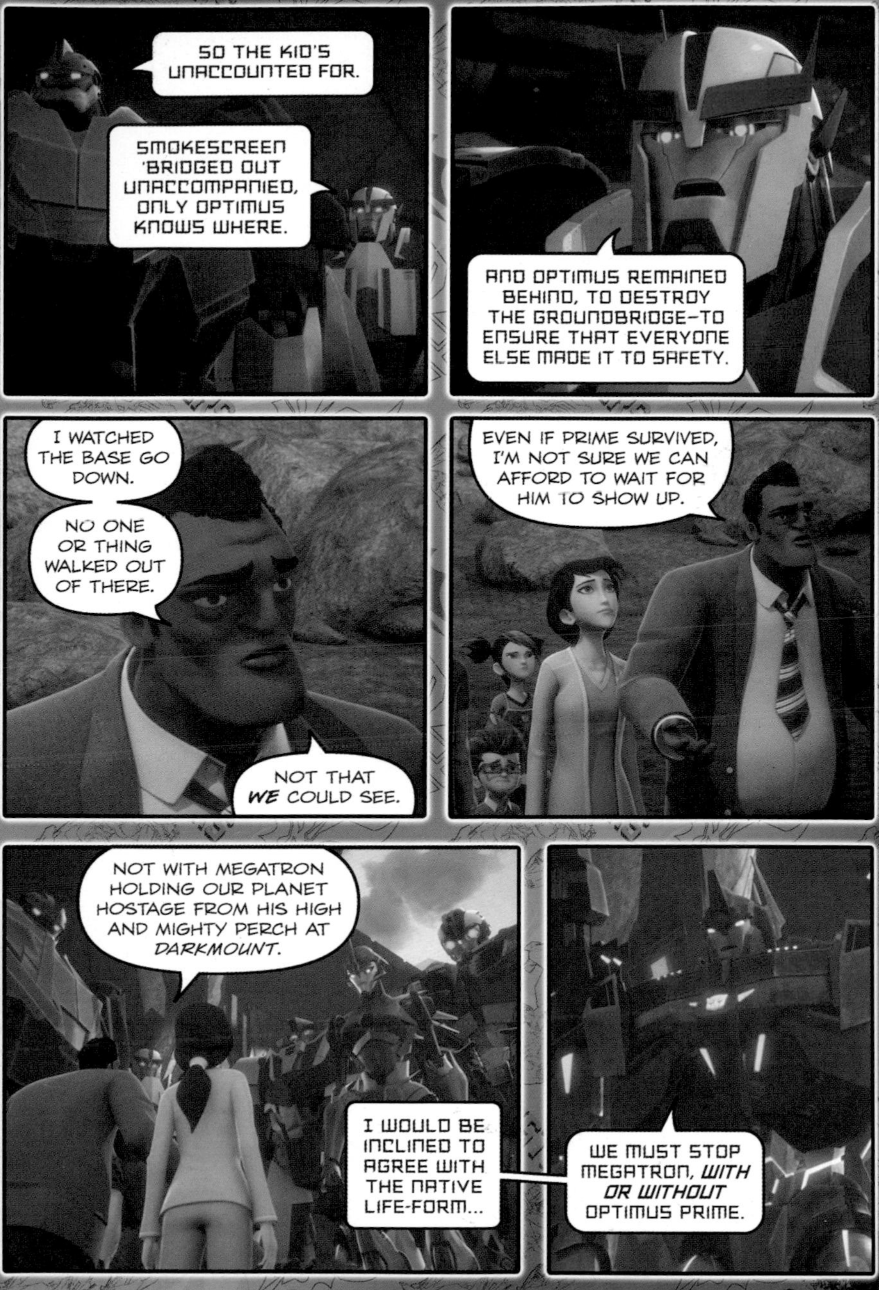
SO THE KID'S UNACCOUNTED FOR.
SMOKESCREEN 'BRIDGED OUT UNACCOMPANIED, ONLY OPTIMUS KNOWS WHERE.
AND OPTIMUS REMAINED BEHIND, TO DESTROY THE GROUNDBRIDGE—TO ENSURE THAT EVERYONE ELSE MADE IT TO SAFETY.
I WATCHED THE BASE GO DOWN.
NO ONE OR THING WALKED OUT OF THERE.
NOT THAT *WE* COULD SEE.
EVEN IF PRIME SURVIVED, I'M NOT SURE WE CAN AFFORD TO WAIT FOR HIM TO SHOW UP.
NOT WITH MEGATRON HOLDING OUR PLANET HOSTAGE FROM HIS HIGH AND MIGHTY PERCH AT *DARKMOUNT*.
I WOULD BE INCLINED TO AGREE WITH THE NATIVE LIFE-FORM...
WE MUST STOP MEGATRON, *WITH OR WITHOUT* OPTIMUS PRIME.

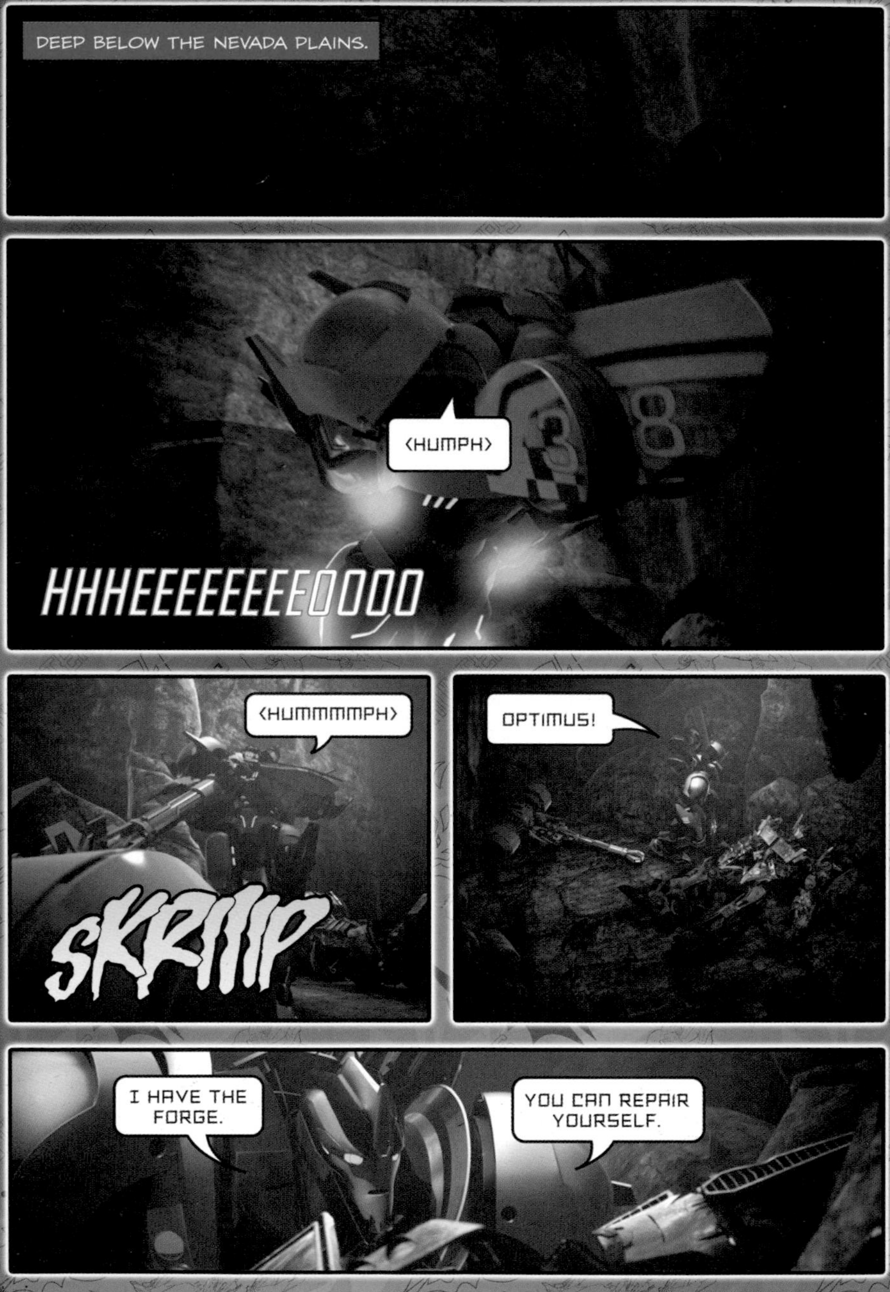
DEEP BELOW THE NEVADA PLAINS.
<HUMPH>
HHHEEEEEEEEEOOOO
<HUMMMMPH>
SKRIIP
OPTIMUS!
I HAVE THE FORGE.
YOU CAN REPAIR YOURSELF.

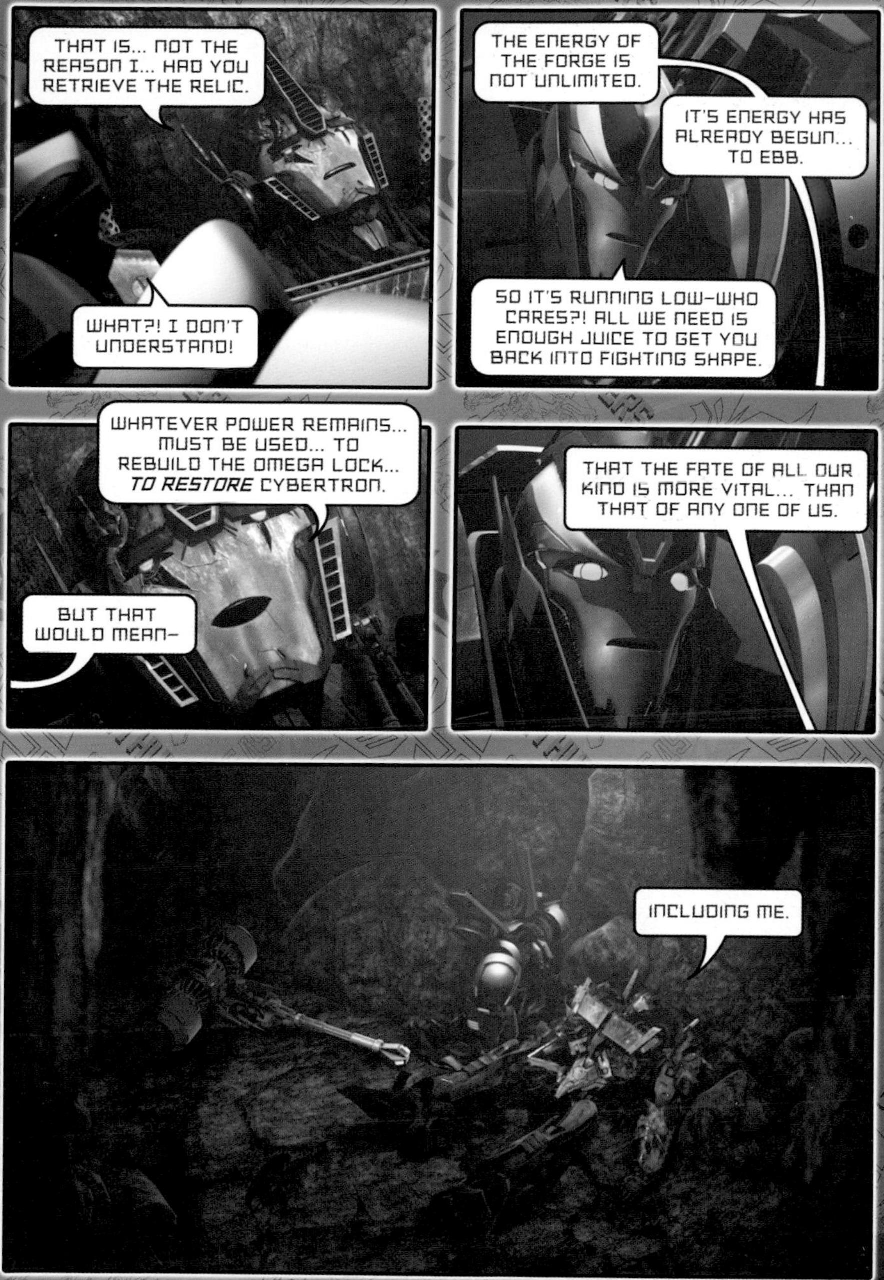
THAT IS... NOT THE REASON I... HAD YOU RETRIEVE THE RELIC.
WHAT?! I DON'T UNDERSTAND!
THE ENERGY OF THE FORGE IS NOT UNLIMITED.
IT'S ENERGY HAS ALREADY BEGUN... TO EBB.
SO IT'S RUNNING LOW—WHO CARES?! ALL WE NEED IS ENOUGH JUICE TO GET YOU BACK INTO FIGHTING SHAPE.
WHATEVER POWER REMAINS... MUST BE USED... TO REBUILD THE OMEGA LOCK... *TO RESTORE* CYBERTRON.
BUT THAT WOULD MEAN—
THAT THE FATE OF ALL OUR KIND IS MORE VITAL... THAN THAT OF ANY ONE OF US.
INCLUDING ME.

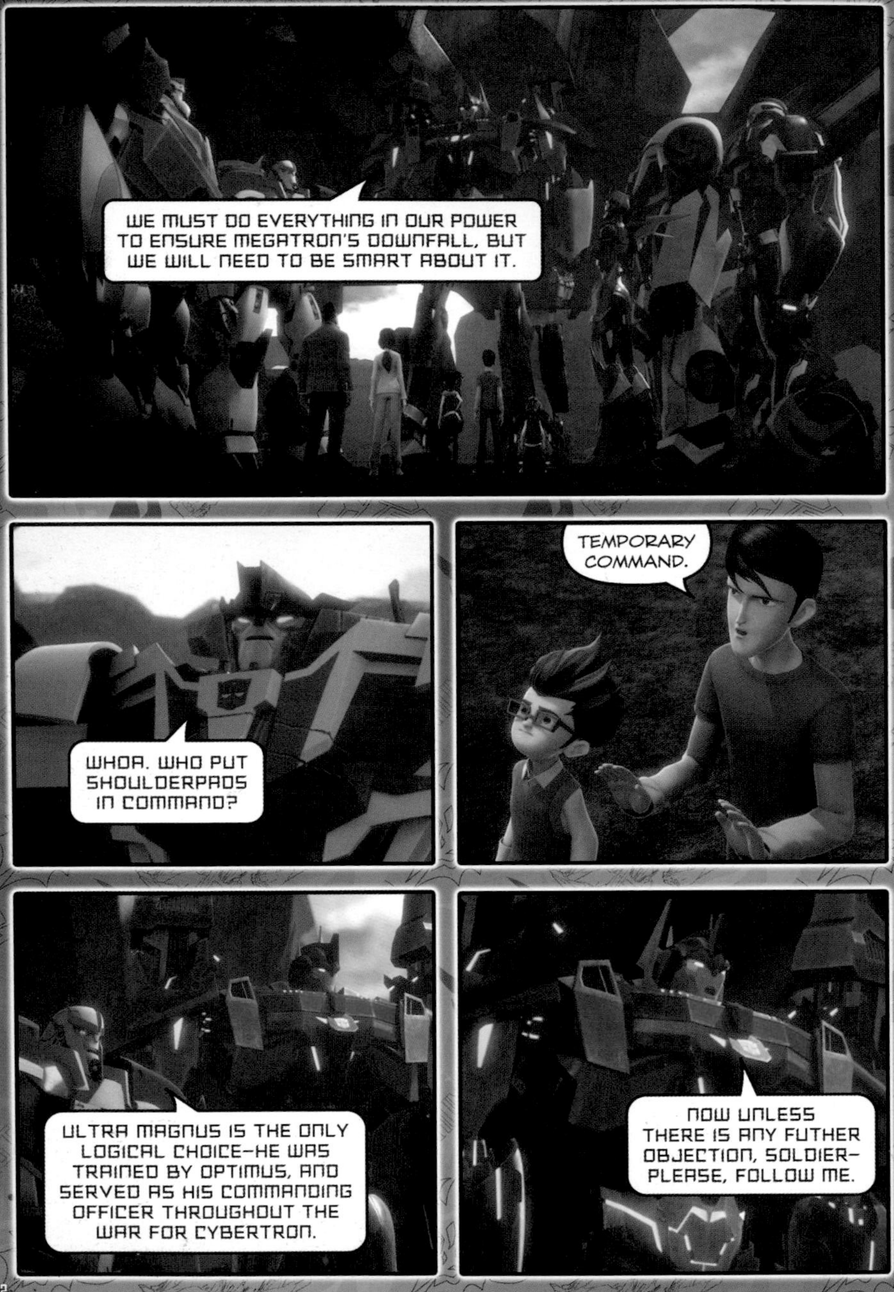
WE MUST DO EVERYTHING IN OUR POWER TO ENSURE MEGATRON'S DOWNFALL, BUT WE WILL NEED TO BE SMART ABOUT IT.
WHOA. WHO PUT SHOULDERPADS IN COMMAND?
TEMPORARY COMMAND.
ULTRA MAGNUS IS THE ONLY LOGICAL CHOICE–HE WAS TRAINED BY OPTIMUS, AND SERVED AS HIS COMMANDING OFFICER THROUGHOUT THE WAR FOR CYBERTRON.
NOW UNLESS THERE IS ANY FUTHER OBJECTION, SOLDIER–PLEASE, FOLLOW ME.

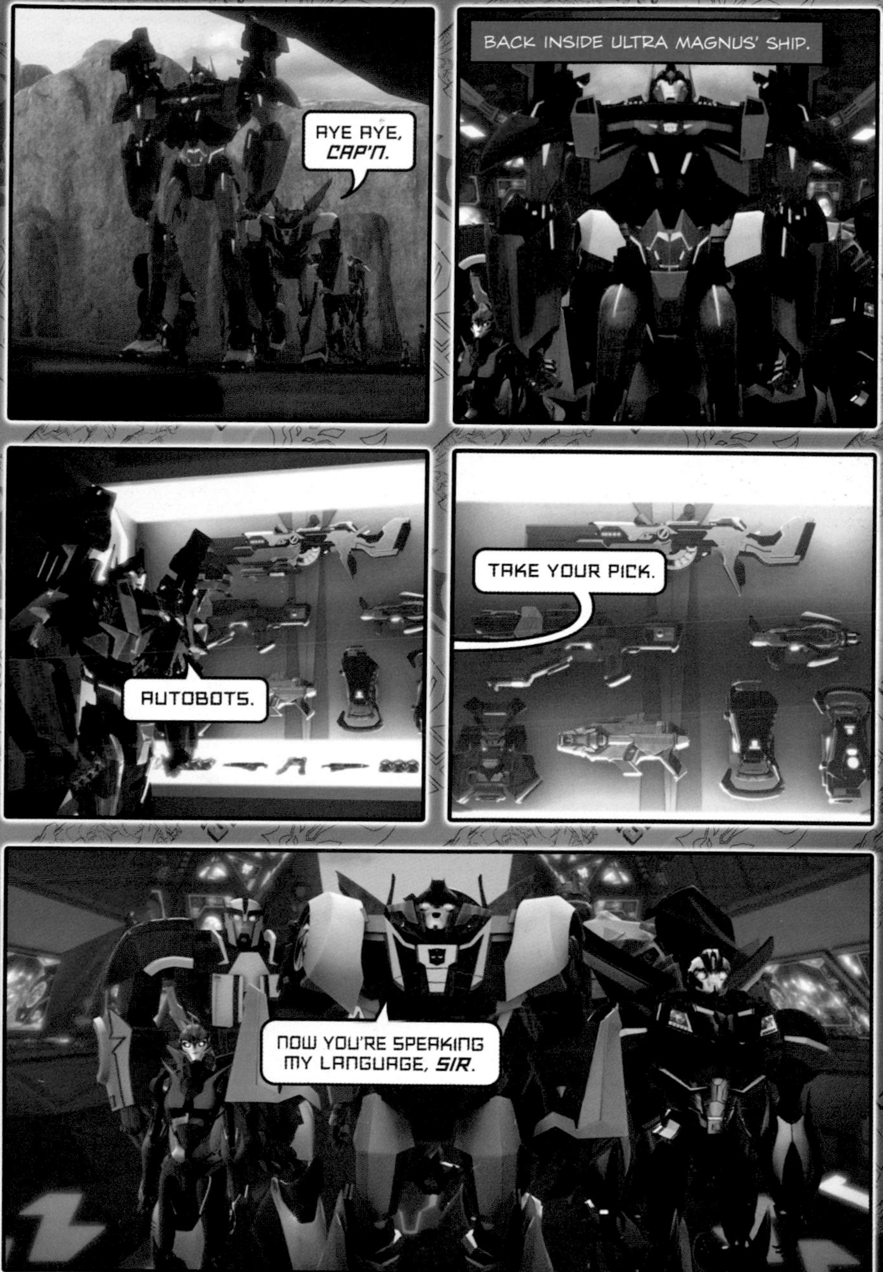
AYE AYE, CAP'N.
BACK INSIDE ULTRA MAGNUS' SHIP.
AUTOBOTS.
TAKE YOUR PICK.
NOW YOU'RE SPEAKING MY LANGUAGE, SIR.

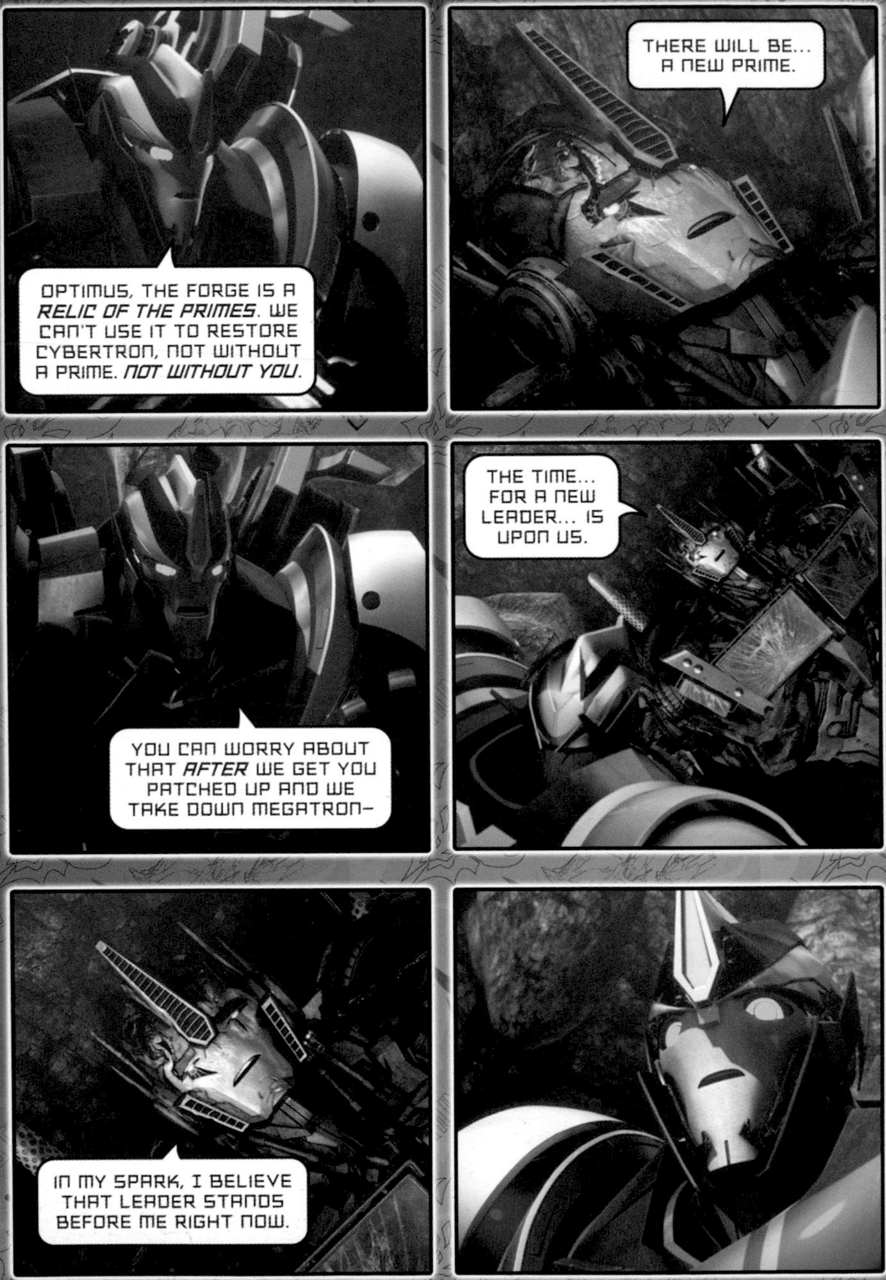
OPTIMUS, THE FORGE IS A *RELIC OF THE PRIMES*. WE CAN'T USE IT TO RESTORE CYBERTRON, NOT WITHOUT A PRIME. *NOT WITHOUT YOU*.
THERE WILL BE... A NEW PRIME.
YOU CAN WORRY ABOUT THAT *AFTER* WE GET YOU PATCHED UP AND WE TAKE DOWN MEGATRON–
THE TIME... FOR A NEW LEADER... IS UPON US.
IN MY SPARK, I BELIEVE THAT LEADER STANDS BEFORE ME RIGHT NOW.

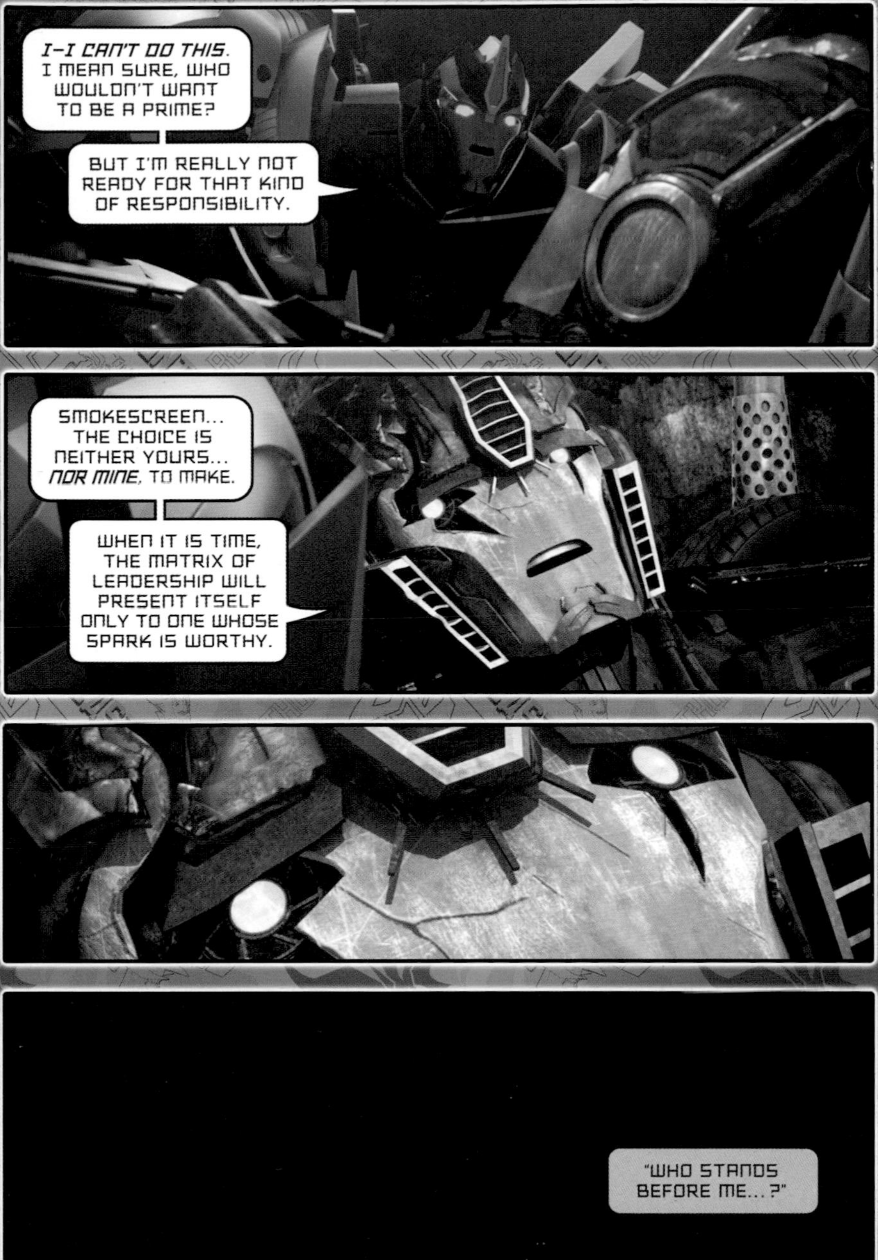

I—I CAN'T DO THIS. I MEAN SURE, WHO WOULDN'T WANT TO BE A PRIME?
BUT I'M REALLY NOT READY FOR THAT KIND OF RESPONSIBILITY.
SMOKESCREEN... THE CHOICE IS NEITHER YOURS... *NOR MINE*, TO MAKE.
WHEN IT IS TIME, THE MATRIX OF LEADERSHIP WILL PRESENT ITSELF ONLY TO ONE WHOSE SPARK IS WORTHY.
"WHO STANDS BEFORE ME...?"

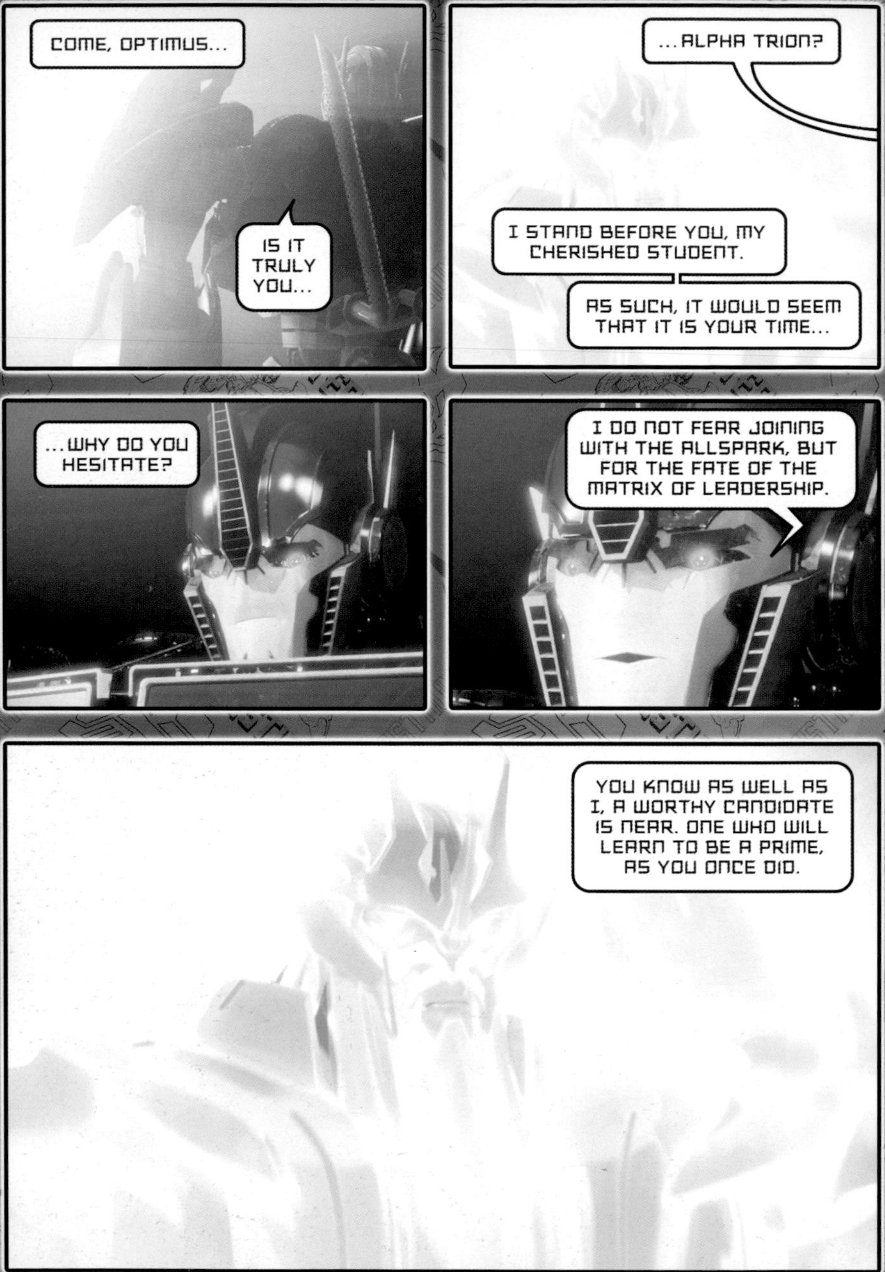
COME, OPTIMUS...
IS IT TRULY YOU...
...ALPHA TRION?
I STAND BEFORE YOU, MY CHERISHED STUDENT.
AS SUCH, IT WOULD SEEM THAT IT IS YOUR TIME...
...WHY DO YOU HESITATE?
I DO NOT FEAR JOINING WITH THE ALLSPARK, BUT FOR THE FATE OF THE MATRIX OF LEADERSHIP.
YOU KNOW AS WELL AS I, A WORTHY CANDIDATE IS NEAR. ONE WHO WILL LEARN TO BE A PRIME, AS YOU ONCE DID.

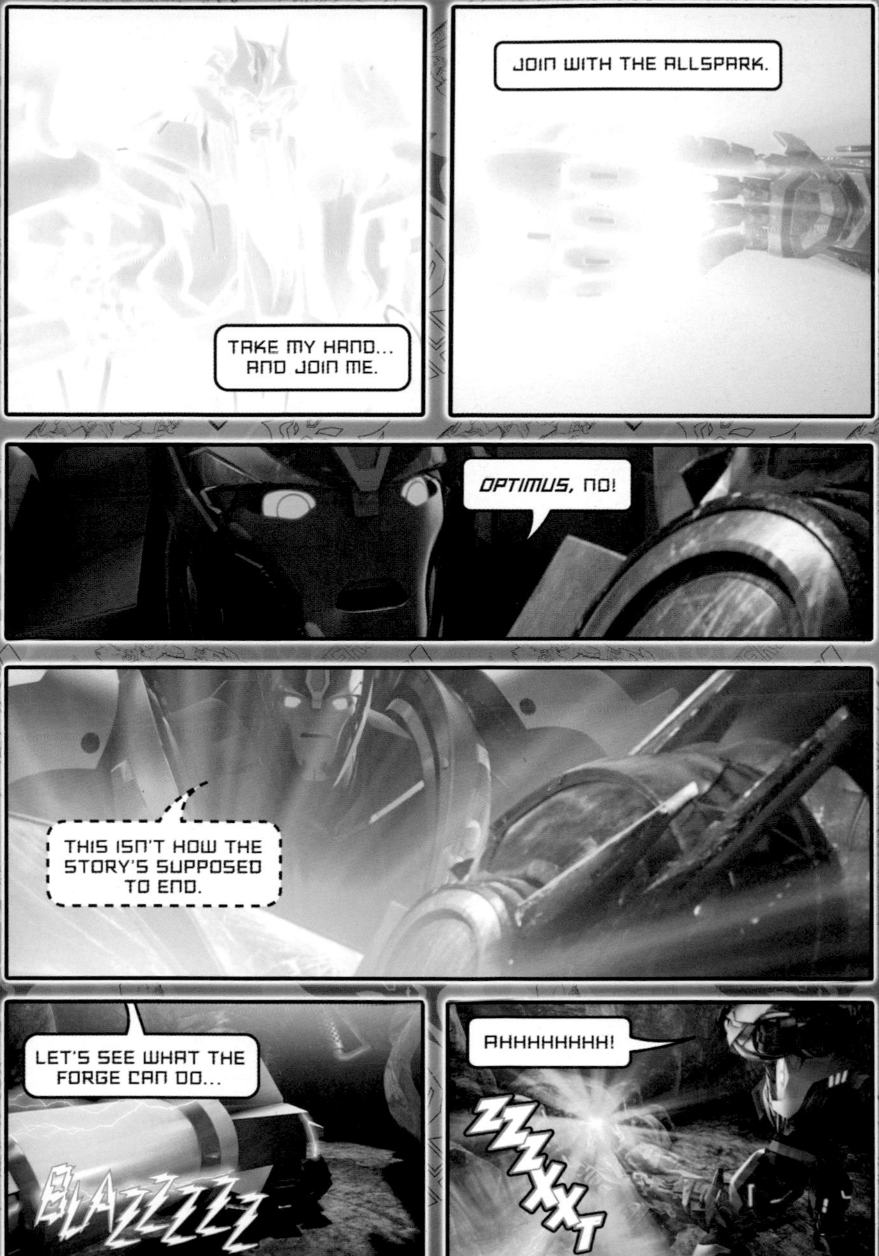
TAKE MY HAND... AND JOIN ME.
JOIN WITH THE ALLSPARK.
OPTIMUS, NO!
THIS ISN'T HOW THE STORY'S SUPPOSED TO END.
LET'S SEE WHAT THE FORGE CAN DO...
BLAZZZZZ
AHHHHHHHH!
ZZZXXT

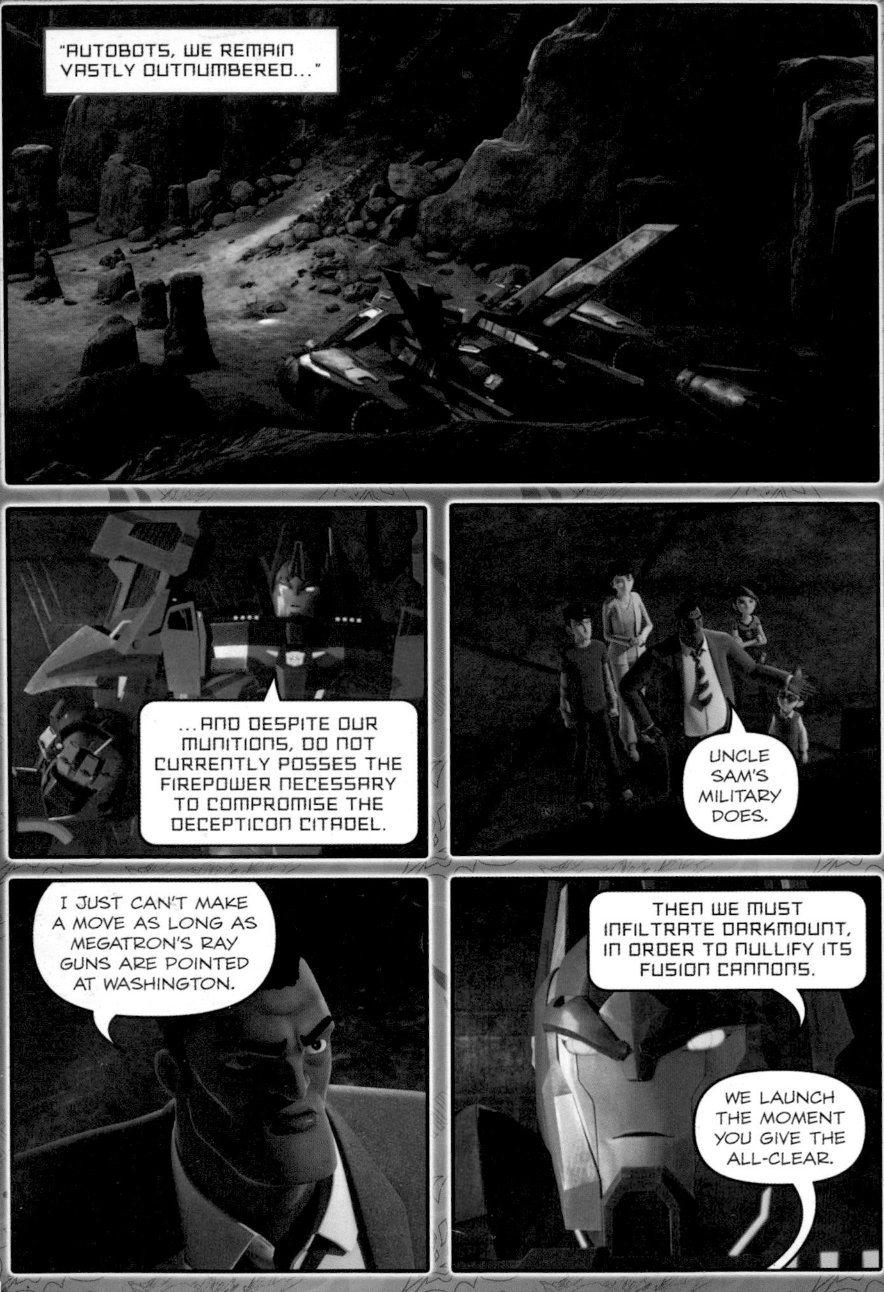
"AUTOBOTS, WE REMAIN VASTLY OUTNUMBERED..."
...AND DESPITE OUR MUNITIONS, DO NOT CURRENTLY POSSES THE FIREPOWER NECESSARY TO COMPROMISE THE DECEPTICON CITADEL.
UNCLE SAM'S MILITARY DOES.
I JUST CAN'T MAKE A MOVE AS LONG AS MEGATRON'S RAY GUNS ARE POINTED AT WASHINGTON.
THEN WE MUST INFILTRATE DARKMOUNT, IN ORDER TO NULLIFY ITS FUSION CANNONS.
WE LAUNCH THE MOMENT YOU GIVE THE ALL-CLEAR.

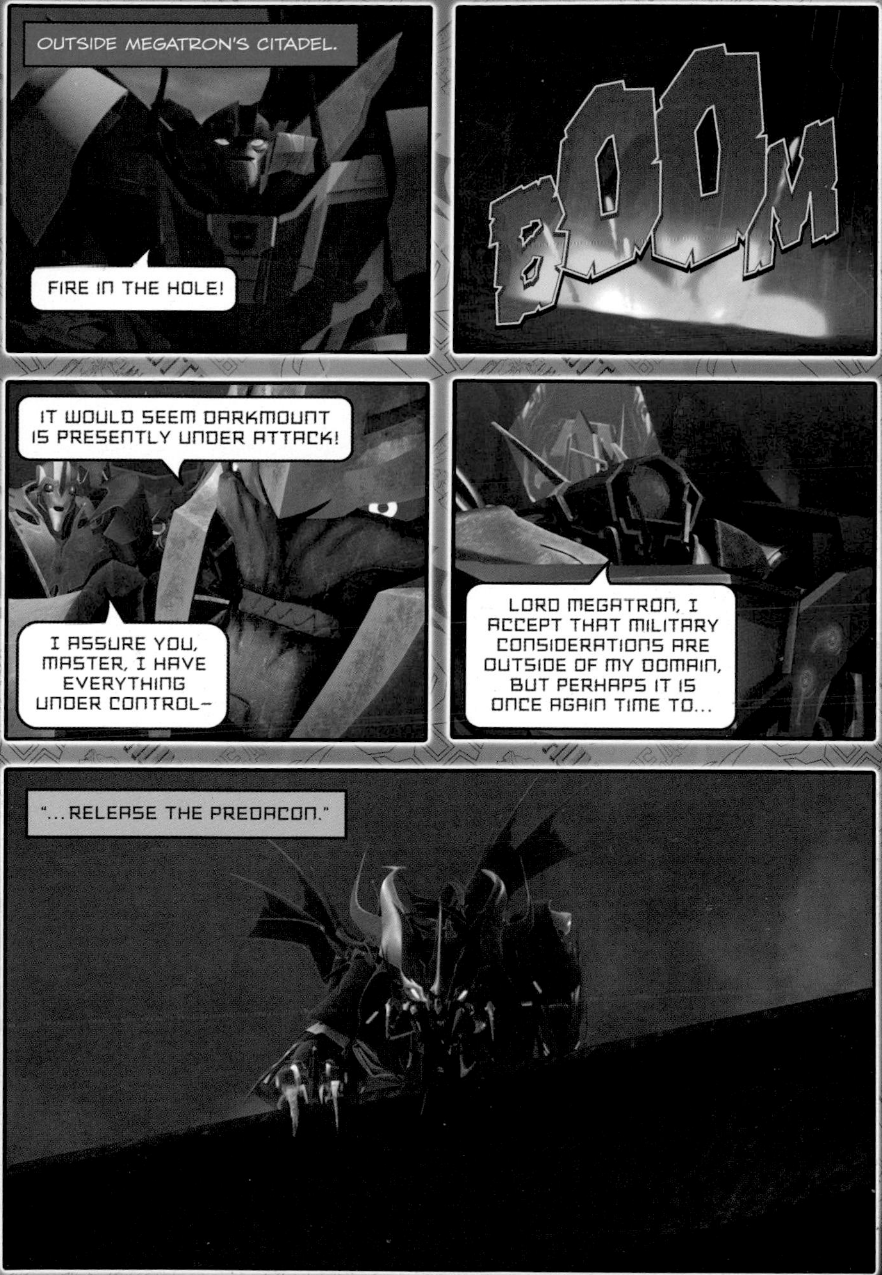
OUTSIDE MEGATRON'S CITADEL.
FIRE IN THE HOLE!
BOOM
IT WOULD SEEM DARKMOUNT IS PRESENTLY UNDER ATTACK!
I ASSURE YOU, MASTER, I HAVE EVERYTHING UNDER CONTROL–
LORD MEGATRON, I ACCEPT THAT MILITARY CONSIDERATIONS ARE OUTSIDE OF MY DOMAIN, BUT PERHAPS IT IS ONCE AGAIN TIME TO...
"...RELEASE THE PREDACON."

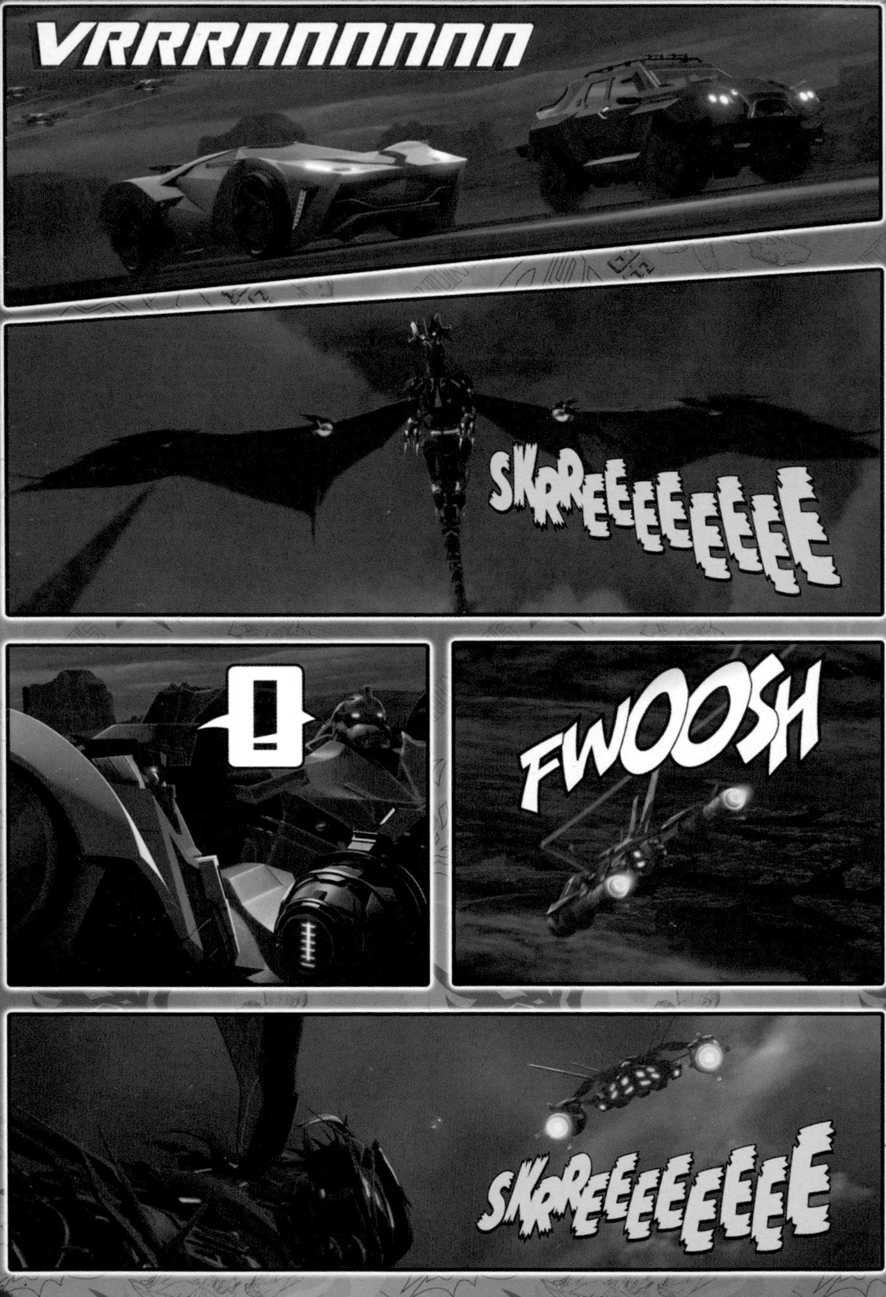
VRRRNNNNNN
SKREEEEEEEE
!
FWOOSH
SKREEEEEEEE

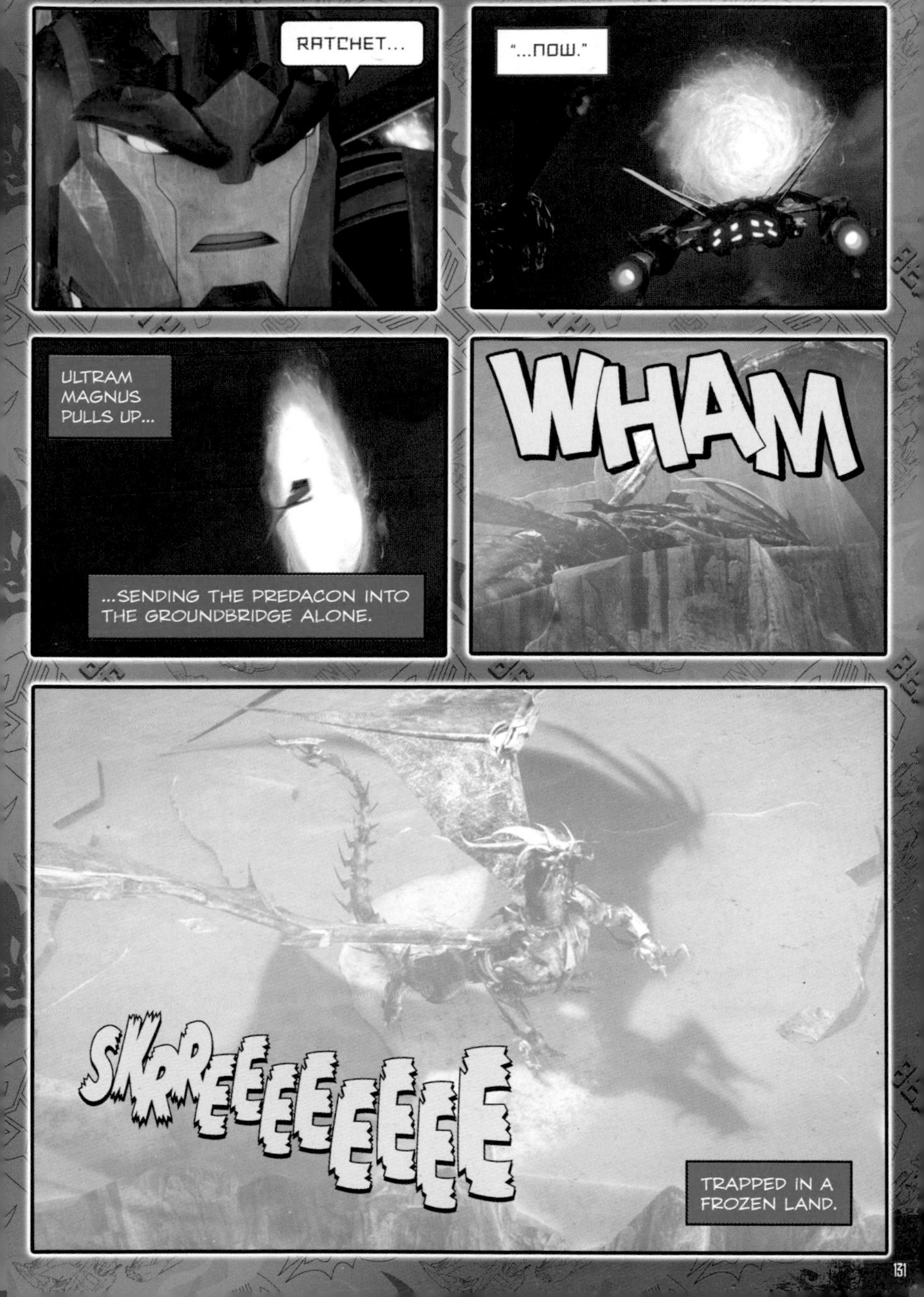
RATCHET...
"...NOW."
ULTRAM MAGNUS PULLS UP...
...SENDING THE PREDACON INTO THE GROUNDBRIDGE ALONE.
WHAM
SKREEEEEEEEE
TRAPPED IN A FROZEN LAND.

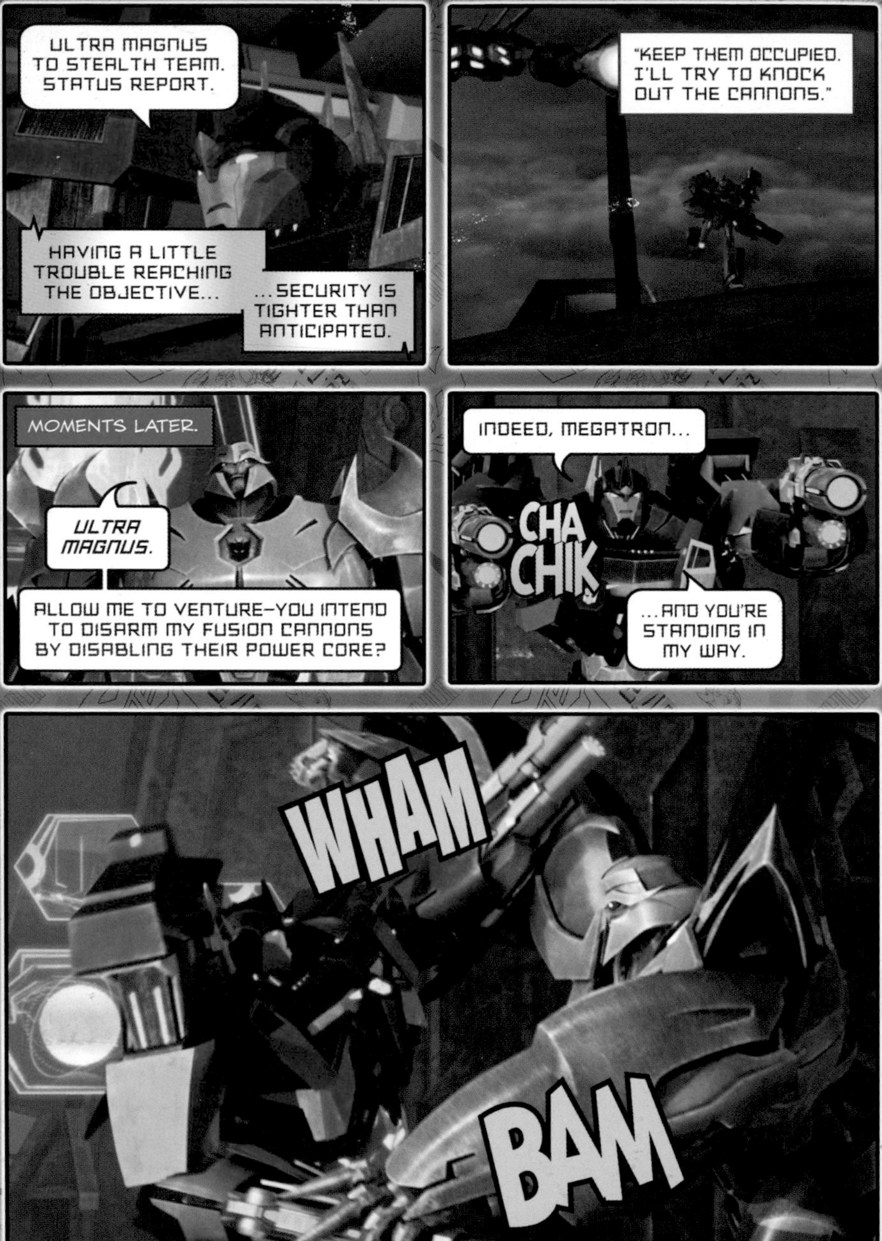

ULTRA MAGNUS TO STEALTH TEAM. STATUS REPORT.
HAVING A LITTLE TROUBLE REACHING THE OBJECTIVE...
...SECURITY IS TIGHTER THAN ANTICIPATED.
"KEEP THEM OCCUPIED. I'LL TRY TO KNOCK OUT THE CANNONS."
MOMENTS LATER.
ULTRA MAGNUS.
ALLOW ME TO VENTURE—YOU INTEND TO DISARM MY FUSION CANNONS BY DISABLING THEIR POWER CORE?
INDEED, MEGATRON...
CHA CHIK
...AND YOU'RE STANDING IN MY WAY.
WHAM
BAM

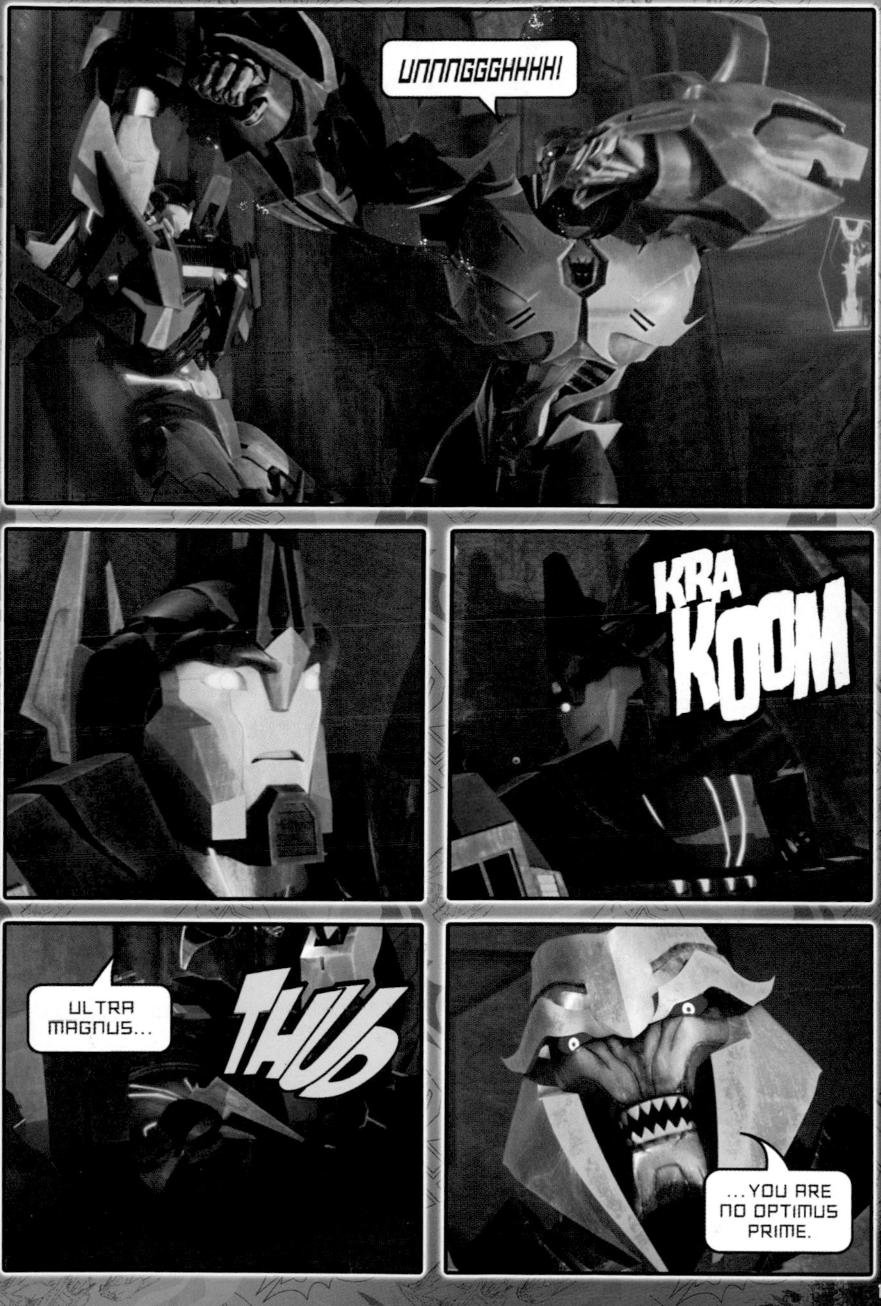
UNNNGGGHHHH!
KRA KOOM
ULTRA MAGNUS...
THUD
...YOU ARE NO OPTIMUS PRIME.

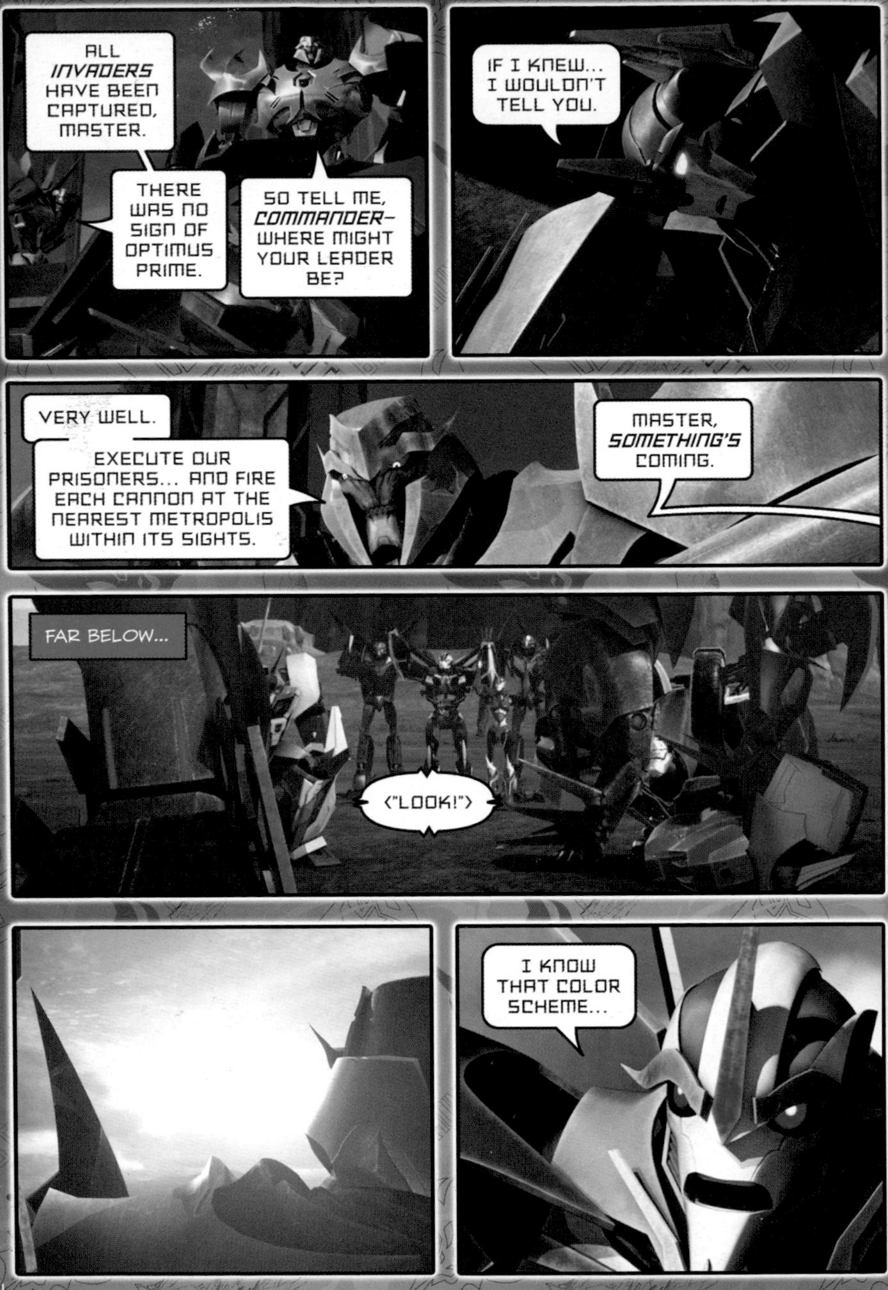
ALL *INVADERS* HAVE BEEN CAPTURED, MASTER.
THERE WAS NO SIGN OF OPTIMUS PRIME.
SO TELL ME, *COMMANDER*— WHERE MIGHT YOUR LEADER BE?
IF I KNEW... I WOULDN'T TELL YOU.
VERY WELL.
EXECUTE OUR PRISONERS... AND FIRE EACH CANNON AT THE NEAREST METROPOLIS WITHIN ITS SIGHTS.
MASTER, *SOMETHING'S* COMING.
FAR BELOW...
<"LOOK!">
I KNOW THAT COLOR SCHEME...

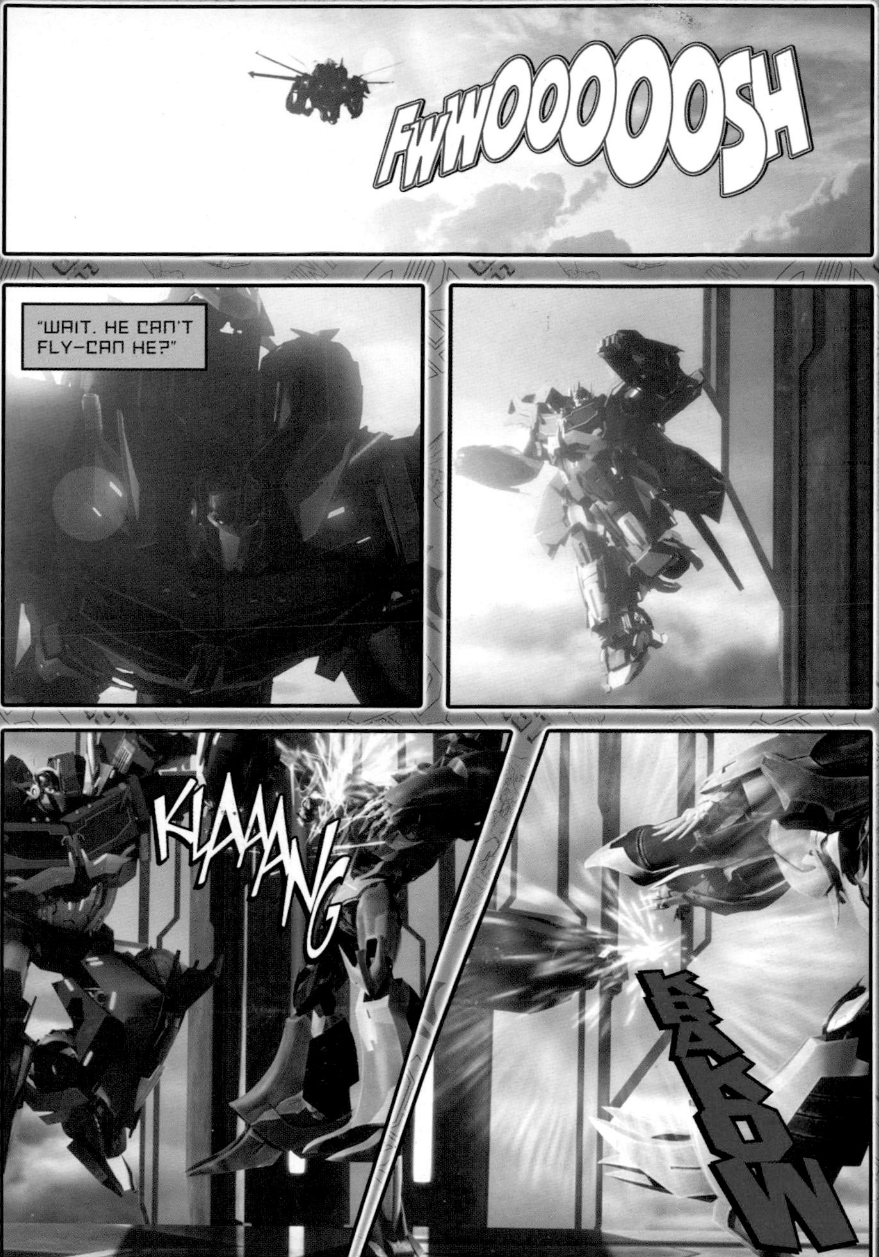
FwWOOOOOSH
"WAIT. HE CAN'T FLY—CAN HE?"
KLAAANG

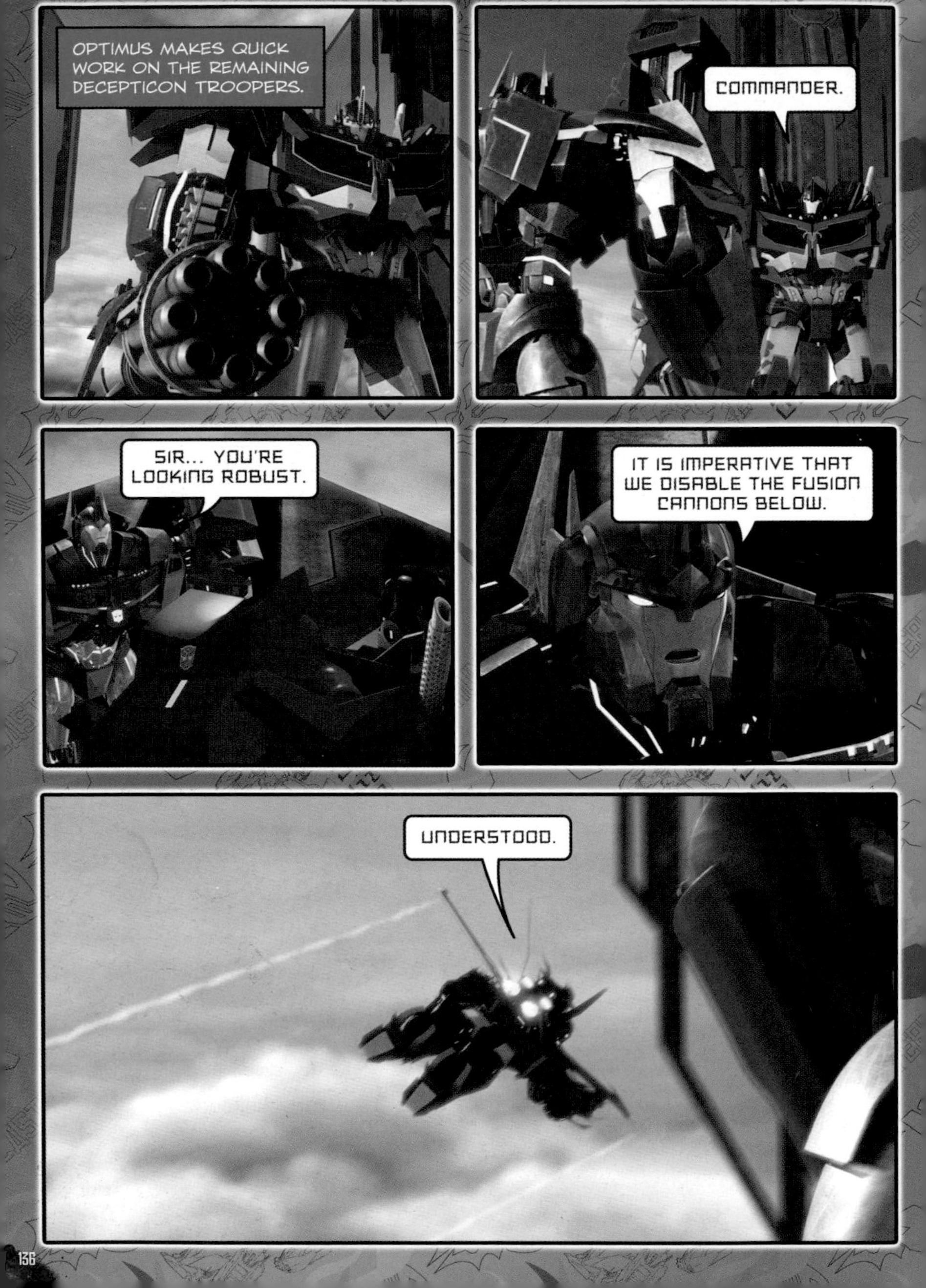
OPTIMUS MAKES QUICK WORK ON THE REMAINING DECEPTICON TROOPERS.
COMMANDER.
SIR... YOU'RE LOOKING ROBUST.
IT IS IMPERATIVE THAT WE DISABLE THE FUSION CANNONS BELOW.
UNDERSTOOD.

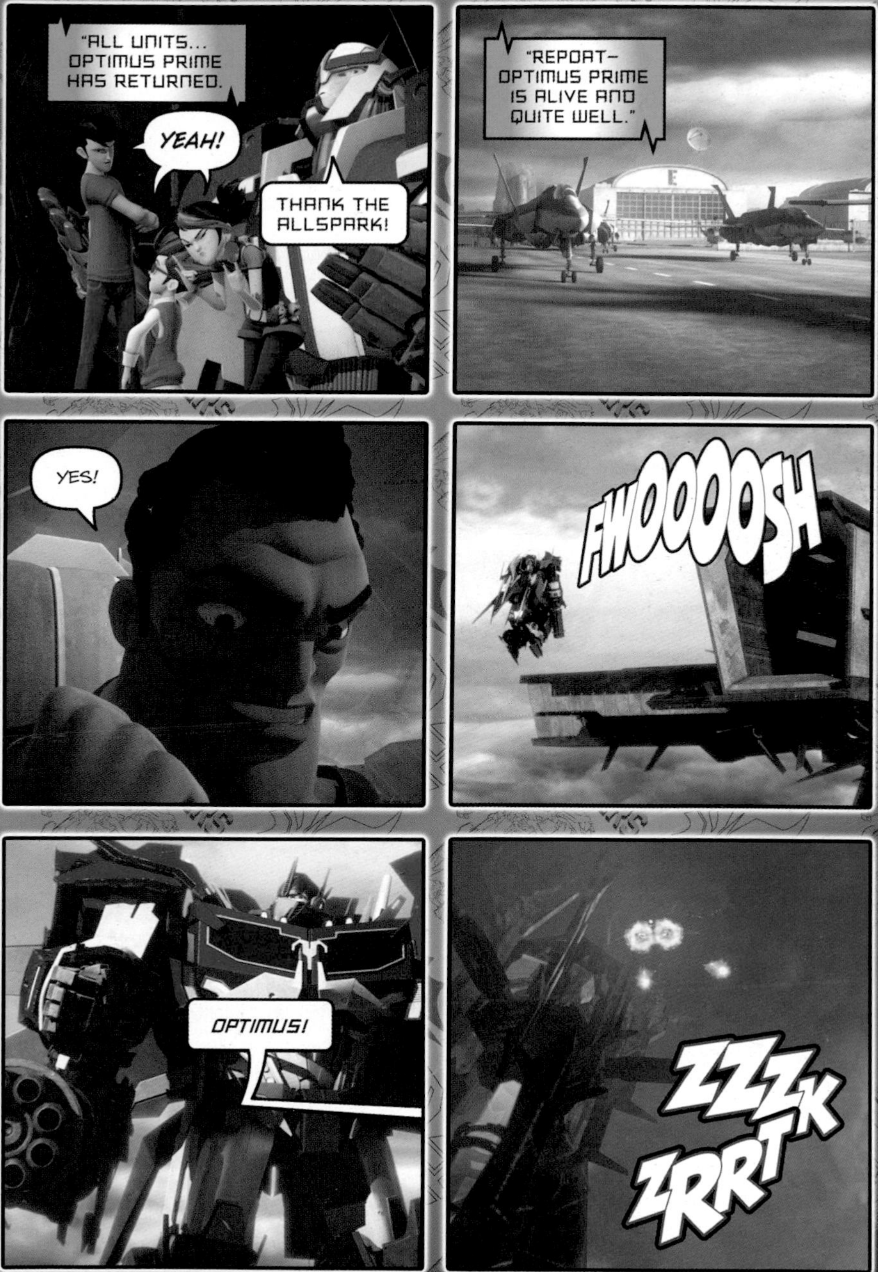
"ALL UNITS... OPTIMUS PRIME HAS RETURNED.
YEAH!
THANK THE ALLSPARK!
"REPORT— OPTIMUS PRIME IS ALIVE AND QUITE WELL."
YES!
FWOOOOSH
OPTIMUS!
ZZZK ZRRT

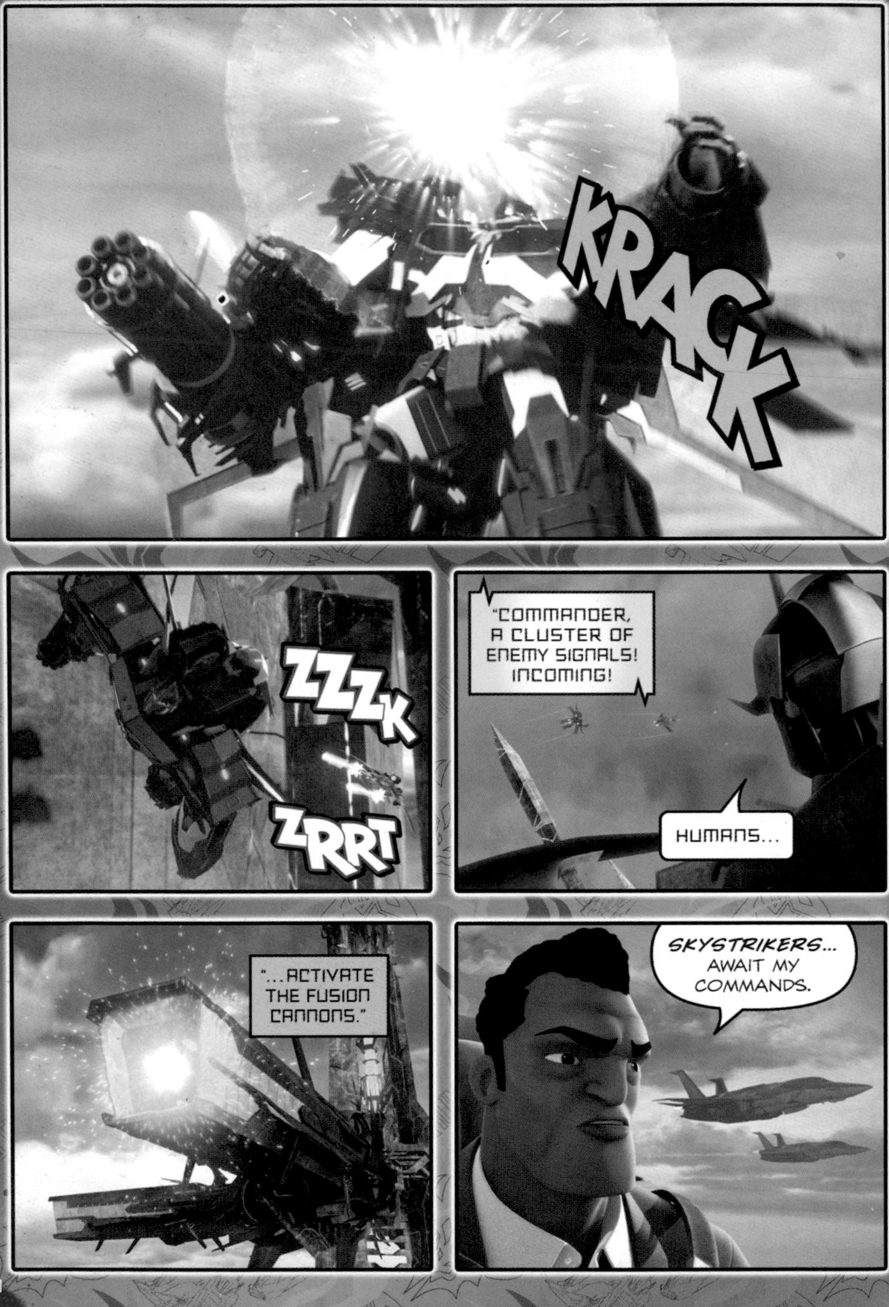
KRACK
ZZZK
ZRRT
"COMMANDER, A CLUSTER OF ENEMY SIGNALS! INCOMING!
HUMANS...
"...ACTIVATE THE FUSION CANNONS."
SKYSTRIKERS... AWAIT MY COMMANDS.

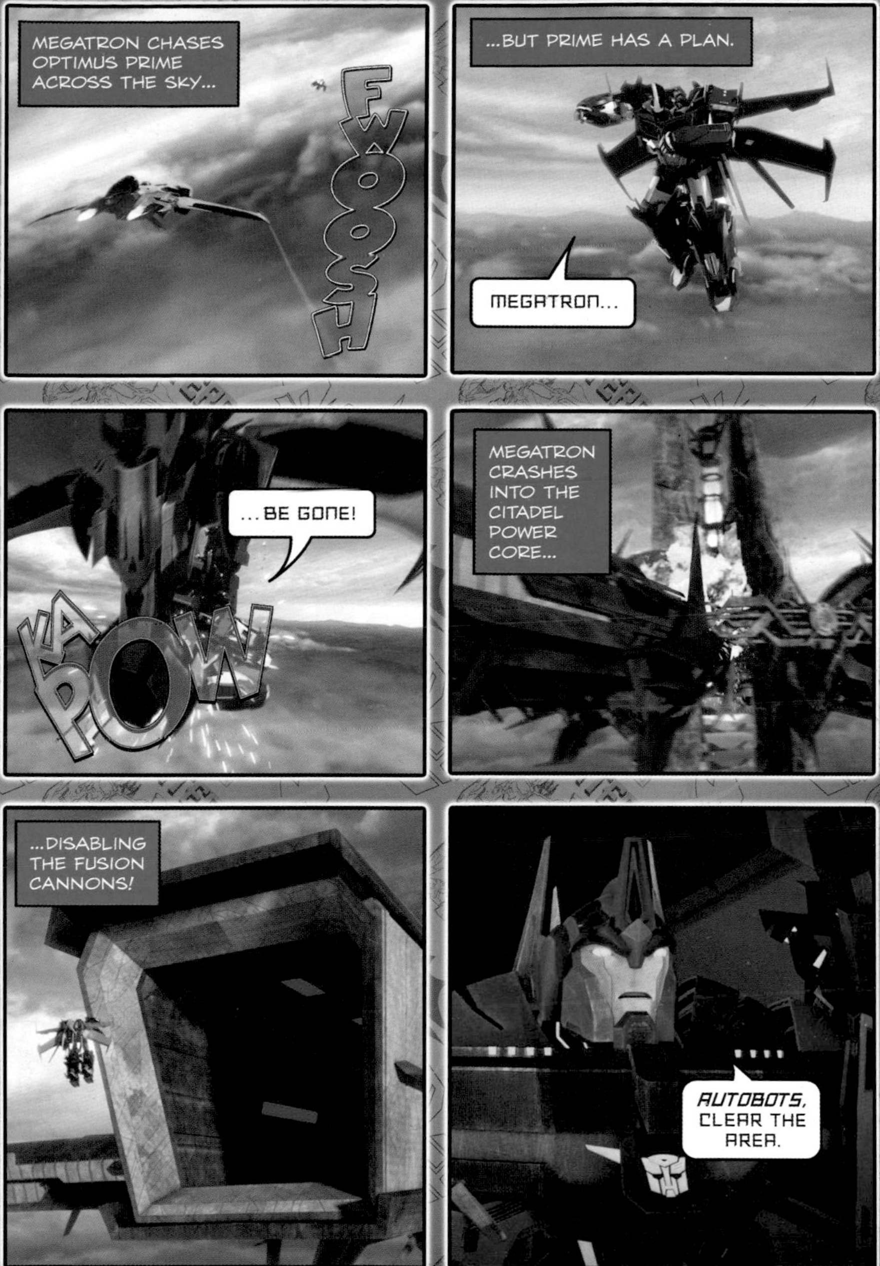

MEGATRON CHASES OPTIMUS PRIME ACROSS THE SKY...
FWOOSH
...BUT PRIME HAS A PLAN.
MEGATRON...
...BE GONE!
KA-POW
MEGATRON CRASHES INTO THE CITADEL POWER CORE...
...DISABLING THE FUSION CANNONS!
AUTOBOTS, CLEAR THE AREA.

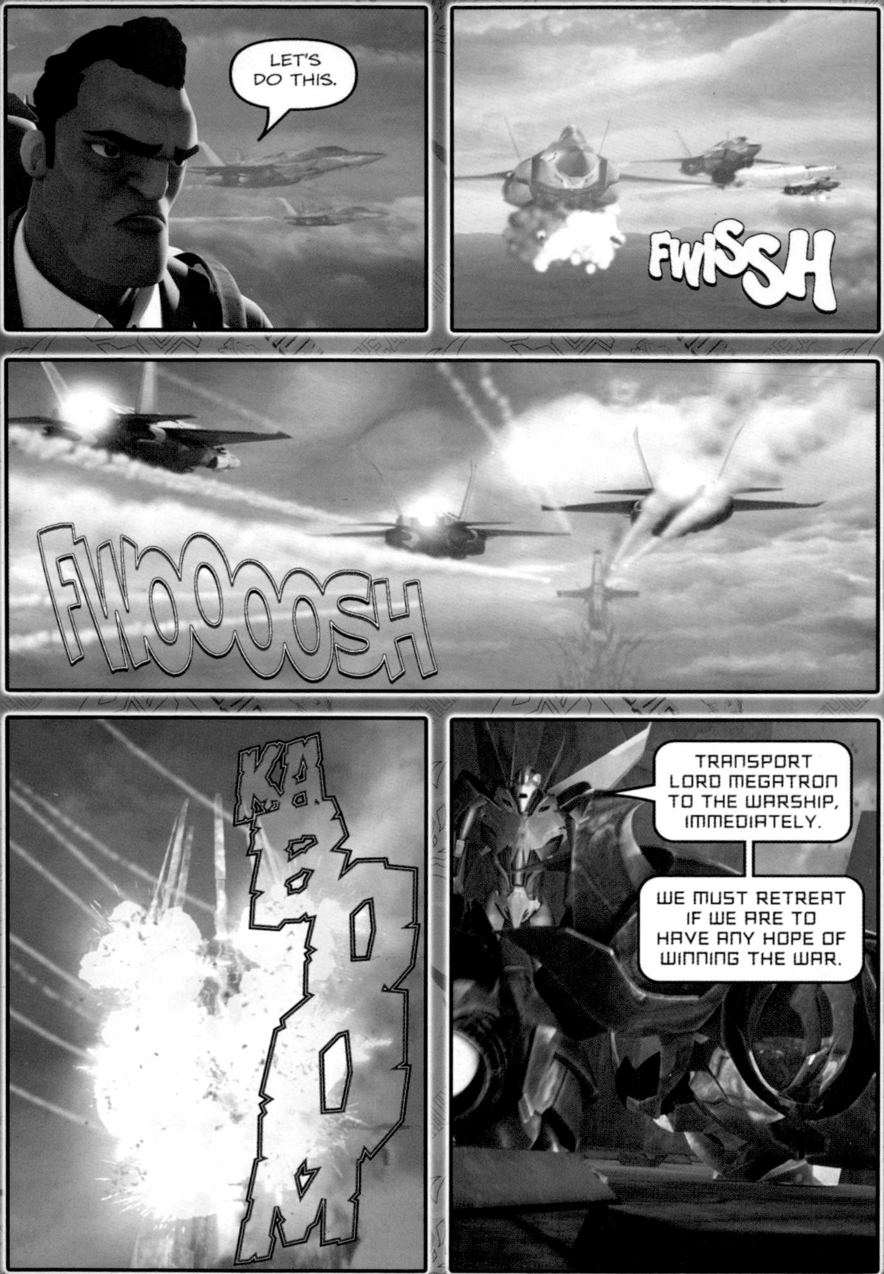

LET'S DO THIS.
FWISSH
FWOOOOSH
KA BOOM
TRANSPORT LORD MEGATRON TO THE WARSHIP, IMMEDIATELY.
WE MUST RETREAT IF WE ARE TO HAVE ANY HOPE OF WINNING THE WAR.

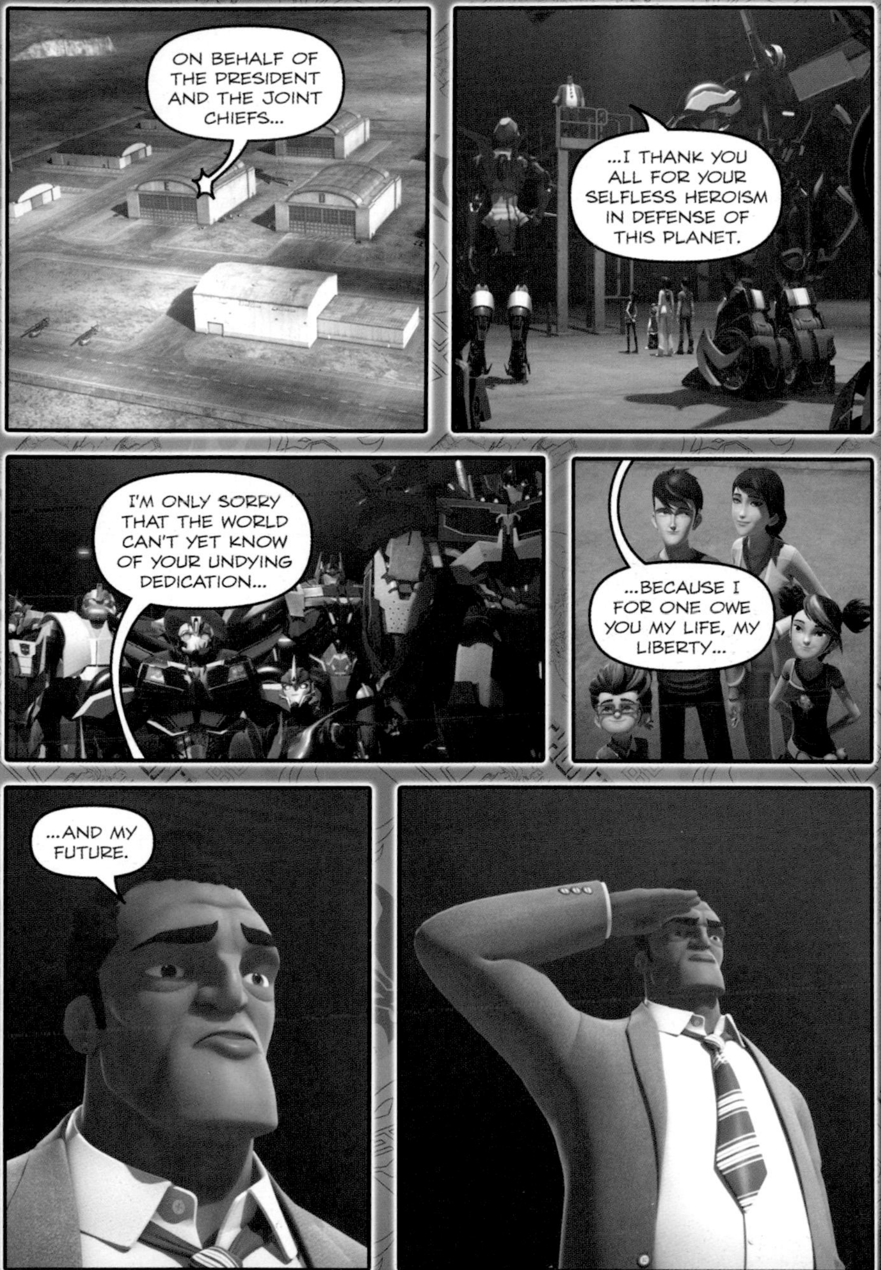
ON BEHALF OF THE PRESIDENT AND THE JOINT CHIEFS...
...I THANK YOU ALL FOR YOUR SELFLESS HEROISM IN DEFENSE OF THIS PLANET.
I'M ONLY SORRY THAT THE WORLD CAN'T YET KNOW OF YOUR UNDYING DEDICATION...
...BECAUSE I FOR ONE OWE YOU MY LIFE, MY LIBERTY...
...AND MY FUTURE.

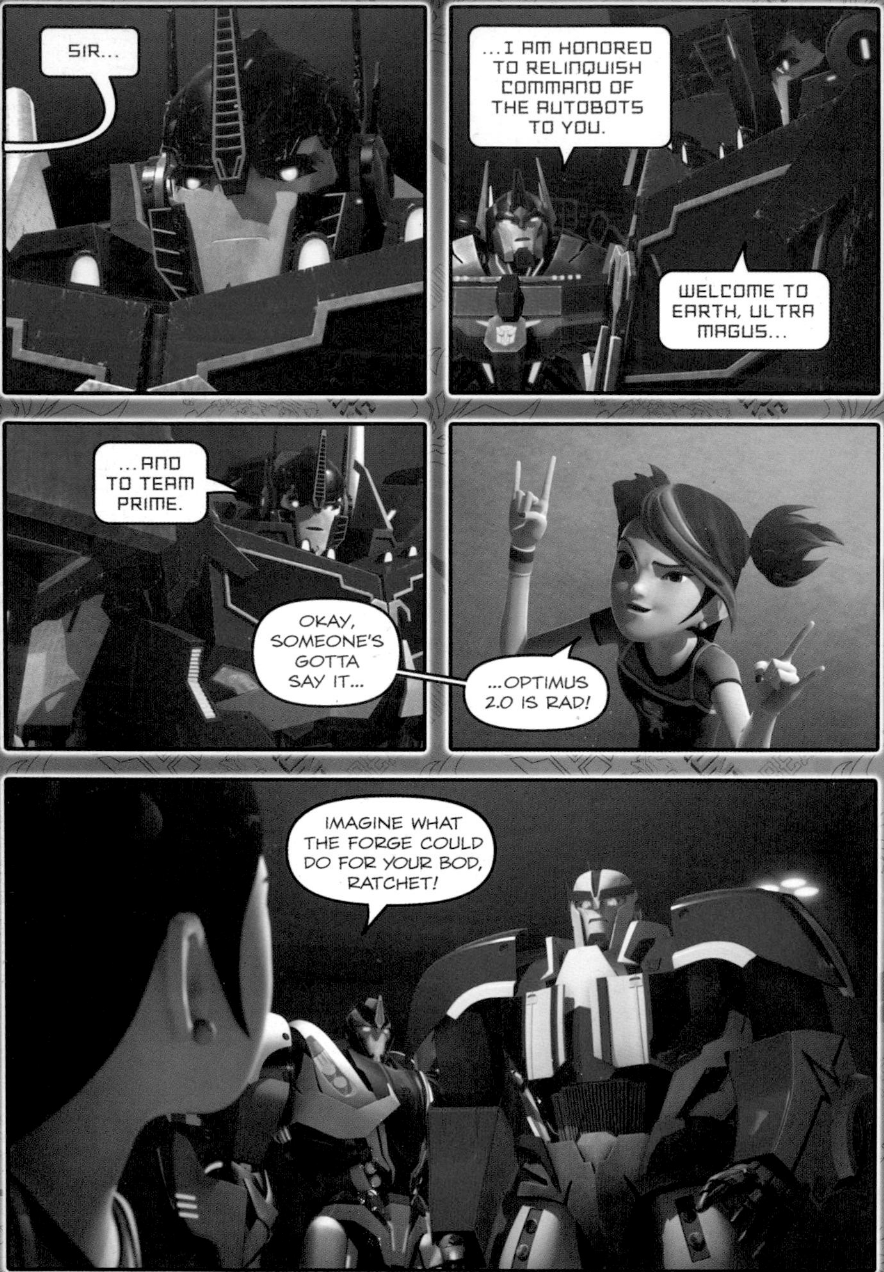
SIR...
...I AM HONORED TO RELINQUISH COMMAND OF THE AUTOBOTS TO YOU.
WELCOME TO EARTH, ULTRA MAGUS...
...AND TO TEAM PRIME.
OKAY, SOMEONE'S GOTTA SAY IT...
...OPTIMUS 2.0 IS RAD!
IMAGINE WHAT THE FORGE COULD DO FOR YOUR BOD, RATCHET!

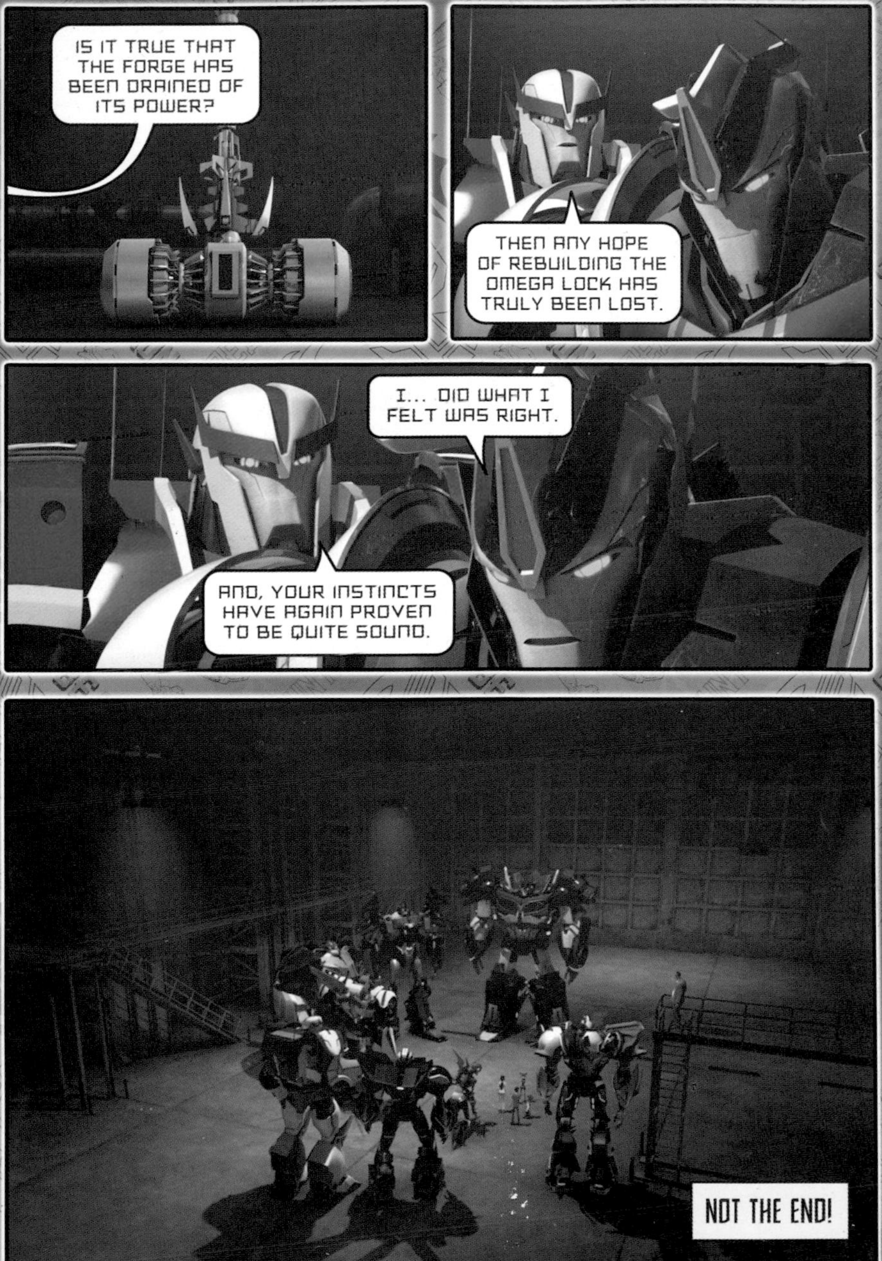
IS IT TRUE THAT THE FORGE HAS BEEN DRAINED OF ITS POWER?
THEN ANY HOPE OF REBUILDING THE OMEGA LOCK HAS TRULY BEEN LOST.
I... DID WHAT I FELT WAS RIGHT.
AND, YOUR INSTINCTS HAVE AGAIN PROVEN TO BE QUITE SOUND.
NOT THE END!

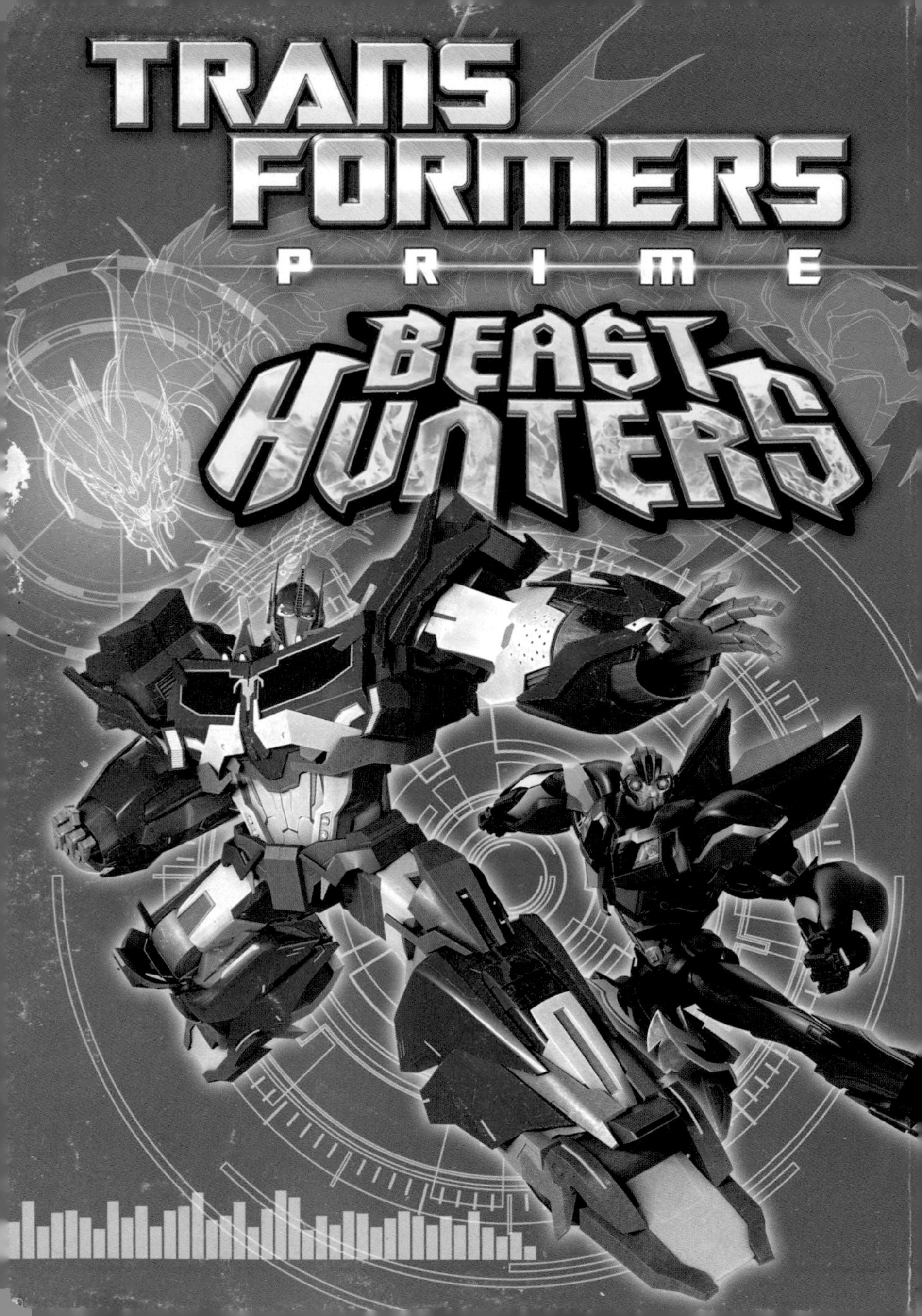
TRANS
FORMERS
PRIME
BEAST
HUNTERS